MW00614306

Wildmane
Threadweavers, Book 1

Todd Fahnestock

F4 PUBLISHING

Copyright © 2018 Todd Fahnestock

All rights reserved.

The characters and events portrayed in this book are fictitious. Any similarity to real persons, living or dead, is coincidental and not intended by the author.

No part of this book may be reproduced, or stored in a retrieval system, or transmitted in any form or by any means, electronic, mechanical, photocopying, recording, or otherwise, without express written permission of the publisher.

ISBN 13: 978-1-952699-28-3

Cover illustration and design by:
Rashed AlAkroka

Maps by:
Langon Foss

To the Clan,
Immortal. Invincible. Vulnerable.

CONTENTS

WILDMANE

Pronunciation Guide

Main Characters:
Medophae—ME-dȯ-fā
Mershayn—Mər-SHĀN
Mirolah—MI-rȯ-lä
Silasa—si-LÄ-sə
Stavark—STA-värk
Zilok Morth—ZĪ-lok Mȯrth

Other Characters/Places:
Amarion— ä-MĀ-rē-un
Ari'cyiane—ä-ri-cē-ĀN
Avakketh—ä-VÄ-keth
Belshra—BEL-shrə
Bendeller—ben-DEL-er
Buravar—BYÜ-rä-vär
Calsinac—KAL-zi-nak
Casra—KAZ-rä
Casur—KA-zhər
Cisly—SIS-lē
Clete—KLĒT
Corialis—KȮR-ē-a-lis
Dandere—DAN-dēr
Darva—DÄR-və
Daylan—DĀ-lin
Dederi—DE-de-rē
Denema—de-NĒ-mə
Deni'tri—de-NĒ-trē
Dervon—DƏR-vän
Diyah—DĒ-yä
Elekkena—e-LE-ke-nə

Ethiel—E-thē-el
Fillen—FIL-en
Grendis Sym—GREN-dis SIM
Harleath Markin—HÄR-lēth MÄR-kin
Irgakth—ƏR-gakth
Keleera—kə-LĒR-ə
Lawdon—LÄ-dən
Lo'gan—lȯ-GÄN
Locke—läk
Mi'Gan—mi-GÄN
Natra—NÄ-trə
Oedandus—ȯ-DAN-dus
Orem—Ȯ-rem
Rith—RITH
Saraphazia—se-ruh-FĀ-zhē-ə
Shera—SHE-rə
Tarithalius—ter-i-THAL-ē-us
Teni'sia—te-NĒ-sē-ä
Tiffienne—ti-fē-EN
Tuana—tü-ä-nä
Tyndiria—tin-DĒR-ē-ä
Vaisha—VĪ-shə
Yehnie—YEN-nē
Ynisaan—YI-ni-sän
Vullieth—VƏL-ē-eth
Zetu—ZE-tü

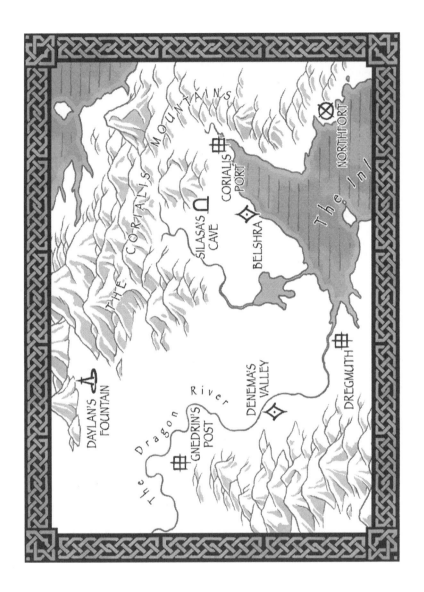

Mailing List/Facebook Group

MAILING LIST

Don't miss out on the latest news and information about all of my books. Join my Readers Group:

https://www.subscribepage.com/u0x4q3

FACEBOOK

https://www.facebook.com/todd.fahnestock

AMAZON AUTHOR PAGE

https://www.amazon.com/Todd-Fahnestock/e/B004N1MILG

Book 1

Wildmane

PROLOGUE

YNISAAN

YNISAAN STOOD on the obsidian floor of the Coreworld, distracted from the task at hand because of what her mother had just told her. The god of dragons, Avakketh, was coming. Time was short.

The god of dragons wanted to remove all humans from the lands. He always had. In his view, humans were animals. They shouldn't build thriving cities. They certainly shouldn't be allowed to harness the GodSpill, giving them the abilities of creation like those of the gods.

Avakketh would attack soon, and when he did, he would succeed. Ynisaan knew this because she had seen the destiny of every human in Amarion come to an abrupt end. The god of dragons had waited three hundred years for the right moment, and he would soon realize that moment was now.

He had waited this long for only one reason: fear of Medophae the godslayer, the shield over the human lands. But Medophae was broken, weak.

Look, Mother said mind-to-mind with Ynisaan, bringing her focus back to the small crack forming on the glistening stone floor, opening a jagged path filled with the black water of creation. These were the flows of destiny, markers that told the paths of humans; not just their present, not just their future, but their capacity to create momentous events and change history.

The Coreworld, where Ynisaan and her mother lived, was a secret map showing the lives of every living thing in Amarion. Aside from Ynisaan and her mother, no one —not even the gods— was aware of the Coreworld except the Obsidians, its immortal guardians. Their eternal charge was to kill any intruders, like Ynisaan and her mother.

Everything in the Coreworld was made of black rock, and it glistened as if wet. Irregular cracks raced across every surface. They ran over the floor, up and down the walls, even across the ceiling. Aside from unicorns, like Ynisaan and her mother, only the gods could even see the cracks and the water within them.

A hundred twisting rooms in this labyrinth represented the lands of Amarion, the human lands. Each crack within each of these rooms represented the life of a single creature—growing, splitting black rock, and filling with water as that creature lived its life.

But if you were a unicorn, there was more. The goddess Vaisha had given unicorns the gift of her own vision. Vaisha had seen possibilities. So, too, could unicorns. When Ynisaan and her mother looked at these cracks, they saw not only lives, but they could see the possibilities of those lives like ghostly cracks moving forward. For some creatures, there was only one ghostly line. For some, there were a hundred, based on choices or events that might happen to them.

If a human's destiny was a single ghost line, it meant that person was done creating, done evolving. She wouldn't change anymore, couldn't affect the world anymore. She had carved out her little niche, kept her head down, and hoped to live to old age.

Ynisaan and her mother searched for the dwindling number of growing cracks with multiple possibilities, representing dynamic mortals who could change events. Such cracks sometimes even traveled from one room to another, intersecting other lives, inspiring those to grow a little more.

But there were so few of them left now in the human lands. Humans were less creative, focused more and more on survival. Their spirits grew smaller, weaker. The lands of Amarion were dying, and humans were devolving, mere generations away from actually transforming into the unthinking animals that Avakketh perceived them to be. Whether by slow, degrading apathy or a war with the dragons, humans stood on the brink of oblivion.

Ynisaan and her mother must find a way to create a new destiny.

Of course, that destiny was so unlikely it was almost impossible, but that was why Ynisaan and her mother were here in the Coreworld. It was why they ran the risks, watched those ghostly lines of possibility, to give humans a fighting chance.

They both watched as the new crevice split the rock of the floor, moving slowly toward the hallway, filling with more of the black water of creation that seeped from the stone. Ghost lines sprouted out from it, destined to intersect with another tiny crack nearby.

It's Orem again, Ynisaan thought to her mother. They had guided this man named Orem to find the godslayer, Medophae, to help Orem pull Medophae out of his self-imposed oblivion and become the hero Amarion needed. It had half-worked. Medophae had left the exile of his cave to choose an exile in a castle instead.

Mother moved ahead to the small, stagnant little crack that Orem's destiny would soon intersect. Her enchanted hooves made absolutely no noise on the rock. As unicorns, Ynisaan and her mother could blend with shadows. They could be utterly silent. If the Obsidians were alerted to their presence, Ynisaan and her mother would be killed.

After a quick inspection of the tiny crack, Mother raised her head in surprise. She had seen something.

Ynisaan came closer, as quiet as a breath, concentrating on the black water pooled in the little crack, spilling over a little onto the floor, looking for the ghost lines. Sometimes it was difficult to see all the possibilities. Aside from the crack being overfull, she could see no special destiny forking away from it.

What is it? Ynisaan asked.

That's a threadweaver, mother said.

By the gods!

Finally, Mother said. *Finally...*

Threadweavers could use the GodSpill, the essence of pure creation spilled from the Godgate onto the mortal plane long ago. But there hadn't been any threadweavers—or GodSpill—in Amarion for three hundred years.

Quickly, Mother said. *Go back to Medophae's flow. Tell me its destiny; tell me if the lines have changed.*

Ynisaan left the room as silent as a ghost, stepping lithely around the flows of destiny without touching them, and into the next room. This was where the long, many-branched crack of the demigod Medophae had stopped long ago, stagnant. As Mother had taught her, she studied the direction of the crack to look in its likely direction, then she concentrated, using her special sight to bring out the ghostly lines—

There was a loud splash down the hall, and Ynisaan's head snapped up. Panic blossomed inside her, and she wanted to gallop back to Mother. But she forced herself to be careful and made her way back silently, peeking cautiously around the edge of the wall.

Mother stood in the room, her forelegs wet with black water up to her knees.

Ynisaan was horrified. You couldn't touch the black water! That was the first lesson—the most important lesson—Mother had drilled into her every day of her youth.

Mother!

Mother seemed stunned, but she finally looked up at Ynisaan.

What did you do? Ynisaan asked.

Mother hesitated a moment, staring at her wet hooves like they belonged to someone else, then she said, *You have to leave. Now.*

What happened?

I was pushed, Mother said.

But there isn't anyone else here! Who—

It was Zilok Morth.

Ynisaan felt cold. The demigod Medophae had many enemies,

and Zilok Morth was the worst.

GodSpill is seeping into the lands, Mother said. Old spirits are rising. I...should have seen this.

How did he even get here? How does he even know about the Coreworld?

Mother raised her head sharply. There was a faint slurping sound from down the hall. *They're coming,* she said in Ynisaan's mind. The Obsidians. Ynisaan's stomach clenched. Together, they moved back into the protective shadows.

Then we return to Amarion, Ynisaan said. We leave the Coreworld and never come back.

They'll follow.

Then we run farther, she said.

Ynisaan, they know I'm here. They don't know you're here.

No! We run.

And let the humans fade away? Let them be slaughtered by the dragon god?

Mother—

If they find me, they won't look for you.

You don't know that!

She spoke the sacred words in Ynisaan's mind. *The gods turned away from our race...*

So we must shepherd the rest, Ynisaan reluctantly finished the phrase. It was why they were here, why they hid from the Obsidians and manipulated human destiny. Ynisaan and her mother didn't have the power to alter the flows, but if they knew what was coming, they could help those who *did* have the power.

The dragon god will stamp out all the other races if he can, Mother said. When he discovers a threadweaver has arisen, he will not stand for it. He won't wait while humans harness the GodSpill again. It is too much of a threat.

Across the chamber, the wet, black walls began to move. The Obsidians.

Don't leave me, she said to her mother, ashamed of her fear.

Hide. Continue our work. Help Medophae. He is the weakest he has ever been, and forces gather against him. He will die if you don't help him, and then there will be nothing to stop the dragon god.

Her mother stepped out of the protective darkness and galloped across the open space, hooves clacking on black rock and splashing intentionally through the destiny flows to draw the Obsidians away from Ynisaan.

Mother!

You are the last unicorn, Ynisaan. Make use of my sacrifice.

Mother darted to the right, and the melting wall dropped wet boulders of obsidian to the ground. They uncurled, rising into stocky humanoid shapes. Their feet hardened, and they charged after Ynisaan's mother.

Ynisaan heard the stomping steps of the Obsidians as they caught her. She heard her mother whinny. She heard the crushing sounds, but mother didn't scream. She didn't scream.

Ynisaan touched her horn, pearly black and intertwined with the same midnight rock as the Coreworld, to the wall. The Coreworld vanished, and she stood in the dry and dying lands of Amarion, bereft of GodSpill these three hundred years.

She bowed her head and silver tears fell, dotting the dirt and scrub grass. Everywhere they dropped, leaves sprouted, stalks rose and flowers bloomed.

Soon, she stopped crying. She was alone, utterly alone. All that remained was her purpose and the hopes put upon her by her family. Mother to daughter, for three millennia, they had sworn that their race, the equines, would be the last to suffer the great fade into non-sentience. And that meant ensuring that the humans woke up again. It meant ensuring that the dragon god did not get his wish. It meant keeping Medophae alive long enough to defend them.

She looked up at the bright blue sky. She would not make Mother's sacrifice in vain.

1

MIROLAH

MIROLAH COULD SENSE the moment before the sunrise. She imagined the birds chirping outside her window, waking her from slumber, but they never did. She was always up before them.

She moved the covers off her legs, pushed her rumpled nightgown down and stood up on the grooved wooden floorboards. It was going to be a beautiful day.

She smiled at the rest of her sleeping sisters, then knelt down quietly, lifted the loose floorboard underneath and gazed at her treasure for a moment. When she first discovered the loose board and the space underneath, it had been full of grit and dust. When no one was around, she had carefully cleaned it, lined it with cloth, and placed her most prized possession inside: a book.

Owning books wasn't against the law exactly, but no one had them. It was said that in far-off Buravar, kings and queens still read books, but in Rith, those who read were shunned, sometimes even killed. It reminded people too much of the threadweavers of old. Not only had they created wonders with the GodSpill, but they had been voracious readers, stockpiling knowledge in great buildings called libraries.

Once, the work of the threadweavers had been prized, but that was before they brought down the gods' own wrath and the great dying, before the threadweavers had destroyed the lands of Amarion.

No, reading books wasn't against the law, but it *was* a sin.

Still, she couldn't stop herself from reading. It scared her, how desperately she longed for the words of those books, how she devoured them. Though she understood that threadweavers were evil, she couldn't see how reading stories about ages gone by was bad. The two did not fit together in her mind. So when no one was around—which wasn't often in Lawdon and Tiffienne's busy house—she read that book over and over. She knew all five of the legends of Wildmane that it contained. She could recite them from memory.

If she was honest with herself, she needed those stories like plants needed the rising sun. Whenever the dark shadows of her past crept into her mind, she imagined herself inside those stories, and the shadows fled. After all, nothing could stand before Wildmane. She would close her eyes and picture him arriving, tall and strong, battling the shadows, sending them running. He would sweep her away to wondrous Calsinac on a flying horse. There she would live as a queen in a castle by the ocean, with red sands stretching to the horizon.

Mirolah heard Casra waking, and she hastily replaced the board and stood up. She made her bed as the now-chirping birds drew her sisters from slumber.

Of course, if the birds did not wake them, then they were not so lucky, because Lawdon would be in shortly after, and his wrath would fall like a hammer upon any of her sisters who were too lazy to get up. Eight of her adopted sisters usually scrambled out of bed before Lawdon's booming voice descended. Mi'Gan, however, was simply not made for the morning. Lawdon's harangue hit her daily. Sometimes Mirolah wondered if Mi'Gan did it on purpose, just to give the old bear something to growl about in the morning.

Mirolah crept down the stairs and to the back of the house,

quietly gathered wood for the morning fire and brought it inside. A stack of three books gathered from Old Rith sat by the fireplace, to be used only as tinder, of course. Books were useful in that way, and using them in that fashion wasn't considered dangerous. It hurt her heart to tear out the pages one by one and light them, but Mirolah had already read each of these books. Whenever Lawdon came back with a new stack to use, she put the newest in the tile shop where it was easier to read them with no one looking. As she got through them, she would move the ones she'd read inside the house. So far, they hadn't caught on.

Soon, the logs were crackling within the stove, and she put the wash water on to boil. Tiffienne would be down soon, and she would want the water hot. She returned to the woodpile several times, until she had a day's worth stacked beside the stove, then she turned her attention to the workshop. Lawdon was Rith's premiere tile-maker, and those ovens needed to be stocked as well.

As Mirolah hauled the wood into the workshop, she heard the house come awake. Shera and Locke talked back and forth in the kitchen, making the biscuits that would be the rest of the family's breakfast. Casra and Fillen thumped through the house, collecting clothes from the previous day.

Mirolah dropped her last armload of wood on the pile and heard Lawdon's gruff voice shake the walls. She couldn't hear the words, but she could guess them. Poor Mi'Gan had slept in again.

Dusting herself off, Mirolah left the workshop and entered the family room once more. She smiled at Fillen, who set a huge wicker basket full of laundry on the dining table.

"You'll get the look again if you leave that basket there," Mirolah said.

"She won't be down for another couple of minutes." Fillen said. "I'll only be a second." And she dashed up the stairs again. Sometimes, Mirolah wondered at her sisters. Tiffienne had told Fillen time and again that the dining table was not the place for laundry, yet every morning Fillen put the baskets in the same place. Mirolah wondered if it had something to do with the regions each of her sisters came from, if being born in a certain place shaped your behavior. Perhaps Quantani, where Mi'Gan came from, started the day later than Rith. Maybe all Quantanis were late sleepers. And perhaps people from Fillen's home, Gildon, always tried to get away with what they knew they couldn't.

Except Mirolah was also from Gildon, and she wasn't like Fillen at all. Mirolah understood why there were rules, and it made life so much easier if you just followed them, worked quickly, and finished your chores. All the time Mi'Gan spent arguing with Lawdon, or that Fillen spent getting caught by Tiffienne, could be spent finishing her chores.

Mirolah waited until Fillen's footsteps faded, then she moved the basket to the floor by the stove. Before she had even straightened up, she heard Tiffienne's slow tread coming down the stairs. Tiffienne was a broad and gentle woman, with eyes that twinkled and a smile that could turn to a reproving frown quicker than you could blink. She never missed anything. Sometimes the sisters whispered among themselves that she could hear a secret being told, even if she was in the farthest room in the house. She was the type of woman who was wonderful to squeeze when you were scared. Mirolah remembered many nights of bad dreams she'd had when she'd first come here. She had found refuge in Tiffienne's arms. How many girls had Tiffienne reassured in the night?

"Good morning, Mirolah," Tiffienne said, looking at the basket by Mirolah's feet. A knowing smile flickered at the corners of her lips. Mirolah blushed. "Are you done with your chores?" Tiffienne asked.

Mirolah nodded. "I was just about to go to the circle."

Tiffienne touched Mirolah's cheek and smiled even more. She seemed about to say something, but didn't. "We'll see you this afternoon then."

Mirolah nodded and fetched her writing desk from the closet. Lawdon had made it for her when she told him that she wanted to begin writing letters for people in the town center, called the "circle" because of how six roads met there like spokes at the center of a wheel.

So far as Mirolah knew, she was the only person in Rith who could read. Nobody in Rith even *wanted* to read, it seemed. The magistrate of the town wouldn't even talk of such things when they were brought up, even though there were scribes elsewhere who wrote letters and enabled communication between kingdoms and villages. It was said there was a stack of letters from other places in the magistrate's building, unopened and unread. People wanted news from Rith. The Sunriders had scattered everybody west of The Bracer—families split, many killed like Mirolah's own parents. Mirolah obsessed about those letters, sitting unopened. What if they were mothers looking for children? Or children looking for their parents?

When, several months ago at dinner, Lawdon had mentioned that the magistrate was a damned fool to cut off communication with the rest of Amarion, that he should acquire a scribe to read and write messages, Mirolah made her decision.

"I can read," she had said, forcing herself to speak. "I can write." She didn't like to be the center of attention, but if there were families looking for each other, she had to help.

It had been a risk, but Lawdon and Tiffienne had helped her, and together they had managed to convince the town, to the glowering disapproval of the magistrate, that having one person who could read and write letters—and letters only—was valuable instead of frightening.

She ran her hands over the dark, smooth wood of her writing desk. Lawdon had carved her initials in the upper right-hand corner. It was a sweet gesture, especially since Lawdon had never written a letter before in his life. Of course, that section of the little desk was ruined for writing upon, but Mirolah didn't mind. It made her smile every time she looked at it.

The little desk had clever foldout legs, so that Mirolah could flatten it and carry it easily to the fountain and back. Keeping the legs against her side, she tucked the desk under her arm and left the house.

Rith's city circle had a fountain in the center, called Vaisha's Fountain after the goddess. It was twenty feet in diameter, with four sculpted dolphins rising up out of the circular base, holding the second tier. Three smaller dolphins rose out of that, holding the third, and so on, until only one sculpted dolphin held aloft the fifth and final tier. She imagined it used to cascade with water, back in the Age of Ascendance. The fountain had been created by threadweavers, of course. There was no underground river bubbling up to operate it. No aqueduct sloped down to feed it. Back when GodSpill could be used to twist the natural order of things, the water had come out of thin air, bubbling up from the top tier and cascading down the dolphins.

But the threadweavers had been executed for their hubris, dropped by the gods in one killing stroke, like marionettes with severed strings. The GodSpill had also been taken away, now absent from the lands of Amarion for as long as anyone could remember.

Vaisha's fountain was beautiful, but it still made Mirolah uncomfortable. If it wasn't in the center of the circle, if the caravans didn't arrive here, she would have chosen a different place to set up her desk.

She squeezed into her normal space between Taegen, the spiced tea vendor, and Baelene, the woman with the pretty ceramic necklaces. They both said good morning to her, and Mirolah smiled and returned the greeting. The first day she'd come to write letters, months ago, everyone had gone silent. Since not a single person in Rith could read or write—even the magistrate—the suspicion about Mirolah had been thick.

In a way, those who loved to read and write, the threadweavers, were what had destroyed the world. Though many used the service Mirolah provided, she never used the word "read" or "write". Rather, she said, "I can help you make a message" or "Allow me to craft your words for you." Thirsting for knowledge beyond what was normal for a human, that was reviled. Helping others was honored.

That first day, she'd not been able to find a place next to the fountain, and no one had been willing to make space.

But that was then. Mirolah had gradually convinced them that she was only interested in helping lost families communicate with each other, even reunite in some cases. Slowly, the other vendors came to realize that she wasn't a threat, and could in fact be an advantage.

Now they reserved her spot. Mirolah was good for business. On busy days, there was always a line in front of Mirolah's desk, and those waiting had a good long while to view the wares of the venders on either side of her.

Unfolding the legs of her desk, Mirolah sat on the edge of the fountain and began laying out her packet of blank parchment and her inkwell. She carefully withdrew a small leather bundle from a pocket inside her vest, pulled the lace and unwrapped her quill pen. It was a fine pen, and had cost Lawdon five full crowns. Mirolah would never forget the day when she had approached Lawdon with her request to write letters at the square. She had been so scared he would say no. After all, why should Mirolah get out of helping the others with the housework and the work of Lawdon's tile shop to run off and write letters for strangers?

But he had said yes. He told her she could begin the following week, one day a week. At first, Mirolah thought he'd postponed her to give himself time to redistribute her duties to the other girls, but the truth became evident when, at the beginning of the next week, Lawdon presented her with the desk, parchment, ink, and this beautiful pen. Mirolah had cried. With his sternest expression, he told her how much everything had cost, and that she must pay back the money by the end of the year.

She paid him back within two months.

Now she wrote three days a week. She was making journeyman wages—a crown and a half a day. She had wanted to give a full crown to Lawdon and Tiffienne for every day she was allowed to write, as payment for everything they had done for her. Lawdon gruffly refused. He said that the labor he was losing from her not being in the workshop was a half-crown a day. He said she could pay him that, but he would take no more. But Mirolah knew how much it must cost him to keep and care for ten girls, only one of which was his own by birth, and Mirolah saved another half crown each day to buy things for her sisters, or food for special occasions. She tried to do it in secret, though Mirolah knew that Tiffienne must notice the extra food, the new clothes.

The last half-crown Mirolah saved for herself, for things she wanted and might want in the future. Perhaps someday she would be able to buy a little house of her own at the edge of town, where she could teach children how to read and to write.

She finished laying out the tools of her trade and turned to the first customer. The square was filling quickly today. It was going to be busy. Two caravans had arrived, and that would mean letters to read and letters to write. It was a good sign that the caravans were running regularly again.

The line had already begun. They gathered orderly and excited in front of her desk. She read letters from as far off as Semiss and Quantani. She had read letters from the kingdoms to the north: Nast, Buravar, Clete, even far-off Teni'sia. She belonged to a larger world, and when she read letters, she could feel it. Mirolah was privy to the hopes and dreams of the people all across Amarion. In her small way, she got to share those hopes and dreams.

She looked up at her first customer and smiled.

"Good morning, Genna."

"Good morning, Mira."

Genna was a tall young woman Mirolah had known since she was ten, since the day after the Sunriders had razed their home to the ground. They had fled Gildon together with a hundred other scared children and a handful of adults to guide them.

She and Genna had been close during that trek, but had been separated when they arrived in Rith. Mirolah had gone to Lawdon's house, and Genna had gone to live with Dester the miller and his wife. Mirolah had always envied Genna's beauty and that long, lustrous gold hair. It wasn't surprising that Genna found a husband so quickly.

Genna's new baby slept soundly in the sling around her neck. The last time Mirolah had seen Genna, he'd been no more than a bulge in her belly.

"He's beautiful, Genna."

She smiled shyly, quietly radiant as she looked down at the infant. "We called him Jacen, after Pacen's father."

"It's a lovely name," Mirolah said, wondering if someday she might hold her own beautiful baby.

"Thank you." Genna handed a letter to Mirolah. She opened it and read it aloud. Genna had an aunt and an uncle who were still alive, helping to rebuild Gildon, and they sent letters every now and then, telling of the slow reconstruction of the village. They sent their best wishes for the new baby.

Mirolah herself did not receive letters from Gildon. She had never had any aunts or uncles, and her grandparents had died long before she was born. The only family she'd ever known was her brother and her parents, and they were dead.

Genna thanked Mirolah again and handed her two hot cheese buns from her husband's bakery. Mirolah took them, wished Genna and the baby well before they moved off into the crowd. She greeted the next person in line and read his letter for him.

The initial rush faded around ten o'clock, at which point Mirolah traded one of the hot cheese buns to the tea vendor for a cup of spiced tea. Smiling at one another, Mirolah and the tea vendor enjoyed their breakfast.

In the midst of her meal, Mirolah felt an uneasiness descend upon her. That feeling didn't happen often, but Mirolah hated it. It felt like a thousand tiny bugs crawling on her. She rubbed the back of her neck and looked around. At the edge of the crowd by Sara Street stood a hunched old woman. Her cowl was drawn down over her face, and she muttered to herself. She hobbled from stall to stall, as if she was looking for something, but not finding it.

Then that old, wizened face turned slowly and locked gazes with her, as though sensing Mirolah's stare. She was one of the Little People!

Mirolah snapped her gaze away from the tiny woman and focused on her desk. She'd always been afraid of the Little People. None of them stood over five feet tall. They had dark gray skin and bright blue eyes, every one of them. And black hair. It was said they had been taken down from the Dragon Mountains during the Age of Ascendance to be used as slaves for the great threadweavers.

Mirolah didn't know why they didn't go back to their homes in the Dragon Mountains after the fall of the threadweaver empires. They were no longer slaves in this land, but still they stayed, roaming from city to city as gypsies. Perhaps they couldn't find a place to settle. Perhaps nobody wanted them. Mirolah herself didn't want the woman, and wished she'd go away.

She sensed the old gypsy's sharp eyes boring into her, but Mirolah refused to look up. The bugs crawled even more frantically across her neck. Even in the clamor of the busy market, Mirolah thought she could hear the gypsy's sharp little steps coming toward her.

The gypsy rapped her small, gnarled knuckles on Mirolah's desk. She looked up, smiled as best she could. The woman's eyes were shockingly blue, like the deep sky on a summer afternoon. Her many wrinkles and gray skin made her look dead. The gypsy smelled like strange spices and intestinal problems. Mirolah wanted to be anywhere but here.

"I want letter written," the old woman said in a gravelly voice. Her accent was sharp; it clipped her words off a split-second before they should have ended. The woman's mouth and teeth were red like her gums were bleeding! Mirolah recoiled.

"Do you have money?" Mirolah returned, defensive. It was rude to ask for money first, but Mirolah was hoping she might offend the old woman enough to make her go away. But the old woman didn't go away. She stared at Mirolah long and hard. Without a word, she reached into her layered robe and tossed a smooth, black stone onto the desk. It clacked loudly and slid up to Mirolah's hand. It wasn't a crown or any other coin Mirolah had ever seen. She picked it up...

The stone swirled with rainbow colors. Mirolah gasped and threw the stone down as if it had burned her. Memories of her little brother flashed through her head. The night he died. The men who killed him, calling him a threadweaver.

"What are you doing?" she asked tersely, trying to keep her voice under control. Those bright blue eyes narrowed to slits. That bloody mouth cracked into a smile.

Mirolah stood up, grabbed her pen and the sheaf of parchment, and tucked it under her arm as she began to fold her desk. The old woman's tiny hand snaked out and grabbed Mirolah's wrist.

"Let me go." She tried to pull away, but the strength in that scrawny claw was not to be believed.

The old woman jerked abruptly on her arm and Mirolah's head

dipped down, close to the old woman's bloody mouth. "You write for me, or I tell everyone what you *really* are," the old woman growled in that gravelly voice.

Mirolah's heart beat fast, and her breath came hard. She looked to her right. The tea vendor's eyebrows were furrowed. He was prepared to come out and help Mirolah, but she shook her head.

"It's all right," she said to the tea vendor. "It's okay. Just a misunderstanding."

Mirolah put on as relaxed and easy a face as she could and pushed down the terror that threatened to overwhelm her. She unfolded the desk and put her things down, spread them out. Her arms moved as if they were made of wood, but she managed to extract a sheet of parchment and lay it flat.

"You say this," the old woman rasped. She spat out a blood-red berry and inserted another one into her mouth, chewing on it. "Sent to Reader Orem, palace at Buravar."

Reader Orem? The old woman narrowed her eyes and poked her thin finger at the desk. "You write it, girl. Do it, or I tell everyone."

Mirolah swallowed. She worked hard to stop her hands from shaking and clumsily addressed the envelope.

"Write this: Prinka find woman. Prinka want gold."

"Who did you find?" Mirolah asked.

"Write. Or I tell them." She gestured at all the vendors around her.

Mirolah wrote the words, then said, "Tell me who this is, or I'm not writing anymore."

The old woman's hand was a blur, snatching the letter and envelope from Mirolah's desk. Mirolah made a grab for them, but they disappeared within the woman's robes.

Mirolah lowered her voice. "Please... Tell me why you need this letter."

"You will find out soon. When Reader Orem comes for you."

The woman turned and disappeared into the crowd. Mirolah looked down at the polished black stone lying on the edge of her writing desk.

Threadweaver...

All she could think about was the night they murdered her brother.

2

MEDOPHAE

MEDOPHAE GRIPPED the iron balcony rail. A cool afternoon breeze blew over him, ruffling his hair and bringing the salty scent of the Inland Ocean, but the pain didn't stop. It never stopped.

Far below, waves rolled and crashed against the cliff. He felt his beloved Bands all around, a presence. He heard her whispering on the breeze. He saw the green of her eyes in the waves. He felt her, like he could reach out and touch her, like he could have her again.

But she was gone. She had trusted him, put her life in his hands, and he'd killed her. He was a bringer of fire and death.

He wanted to be ignorant again. He wanted to believe that his every action didn't lead to ruin for those around him. The memories whispered to him; they wanted him and he wanted to surround himself in them, to wrap himself in his past.

He looked at the gray cliffs, the rocky shoreline below, and imagined they were the red sands of Calsinac, back when *she* had been with him, back when he'd been happy. He started to smile, almost able to see her on that beach, her short blond hair whipping in the wind...

He shook his head fiercely. Calsinac was gone, a ruin. Anger slid through him like a silk scarf stuck with thorns. His friends, his subjects, even his nearly-immortal lover, had all been destroyed because of him. So many had believed in him, had loved him, and in the end he'd killed them all.

I killed them all....

The god Oedandus woke inside Medophae, sensing the anger.

You are the hand of justice, the god said. Kill them. Kill them all.

The rail squeaked, and Medophae looked down. He had twisted it, making deep grooves with his fingers. He let go and stepped away.

"Medophae."

He spun and clenched his fist as a woman stepped into the ring of lamplight. She was petite, with delicate features and red hair coiled artfully on her head. Two ringlets trailed down from a light golden crown, framing her pale face. She wore a green dress fringed in gold, tight about her slim waist and upper arms, flared at the wrists. She stood with head high, confident, and her green eyes watched him. Green eyes. Like his beloved.

This is not Calsinac, he thought to himself. This is a different time.

But her eyes... His heart felt lighter just looking at them, as though he might touch his beloved again, if only—

She isn't Bands, he thought. Say her name.

It came to him suddenly, like a gasp of air to a drowning man.

"Queen Tyndiria," he said.

Other memories followed then, recent ones. Safer ones. They told him where he was, *when* he was. He lived in Teni'sia, a northern kingdom nestled in the cliffs by the Inland Ocean. He was captain of the royal guard and protector of Queen Tyndiria. Sweet Tyndiria, the green-eyed girl who became a woman in a time of war. The teenage leader who held up a toppling kingdom.

The Sunriders had swept through Amarion over the last decade, laying waste to villages, pulling down kingdoms. They had tried to pull down Teni'sia, too, but the steep mountains and the cleverness of Tyndiria's father had held them at bay. After two years of raids, the horsemen finally moved on. By then, barely half of Teni'sia's young men returned to tend the cliff gardens and sea nets. Tyndiria lost her father and brother to the battlefield and her mother to a fire. She would have also lost her kingdom and her life if not for Medophae.

He could still see the tiny, sixteen-year-old Tyndiria standing in front of a towering Magal Sym, strongest of her nobles and the most vocal on the King's Council. He had demanded that, until Tyndiria came of age, she needed a regent. Tyndiria declared she would take the reins of the kingdom, and that Magal Sym was welcome to advise her in his current capacity, but she would require no regent at this time.

She hadn't known that, of her remaining seven nobles, barely half were still loyal to her. She didn't know that most of her royal guards had been bought, that an assassin waited to claim her a dozen paces down the hall. She was a fledgling sprout, pushing up through the soil, unable to see the boot hovering over her. The coup against her was all but finished, and all that needed doing was a quick stab of the assassin's knife.

But Tyndiria didn't know, and when she spoke, she spoke like a queen, like the kingdom was—and should be—a sane place. Such an act of blind courage ignited the fire inside Medophae, and he had broken his oath. He had interfered in mortal affairs again.

He followed Tyndiria without her knowledge, found the hidden assassin and eliminated him. He eliminated two others in the next two days, then identified Tyndiria's treacherous guards and made them disappear. He shadowed her, a silent guardian turning aside any threat to the young queen. Frustrated, Sym finally attacked Tyndiria in force, in broad daylight.

There could be no more standing in the shadows for Medophae, and he had made himself known. Seventeen soldiers and a power-hungry noble surrounded the young queen in the royal garden. Her two guards, bought by Sym, had backed away, leaving her alone with her ladies in waiting. The injustice infuriated Medophae, and the dark voice of his god rose inside him. And he killed them: seventeen soldiers, two traitorous guards, and a power-hungry noble.

I killed them all....

"Medophae?" Tyndiria broke his reminiscence. He shook his

head, brought himself back to the study. The queen's gaze flicked to the mangled rail, to his hands, to the ocean beyond.

"I am at your service, my queen," he said.

"Your queen..." She moved to the balcony, watching the horizon like she was overseeing the sun's travel. "Do you know where you are, my lord?"

"Of course," he said. "Your kingdom. Teni'sia."

"Do you know how long you have been standing here?"

He didn't know. "An hour, my queen," he said.

"Since morning."

He glanced at the afternoon sun. "I'm...sorry, my queen. I have neglected my duties."

"Stop it," she said harshly. "Don't talk to me like you're one of my subjects." She ran light fingers over the mangled rail. "I would help you if I could," she said softly.

"Your attention must be on your responsibilities."

"I think a demigod in our midst qualifies as one of my responsibilities." She turned and leaned against the rail.

Her eyes longed for him, and his heart beat faster. She saw the eighteen-year-old boy he had been when he was made immortal, not the tortured, ancient soul he had become.

And her tone, the way she approached him... Guilt twisted inside him as more memories flooded in... Tyndiria and him... They were lovers.

He struggled, trying to remember how he had let that happen. The lonely moment in her study. Her approach. Her green eyes, looking up at him. So green. Just like *her* eyes. Then her lips were on his. He should have pushed her away. He should have ended it, but he wanted her. He hungered for her, and when her lips met his, the pain vanished. He pulled her to him, kissed her like she was Bands. For one sweet moment, he was back in Calsinac—

"Medophae." She broke his reverie, putting her fingers on his chest. They were warm through the linen of his shirt. "I can help you."

He leaned down, kissed her, and she went soft in his arms. Her fingers slid into his hair. Her affection was salve to his soul. He wanted to live within it, but her touch didn't heal; it only numbed the pain.

And he was the bringer of fire and death.

I'll bring death to you, he thought. It is inevitable. Not even Bands could escape.

"I don't want to hurt you," he whispered into her neck, hating his need, hating what it would do to her.

"You don't," she said.

"Not yet..." he whispered.

"I made this choice, Medophae. I know who you are, and I made the choice."

Hers was the conviction of the young, the invincibility of the ignorant. At eighteen, she believed in herself, in her mighty little sprout of goodness. He wanted to believe in her, too. He wanted to be ignorant, to believe that goodness would prevail in the end.

He let go and looked away. She would never leave him, because mortals couldn't make themselves do it. And he wouldn't leave her because he needed her. Because her goodness eased his agony. Because he was weak.

She took his chin in her hand and brought his gaze back to her. "I do not ask you to be something you are not." She leaned her forehead against his. "You make me happy. I want to make you happy. Let me. Tell me why you hurt so much," she whispered. "Even if I cannot help, let me try. Please."

It was like looking at a well-worn path he had walked a hundred times. He knew where it went, knew where it ended. But there was no other path. Every path ended badly.

He tried to focus on the present, tried to—in this moment at least—be the man he ought to be. Tyndiria wanted answers, wanted memories from his past. Those, at least, he could give.

"I was...in love," he said.

"The Lady Bands," she said. She knew the legend of their romance, of course. All of Amarion knew the legend of Wildmane and his lady love Bands, but they didn't know truth. They didn't know how it ended. They didn't know that he had killed her.

"She trusted me," he said. "Like you trust me now, and—"

A knock sounded at the door. Tyndiria went stiff. Frustration flashed across her face. She turned to order the offending knocker

23

away when Medophae's page, Casur, spoke through the door.

"Captain Medophae. Come quick. Guardsman Galden has been murdered!"

3

MEDOPHAE

WIND SWEPT in from the ocean, swirling the white and black sands of the steep beach to the north of Teni'sia. Ten-foot waves rose and crashed, creating a roaring background to the violent scene. Galden's bloody remains lay upon the sands only ten paces from the northern cliffs. Sand collected in small drifts against the windward side of his body. Galden had been left just as the patrol found him. Medophae would have to commend Lo'gan for that.

Half a dozen of the Queen's Guard stood around, waiting for Medophae's orders. The surf dragons had been a mild problem as long as Teni'sia had stood, but not a deadly one. Of course, they were not true dragons, just serpents with arms and legs that could grasp and cut their prey. Like most predators, they only sought out prey smaller than them, but they could be aggressive when cornered. The worst Medophae had ever heard was a careless young man who had teased a surf dragon and lost a hand for his idiocy. They were a danger to children who swam in the Inland Ocean, but not adults. In the history of Teni'sia, there was only one death from a surf dragon.

"When did he go on his sweep?" Medophae asked.

"Noon, sir," Lo'gan answered.

Medophae nodded. He knelt in the sand and looked at Galden's face.

The entire left side had been ripped open and a small pool of blood stained the sand behind his head. Another slash went from Galden's shoulder down to his belly. The third and last claw strike went across his throat, but there was little blood, which meant he was dead before that strike.

He touched the shoulder wound. The cuts were deep, the arm bone shattered. The claw marks on Galden's face had cracked his skull. That was the wound that killed him, probably instantly. The power behind those strikes was too great for a surf dragon. Surf dragons latched onto their prey with their jaws, raked them to death with their claws. Medophae had seen a surf dragon attack a seal once. The struggle was fierce, but slow, an endurance battle until the seal bled out.

Galden had died because his head had been smashed and his throat torn out, not because he bled to death. And here he was, lying on the beach, whole except for his wounds. A surf dragon would have eaten the kill.

His guards wore grim faces at the sight. Medophae wondered what they would think if they knew that he had delivered far worse wounds than this, if they knew he had walked across battlefields where the ground was slick with blood a mile long from carnage he had caused. Medophae remembered little from his rages, only the aftermath. When violence sang in his mind, it was the only song he could hear.

He snapped out of his reverie, shoving the unhelpful memories down and focusing Galden's body. He swiveled about and looked at the cliff caves to the north. It was where the surf dragons used to make their nests. There hadn't been any dragons in those caves for years because of the periodic sweeps the city guards made, but there was something there now. Medophae's gaze were drawn to a high cave opening in the cliffs. There was something in there. Something—

"Sir?" Lo'gan interrupted. He followed Medophae's gaze.

"We'll make a sweep with a hex guard, sir. We'll find it. We'll kill it. Don't worry." The original architects of Teni'sia had appreciated geometry, and any grouping of soldiers or guards were named based on a geometric shape. It had taken Medophae sometime to get used to that, but Lo'gan was telling him that he would take six guards to search for the creature.

Medophae paused, shook his head.

"Sir?"

"We'll wait until tomorrow," Medophae said. "I will accompany the hex."

Lo'gan frowned. "Sir, my guards and I can handle it. It would be ill advised for the Captain of the Guard to undertake such a task."

Lo'gan saw the same things Medophae saw. Lo'gan knew that, if this had been done by a surf dragon, it was unlike the others. He wished to protect his captain.

Medophae glanced again at the high cave. The back of his neck tingled in a way he hadn't felt in years, and it made his stomach queasy. No, he wasn't taking anyone with him when he hunted this creature. "They can take the body now. Prep it for burial tomorrow."

"What will you do now, sir?" Lo'gan asked.

"We visit Galden's wife."

MEDOPHAE WAS aware of Lo'gan's curious gaze on him as he hesitated in front of Galden's house. Medophae felt the emptiness that always filled him when he was forced to do this. How many of these speeches had he made? He never found the right words. One would think after this much time, he could find the right words.

"Is this the first time, Captain?" Lo'gan asked. Medophae grunted, but didn't look at Lo'gan. In Lo'gan's eyes, Medophae was a young, inordinately capable captain. Medophae's body remained the same age it had been when Oedandus had claimed him. Medophae would always have the physical form of an eighteen-year-old. Of course, because of his commanding presence and

27

experience, Lo'gan probably assumed he was at least twenty-five, simply young-looking.

"If you would permit me, sir, I will tell her." Lo'gan said.

"Thank you," Medophae said, waving a hand. "I am fine."

"Of course, sir. Please forgive me." Lo'gan stepped back and stood at attention, his eyes focusing straight ahead. Medophae knew there would be no more nervous shifting, no more offers to help. Lo'gan was a soldier's soldier, and would stand there until the mountains fell into the ocean, or until Medophae gave him another order.

What are the words, then? What were the words you used after the Deitrus Shelf, when your entire army was slaughtered? What were the words you used to comfort the Duke of Gorros when Baron Shandeer impaled his son on that curved sword? Can you remember? Can you ever remember anything important?

"Let's go," Medophae said. Lo'gan nodded and accompanied him up the walkway.

It was comprised of old wooden planking, faded and worn by the weather. The planks ended halfway to the small house, replaced by cobblestones. The stones looked new, a project in the making. A project Galden would never finish.

Galden's house was small. The stones were old, but the moss had been scraped and polished away. Galden had loved his home and took pride in his station in life. Times were hard in Teni'sia—were hard all over Amarion—but he had spent the effort to make his small piece of the world a little brighter.

There was a pot of flowers in the front window, open to the breeze and the sunlight. A splash of color on weary lands.

The woman saw them walking up the path before they reached the door. She stepped out onto the porch, a baby in her arms. A five-year-old boy came out behind her, stood with his hands at his sides, watching them.

The woman didn't know she was a widow yet. She recognized them as Teni'sian guards, her husband's peers, and her smile was warm. She paused a moment, and her smile faltered as she recognized Medophae. She quickly smoothed her hair and tried to find the most dignified way to hold her baby while trying to

28

straighten her dress. A blush turned her cheeks red.

Medophae paused at the steps. He wanted to smile at her, to make her happy for just one instant before he told her. He could do it. He had that sway over people, but it would be a flame born only to be snuffed. This was not a happy occasion.

Worry flickered in her eyes, and her embarrassment dissolved. "What, m'lord?" she said, her brow furrowing. "What is it?"

Medophae took a slow, calm breath and let the words come one more time.

"Deetra?"

"Yes, m'lord, I am Deetra. What is it?" Her hands twisted around the baby's blanket. "Is it Galden? What is it?"

Medophae nodded.

"No..." She shook her head. "Nothing is wrong. I saw him this morning."

"Deetra, perhaps you should sit for a moment," he said calmly.

"No. I want to stand," she said. "I want to stand. Oh gods..."

Medophae paused, but he could see that every moment he hesitated was excruciating for her. This never went well. There was never a good way to do it.

"Deetra, your husband was killed during a sweep of the—"

"No!" She screamed. Her legs gave way, and she stumbled backward. The baby tumbled from her nerveless fingers. He stepped forward smoothly, catching the baby with one hand and Deetra with the other. The baby began crying. Medophae turned and found Lo'gan at his side. He gave his lieutenant the baby and gently sat Deetra in the chair beside the door.

She looked at Medophae in horror, shaking her head. Her wide, blue eyes searched his face. "Oh gods..." she said. "Tell me you're lying. Say it's a lie." Her voice was small.

"Deetra—"

"*You're lying!*" she screamed. She leapt up from the chair, knocking him back. Her fists flew at his face, at his chest. Lo'gan stepped forward to stop her, but Medophae caught his wrist and sent him spinning away. Deetra's strikes were wild and passionate. Medophae winced as she hit him, but he let the blows fall. After a short time, they became feeble, and the woman slumped against him. He wrapped his arms around her and held her tight. She sobbed into his shoulder.

"No..." she whispered, her body shuddering. "Please..."

"I'm sorry, Deetra. Gods, I'm so sorry," he said, fighting to speak over the lump in his throat. Her long brown hair swept down the front of his chest and over his arms as she shook. He didn't know how long he stood there, holding her, but eventually, someone removed his arms.

He looked up. Another woman had arrived. She was small, older, with graying hair and dark brown eyes. She led Deetra toward the door. Medophae turned to Lo'gan.

"The next door neighbor, sir. She came when she heard the screaming."

"Yes..." He turned away from his lieutenant. He put his hands on the porch rail. The tears welled up, burning his eyes. He let out a slow breath and blinked them back.

"Sir, are you all right?"

He nodded, took another breath. "Come back in a few days, Lo'gan. After the funeral. Let her know that Galden's wages will continue to come to her. Tell her that the Guard takes care of its own."

"Yes, sir. Of course." Lo'gan paused, then said, "And tomorrow, sir?"

"Tomorrow?"

"Yes, sir. Tomorrow we find the beast and destroy it."

Medophae nodded slowly. Not on your life, Lo'gan. Not on yours or anyone else's.

The beast dies tonight.

4

MIROLAH

MIROLAH WAS SOAKED to her skin, but she didn't care. When the heavy clouds had rolled in more than an hour ago, she had closed up her table, stashed it inside Lawdon's workshop without letting anyone in the house know, and gone for a walk.

The rain still fell steadily, giving the hard-packed dirt streets a slippery sheen of mud. If it persisted, they would soften, sucking at horses' hooves and miring wagon wheels. Lawdon hated the rain. It made travel difficult and his business depended on delivering tiles to his customers.

But Mirolah loved it, and even though she was cold and thoroughly wet, she paused across the street from her home and leaned against the wall of the bakery that had closed an hour ago. Her house was a rather plain, two-story structure with a single-level workshop jutting out from the left side. That was where Lawdon formed and baked his tiles. When she first joined her adopted family, Lawdon had collected most of his tiles by sorting through the wreckage of abandoned buildings in Rith and even Old Rith. Since the Sunriders moved on and commerce began flowing again, every year brought more people to Rith. New people meant rebuilding old houses, giving them new roofs, or in rare cases building new houses. The usable tiles from Old Rith were almost depleted, and Lawdon was one of the few in town who could make new ones. There was always a demand for his work, and she was happy for his success. No one deserved it more.

Rith was rebuilding, growing. The difference between now and the last decade was subtle. More wagons. More people. More colors—from plants on window sills, and from a rare bolt of bright yellow cloth brought into the city and turned into twenty dresses, one worn by every woman who could afford it. But the most colorful addition to the streets was the smiles. Those had not been present when Mirolah first came straggling into Rith, hungry, scared and silent. For the first time, Rith had begun to feel safe to her.

The rain had brought a premature darkness to the city, but it wasn't quite dusk. Though she couldn't see it, she could feel the sun behind the clouds, blazing a sunset that no one would see. With the rain-blurred view of the city, she squinted her eyes and imagined how the broken buildings must have looked during the Age of Ascendance, when a festival of colors was an everyday sight, when exotic trees and plants laced throughout the city, and houses shimmered with whatever use of GodSpill its owner had set upon it. When threadweavers appeared through portals or trundled down the street in carts drawn by nothing but air.

People back then had created so many books. She couldn't imagine how many scribes must have worked days and years and even lifetimes creating books for there to have been so many.

But such things were hated now, mostly. Almost no one could read, and any books that looked like they had even the slightest reference to GodSpill were piled next to the hearth, their pages used as kindling for fires. Lawdon had a pile of them of his own, taken from an old library he found while looking for tiles. She had peeked in them when no one was around. She'd read about the threadweavers and what they could do. She had read about heroes from the Age of Ascendance, when kingdoms spanned miles and miles. She had committed the names of her favorites to memory.

The information the books held was wild and foreign, and it set her imagination alight. They told stories of wondrous things that could be done during that time, ordinary people using GodSpill for the most mundane of tasks, like commanding a broom to sweep a floor all by itself, like making water flow upward instead of down.

It was said the gods had punished Amarion for its hubris during the Age of Ascendance, for overreaching and acting like gods themselves. But Mirolah had read one bedraggled text that said the loss of these fantastic powers was because a group of threadweavers—a name for skilled users of the GodSpill—had capped something called Daylan's Fountain. The writer of the book claimed that this was what had stopped GodSpill from flowing into the lands, not the wrath of the gods themselves. It was insanity, but it compelled her.

When the gods delivered their wrath, thousands died on that very day, just dropped dead as though they were marionettes whose strings had been cut. The threadweavers who had immorally used the GodSpill for their own selfish desires died. It was as though their blood had been sucked from their veins. Almost everyone was a threadweaver during the Age of Ascendance. All of humanity's leaders—its most learned women and men, its wealthiest tradespeople, its most influential royalty—they all died. The writer of that book estimated that ninety percent of all the people in Amarion had died.

Entire cities were abandoned, and the great kingdoms of Amarion dwindled to a few patches of frightened humanity, like in Rith and Buravar to the north.

No living person remembered what Amarion had been like during that time, and it was dangerous to wonder about it. Mirolah kept her reading secret. GodSpill was not spoken about in Rith, except to be used as a curse. What were once called threadweavers were now referred to as rot bringers. The very notion of trying to understand GodSpill was a crime in Rith.

It was a crime to do so, but sometimes Mirolah wondered about all of the writings that had been lost over the centuries, all the books that had been burned. It was said there was a library in Buravar, a small one filled only with the histories of the time after the judgment of the gods and the subsequent penance of humankind.

Only verbal stories now remained, mostly of heroes. Never of threadweavers. While threadweavers were cursed, called rot bringers, people clung to heroes. They were bright and colorful and always fought for the good. One of her favorites was Vlacar, who was something called a paladin, but also the archer duo, Bardus and his brother, nicknamed "Clincher," who traveled all over the lands and beyond with twin bows that never missed. There was Sasha Braen'dite, who closed the Godgate and saved humankind from being overwhelmed by the crack in the Godgate. There was also Meetris Deneer and his dancing sword. And, of course, her favorite: Wildmane and his lady love, Bands, the dragon who could shapeshift into human form. Wildmane was her favorite. There were so many stories about him.

The legends didn't create danger or apprehension like the books did. Instead, they gave hope; they ignited belief that better days would come, that there were women and men of strength, so much strength that they could lend it to others.

Mirolah blinked, focused again on the rain, imagining shimmering cobblestones over the muddy road, bright paint on every building. She pictured rich blue fabric draped over white horses as they clacked up the street in procession, noble riders holding lances straight up, colorful pennants snapping in the breeze, burnished armor glinting in the sun. People cheering. Children laughing and running through safe streets.

She closed her eyes, and the vision vanished, transforming back to the gray rain and dirt-smudged buildings. There was no glorious parade, only an empty, muddy street....

Mirolah drew a quick breath. A slender, cloaked man stood in the doorway of her home across the street, watching her.

Of course he's watching you! He's probably wondering if there's something wrong with you, standing in the rain like an idiot.

She broke from the wall and splashed across the street. He was probably just a customer, but she kept one hand on the small knife Lawdon had given her.

"Good evening, young lady," he said in a deep voice that

rumbled her chest. It was the type of voice she would expect to hear come from a giant of a man, seven feet tall and three hundred pounds, not a slender man barely taller than her. Under his cowl, the man's brown hair curled down the sides of his face and ended just above his shoulders. His skin was tanned and weathered, and laugh lines wrinkled the edges of his eyes. He had a bent nose, as if it had been broken sometime in his past. The man inclined his head, touched the handle, and opened the door for her. As he did so his plain, brown cloak opened, and she saw a finely tooled black vest over a white shirt. Expensive clothes, far more expensive than most clothes in Rith.

She realized that she was staring and rushed to find her tongue. "Good evening, sir," she said. "Please, come in. There's no reason for you to stand in the rain." She glanced into the house. Casra was spreading the tablecloth over the dining table, readying for supper, and she looked up, her eyebrows rising. The man moved inside the room, and Mirolah closed the door.

"Thank you," he said.

"Did no one answer your knock?" Mirolah asked, holding out her hand for his cloak, which he gave to her. His rich clothes were dry underneath, and she realized his seemingly plain cloak had been treated with some kind of oil to repel the rain.

"I enjoy storms," he said. "It evokes my imagination. When I look at the rain, I see heroes."

That was odd. She found it eerie that she had been doing almost exactly that. She removed her own cloak and hung it, dripping, next to his. Her own clothes were wet; she would need to change before supper.

"What about you?" he asked. "I wondered if we were looking at the same thing. Heroes in the rain."

"I was just..." She stammered, trying to think of something safe to say. Telling him that she envisioned the Age of Ascendance was not a safe conversation.

"The rain is something like a new canvas, isn't it?" he asked.

"Canvas?"

"In some places, they make pictures on canvas. Did you know? They smear pigments across it to make images."

"You're talking about paintings."

"Just so. Rain makes the lands like a painting, don't you think? Everything fades a little, becomes less distinct. When it storms, I imagine painting the world differently, changing a little something here, a little something there."

She didn't like how he seemed to know her thoughts, to know what she had really been doing across the street. "Lawdon hates the rain," she said quickly. "It makes business difficult. If you're hoping for a delivery from him, you may have to wait."

Tiffienne bustled into the room, carrying a bucket of rainwater. They had a well, but she liked to collect water from the sky. "Oh, Mirolah," she said, noticing her. "Good that you're home. This man has been waiting for you."

Time slowed for her. "For me?" No. That could only mean one thing. This was the man that horrible Prinka woman had called. This was Reader Orem.

"Yes, dear," Tiffienne said, not noticing that Mirolah had gone stiff. "He's been waiting for you for an hour now. He went by the town circle, but you'd already left. Where have you been?"

"I...had some things to get..." she said, then realized she had nothing in her hands, "...straightened out in my head," she finished lamely. "I went for a walk."

Casra rolled her eyes. Tiffienne pretended not to notice the blatant lie, and she turned to the man. "Are you sure you won't stay for dinner? It will only be another half an hour or so."

"Honestly, I cannot. Thank you so much for your kind offer."

"Well, don't let us stop you," Tiffienne said. "Casra, come with me."

Casra pulled her gaze away from the man, then adjusted a plate on the table. "But I'm not done," she said.

Tiffienne gave her a pointed look.

Casra glanced at Mirolah, then at Tiffienne. "Fine." She pouted. The two left the family room and disappeared up the stairs.

Mirolah desperately wanted to call out to Tiffienne not to go. Instead, she slowly turned to face the man.

"You're him, aren't you?" she asked. "That horrible old woman sent you."

"You can call me Orem." The man's eyes were dark brown and gentle, his deep voice soothing.

"Reader Orem," she said, looking over her shoulder as though someone would catch her saying that near-blasphemous title.

"That's just a nickname. It wasn't meant to flatter, but I've grown fond of it. Unfortunately in this time, some people don't trust those of us who can read."

"They trust us as long as we don't read books. They trust me."

"I'm sure they do."

"But you read books, don't you?"

"Every book I can find." He glanced at the three thick volumes at the hearth. His wistful gaze at the impending destruction of those books made her feel guilty.

"Why?" she asked.

"Because there is knowledge in them."

"Too much knowledge destroyed the world."

"*Almost* destroyed the world," he corrected her.

"Some knowledge is only meant for the gods. That's the lesson humankind has learned the hard way."

"Perhaps."

"Trying to use what spilled through the Godgate centuries ago is dangerous. It's immoral."

"Reading isn't threadweaving."

"Don't say things like that," she hissed, looking around in alarm. No one used that word!

"But it's true. Reading isn't the same. If it was, I'd be a threadweaver of great power by now."

She winced and stepped away from him as though he was pointing a spear at her. "Stop saying that. People get killed for such things!"

His eyes were just a little bit sad, like he was looking into her heart, like he could see her fear of what they did to her little brother, Dorn. She didn't want him in her house. It was like being trapped in a cage with a wild animal. If he would say the word "threadweaver" aloud, what else would he do? She glanced at the stairs, then at the kitchen doorway, but it was as though the house was suddenly empty.

Orem sat down without invitation, put his hands quietly on the table, and laced his fingers together. "Do you still have the stone Prinka gave you?"

"No," she lied quickly. She didn't want the stone. She wanted to have left it at the town circle, but she couldn't make herself do it. The truth was that the stone sat snugly in a thick pouch against her chest. She had slept with that pouch for the last five nights. For some reason, it felt good to have it near her, and that haunted her. If anyone caught her with it, they'd know she was just like Dorn.

"May I see it?" he asked gently.

"Why don't you just go?" she asked bluntly, wanting to offend him, but he just chuckled.

"If you like," he said. "But it won't make the stone go away, especially when you keep it so close. And it won't keep the others away, the ones who will come looking for you."

"Others? What are you talking about? I didn't do anything!"

"Bad things don't happen just because of what you do. Sometimes they happen because of who you are. The lands are not fair. Or gentle."

She saw little Dorn's face, his happy face, just before they killed him. It was like he was reading her mind. "Stop it," she hissed.

"Having as much knowledge as you can is the only way to see clearly. I claim the title 'Reader' with pride. It means I know more, and that's what I wanted. It's what I've earned. I worked very hard to know what I know."

"Are you bragging?" she asked.

He paused, still not offended. Mirolah didn't know how she could be any more rude.

"Tell me," he said. "How did you learn to read and write?"

She felt heat in her face as she flushed. "I just know. Why do you care?"

"It is strange for someone like you to be here, in this town, and know how to read."

"I'm not strange!"

"Were your parents nobility?"

"No."

"Did they work for nobility?"

"I don't want you asking so many questions about my life. I don't like it, and I don't like you," she said. She thought of her mother and father, dying at the hands of the Sunriders like so much wheat cut down by a scythe. Those stories weren't for him.

"Then how did you—?"

"If I tell you, will you leave?"

He paused, then slowly nodded, again with the sad eyes. "Of course."

"There was a book, okay? It was a book describing how to make a mill and a water wheel. It was *not* some book about GodSpill. My father and his brothers wanted to remake the mill, so they had the book because it had pictures. But they couldn't get the plans to work. So I..." she trailed off.

"You helped them."

"I read it. There were instructions in the words that were missing in the pictures."

"How did you do it?"

"I don't *know*. The more I looked at it, the more it made sense. That's all."

He put a hand to his chin, tapped a finger on his lower lip. "That's a rare gift."

Her heart raced. "You want to be a rot bringer and harness GodSpill. That's evil!"

"A rot bringer?" He seemed amused by that term. "Is that what they call the threadweavers of old?"

She wished he would stop saying that word! "You promised you'd leave if I told you. You're still here."

He nodded. "Fair enough. I will leave. Before I do, may I look at the stone?"

She clenched her teeth. She thought about not giving it to him. Instead, she reached into the pouch around her neck, took it out. Bright rainbow colors swirled inside the stone.

Orem gasped.

"The colors," he whispered, wide eyed and captivated. He reached out a shaking hand for it. "May I...?"

His reaction to the stone spooked her. She grabbed his hand and pushed the stone into it. "Take it. I don't want it."

The stone went black.

"What did you do?" she asked.

He stared at it ruefully. "Nothing. This stone is black. You are the one who fills it with colors."

"I didn't fill it with anything!"

"It's called a laughing stone," Orem said. "A quicksilver's toy. The quicksilvers made them for their children, who would slowly learn to bring out a single color in the stone. Every child had her own unique color. With practice, they could change the shade and brightness of the stone with the sound of their laughter."

"Well, take it. I don't want to see it ever again." Again, it was a lie. She longed to grasp the stone again. It scared her, but at the same time it was like a link to her brother. It felt like him. It reminded her of him.

Visions of him leapt through her head, of when they killed him. Little Dorn, smiling at the group of refugees who had gathered around. He'd made colors brighter than the laughing stone. He'd made them leap through the air, made the colors dance. Dorn had been so proud of himself. But it was GodSpill he was using. She remembered the hairs raising on her arms, the power in the air. Everyone could feel it. It felt like terror.

She had screamed when the first rock hit Dorn in the head. She had thrown her body over his, but they'd pulled her away. Big men. Angry women. She tried to stop them, but they had been so large. The stones hit Dorn, over and over again. With stones gripped in fists, they beat him until he died.

"Mirolah." Orem broke her reverie, his voice earnest. "I spent one hour every single day for a year trying to affect this stone. After all that time, all I could do was change it from black to gray." He paused. "But it bursts into a rainbow when you touch it. A *rainbow*." He seemed awed. "I've never seen that. I've never even *read* about that—"

She slammed her arms on the table. "You promised! Now go!"

She heard a footstep behind her, and she turned to find Lawdon standing in the kitchen doorway. He had a tile-shaping tool in his hands, a long steel rod with an edge. To Mirolah's left, Tiffienne stood at the bannister, and Mirolah's nine sisters were stacked up the stairs like birds, each one peeking through the rails.

Orem drew a slow breath. The wrinkles around his eyes were pained. He set the black stone on the table next to her hand and let it go. Dull colors began to swirl. She snatched her hand away, and the stone faded to gray.

"There are real heroes in the world still, Mirolah," Orem said softly. "Not just phantoms in the rain. And we need them more than ever."

She held her chin up high.

He nodded, then stepped back from the table, deftly hooked a finger under the collar of his cloak and slipped it off the rack. "I know that truth can be frightening," he said. "But ignorance can be deadly."

Without another word, he swung the cloak over his shoulders, opened the door, and disappeared into the rainy night.

She waited for a long moment, then snatched up the stone, ran to the door and flung it open. The rain was falling heavily now. She could barely see the bakery on the other side of the street. Reader Orem was gone.

She hurled the stone into the mud with all her strength, turned, and slammed the door, leaning her back against it.

Her breath came hard as she looked at her family, who were all staring at her with gazes of wonder, surprise, or compassion. She tried to force the thought of the laughing stone from her mind. She had wanted to throw it farther. She had wanted to lose it in the rain.

But she could picture the exact spot where it had splatted in the mud.

5

MEDOPHAE

A RAVEN CAWED at the top of the cliff, disturbed from its slumber as Medophae pulled himself over the lip of the cave, a hundred feet above the roaring surf. Even in the dark of night, the jagged cliff offered plenty of handholds and footholds, and the climb had not been difficult. He unslung his pack, unstrapped his sword, and buckled it around his waist. Next, he withdrew his flint and steel, and a torch. In a moment, a tongue of flame flowed upward from the thick, pitch-covered stick, sending light and sharp shadows stretching down the tunnel.

He stooped and started forward. It twisted this way and that, sometimes narrowing so severely that he was forced to crawl, pushing the torch ahead of him.

His memories hovered around him, memories as old as Bands, memories from another age. He was close now. Whatever had killed Galden was ahead, and if it wanted to try its hand at killing Medophae, he welcomed it.

He stood as the passage opened into a huge cavern. Air flowed past, carrying the smell of rotting flesh. Just within the perimeter of his light, he saw a human arm, torn meat at the shoulder, decaying fingers curled in pain long past.

Perhaps this was from a vagabond from the abandoned kingdom of Diyah? Or a Teni'sian fieldworker not reported missing? He moved closer, found half of another human body. The sweet, cloying stench thickened around him. There were also the corpses of a deer and a lyonar. This hunter was no surf dragon. This hunter was fast, and it killed for sport. Most of these corpses were barely eaten.

He pulled a length of rope, a slipknot tied in each side, from his pack. Something scratched the ceiling overhead, the faintest whisper of claw on rock.

Medophae threw his shoulder to the cavern floor, leaving the torch behind. A purr tickled his ear as something large flew over him, striking the torch where he had been a moment ago. The torch skittered across the floor and hit the wall. Medophae rolled to his feet and drew his sword from its scabbard, steel ringing in the quiet. He held the length of rope in his other hand.

The torch guttered, illuminating an oval portion of the wall and curved ceiling. He scanned the highest perimeter of the light, edged his way backward, trying to see any movement in the blackness.

There was a light scrape on the rock wall behind him.

The creature was fast—!

Razor claws dug into his neck. The thing landed heavily on him, driving him to his knees. He tried to shake it loose, but its claws sank deep into his ribs. He stifled his scream, kept his mind on the fight. Flipping his sword around, he stabbed the thing, and the blade sank deep, hitting muscle, bone.

The creature howled, letting go and retreating into the darkness again. It had two arms, two legs, longer and thinner than a human. Medophae waited, tense, feeling the warm blood flow down his side.

"Come..." he growled into the dark, gritting his teeth against the punctures and slices.

A hiss answered him.

A dark shape flew out of the shadows. Medophae slashed...

...and his sword struck the rotting corpse the creature had

43

thrown at him.

It attacked instead from the side, wrapping itself around him. Its hind claws sliced into Medophae's thighs. Its front claws gripped his neck, and it sank needle-like teeth into Medophae's throat.

A scream filled the cavern, and Medophae distantly realized that it was his own.

The teeth ripped through Medophae's neck muscles, arteries, windpipe. A killing blow for a mortal. But not for Medophae.

The rage exploded inside him, a golden fire that blew apart his sanity and took hold of his body. The door inside him—that he tried so hard to keep closed—slammed open, and Oedandus, Medophae's god and ancestor, awoke.

He dropped his sword. It made no sound as it hit the stones. He could not hear the purring breath of his attacker, could not hear even his own breathing. There was only the burning. It moved outward from his bones, raced through his blood, lit his muscles alight, and leaked from his pores. The golden fire raced across Medophae's skin as though he had been soaked in oil, engulfing his arms and chest.

His glow lit up the darkness, and he grabbed the monster. It tore away a chunk of his neck and went for another. Medophae howled, a grotesque gargle through the hole in his throat, and he ripped the creature away, flaying the flesh from his own back as he slammed it to the ground. It hissed, tried to scramble away, but Medophae had a grip on it now. And Oedandus was with him. It wasn't going anywhere.

Destroy it, the voice growled in the back of his mind. *You are the hand of justice.*

Golden fire flared from Medophae's hands as he bore down on the beast. The creature's arm snapped. Ribs crunched. The monster fought desperately now, scratching against rock and dirt, clawing at Medophae's stomach, biting his forearms. He couldn't feel any of it.

He lifted the creature and brought it down onto his knee. Bones snapped. The creature howled.

Again, the dark voice said. The vengeful fire gushed through his body, filling him with unfathomable power.

He raised it overhead, slammed the creature onto the stone.

Destroy them all, the voice said.

Medophae bent the creature, snapped it, twisted it. He was divine vengeance, and this creature was an abomination. The monster's agony thrilled him with holy joy.

He lifted it, slammed it down. And again, and again. Finally, the beast was nothing but a limp bag of broken bones, slick with blood.

Justice... The dark voice retreated, far back into the deepest part of Medophae's mind. The golden fire flickered and died away, and Medophae's sanity returned. He stumbled back from the mangled mass. Black blood covered his hands and arms. His breath whistled out of his throat like wind through a broken window. He clenched his gory fists in front of his face, fell to his knees and slowly...slowly...took control again.

He knelt there a long time, waiting. The golden fire flickered about his injuries, and the blood stopped flowing. The wounds healed. Skin, bone, and cartilage knit together, returning Medophae's body to its original state, to that eighteen-year-old adventurer he had been when Oedandus had found him and claimed him. He touched his hair, and it was long again, straight and golden down to his shoulders.

He pushed himself to his feet, walked to the torch, and picked it up. He shined it upon the broken body.

It was a darkling, one of the god Dervon's creatures. But there were no darklings anymore. They were made creatures, reliant on GodSpill. And there was no GodSpill in the lands anymore—no threadweavers, no quicksilvers, no vampires, and no darklings.

"How are you here?" Medophae rasped at the dead creature. "You can't be here...."

6

ZILOK MORTH

"SEF."

"Yes, my master."

"Where do you suppose that darkling came from?"

"I do not know, my master."

"Darklings only operate at the end of a leash. Someone sent it. It is enough to stir the blood."

"Yes, my master."

"Metaphorically speaking."

"Yes, my master."

"It interests me that another like me may have risen, powerful enough to summon a darkling. It is no coincidence that the Wildmane and this darkling met. We must assume the darkling's master hunts our prey. I do not like this, Sef."

"Yes, my master."

"The best-laid plans can be upset by a sloppy interloper. If we have stumbled across a ghost with a grudge who insists on flinging darklings into the Wildmane's path, then we must account for this."

"Yes, my master."

"We must use him, make him a part of our plan."

"Yes, my master."

"Removing the Wildmane's secret admirer in the Coreworld was our first step. Our second shall be to find this darkling's master. Third, we must understand why the GodSpill has returned in the first place."

"Yes, my master."

"Every great action has a trail of smaller actions behind it. We will find this trail. We will be meticulous, Sef."

"Yes, my master."

"We will be vigilant."

"Yes, my master."

"We will see all problems before they arise, or the Wildmane will escape us again. He suffers. He broods. He wishes he was not the house for the feral god Oedandus. He wants to be mortal. He wants to die. We will help him, Sef."

"Yes, my master."

"We will pare him down to his quivering, mortal body, and we will settle accounts."

"Yes, my master."

"We will take from him what he took from me."

"Yes, my master."

"Now, Sef, there is reading to be done. Even the scribblings of fools can hide wisdom, if one knows how to look. We must know what has transpired during our absence."

"As you say, my master."

"Yes, as I say."

7

TYNDIRIA

TYNDIRIA AWOKE, a light chill on her bare skin. She liked coming to the surface of a deep sleep to goosebumps on her arms, then snuggling into the warmth of her down covers. Her wooden shutters stood open to the starry night like a gateway. She liked that chill, and to feel the gradual cooling of the air night after night as the last remnants of summer vanished. The transition was so brief that she woke each night just to feel it slipping away. And when the cold finally came, it was as though her ephemeral summer had never been.

Fleeting moments were that much sweeter for their impermanence. At eighteen, she knew that lesson well. She'd loved her mother and brother, and her father especially. And their loss had only made them more precious in her mind, only made her cling to their lessons more fiercely. Nothing lasted; one must enjoy the summer before it was gone.

She turned over, looked at the man in the bed next to her.

When he commanded her guards, he was implacable, like a mountain rising from the True Ocean, immovable. When they made love, he was playful, artful; he worshipped her and she felt like a goddess. When they lay down to sleep, he was her protector, enveloping her in his arms until she drifted off.

But when he slept, she could imagine he was her own age. The mantle of his many lives fell away, and he seemed the eighteen-year-old he had been when he was made immortal: young and long-limbed and muscled and... She wanted to take a bite out of him.

She reached out a hand to touch him, but didn't. She just let it hover over the smooth, bare skin of his muscled back. Her heart was full, spilling over. Every moment with him made her better. His lips on hers thrilled her. His quiet manner taught her presence, the ease of real leadership. His restraint taught her willpower, that it was at the core of everything a leader must be.

He was her precious summer, and she knew, like the summer, he would one day be gone. She knew it the first moment she saw him, and again when she opened the dusty Teni'sian library that had been walled off for decades and did her research. That was when she discovered who he really was. The legends of Wildmane were well known. But historical accounts of the man were rare; almost no one knew them.

Once she learned he was the demi-god from the stories, the prudent thing to do would have been to lock her heart away and look on him as a royal asset.

But she had wanted him. Oh, she had wanted him, and so she had taken him. His heart was a cracked china cup. The love and certainty that had once filled it had been drained away long ago, and his fragile heart was held together by a flagging will. He longed for his lost beloved, and she had seen his weakness. He was willing to pretend his beloved was still here, if given the chance. He was willing to pretend with another.

And so, one day, Tyndiria had stepped into that role. She filled his broken cup. She captured him, and she stole a brief season of happiness.

Now she bore her victory, twin marks on her soul. A brushstroke of ecstasy and a slice of agony, running side by side.

He would leave someday. Whether he rode away tomorrow or

held her dying, wrinkled body on her seventieth birthday, Medophae would leave her behind. But she had the wisdom to hold that hurt as precious as she held the joy.

Medophae shuddered, and she drew back her hand. The tremor was small, and if she had been asleep, she wouldn't have noticed it.

He turned, and his eyelids flickered. Then, as if he had never been asleep, he said in his rich, compelling voice, "Diria... You should sleep, my queen."

She didn't speak. Instead, her fingers traced his collarbone, then the edge of his jaw. Mere hours before, he'd come to her in the middle of the night, bloody. She had called for a servant to bring water, and she had helped wash him clean. He had told her about the darkling, about what it did to him, and that he had destroyed it: a creature from the Age of Ascendance.

Now, this moment with him, it was like a breath drawn in deeply and held, waiting to exhale. Somehow, there was GodSpill in the lands of Amarion again. Medophae denied it, said it was a strange fluke, but it was the only explanation for the arrival of a darkling, a supernatural creature that had once only existed in legend..

Her season of summer was turning, and what she had stolen must be returned. The lands were coming for him.

"Were you dreaming about the darkling?" she asked.

He let out a long breath, but he said nothing.

"Were you thinking of *her?*"

He shook his head. "You don't want to talk about that."

"I want to know. Will you not share it with me?" Medophae's loss of his beloved Bands was intertwined with his core; no history book told that tale. No one knew except Medophae.

He paused. "In truth, I am trying to forget it."

"I watch you hold it in so tightly. To talk might release it. Try. Try with me."

He shook his head. "I just want to forget."

"Turning your head from danger does not create safety, only the illusion of safety." She repeated the words he had spoken to her two years ago when she had first taken power in Teni'sia.

He chuckled. "Crackpot wisdom. Who told you that?"

"Some man I met."

"Who probably couldn't be trusted with two copper pennies and an errand to buy bread." The corner of his mouth turned up in a smile.

It was like the sun's own warmth, and she laughed.

"Tell me you didn't give him the coppers," he said.

"I gave him my body." She ran her hand over his chest.

He rolled on top of her, kissed her. "Foolish. You realize you're never getting it back, right?"

"That's okay," she murmured as he kissed her throat, her jaw, her ear. "I didn't want it anyway..."

She told herself she didn't care that he had steered the conversation away from Bands, away from the tragedy that had cracked his heart. She had made him smile. If nothing else, she had helped him close his eyes and look away from the danger, and maybe that was all she could do. Maybe that was her purpose in his life. Maybe that was enough.

She had stolen her precious season; she bore the two bright marks on her soul. And it was so hard to remember the agony when all she could feel was the ecstasy.

8

MEDOPHAE

THEY DIE. YOU LIVE. *It's always the same.*

Medophae sat up quietly. Tyndiria slumbered, tangled in her sheets. Her crimson hair spilled across the pillow like a fan. She'd fallen asleep with a smile. Happy for the moment. That was all he could do for her.

He couldn't save her from death. He couldn't save any of them. Once, Medophae believed he could. He had tried to be a force for good in the world. He'd tried to save hundreds, thousands at a time. He had stood between kingdoms and the armies of conquerors, only to later watch those same kingdoms turn conquerors themselves, or crumble from disease, or fall into chaos.

But he could protect at least one person. With all of his power, he should be able to do that. If he stayed vigilant, careful, and if he did not attract attention, he could ensure that at least Tyndiria lived a long, happy life.

This was the gift Orem had given to Medophae, bringing him into this tenacious cluster of humanity in Teni'sia. Tyndiria had evoked interest within him, something he'd thought long dead. He found himself caring about her, against his will, because she was what he should be. She was unreasonably hopeful and brave. She was a shining example of goodness. And if he couldn't manage to be the Wildmane the stories sang about, if he couldn't exemplify those heroic qualities, at least he could protect someone who did.

He went to the balcony and looked down at the distant, roaring surf. But still, he doubted himself. Did he ever really help at all? *What if I'm the real danger? What if the darkling is here because of me?*

Wasn't this how it began in the first place, lifetimes ago with Zilok Morth and Bands, Vitrio, and Quinn? They conspired to slay a god of horrors, to make the lands safer for humankind, to do good, but their temerity called down the lightning. And when it came...

Vitro and Quinn had died, Zilok was forever scarred, and Bands lay in a coma for months.

And Medophae lived, returned to health, to exactly the way he had been because Oedandus would not let Medophae change or grow old or die. Ever.

Golden fire crackled around Medophae's body as Oedandus awoke to his anger.

I hate you, Medophae said to the senseless god. You're the reason I lost everything.

He opened a thick leather pouch, well-worn from the centuries it had spent with him, and upended it. A dusky red gem slipped into his palm. Crimson smoke swirled within, and he could feel its warmth. Did that mean she was still alive?

Because Medophae gave in to his folly, because he played the god, he had brought the lightning, he had drawn all those who longed to challenge power. And finally came the sorceress Ethiel, who fancied herself Medophae's one true love. No gentle refusals could turn her aside. No forceful rebukes diminished her zeal. And finally, her mind poisoned by insanity, she'd made it her life's purpose to undo whatever Medophae tried to do, and finally to take Bands away from him.

And somehow...she had succeeded. Ethiel had created a spell so powerful that it captured a dragon and a god and held them inside this mystical red gem, and no matter what Medophae did, he could not free them.

The damning golden fire flared about him, illuminating the balcony as he leapt to the rail and cocked his arm back to throw the gem to the horizon.

He could throw the gem away and leap after it. Certainly even he could not survive if he swam fathoms deep and drowned. And when Oedandus revived him, he would swim deeper and drown again. And again and again until he *stayed* dead. And if that did not work, he would beg Saraphazia for death. Certainly the goddess of the True Ocean, Oedandus's sister, could kill him....

Medophae remained that way, struggling against himself, willing himself to do the deed. His biceps trembled as he clenched the stone. His lips pulled back in a soundless snarl.

A low breath escaped him, and he fell to his knees. He couldn't do it. He was nothing without Bands. In all likelihood, she had died centuries ago, nothing more than a corpse trapped in that jewel, but he couldn't let her go.

Gingerly, he slipped the stone back into its pouch.

"Medophae..."

He twisted on his knees, then sucked in a breath.

Ethiel's red hair stood out like a flame in the darkness. She was alive! She was here!

He leapt to his feet. Golden fire raced over his chest, down his arm to his fist. Golden fire elongated and formed into a sword, hissing and spitting flecks of flame.

Tyndiria gasped and stumbled backward.

You are the hand of justice, Oedandus's dark voice inside told him. *Kill her.*

Medophae blinked, shook his head.

No. It wasn't Ethiel. It was Tyndiria. Ethiel was gone. This was Tyndiria's castle, her bedchambers. She was his lover.

The queen stood, uncertain, in the center of the room, clutching a blue satin sheet to her breast, her dark red ringlets in disarray.

"Tyndiria..." he said. "I'm so sorry. I'm—"

"No don't..." she said. "Don't apologize." She came forward a step, reached out a shaking hand as though she could touch him from ten feet away.

He crossed the distance and took her in his arms. "I would never hurt you," he said. "I would rather die."

She hugged him tightly. "I was afraid." She mumbled into his broad chest. "So afraid for you. You were suddenly a stranger, and I feared what you would do to yourself."

He cradled her, pushing his memories to the back of his mind where they could not rule him, where they could not make him do something he would regret forever. But they were bright and alive inside him, and he relived that horrible moment when he lost Bands. As he pressed Tyndiria to his chest, holding onto her like she was his last thread of sanity, he saw that moment like it was all happening again:

Medophae drove the godsword through Ethiel's chest. She gasped, her hands splaying as though she was tossing something invisible at him.

A deep red light swelled behind him. It pulled at him, but Bands hit him like a flying boulder, shoving him out of the way as the portal flashed. Bands and Tarithalius vanished into it like drops into an ocean, and Medophae skidded across the floor. He leapt to his feet, annoyed. Ethiel had scored a point, but there was no cage made of GodSpill that could hold a dragon and a god.

As Ethiel coughed blood on the steps of her own throne, her smile was smug through the pain, like this was all part of the plan. Her laughter echoed in the cavernous room, then she spoke the last words she would ever say, the words that would, over the coming century, crush Medophae into despair.

"Only you can bring them back, hero. Only you." She coughed, mixing blood with her words. "Solve the riddle and set her free. Take these words and unwind them, and she is yours: You must give to someone that which you have already given away. And you must cast away what now sustains you. This is my riddle. This is my vengeance upon you for every act of brutality you have visited upon me. But I promise you, this time your rage will avail you nothing." She coughed, red spilling down her chin. "You can only kill me once, hero. But I..." she coughed again. "I shall stab at you from the grave. Instead of her soft, false skin against you as you sleep, you will feel my blade, thrusting. Again and again and again, forever. Solve the riddle, hero. I hope you do. For it shall not matter..."

Medophae pressed Tyndiria to his chest.

It shall not matter...

9

MIROLAH

MIROLAH LAY AWAKE most of the night, certain that Orem was hovering outside her door. Every time she closed her eyes, visions of Dorn's death forced their way into her mind's eye. She heard the angry voices, felt each kick into his tiny ribs as if they were her own. She felt like she was suffocating.

Finally, she crept to the window of the long room she shared with her sleeping sisters and peered out. No one was there, just the empty street, the quiet night. The air was cold and full of that wonderful after-rain smell. Despite herself, she strained to see if the laughing stone was still lying in the mud where she had thrown it. She couldn't see it in the dark, but she could feel it. Waiting for her.

She returned to her bed and suffered through another hour of tossing and turning before she gave up. Quietly, she climbed out of bed, sneaked downstairs, removed the heavy wooden bar from the door and hurried out into the street. Her bare feet sank into the cold mud, but she squished forward, toward the center of the street, and searched for the stone. Her foot touched something small and solid, and a flash of rainbow light splashed across her leg, She snatched up the muddy stone and hurried inside, barring the door behind her.

She washed up as quietly as she could and stole back to her bed, clenching the stone tightly in her fist. Once safely under the covers, she let the rainbow spirals dance in her hand. They were beautiful, and at the same time she hated them.

But she held it there, and soon, she sank into a dreamless sleep.

In the morning, she pretended that nothing had ever happened, that no man named Orem had visited her, and her family quietly pretended the same. She did her chores like it was a normal morning, then she went to the fountain.

A hint of red from the sunrise lingered in the east as Mirolah set up her writing table. It would be a busy day. A caravan had pulled into town last night from Buravar. A messenger would be by soon with a whole stack of new letters for her to read.

She glanced around the market as she set out her ink and papers. Her conversation last night with Orem had set her on edge. A few weeks ago, she had been content. Then he had burst into her life, and now every stranger looked dangerous. She felt tight from the top of her throat to the bottom of her stomach.

The market square was busy by the time the caravan master's daughter arrived with the bundle of letters. She was small, with a missing front tooth and dark curls cropped short around her face. In some ways , Mirolah envied the little girl growing up with the caravan, her whole life spent on the road. Mirolah already had half a dozen customers waiting to hear news from afar, so she gave the girl five silver crowns.

The second the girl was gone, Mirolah's customers clustered around her desk, anxious for news. She quickly flipped through the pile of letters, handing out the letters to those waiting. Some came from the nearby towns of Pindish and Cirienne, one from as far away as Clete. Her anxious fingers froze when she came to the letter at the bottom of the stack. Her chest locked up and refused to breathe. It was addressed to her. She slowly turned the piece of folded parchment over to see the sender's name on the far side. It bore a wax seal she did not recognize and the name P. Orem.

"What is it, Mirolah?" Taegen, the tea vendor, asked. He was looking over her shoulder hoping for a letter from his brother in Buravar.

"There's one for me," Mirolah managed to say.

"Lucky girl," he said. "Is it from family?"

"No," Mirolah admitted, still in a daze. "It's from a man."

Taegen smiled and nodded his head. "Good for you." He turned to the customers around her table. "Give the girl some room," he said, shooing them away. "Let her read in peace."

Most of them politely retreated, going to look elsewhere around the market. A few stayed, annoyed but not speaking.

Mirolah picked up the small knife from her desk and carefully broke the wax seal. She opened it up to find only a few words inside. She read them twice before refolding the letter and placing it in the pocket of her dress. Rising to her feet, she carefully started packing up her things.

She felt a hand on her shoulder and yelped.

"Where are you going?" one of her customers, a man with a long moustache, asked.

"I have to..." she said. "Please come back tomorrow."

"What? But I want to hear this now," he said.

"Are you all right, dear?" Taegen asked. "You look as though you've seen a ghost."

"I want my letter read," the moustache man said.

"Oh, a day's not going to kill you, Ramkin," Taegen admonished. "Give her some room."

The man grumbled, but he stepped back.

Mirolah started quickly throwing her things together.

"Is it bad news?" Taegen asked.

"I don't know," Mirolah said as she tucked her writing table under her arm and hurried away.

MIROLAH WENT HOME AS QUICKLY as her legs would carry her and hid her desk in the back courtyard, hoping no one would see her and ask difficult questions. Tiffienne came out of the house to toss scraps into a bowl for the cats and nearly saw Mirolah, but she ducked behind a stack of old tiles, not even breathing for fear of being discovered. She couldn't help feeling like a thief. She'd never run from a day's work in her life. Tiffienne fussed over the cats for a few minutes before going back inside.

Mirolah sneaked out of the back courtyard and took the long way around the house so she wouldn't have to walk past the open shop door. She hurried through the streets of Rith, glancing behind herself every few steps to make sure she wasn't followed.

She soon found herself walking the street through the ruins of Old Rith. She might have been near here once, years ago, collecting tiles from abandoned buildings with Lawdon, but she couldn't be sure. Most of the buildings were crumbling into the street, and nobody lived there anymore.

The letter had been from Reader Orem, asking her to meet him at the Blue Tower in Old Rith. She had seen the crumbling monument from a distance hundreds of times, but had never actually visited it. Its pale blue walls were visible from most of the city, rising high above everything around it. She had heard that Rith was once full of towers, but this was the only one that remained.

He'd asked her to meet him, and she had no doubt he would want to talk about dangerous things like threadweaving. She considered ignoring him, but she suspected, if she did, he would send her another letter or show up at her house. Or worse, he would come to the fountain. In the end, it was best to meet him alone. He could be a danger to her alone, but he was certainly a danger to her when others were around.

Today, she had to make him understand that she was not interested in him, or his wild conversations about reading and GodSpill. She wanted nothing to do with it whatsoever. That was her task.

She reached the base of the tower. The round spire rose ten stories above her head, yet it was barely more than thirty feet across. The bottom of the pale blue walls were scratched and scarred as if attacked by a hundred axes. Farther up, higher than a man could swing an axe, the remains of a beautiful mosaic rose above the gouges. She saw what looked to be the green wings of a dragon flying toward the setting sun. Most of the image had been destroyed, but the small part that remained captivated her. The craftsmanship was stunning, the colors vibrant and rich, and the details were lifelike for something made of little pieces of colored stone.

"Do you recognize it?" Orem asked from behind her.

She spun around to find him standing behind her. He looked different in the daylight, younger. Not quite so intimidating. Last night, he had seemed like a wealthy highwayman, charismatic and deadly. Now he seemed like a lesser noble from Buravar, perhaps a court storyteller. He was thin and barely taller than her.

He smiled, and a dimple appeared on his right cheek. He left his hands open at his sides, and stood just far enough away that she did not feel nervous. She tried to meet his gaze, but the heat of embarrassment rose in her cheeks. She looked away. She'd felt the way some men looked at her since she'd become a woman, gazes flickering with desire, thoughts of naked flesh. She understood that kind of gaze, and in some cases even liked it.

Orem wasn't looking at her like that. This was different.

He does not want my kiss or his hands on my body. He wants something deeper. He wants my secrets, and he cannot have them.

"It is a mosaic of Wildmane when he was just a boy," Orem continued, moving past the awkward pause as though it hadn't happened. "You know the legend of Wildmane?"

"Yes."

"This depicted when he first rode the dragon, Bands. That small bit is one of the few mosaics to survive. The whole city used to be full of mosaics like this. What wasn't lost in the GodSpill Wars or the Devastation Years was defaced by the Sunriders when they rode through."

He took a step closer to her. She didn't retreat, and she stayed wary. Last night he seemed like a complete stranger, but he seemed less so now.

"Why would they destroy something like that?"

"The Sunriders worship Wildmane as a god. And they believe creating an image of someone steals some of their power. They considered this to be sacrilege."

"So they honor him by tearing down this beautiful artwork?"

"Yes. They don't keep images of others. They believe life should be lived like wind blowing over the grass, and despise any attempt to preserve the past or predict the future. They believe it sucks the beauty from the present, lets evil seep into their minds."

"They've destroyed something beautiful. It's terrible."

"What makes you so sure your way isn't the terrible one?"

She looked at him in surprise. "Because they burn, kill, and destroy. They are ugly and brutal. We build, create, nurture, grow. Those are all beautiful things."

"I couldn't agree with you more," he said with a smile. "I am not defending them. I strive to understand them. These days, understanding is in short supply."

She paused, and realized this conversation wasn't going how she expected. She planned to ask him to leave her alone, but she found herself curious about his next words. He was intriguing and frustrating. He could never convince her that Sunriders needed only understanding to be human, though, or that their ways were simply different. She had watched the Sunriders cut down her parents.

"Some things don't need to be understood," she said. "They're just evil."

"I don't believe you believe that," he said calmly.

"Excuse me?"

"You mastered reading and writing in an illiterate community. Why?"

"That doesn't matter."

"Because you want to understand. You want to know more. You crave it. They said that threadweavers sometimes became addicted to learning—"

"I'm not going to talk to you if you're going to say such things," she cut him off. "Don't compare me to...them. I'm not a rot bringer!"

He bowed his head. "Of course. My point is that learning to read and write is difficult. Nearly impossible if you don't have a teacher."

"It just came easily to me," she said, but she remembered her thirst to understand. She hadn't just picked up the book about the mill and water wheel and read it. She'd spent days and days studying it until it started to make sense.

"You taught yourself because you had to know," he said as though reading her thoughts. "Because it drove you. That is the only way you could have managed it. And now you make your daily wage due to the very fact that you understand more than those around you."

"Okay," she said. "This is enough. I want you to leave me alone. Why did you ask me here?"

"I wanted to show you something."

"Well, I can't look at it. I'm sorry."

His eyes were warm, and she thought she saw pity in them. Pity for her. "You have worked very hard and done very well for yourself. You are strong, independent. But you don't yet know how amazing you are."

"You're wrong about me. I don't have to know. I don't *want* to know how amazing you think I am, or what those cursed abusers of GodSpill did long ago that you like to read about," she said. "Why can't you understand that? Find someone else. I am happy. The only thing that makes me unhappy is you."

"I understand," he said softly. "I was afraid once, too. You're smart. You think I am dangerous to you, and you care far too much about your adopted family to put them in danger."

"Are you dangerous to me?"

"Yes," he said. "Or rather, the knowledge I have to give you is dangerous to you."

She closed her eyes, wishing he wouldn't say anything more.

"But if you run from fear, you'll run your whole life. Despite what you say, I don't believe you actually want me to go. If you tell me to leave, and you really want me to, then I will. And I won't bother again."

"I *do* want you to go! How many different ways can I say it?"

"Then why do you still have the laughing stone?"

Her hand went involuntarily to the pouch around her neck.

He held out his hand. It was rough and tanned, callused from his travels. "Come," he said. "I want to show you something."

She shook her head. She didn't want anything to change. Dorn had died because of what he knew. She didn't want to die, but, at the same time, he was right. She wanted to know more.

She put her hand in his, and she could scarcely believe it.

He led her around the tower to an old wooden door rotting off its hinges. He opened the door, handed her inside, and she stepped into the darkness alone, running her hand along the wall, waiting for her eyes to adjust.

"There is a stairway off to your right," he said, coming up alongside her and taking her hand again.

He squeezed her hand, then led her to the top of the tower, around and around the staircase. Her legs were burning when they reached the top, and he opened the doorway to blinding light.

She blinked, stepped through, and then she could see his face again. Little crow's feet appeared at the corners of his eyes as he smiled.

"You said you were dangerous to me. Why am I trusting you?" she whispered.

He gave her hand another squeeze. "Because I looked at a black stone and knew it should have colors. Because you touched a black stone and made a rainbow."

10

MIROLAH

HE HOPPED UP on the blue stone rampart that ran around the edge of the tower. She could see the entire city from here. Rith was built in a huge, gradually sloping bowl with a small lake in the center. Everyone lived on the north side of the bowl, and she could see smoke rising lazily from their chimneys, people milling around the market at Vaisha's Fountain. The rest of the city was empty, almost entirely destroyed during the Devastation Years and the following Sunrider Wars.

"I can see Lawdon's workshop," she said, pointing off in the distance.

"Where?"

"Right there, just up from the market place. Those two chimneys. Those are ours."

He nodded.

"I helped make the tiles for half the roofs in the city."

She went to the other side of the tower and looked to the north. The trade road twisted and wound through rocky hills dotted with sheep. A caravan made its way into the hills, heading further up

The Arm. Storm clouds crouched on the horizon.

"I can't believe I've never seen this before," she murmured.

He had an amused smile on his face, and she suddenly felt twelve years old.

"Come take a look at the rest of the city," he said, "And tell me what you see."

She walked over to where he sat, perched on the rampart. She gathered her skirts in her hand and hopped up to join him.

It was marshy in the center of the bowl around the small lake. Vines and moss had taken over the ruins. Some of the buildings had crumbled with time, but some had been blackened, twisted, and melted by the GodSpill Wars hundreds of years ago.

"It's built in a spiral," she said suddenly. She had always thought the city was in a natural valley, but from this vantage, it was obvious that the circle was too perfect. There was only one Main Street, winding around and around. It made half a dozen revolutions as it radiated outward to higher and higher parts of the bowl, bisected by seven straight, wide streets leading outward from the center like the spokes of a wheel. Mirolah had always known the streets were curved, but she never realized they were the same street.

"This place has only been called Rith for the last few centuries," Orem said. "It used to be called Historia, the City of Time."

"Why change the name?"

"It was lost. Those who once lived here were killed in the GodSpill Wars; there was no one to pass on the name, and those who have made their home here do not read. Now they have resettled here, creating a city. Not yet a thriving city, maybe, but it is growing."

"It wasn't a city before?"

"No. Historia started as a giant piece of art, a living, growing sculpture depicting the history of Amarion. Those who lived here were either sculptors or supporters."

She looked at the precision of the entire city, radiating out in a spiral, and realized that the threadweavers of that time must have created the entire valley just so. It was staggering that anyone could *make* a valley.

"They could create the impossible back then," she said.

"Yes."

"And it destroyed them."

The man was silent for a moment. "Almost everyone judges the Age of Ascendance by the way it ended. Don't forget the decades of wonder and prosperity beforehand."

"Decades of abuse of the GodSpill," she murmured. "In trade for centuries of suffering."

"You see only the scars. Look harder. See the whole."

"What do you mean?"

"Look down there, the lake. See the small island poking up through the center?"

"Yes."

"It's not an island. It's a statue. It's where the story begins. Before it collapsed, it was a statue of the goddess Natra making the world. It stood over one hundred and fifty feet tall."

"From a lake?"

He laughed. "It wasn't a lake then. It was a fountain like Vaisha's Fountain used to be, but as tall as the sky. It had an endless supply of water flowing through it. When the GodSpill was sucked from the lands, the water fell and it became a lake. I would love to have seen it in its day. Natra at the center of the world, creating it from her fingertips. Dragons, whales, humans, aath trees, equines all leapt from her fingertips. It was said to spout water from a hundred places, filling the air with swirling mists. You could never see the entire thing at one time. It was constantly emerging and disappearing, changing before your eyes. At night, the water glowed five different colors, and you could see it from miles away."

She tried to imagine it, but it just didn't seem real to her.

"How? How did it work?" Dorn had made colors dance through the air. How did GodSpill move stone?

"The same way we build things now, one stone at a time. But back then, there were stoneweavers, master masons who could turn granite to clay and back with the power in their hands. People would come from all over Amarion and sometimes beyond, each bringing a stone from their homeland. They would present the rock to the master sculptor. She would listen to the rock, feel its proper place within the sculpture, then she would hand the piece to one of her children, the stoneweavers. They would climb high up onto the sides of the statue and place the stone in its proper place, smoothing the rough edges and melding it with the others around it."

She imagined the mists, imagined the giant statue of Natra, children scrambling up it like spiders, fitting stones.

"It was the very best of what people can do together. This miraculous power, the ability to use GodSpill, it did more than meld stone. It melded people, gave them a common vision and the power to make dreams come true. People today worry about their next meal. We don't look at the stars and dream anymore. And we are the lesser for that."

She looked into his eyes. They shone, like a thousand candles were glowing inside his body.

"Losing the GodSpill crushed us, but worse, we lost our dreams. We became afraid, and fear makes people small. It clouds their eyes so that they cannot see dreams becoming reality."

Being next to him was like standing in the blasting heat from Lawdon's kiln. His intensity never let up.

She turned her back and took a few steps away, put a hand on the blue marble, felt its cool solidity, held onto it like an anchor. She had a vision of Orem walking up behind her and putting his arms around her shoulders. But he didn't.

"What about the rest of the city?" she asked.

"The entire city radiated outward from Natra's statue," he said, pointing at the center of the lake. "Underneath that water, at the base of Natra's statue, the street begins. A single wall runs along one side of the street as it spirals outward. The history of the world is depicted on that wall, one huge mosaic running for miles in a circle. It started with the arrival of the gods, the creation of the sentient races, the War of the Behemoths, the creation of the Godgate, Vaisha the Changer's experiments, the Age of Awakening. It is all there, all the way up through Wildmane's slaying of the god Dervon and the founding of wondrous Calsinac. They had planned to expand the city forever, telling the history of the world as it unfolded..." He pointed at the dilapidated streets that emerged from the water, muddy and broken, curving into the rest of the city of Rith. "But it was not meant to be. The mosaics above water were destroyed, and no one can see the ones below anymore."

The sun shone overhead, but to the east, a storm approached. Dark curtains of rain fell upon the distant hills.

"It's all gone now," he said wistfully. "All that remains are the tips of a dragon's wings."

She watched Orem's back as he looked off into the distance, noticed the width of his shoulders, the way the wind barely ruffled his thick, curly hair.

"How do you know so much?" she asked him. "Some of the historical events you speak of... I've never heard of them."

"I've been hunting for as long as I can remember."

"Hunting?"

"I read every book I could find, spent my inheritance like water, walked more miles than any foot should have to suffer. I slept in ditches and rode all night through the rain. I talked to every city elder, crackpot witch woman, and charlatan illusionist I could find. And I never found anyone who could actually find or use GodSpill."

"What were you looking for?"

He let out a sigh. "Something better."

She turned a curious gaze to him, but didn't say anything.

"There are times I thought myself crazy, but every day of my life I have woken up in the morning, knowing this is not how the world is supposed to be, feeling a sickness in the lands, a wound deep down, a dryness that no amount of water can fix. A voice in my mind is constantly telling me that there is something more out there. Something that is just out of sight, just beyond the tips of my fingers. This dry, scraping existence that we call life is not what it was meant to be."

She swallowed, and her heart beat faster.

"I have seen a glimpse of what Amarion could be. I tried to turn away from it, tried to ignore it, but I cannot. There is only one thing in this world I ever wanted, only one dream that ever touched my heart. I want to bring the GodSpill back. We're hollow without it. I would die just to spend one day in a world where anything is possible. For years, I have known we can recapture this power, we can bring back what makes dreams come true. Sometimes, it is so close I can taste it. But I have never held it." He took her hands in his. "Not until now."

She stood up, tried to pull her fingers from his, but he wouldn't let go. The sun had been swallowed by the clouds, and lightning flashed in the distance. Raindrops splashed off her nose, stung her eyes.

"Please," she whispered, pulling again.

"Mirolah," he begged her. "Come with me. This is a fork in the road. We can bring the GodSpill back."

"I have to go," she said. "It's raining."

He let her go of her hands and held his up to the sky. "Let it rain." he cried. "Let it pour down. There are heroes in the rain, Mirolah. We see them! We can bring them back!"

He turned his face upward, opened his mouth as lightning flashed and thunder rumbled, coming closer.

She dashed for the stairwell, ran down around and around, until she burst out onto the street.

She ran all the way home. Wind and rain battered her from all directions, soaking her clothes, making her legs numb and wooden. She had left her writing supplies out in the back courtyard. They would be rain-soaked and ruined.

She turned off the muddy street and plunged down a flight of stone steps. Home was only a few minutes away. At the bottom of the steps, she turned a hard right and slipped in the mud. She fell to the ground, landing on her elbows, splashing mud into her eyes and mouth. Everything washed over her like a wave, and she started crying. She did not want anyone to know about the GodSpill hidden inside her. She did not want to die like Dorn.

She imagined people rushing out of their houses, circling around her, calling her a threadweaver, kicking her in the gut, yanking her around by the hair. She imagined Lawdon, looming above her, raising a stone high and bringing it down on her head.

She lay in the mud and cried, letting it all pour through her. She was shocked back to her senses when a harsh voice said to her. "Foolish girl, crying in the rain."

She peered forward through squinted eyes to see Prinka standing before her, that leering red grin and craggy face.

Mirolah scooted back in the mud.

"You can't run from him," the twisted old crone said, moving forward and crouching. "His words have power. They can't be ignored."

She grabbed Mirolah's arm and yanked her up, out of the muddy water. How could such a tiny woman be that strong? Mirolah tried to pull away.

"He has planted his seed within your heart," Prinka said.

"Leave me alone!" She shoved the old woman away with all her strength. Slipping and sliding in the mud, Mirolah ran off.

"You are already with his child!" the ancient woman yelled after her. "You will give birth to his world!"

She pressed her hands to her ears and ran.

11

MEDOPHAE

MEDOPHAE OPENED his eyes to the curved stone ceiling over Tyndiria's bed. She slumbered peacefully next to him, and he took a moment to stare at nothing. To think of nothing.

He rose, carefully and slowly, and the bed did not move. He donned his simple captain's uniform: a white shirt trapped by a leather vest. Simple black breeches, black boots. Tyndiria would have outfitted him in a noble's finery if he had let her, but Medophae had been firm. If he was to be her Captain of the Guard, he would wear the same uniform as her other guards.

Eventually, he had made a small concession to her. She had demanded that he wear some sign of his rank. She suggested a fancy hat. Medophae told her a true leader should be known by every one of his soldiers without a symbol to remind them. The person should be the symbol.

She reminded him that the people liked—even needed—to see an immediate reminder of their leader's strength and authority. It created clarity, promoted reassurance.

In the end, he had lost the argument, but he had not taken a hat as his symbol. He had an "X" harness made. Tyndiria had snorted and forbade him to use it. It was barbaric, she said. He was born in a barbaric age, he countered. She said it made him look like an ox ready to plow a field. She suggested the vest and a blue silk sash. Medophae decided he could live with that.

He tied the sash on and gently buckled his sword belt. He paused at the door. Sometimes when he left like this, he felt like a thief stealing away. A one-night lover who used her and moved on.

He walked softly down the corridor. This entire section of the castle contained Tyndiria's private quarters. Across from her bedroom was her library. Down the hall was her study. Her chambermaid had a small room adjacent to Tyndiria's. Behind Medophae, all the way to the end of the hall, was a room that Tyndiria referred to as her "quiet room." No one entered that room except for her, not even Medophae. He still didn't know what she did there. When he asked, her only response was, "It is the part of my life that is personal. It is the only part that doesn't belong to the people." He had never asked again. He understood the need for privacy.

This section of the castle was completely removed from the rest. There was only one hallway leading in or out, for obvious reasons of security. Two of Medophae's guards stood at attention at this entranceway. There were two more hidden in the hallway close by. Besides Lo'gan, Medophae's second in command, the two visible sentries were the best guards Medophae had. As quiet as he had tried to be, he was sure they had known he was in the hallway the moment he stepped from Tyndiria's bedroom.

"Good evening, Aeder, Mik'syn," he said as he came up to them.

"Good evening, Captain," Aeder said.

Mik'syn nodded and said in his low voice, "Sir."

Aeder was typical Teni'sian stock. At six feet, he was still a head shorter than Medophae. He had shoulder-length blond hair and bright blue eyes that betrayed his affability. Aeder was one of the most personable soldiers in the Guard. He had an easy way about him in everything but fighting, and his physical strength was awesome. During a sparring match once, he'd broken Medophae's blade with a mighty foot stomp. Afterward he had apologized profusely. Aeder had thought the shock of the kick would cause Medophae to drop the sword. Medophae had been laughing too hard to reprimand the unorthodox maneuver.

Mik'syn, contrary to Aeder, was quiet. He never spoke more than he had to. He was medium height for a Teni'sian, and he was thin. His chin-length brown hair framed blue eyes. Truth to tell, he didn't look very intimidating. He looked rather like a kid in a guard's uniform, but he was the second finest swordsman in the kingdom. He was as fast as Aeder was strong. Only Lo'gan could best him on the sparring field. He was what Medophae called "a hidden edge." That was why he was guarding the queen. He and Aeder made a complementary pair. One had brawn, the other speed, and both had quick, attentive minds.

"Anything unusual tonight?" Medophae asked.

"Nothing, sir," Aeder said. "Quiet as quiet can be."

Mik'syn nodded.

"How are you doing?"

Aeder smiled. "Just fine, sir." Mik'syn nodded.

"How is Fala'si? She is coming close to time, isn't she?"

Aeder reddened slightly, but he seemed pleased that Medophae had remembered to ask. "I suppose so, sir. I don't know much about that sort of thing."

"Only how to start it off, hmm?"

"Yes, sir." Aeder laughed.

"You take good care of her. That's an order. The more little Aeders we have running around the kingdom, the better off Teni'sia is going to be."

"Yes, sir."

Medophae gave Mik'syn a nod of camaraderie. He had learned early on that Mik'syn responded better to distant forms of socializing. He wasn't comfortable answering pleasantries, but nobody liked to be ignored.

"Good night, gentlemen," Medophae said, and headed for the ramparts. Though the threat of the southern tribesmen was gone, there were other threats to Teni'sia. Magal Sym was still out there somewhere. There were at least two militarized groups of outlaws in the Coov'rein Forest who would love to loot the wealth of Teni'sia. Of all the kingdoms on The Arm, Teni'sia had come through the Sunrider Wars with the least damage, and so was perceived by surrounding kingdoms as wealthy, a jewel in the midst of ruin.

Medophae descended the northern stairway as always. Tyndiria shared the upper level of the castle with her tutor, his assistants, and the main library. It was the only level of the castle that peered above the protective walls of Teni'sia. There were fifty-two steps from the Queen's Landing to the archway that led into the ramparts. Medophae had counted them often enough: fifty-two steps and four solid doors that could be bolted and barred, effectively becoming a part of the thick stone walls. If ever an invasion were to get far enough to threaten the queen, they would have their work cut out for them.

Medophae stepped out into the crisp night air. Spring was a beautiful season in Teni'sia. He enjoyed something about every season, but if he had to pick a favorite, spring would be it. The smell of newness called to him. He loved the storm clouds that gathered on the horizon every afternoon in Teni'sia. He loved the cool, clear nights like this.

Deni'tri saw him the moment he stepped from the archway, expected him. Medophae stepped from that arch at roughly the same time every night. She moved toward him with a smile.

Deni'tri was one of the few women in the Queen's Guard. She was young and passionate and completely driven to be a fighter. He didn't know much about her history, but he surmised that something in her early youth had inspired her to be a warrior. Any time one of the other soldiers asked her why she wanted to be in the Queen's Guard, she asked them why *they* wanted to be in the Queen's Guard.

She was a comely young woman, but large and well-muscled. She was not the best swordsman in the guard, but she was not the worst, either. She also had other assets. For one, she was ambidextrous. She could switch sword hands and suffer no loss of skill. Second, she was a weapon's master. She carried a small arsenal with her: three different lengths of daggers, a long and short sword, and a throwing hatchet. He didn't like carrying more metal than he had to, but each fighter had their own style.

He had worried a little when Deni'tri had signed up. She had no husband, and she didn't want one. She had undergone a good share of coupling offers in her first few weeks in the guard. He had considered intervening, but decided against it. If she could not make her own place, then there was no place for her. He would not always be around to mediate difficulties between the guards. He let her resolve it, and resolve it she did. One night a guard seeking her attentions had made the comment that she had the smoothest skin in the land, and hair that shone like the golden sun. The following morning, Deni'tri showed up with a shaved head and three deep, symmetrical cuts on her face: one on each cheek and one across her forehead. The wounds still oozed blood as she set about her duties that day.

Medophae was just as shocked as everyone else, but he said nothing. Her message was clear: "I am dedicated to my profession. Do not distract me with unwanted offers." Not one of the soldiers approached her sexually after that. He surmised that the men secretly feared her for that gesture. After all, if she was willing to disfigure herself to draw this definite line, what would she do to them if they crossed that line?

"Good evening, Captain," Deni'tri said. She gave a relaxed look behind her and down the wall, then casually leaned against it and gave her captain an easy smile. Medophae smiled in return. He liked Deni'tri. When she'd first shorn and scarred herself, he'd wondered if she was a little scrambled in the head, but she wasn't. She simply knew what she wanted, and there was no artifice in her. She either stepped with force, or she didn't step at all.

"Quiet night?" Medophae asked.

"Yes and no. There are no Sunrider hordes beating at the gate," Deni'tri said. "But the crickets are loud tonight. A storm is coming."

"A storm."

"Yes sir. The crickets."

"Can predict a storm?"

"Every time, sir."

"Very well."

They both fell silent. Eventually, he asked, "Do you enjoy midnight duty, Deni'tri?"

"I enjoy all the duties, sir."

Medophae nodded. They both stared out over the wall into the ocean. He considered the northeast walk the best post. One could see the northern mountains and the sea as well. The craggy cliffs and the swelling ocean were breathtaking from this vantage.

"How is the queen tonight?" she asked.

"She is well. I will tell her you asked after her."

She nodded, and the ensuing silence was comfortable. Deni'tri was not the easiest of his guards to talk to.

"Sir?"

"Yes?"

"May I ask you a question?"

"Of course."

"It's a personal question, sir."

"You may ask." The corner of Medophae's mouth turned up in a half smile. Many of the guards speculated about the relationship between their captain and their queen. "I don't promise to answer."

Deni'tri nodded. "How old were you when you first went into a real battle?"

He hesitated. It was not the question he expected. But the memory of his first battle was as clear as if It had happened yesterday. "I was...eighteen."

"You were old, then."

He laughed. Deni'tri herself was eighteen.

"I didn't think so," he said.

Deni'tri sighed. "Sometimes I think I will never see a real battle."

He put a hand on her shoulder. "Don't look for a fight simply for the fight's sake, Deni'tri. Nothing good comes from that. To be prepared is enough."

She broke gazes with him and looked over the water. "That is easy for you to say, sir. You have been tested. You know your own mettle. What if I never have a chance to know? What if Teni'sia remains peaceful for the rest of my life?"

"Pray that it does. We are here to *ensure* that it does."

"I know, sir. It is simply that...I wonder. What if I am a coward at heart and I never know it?"

He wanted to laugh, but he didn't. What Deni'tri was saying was serious to her. And it wasn't an unreasonable question. Medophae had seen hardened veterans break ranks in sudden terror. He had seen green farmers with spears hold their ground against the charge of a dozen Sunriders.

"One can never truly know such a thing, even having been tested once or a hundred times. It's a new challenge every time you take up a weapon against another person. If you worry that you are a coward, then consider this: a coward would not ask such a question of herself, at least not aloud. Certainly not in front of her commanding officer."

"Thank you, sir."

He nodded. "I will see you at sword practice tomorrow."

"Of course, sir."

He left Deni'tri and continued up the ramparts.

Is that how you would have done it, Bands? Medophae wondered. Are those the words you would have used to reassure someone under your protection?

No. You would have simply stood near them. They would have felt better somehow. Was anyone ever uncertain when you were around? Certainly I was not.

He let out a sigh and increased his pace. The walk from the northeast post to southeast post was entirely too long for a pensive night like this—

A flash of silver caught Medophae's eye, and he followed it. Someone pressed themselves into the shadows of the castle wall up ahead.

Medophae's sword rang as it slid from its scabbard.

He stilled himself so he could hear better, his stance wide and his arms relaxed. For the first time that night, he felt utterly calm. His sword point touched the stones between his feet, and he waited for the intruder to make his move.

The figure stayed where he was, perhaps hoping that Medophae had not seen him.

"Stand forward and identify yourself," Medophae said with

quiet force. He expected the intruder to run, or to make a desperate attack. Instead, the small figure moved calmly into the moonlight.

It was a quicksilver.

He felt a draft of cold air slither across his soul, a whisper of destiny, and his stomach clenched. First a darkling, then a quicksilver. Like the darklings, the quicksilvers had died or fled three hundred years ago with everything else that relied on the GodSpill to survive.

The boy was young, no more than twelve. His hair flowed to his shoulders, a river of silver split only by his pointed ears. His silver eyes shone like tiny moons in his alabaster face, which was hard with sharp cheekbones and a nearly pointed chin.

"I am Stavark," the quicksilver said. His melodious voice hearkened back to Medophae's past, to a time when quicksilvers were always seen among humans. Laughing. Playing with human children, dazzling them with their speed.

"Where did you come from?" he asked.

"You are the Rabasyvihrk?"

It was what the quicksilvers called him, a word from their twisty language. It meant "Lightning Man of the People Who Love Beauty."

Medophae didn't say anything.

The boy squinted and cocked his head. "Your hair is short."

"I cut it."

"Every day?"

"It doesn't grow that fast." Only once a week— Stop! Medophae told himself. Let him think you are someone else. Let him continue on his way.

"You do not shine," Stavark said. "The legends say that the light of a furious sky surrounds you."

"What do you want?"

"Reader Orem wants to meet with you."

Reader Orem. The man garnered the nickname on his travels, flaunting the fear of the people, and he was naive enough to be proud of it. He felt it connected him somehow to the threadweavers of old. If he had known those vain, selfish people, he would not be so proud.

"Where is he?"

Stavark's silver gaze swept over Medophae, his arms, his chest, his hand where it gripped his sword.

"He said you must come," Stavark said. "The girl is in danger."

"What girl?"

"Why do you ask questions? You are the Rabasyvihrk. You are the protector."

"I don't jump through hoops for Orem."

Stavark's face soured. "You do not sound like the Rabasyvihrk."

"I'm *not* the Rabasyvihrk!" Medophae growled, butchering the pronunciation of the slippery word. He had never been good at the language of the quicksilvers.

"Why do you lie?" the boy asked, furrowing his brow, clearly disappointed. "You are the—"

"Go back and tell him you did not find me."

Stavark paused, cocking his head as he watched Medophae. "Orem said you might say no. I did not believe him. But he told me to tell you that you must still come."

"Did he?"

"He said that you owe him."

"I *owe* him? Did he tell you that he would be dead if not for me? How exactly do I owe him?"

"He told me to tell you: 'Tyndiria.' Is that a person?"

Medophae raised his chin. "Fine," he said in a low, passionless voice. "I will meet. Where?"

"In Clete. I will show you," Stavark said.

Clete was a two-day ride. One day at a full gallop.

"Will you come?" Stavark asked.

Very well, Orem, Medophae thought. "I will come."

Medophae strode down the battlement, and the young quicksilver followed silently.

79

12

TYNDIRIA

TYNDIRIA AWOKE the moment Medophae entered the room. Something was wrong. She was aware of his routine. Every evening he left her bed to make his rounds, visiting every guard post, giving each guard a smile during their long vigil. He would always return with the sunrise.

The sun had not yet risen. She sat up in bed as he gently closed the door. Her dark red hair tumbled down to her shoulders in disarray. Only Medophae and her handmaid saw her like this.

He stood just on the inside of the room, hesitating. He looked grim. She studied him for a long moment. He had changed his clothes. Instead of the plain guard uniform that he insisted on wearing, he now wore a loose but sturdy tunic, riding breeches, and tall riding boots. A thick, black belt wrapped his waist. She had seen him wear this into the field with his men before. He was going somewhere. He was leaving her.

Neither of them spoke, and the silence confirmed her guess. He was waiting for the right words. He might find them. He was good with words sometimes. But she let the silence drag and let him struggle. She simply looked at him. It was her last chance to memorize every bit of him.

His golden hair was cut short above his ears. The back of his neck was closely shaved, but his long bangs hung low, and perpetually fell into his eyes. Oh, how she loved to push those bangs away from his beautiful face. He had to cut it that way every week. His hair grew at an alarming rate. She remembered when he'd told her why, after she had guessed him to be Wildmane from the legends. He explained how his hair had been past his shoulders when he became what he was, and how it constantly tried to return to that state. She remembered how his lips moved when he said it. Oh, how she had wanted to kiss him. She had dreamed of it then, those enigmatic lips that bent down slightly at the ends. What would they feel like?

She knew now. They were soft, energetic, experienced. They tasted sweet, yet somehow salty like tears. There was always a touch of sadness in Medophae's kisses. She had come to crave the flavor of his sadness. She knew every inch of him. *Oh, my eternal boy...*

How she loved to rub the smooth skin of his cheeks that would never grow a beard. He had the face of an eighteen-year-old boy, all vitality and energy and delicious angles. He had a strong jaw that promised to square off even more profoundly in a few years. Of course, those few years would never come for him.

His body was young, but his eyes gave him away. They weren't the eyes of a boy, nor of any grown man she'd ever met. They were the eyes of a stranger, someone who had seen things she couldn't imagine. They held what she had tasted in his kiss, ocean-blue eyes with an ocean of sadness behind them.

He moved forward, and she closed her eyes, holding him in her mind, keeping him that way forever.

He sat on the bed with her, and she opened her eyes again.

"Tyndiria, I have to leave for a few days."

She said nothing, and he continued.

"Orem sent somebody to ask me to meet with him. He said it was important." Medophae snorted. "Of course, to Orem, everything is of the utmost importance." He threw the words into the room as if they meant nothing. He was annoyed, but there was something under the annoyance, something profound. Her heart sank, and her stomach shriveled. It had come. Today, this moment, was the day he left forever.

Why was it so difficult? She had known it was coming. He did not belong to her. He belonged to the lands. To the gods.

She'd known she'd only have him for a short time, that she must enjoy him and let him go when it was over. No regrets.

But her heart was breaking.

"I see." She finally managed to say. She was happy to note that her voice came out steady and strong, the voice of a queen.

"I'll be back in a few days, no more."

"Will you?" she said, and she cursed herself for a fool. It was what an immature young girl would say, trying to hang onto a lover whose heart had already left. But she couldn't help it. Her longing and anger slammed around inside her like drunken sailors. It was all she could do to keep from crying.

He looked at her strangely, as if he didn't understand why she was angry. Finally, he spoke in that unquestionable voice of his, the voice he used to reassure his guards in the face of fear. "Tyndiria, I'm not going away. Is that what you think?"

She cleared her throat, but she knew she couldn't speak without her voice quavering, so she said nothing.

"Don't," he said emphatically, and she listened to the passion in his voice. Medophae could convince anyone of anything. "The only reason I'm going is because I owe Orem for bringing me to Teni'sia, for bringing me to you. This is my home now. You are my purpose."

She bit her lip. The tears came this time, and she didn't try to wipe them away. She let them slide down her cheeks and onto the sheet. His face softened with a small, relieved smile. He must think they were tears of joy. He didn't understand what was happening at this moment.

Teni'sia was not his place. Of course, he had tried to fit in, and he had convinced himself that he had, but she knew it was a necessary lie, the only thing that protected him from his sadness.

Wish him well, she told herself. *Don't be an idiot. Smile at him, and wish him well. If you don't, you will hate yourself when he leaves, and he will think less of you. You cannot hold him. The entire realm could not hold him if he wished to go.*

Tyndiria gave him a smile, even though her tears betrayed her. She acted as if they weren't streaming down her face.

"It'll be okay," he said, smiling as he reached out and brushed the tears away. "I'll be back before you know it."

You're stupid. You're stupid, and you don't understand anything, and I love you so much....

She nodded and gave him another smile. She couldn't bear to speak.

He kissed her lightly on the lips and stood. "I have to go. I have a long ride. Lo'gan will see to my duties while I am away. I'll see you in two or three days."

He turned and went to the door. As his hand fell on the handle, she rose. The sheet slipped away, and she stood naked in the room.

"Medophae," she said.

He turned. Again, that quizzical look crossed his features. He sensed something was wrong, but he didn't know what it was.

"Are you okay?" he asked.

She nodded. "Yes. Kiss me."

He let go of the handle and crossed the room to hold her. His blue eyes looked deep into hers, and she drank one last drink of him. "Kiss me once," she whispered, closing her eyes. She felt his lips on hers, his tongue on hers. The kiss lingered beautifully.

Finally, she ended it. She pulled away.

"Good luck, Wildmane." She squeezed him tight, felt the mighty muscles of his arms, his back, his chest. "I love you," she whispered so that he could not hear.

When she let go, he grinned down at her.

"You'll see me soon. I promise."

Oh, Medophae. You do mean it. And the tone of your voice could make anyone believe. I want to believe.

Then why did she feel like she would never again look at his beautiful face?

13

MEDOPHAE

MEDOPHAE AND STAVARK rode through the night and the rest of the next day. They stopped only to water and rest their horses. Medophae was impressed with the young quicksilver's stamina. Quicksilvers were known for their speed, not their endurance. His thin, white face slowly became drawn and tired, but he didn't say a word.

The stretch of land that separated the Inland Ocean from the True Ocean was called the Jaw. There were four small kingdoms on The Jaw: two on Northjaw—Clete and Teni'sia—and two on Southjaw—Nast and Buravar. All of the kingdoms were friendly with each other since the Sunriders had come north. There had been five originally, but the Sunriders had destroyed Diyah. There was nothing left but ruins.

They kept to the roads mostly, but circumvented the smattering of tiny villages between Teni'sia and Clete.

The trip continued through the day without incident. Riding, resting, then riding some more. The sun was setting by the time they arrived at Orem's meeting place, a small clearing outside the tiny town of Deridin.

Medophae reined his horse in and dismounted. Orem already had a fire burning with plenty of wood for the night to come. Well-prepared. Of course.

Stavark wearily wrapped his horse's reins around a nearby tree branch and moved over by the fire.

Medophae took more time with his horse. He knew that Orem would be anxious to talk, but Medophae was feeling belligerent, so he made Orem wait.

Medophae stroked his gelding's lathered neck, removed the saddle, and carefully checked each hoof. Finally, he looked up. Orem had his arms crossed now, backlit by the fire, barely more than a shadow in front of the flaming glow.

He and Orem had saved each others' lives. Orem had pulled Medophae back into the land of the living, had brought Medophae from the cave where he had been reduced to something just above an animal to Teni'sia, where Tyndiria stoked the coals of his heart to life again.

Medophae had literally saved Orem from being ripped to pieces by a pack of skin dogs. Orem had been starving and half-dead from the cold in the Spine Mountains, exploring dangerous places where he had no business going.

Medophae had been hunting close by when he heard the commotion. A pack of starving skin dogs had hunted Orem for more than a mile, driving him on and wearing him down. The brave scholar-turned-woodsman kept them at bay for a long time. The dogs almost had him when Orem made a desperate jump across a narrow ravine. He bought himself another few precious minutes while the dogs found a way around, but it cost him a sprained ankle.

Medophae had followed for a short time. He watched the hunt with the dispassionate gaze that he had watched several other hunts of this pack of skin dogs. He knew what he was about to witness, and he perched on top of a boulder to watch Orem's inevitable end.

Medophae had been a different man back then. He watched the seasons change, watched the turn of nature: the growth of the grass, trees, the death of the leaves in autumn. He watched birds feather nests, mice search for food, and the skin dogs hunt deer. He watched it all with equanimity. Life happened, and there was nothing that could—or should—be done.

That the skin dogs hunted a human this time didn't concern him at first. Medophae watched Orem—bleeding, cold, and clearly exhausted. Each time the dogs went in for an attack, Medophae thought Orem would go down for good, but each time, he fought his way back to his feet, drove the dogs back. His passion for life evoked something in Medophae, broke a barrier inside himself.

He'd been almost an animal himself at that point, but suddenly he felt the threads of his old life wrap around him, dress him up as he once had been: a protector. A man who cared about the lands. A man who cared about the lives and deaths of others.

Medophae had leapt into the midst of the pack and cowed them. The skin dogs knew Medophae, and they deferred to him. He had established his dominance over them many years before.

He brought Orem back to his cave. He cared for Orem until the man was strong enough to fend for himself. And in that cave, while Orem convalesced, the conversations began.

How many years ago had that been? Five years? Ten? Medophae could not keep track of the years anymore.

He let out a low breath and started toward the expectant Orem. The moment Medophae leapt into the midst of those skin dogs was the moment he leapt into the world of humans again. That was how it always started. One action. And the way it always ended was disaster.

"Medophae," Orem said.

"Orem," Medophae nodded.

They shook hands firmly.

"Thank you for coming."

"Your messenger is persuasive."

Stavark sat by the fire, gazing unblinkingly into the flames as he chewed solemnly on the meal Orem had prepared. Stew with venison, by the smell.

"He made it sound like you were calling in a favor," Medophae said.

Orem studied Medophae for a moment. "I told him to put it that way only if you forced him to."

"If I didn't immediately dance to your tune, you mean?"

Orem paused, straightened his shoulders. "Please, Medin." Orem resorted to the nickname, and Medophae felt his hackles rising. That was what Bands used to call him, and Medophae had incautiously told Orem about it. He'd compounded his mistake by failing to tell Orem to stop. Now, he used it like a club to remind Medophae they had been close. "I don't want to begin this way. Will you sit by the fire? Are you hungry?"

Medophae followed Orem to the fire. He handed Medophae bread and a wooden bowl full of the stew. He took a spoonful, chewing slowly. It was tasty. Orem had always been a good cook.

"I want you to help me," Orem said.

"Someone you want protected. A girl, the quicksilver said."

Orem hesitated, "Yes."

"I'm not a bodyguard." He paused, realizing that actually, that was precisely what he was. "I'm not a bodyguard for hire. I have a life in Teni'sia, a life you gave to me. My place is there. I'm not interested in your quest."

"Your place is Amarion. You are our protector. Not the protector of just one kingdom. History is happening right now, and we have a chance to affect it for good. Look!" He made a gesture at the impossible quicksilver sitting at the fire.

"That must have been such an encouraging moment for you, finding him. Where was he?"

"There are many of them, living in the Spine Mountains."

"Ah."

"Have you seen creatures? Children of Dervon? Those who need GodSpill to live?"

Medophae hesitated. "No," he lied. He didn't mention the darkling. He did not want to give Orem any more sticks for his fire.

"It's everywhere. If you try hard enough, you can feel it in the air," Orem said.

"If you try hard enough—and you do—you can feel whatever you want to feel."

Orem pressed his lips together and sat back, annoyed. "I bring you a quicksilver, and you still refuse to believe."

"It doesn't mean anything."

"Well," Orem said tightly. "Since you're going to be pig-headed, let me tell you what I know. GodSpill is returning. It's leaking into the lands, coming from the Fountain, but the only creatures appearing near that place are darklings."

"When were you at the Fountain?" Medophae asked, surprised. Nobody went close to the Fountain. In the beginning, those who had gone didn't return, and if they did return, they were deformed or diseased.

"This winter. I spent months in the library in Denema's Valley, researching, gathering information. I know what is happening. The Fountain is breaking down."

Medophae's heart beat faster. If there was GodSpill, then there would be threadweavers, someone to look at the gem...

He clenched his jaw.

No.

He had been down this path before. He had traveled that same road for one hundred and thirty-one years during a time when the most powerful threadweavers in the world were alive. This was a fool's hope. "It's not my responsibility," he said.

Orem sat back. "Except that it *is*."

"Why?" Medophae shouted, standing abruptly, dropping his bowl and spilling stew into the dirt. "Because *you* say so?"

"Because you have the power to do something about it." Orem stood with him.

Medophae bared his teeth. "I thought that once, but it's a lie. Nothing I do matters. Nothing *you* do matters. It never did, and it never will." He turned to go to his horse.

"These darklings, they're not going to stop." Orem's voice chased him. "You'll find them at the gates of Teni'sia soon."

"Then I will fight them when they arrive," he said, tossing his saddle on his horse and working the cinch.

"Only then?"

"That is my place. You are the questor, Orem. Not me. Not anymore. I've made that as clear as I can."

Orem was silent for a moment. "I want to destroy the

Fountain," he blurted.

Medophae stopped, turned.

"If we destroy it, the lands will return to normal. They'll go back to the way they were in the Age of Awakening. Before Daylan Morth and his Fountain. Amarion will become what the gods originally intended."

Medophae looked into Orem's eyes. There was true conviction. It wasn't just a line to get Medophae's attention. Orem was seductive. He believed these things, so much that he made you want to believe, too.

Medophae shook his head. "You think no one has tried before now? The Fountain is too strong. Daylan Morth was the most powerful threadweaver ever. He was nearly a god himself. The Fountain cannot be undone."

"In the beginning, maybe," Orem said. "But it's been three centuries. It is breaking on its own. That's why Stavark can access the powers of his birthright here in Amarion. It's why darklings roam the land. And who knows what else might have emerged that we don't even know about? It's already happening, but we need to make it happen faster."

"So you're going to, what, take a chisel to it? You need a threadweaver. You don't have one."

"I have one."

Medophae's breath caught in his throat. "The girl..." he whispered, putting it together. He turned back to his horse, untied the reins from the tree. "No."

"Medophae," Orem said. "She needs you."

Medophae closed his eyes. A threadweaver. A woman. She probably had a name, too. A family. Children maybe. Medophae prayed that Orem didn't say her name.

"She hasn't learned much, but her natural aptitude is astonishing. If she doesn't learn soon, the GodSpill will begin teaching her by itself. I gave her a laughing stone, and it all but exploded in her hand."

"She made it turn a color?" he said in a low voice.

"Medin, it burst into a rainbow."

"A rainbow?" He had never even heard of that.

"This is the welfare of humankind we're talking about," Orem said.

Medophae hesitated. A threadweaver. And he could help. He could protect the girl against anything. Killing darklings was something he could do better than anyone. They could walk right up to the Fountain and tear the thing down. Amarion would go back to what it was...

Or... He could fail. He could take the curse of his life and throw its shadow over even more people.

"No. I don't do that anymore," he said, lifting the reins over the horse's head. "The ocean remains the ocean. Make waves or lie still, the ocean will always remain the ocean."

"You're hiding with Tyndiria just like you hid in that cave where I found you," Orem said. "You're afraid of trying, afraid you'll fail."

"Yes. That must be it. Goodbye, Orem." He put a hand on the pommel.

"It's *her*, isn't it?" Orem said.

Medophae paused. Just get in the saddle and ride away. Don't wait for Orem to make his mistake....

"It's Bands. It's that wispy hope of a life that is gone. It's that damned red jewel. Are you seriously going to let others die because of an ancient mistake? She's gone. You're not. That's it. You can't save her, but you can save—"

Medophae crossed the distance like a charging bear. He grabbed Orem by the vest and slammed him into a tree. The man gasped. Golden fire crackled about Medophae's chest and arms as he lifted Orem into the air.

Stavark vanished from the fire in a silent explosion of silver light. He streaked across the camp and suddenly stood next to Medophae, a knife held high against his throat.

Medophae ignored the quicksilver. Orem, his eyes watering, stared at Medophae defiantly.

"You know nothing of which you've spoken," Medophae hissed.

"I know enough." He gulped roughly against Medophae's fist. "She would disapprove of you hiding away—"

Medophae pressed his fist against Orem's neck, choking off the words.

"If you hurt him, I will kill you," Stavark said, pressing harder. The knife bit, and Medophae felt a wet trickle of blood down his neck.

"You don't know when to stop," Medophae growled to Orem.

"I will never stop," he said.

"I should have left you to the skin dogs."

"I know you can kill me. You can kill anyone you choose—"

Medophae dropped him to his feet and walked back to his horse. Stavark moved to stand between the two of them, his knife up in Medophae's direction.

"You could use those powers for good, Medophae," Orem said. "Instead of for nothing. The darklings are stronger than me, stronger than Stavark. But they're not stronger than you. We need you. Mirolah needs you."

Mirolah. The threadweaver. The girl. That was her name.

"You belong to Amarion," Orem said, following him, pushing it. He always had to push it. "Not Teni'sia. You're angry because Bands would want you to go—"

Medophae spun and struck Orem across the face.

Stavark attacked Medophae in a flash of silver light, his curved sword whipping out of his scabbard and arcing down. The blade bit deep into Medophae's arm, slicing through flesh and lodging into bone. With a growl, Medophae ripped the sword from the boy's grip.

Orem stumbled back, tripped, and fell to the grass. He lay there, senseless.

Medophae yanked the sword from his arm and snapped it across his knee, golden fire crackling around him. Stavark turned to silver light, streaked to Orem in the blink of an eye. He stood over the dazed man, panting. He had his dagger out again, ready to defend Orem with his life.

Orem just wouldn't stop. He never stopped. Nothing was sacred to him except his damned quest, and he would ruin as many lives as needed to see it fulfilled.

Well, Medophae had ruined enough lives already. Orem could

pursue his folly alone. Medophae leapt into the saddle and rode away.

14

ZILOK MORTH

"SEF, WHO IS THIS Reader Orem?"

"I do not know, my master."

"Who do you suppose gave him such a name? Do you think he chose it for himself?"

"I do not know, my master."

"I suppose he gains satisfaction from it. He likes to think of himself, maybe, as a threadweaver? As a man of learning? But he has no idea what a threadweaver really is."

"Yes, my master."

"And what of this other, this threadweaver Orem has supposedly found? Could she be at the end of the darkling's leash?"

"I do not know, my master."

"I always love to see what the latest generation has wrought in the way of threadweavers. All too often they are terrible disappointments. But this is a new century, Sef. The possibilities are limitless. I wonder what she is like."

"I do not know, my master."

"Young. Gifted. I could teach her, Sef. I could teach her things that even a threadweaver from the Age of Ascendance could not teach her. I could teach her things that even my esteemed great-grandson could not teach her."

"Yes, my master. Shall we take her?"

"And what would I do with an apprentice?"

"As you say, my master."

"Yes. As I say. And what of the Wildmane? He is torn. He feels he should go, but he is afraid. This is...disappointing. He is just a shadow of his former self."

"As you say, my master."

"Well, that is just...perfect. We will give no leniency to the Wildmane."

"No, my master."

"This 'Reader' Orem tried so valiantly to change his mind."

"Yes, my master."

"We will show him how one changes a mind."

"Yes, my master."

"We will illustrate what a real threadweaver is."

"Yes, my master."

"And we begin our plan for the Wildmane."

"Yes, my master."

"This 'Reader' Orem does have one thing correct. Knowledge is the real power, Sef. GodSpill is incidental. That is the first of the threadweaver secrets. Let us visit this young threadweaver 'Reader' Orem has found. Let us see if she knows this secret."

"As you say, my master."

"Yes. As I say."

15

MIROLAH

MIROLAH HEARD THE RAVEN cawing when the sun was high in the azure sky. She remembered the days of the horsemen when the sky had been gray every day from the smoke of destroyed villages and farms, but those days were gone now, and she prayed they would never return.

A few thin, white clouds drifted across the blue, and the sun warmed her nicely. The svelte raven wheeled and changed course. It swooped in, landed atop a nearby building, and cocked its head at her. Mirolah smiled and turned back to follow her sister, Fillen. The marketplace was busy today. People brushed up against her as they moved about their business, chatting with friends or haggling with vendors. The smell of Katstan's lamb-on-a-stick hung heavy in the air. Mirolah caught a glimpse of old Glif juggling fruit from his cart. Children gathered around him, rapt with attention. Fillen giggled in delight as they walked amongst the various carts. Mirolah waved at Taegen, the tea vendor. He nodded back and winked even as he continued speaking with his current customer. Fillen didn't wait for Mirolah to stop and chat, but dragged her onward. Mirolah loved going to the market with any one of her sisters, but with Fillen especially. Everything was a new adventure to her. She didn't get to leave the house as often as Mirolah, and so the marketplace was still a novelty for her. Mirolah remembered when it was so for herself, but that was long ago. She knew all the vendors by their first names. She knew what they sold. She knew who offered a good price and who did not.

Fillen stopped at the spice vendor's tent and began smelling each of the spices. New caravans had come south from The Arm last month, and the spice vendor had set up shop. In all likelihood, Fillen had never seen his wares. She sniffed each over and over again, smiling from ear to ear. Mirolah simply waited. She could wait forever like this. Simply watching the happiness on Fillen's face was enough. Could she ever grow tired of that?

After many minutes, Fillen was finished with the spices. She spun around, her dark coal eyes glistening with vigor. "What next?" she asked.

"I have seen them all," Mirolah said, grinning. "I will follow you."

"The jewelry maker," Fillen said. It was her favorite. Fillen never tired of caressing the polished stones and tooled silver. Of course, Fillen could not afford anything in the jewelry maker's tent. Mirolah knew the jewelry maker well, and he trusted Mirolah. Fillen could try on anything she wanted.

Fillen grabbed Mirolah's hand and bounced through the throng with her in tow. Mirolah laughed as she jostled people in her sister's wake.

"Slow down!" she said, laughing.

"I can't. I can't be slow today! Come on, Mira!"

They finally managed to squeeze into the jewelry maker's shop, and Fillen spent an hour trying on bracelets and necklaces. She held earrings up to her ears and pressed anklets against her shins.

"Ah, if I were wealthy..." Fillen said, "I would dress up with every bit of this and simply sit in front of a mirror all day."

"I believe you would."

"Do you think I ever shall be, Mirolah?"

"Wealthy?"

"Yes."

"Anything is possible, as Lawdon is so fond of saying," Mirolah said, then whispered into Fillen's ear. "If you bat your eyelashes enough, I think the jewelry maker might take you to wife." Fillen glanced up at the short, portly jewelry maker. She made a sour face.

"He's three times my age, Mira!"

They both giggled and continued to try on the jewelry.

The sun had begun to set, and the shadows stretched long across the ground by the time they left the jeweler's tent. Many vendors were already packing up their goods and striking their tents.

"We should get home," Mirolah said. Tiffienne would already have begun supper. Both Mirolah and Fillen should have been there to help, though Mirolah knew that Tiffienne would be lenient. It was Fillen's outing for the week. Tiffienne never reprimanded the girls after a day of fun, no matter the transgression. She said there was precious little fun had these days, and there was no point in fixing a bad impression at the end of a good day.

Still and all, they would get away with dodging supper preparation, but they shouldn't be late for the eating of it. That would simply be rude.

"Come on. Let's hurry," Mirolah said.

"Let's take the short cut home, Mira!" Fillen exclaimed. Grabbing Mirolah's hand, she started off at a fast walk. Again, Mirolah was dragged behind. They left the market and cut through some of the old, broken-down buildings. They raced through the back streets, passing an occasional villager who was doing the same. Fillen danced lightly up the stair-step formation of a ruined wall and Mirolah followed. They giggled as they rose the first few feet in the air, then became silent in concentration as they traversed the tallest section. Their laughter resumed when they came down the far side and began skipping into the alley.

"Hurry!" Fillen said, who was several yards ahead of Mirolah. She held out her hand. "It's getting dark. We won't be able to see enough to get home if you keep dawdling like that!"

Mirolah laughed. "I could find my way home from the market

in my sleep," she said. "I could—"

A cold wind blew through her. She slowed and turned around, but there was no wind.

"Did you feel that?" she asked Fillen.

"What?" Fillen giggled and walked back a few paces to stand next to her.

"The wind."

"I don't know. Why? What's wrong?" Fillen's laughter vanished. Mirolah rubbed her arms. She was cold. Why was she cold? It was warm out. "There was a wind. Did you feel it?"

"No," Fillen said. "Mira, you're scaring me."

The alley stretched out empty behind them. A moment ago, it had been warm and friendly. Now there was nothing but shadows and coldness, and it was deathly quiet. The two girls stood alone. The old walls hunched in the darkness like malevolent beasts.

Another wind passed through her, just as chilling as the first.

"Oh gods..." Mirolah said, because she hadn't felt anything on her arms. "Did you feel it?" she whispered, though she knew what Fillen was going to say. There was no wind for Fillen, because this was something unnatural. Mirolah knew it like she knew the moment before the sun rose."

Fillen was looking around fearfully at all the shadows. "I don't like it here, Mira. Let's go. Let's go now."

A great flapping of wings surrounded them. Mirolah screamed. Fillen screamed. They both spun about and watched the raven settle on the wall above them. Mirolah would swear it was the same raven she had seen earlier, but this close it was enormous. It grabbed the broken stone with one claw then the other as it settled itself. Once it was adjusted, it cocked its head at them and watched. Mirolah looked closer. The raven had ice-blue eyes. She'd never seen a raven with blue eyes before.

"Mira, let's go." Fillen tugged at her hand, but Mirolah was entranced by the bird. It stared right at her.

"It's looking at us, Mira! Let's go!" Fillen begged.

"Do you see its eyes?" Mirolah murmured.

"So come back and look at it in the daytime. Please, Mira!"

"Ravens don't even fly at night," Mirolah murmured.

Fillen's voice broke. "Mira, I'm really scared!"

Mirolah nodded dumbly, stepped backward a couple of paces. The raven hopped along the wall, pacing them. That was enough to break the spell. She turned with Fillen and began running down the alley. Suddenly, that chill wind blew through her again, so cold it hurt. She gasped and stumbled. What was that?

The raven cawed loudly and took flight, following them.

Jagged walls blurred past like a giant's teeth as they ran. They dodged around piles of stones and rotting wood. They could both see the light of the main road ahead. It called to them like a mother's arms. Mirolah craned her neck to find the raven, but the sky was dark now.

They burst into the light of the main road, gasping and looking around wildly. A lot of people were coming home from the market themselves. A few pushed carts up the wide, packed earth. Mirolah recognized Jarvik, leading his ancient mule.

She and Fillen stood there breathing heavily, holding each others' hands tightly.

"Where did it go?" Fillen asked.

"I don't know," Mirolah said. "I don't care. Let's go home. I'll feel better when we're inside."

They started down the street, and Mirolah began to feel normal again. The main street was lit, and the flickering glow of the torches drove her fears away. Mirolah silently reprimanded herself for being scared of a stupid raven.

"We're silly," Mirolah said to her sister. "Look at us, almost grown and screaming because a bird landed near us in the dark. Lawdon will laugh at us."

Fillen giggled nervously. "Well," she said, "it was a big bird."

"Next time, let's hit it with a big rock."

"Yes. No more walking into dark streets without a good bag full of rocks."

Mirolah smiled and agreed. Fillen skipped a little and Mirolah followed her.

"Let's not tell Lawdon," Fillen said. "He'll make fun of us."

"Yes—" There was a low *thump* behind Mirolah, and her reply stuck in her throat. The cold wind blew through her again, fierce and shocking. Her hand clenched Fillen's as she turned them both around.

In the alley they had just left, a nightmare crouched low against the corner of the building. Its long, black limbs bent at the elbows and knees, and it held itself above the dirt like a spider. Its head was a tiny ball hunched into its shoulders. Thin eyes glowed red in the darkness, and they stared straight at Mirolah. It opened its mouth and rows of needle-like teeth glowed white in the firelight. Saliva dripped from its open mouth and splatted on the ground as it let out a breathy purr.

Fillen screamed.

Mirolah envied her. She wanted to scream, wanted to move, but she was transfixed. That thing wasn't human. It was a monster from stories written long ago about supernatural creatures who had all died long ago.

Other people on the street ahead of them heard Fillen's scream, and they turned. Gasps and another scream filled the air.

The thing leapt from the darkness and bounded toward Mirolah and Fillen.

Fillen screamed again. They spun together, stumbling over one another as they tried to run away. Fillen twisted her ankle and went down. In the grips of utter panic, Mirolah leapt past her. Fillen wailed in fear. She jumped to her feet only to gasp and go down again.

Mirolah kept running. That thing was back there. That thing was coming!

"Gods, Mira! Don't leave me!" Fillen's terrified shriek broke through Mirolah's panic. She skidded to a stop and turned around.

The thin, black monster had reached Fillen, crouching like a spider and cocking its head as it looked down at her. An insidious purr rolled out of its throat. Fillen sobbed and pushed herself backward, scrabbling in the dirt to get away.

Somewhere above, a raven cawed loudly.

The monster reached out one long-fingered hand for Fillen's leg.

"Fillen!" Mirolah screamed. "No!" She wanted to help her sister, but her bowels had turned to ice. She couldn't force herself nearer the monster.

It snatched Fillen with one hand and dragged her toward itself. Fillen kicked it in its little head, but it was as if she was hitting leather-covered stone.

The shouts and screams of the villagers behind Mirolah grew louder as more people clustered close in awe.

The monster's claw flashed out and sliced open Fillen's belly. A little breath popped out of her mouth, and her eyes flew open in disbelief. She screamed raggedly, and others on the street screamed with her.

"*No!*" Mirolah shouted.

She pushed back her fear, pushed back the cold feeling. All she could see was the monster and the dark, shiny slash across Fillen's middle. The buildings faded and the air between her and the monster became brighter. She sent her hate and rage across that bright bridge. The monster looked up. It opened its mouth to her, exposing needle-like teeth. Its saliva dripped onto Fillen's thigh.

Mirolah walked toward it with her hands held out. The bright bridge intensified. The cold feeling inside her turned hot. Her face flushed, and her hands tingled.

The monster crouched lower to the ground, a dark cluster of shiny sticks. The purr deepened to a growl, and it rocked from side to side. Dark red blood welled up from Fillen's stomach, soaking her dress and leaking into the dirt. She keened and pulled weakly against the monster's powerful grip.

Mirolah struck at the creature across the bright bridge. She imagined a flaming sword slicing it. She imagined a huge boulder bashing it. She imagined fists pummeling it until it let Fillen go.

The monster flinched and skittered backward, dropping Fillen's leg. Again, she smote it with her imaginary sword.

The monster flinched again, but began creeping forward again. This time, it ignored Fillen, its glowing gaze focused on Mirolah.

She shouted and retreated, pushed at it through the bright bridge between them, trying to hold it, to keep it back.

It leapt at her.

"No!" she cried, turning away and throwing up her arms.

But the claws did not reach her. She turned, breathless, to find the monster struggling mid-air as though caught by an invisible hand. One of the monster's claws hovered inches from her face, quivering.

Like a stick marionette, it crashed to the ground in a limp pile, then stood up straight. For the first time, Mirolah realized it looked somewhat like a person; a tall, thin nightmare of a person.

Cords of thin muscles rippled under the shiny midnight skin as it fought whatever force had taken hold of it. One arm moved shakily across its belly and the other behind the small of its back. The monster growled defiance, but it bent one knee and knelt before her as if she was its queen.

She couldn't believe her eyes. Behind her, the raven cawed, and that cold shiver went through her. Mirolah whipped her head around. The big black bird perched on a nearby building, watching the monster. It turned its gaze to her.

The monster dropped to a crouch, in control of itself once more. It considered Mirolah, but did not threaten her or Fillen, who crawled pitifully away, leaving a thick trail of blood. The monster let out a purr, then turned and bounded into an alley.

Somewhere above, the raven cawed again, but when Mirolah looked for it, it was gone.

16

MIROLAH

MIROLAH COULDN'T HEAR ANYTHING. It felt like time had stopped, and she stood stunned, watching the alley where the monster had gone. Her thoughts hung in her mind like winter breath, unmoving. It couldn't be real. None of this was real.

Then she turned and saw her sister lying in a pool of blood.

Sounds returned in a crashing cacophony: the shouts of the villagers, the movement of frantic bodies, horses whinnying.

Mirolah wailed and crashed to her knees next to her sister. "Fillen!"

Fillen had turned on her stomach to crawl away from the monster. Her feet pushed, trying to move her body forward, but she couldn't. Her lips drained blood onto the street, and she blinked against the dirt. "Mira," she croaked.

"Gods, Fillen! Oh no. Oh no. No no..."

"It hurts, Mira..."

Mirolah could barely hear her sister's words over the growing din of the villagers behind her, clustering near.

"Oh Fillen. Oh gods... I'm so sorry."

"I feel it now, Mira. The cold wind. It's so..." Fillen's lips stopped moving. The blood stopped coming. Her eyes turned glassy.

Mirolah couldn't breathe. She gasped, but she couldn't get enough air.

"Please, no. No, no. We'll fix it," she sobbed. She grabbed Fillen's hand and squeezed, rocking back and forth on her knees, crying as the fingers turned cold. "It'll all be all right..."

She didn't know how long she sat there, crying. The crowd thickened around her. Suddenly, someone grabbed her arm and hauled her roughly to her feet. She turned to stare into the gruff and angry countenance of Michin the baker.

"What did you do?" Michin said. "What kind of nightmare did you bring down on us?"

She looked at him in a daze. "My-my sister..." She looked at the faces around her. Fear. Shock. Anger. Everyone was glaring at her.

"The monster did your bidding. How did you do that?"

What Michin was saying sank in.

"What? No," she protested. "I didn't do anything!"

"She controlled it!" A woman's high shriek rose from the din of noises. "It bowed to her. You all saw it bow to her."

Mirolah stepped back, but Michin didn't let her go. He clutched her so hard it hurt. Mirolah looked down at his grip, then up into his face. He was afraid. Afraid of her.

The throng of villagers pressed closer. Mirolah saw faces she knew, but none were friendly.

"It bowed to you, like you were its master," Michin said, shaking her.

"It wasn't me," she cried. "I just... I just tried to stop—"

"It's GodSpill," old Jarvik growled. "Actual, damnable GodSpill. She's a rot bringer. I knew it. I heard tales of her brother. He was a rot bringer, too. She's got the same."

The woman's high voice cut in again. "You all saw her!"

Someone grabbed Mirolah's other arm and pulled her around. The shrill woman's face came close to her own.

"What did you do? You've brought an evil down on us."

"No!"

"What should we do?" Michin asked. "If we let her go, what if she just calls it back?"

"I didn't bring that thing!" She yanked her arm, but Michin held tight. Mirolah began crying. "That's my *sister!*"

"We'll take her before the council, and they'll rope her," he said. Suddenly, Michin gasped as someone cuffed him on the back of the head. His grip faltered on Mirolah's arms. Lawdon knocked Michin's hands away, growling as he shoved the baker back into the crowed. Lawdon draped a protective arm around Mirolah's shoulders.

"What's going on here?" His booming voice cut through the din. "You bloodthirsty fools!" The shouting crowd quieted. "This is my daughter..."

Lawdon's gaze fell on Fillen's body. It seemed to knock the wind out of him, but then he turned his fierce gaze back on the crowd. "Call the night watchman," he demanded as he guided Mirolah through the angry faces.

The villagers mumbled to themselves. A young man broke from the throng and ran off in the direction of the guardhouse. No one moved to stop Lawdon as he led Mirolah away.

Neither of them spoke as he brought her back home, which was only a few houses away. All the girls were in the dining room, staring out the two large windows at the crowd in the street. Tiffienne stood nervously by the door. She led Mirolah to the dining table and sat her down.

Tiffienne's hands absently wrung an old dishrag as she looked at Lawdon. "What is it?" she asked. "What's happened?"

Lawdon's voice, so powerful and commanding a moment ago, was quiet. "I don't know. I'm going back to find out. Stay here and don't let anybody in. There's madness in the air. Get Mirolah upstairs; get her cleaned up. She's been through something, though I'll be damned if I know what. We'll have that later."

He glanced at Mirolah, who sat at the far side of the dinner table, staring unblinkingly at her folded hands. She looked up at him. He was uncertain, maybe even afraid of her like the other villagers. Just like the refugees had been afraid of Dorn.

She put her head in her hands and cried. She could hear

Lawdon talking to Tiffienne.

"I'm going," he said gruffly. "Remember what I told you."

Tiffienne said nothing, and Mirolah looked up when she heard Tiffienne close the door and bolt it.

"Come along, Mirolah," she said, smiling as though it was time to do the laundry. "Let's get you cleaned up."

Mirolah meekly followed her upstairs.

Tiffienne sat her on the bed. Casra and Locke peered into the doorway of the girls' shared room, but didn't say anything.

Tiffienne continued to speak to Mirolah in quiet, calm tones. Her voice was a mother's voice, ever patient, ever loving.

But she hadn't seen what happened. She hadn't seen Fillen stiffen in a pool of her own blood. She hadn't seen the monster. If she had, would she be so gentle with Mirolah? Or would she have the same look that the villagers had, that Lawdon tried so hard not to have?

"What happened?" Locke asked timidly from the doorway. "Where's Fillen?"

"Best you keep your curiosity to yourself," Tiffienne snapped. "If you're so bored you can linger in doorways, go put some water on to boil and bring a basin full up here. Quickly now."

Locke and Casra flinched like she'd hit them with a whip. They vanished from the doorway.

Tiffienne turned her attention back to Mirolah. "Give me that shirt, Mira. It's filthy."

Mirolah pulled her tunic over her head.

"I didn't do it," she said meekly as she pulled her hands out of the bloody sleeves. "What they said I did. I didn't do it."

"Well of course you didn't." Tiffienne took the tunic and tossed it onto the floor.

Mirolah closed her eyes and a sob escaped her. "You don't even know what I'm talking about," she whispered.

The bed creaked as Tiffienne settled herself next to Mirolah. She put her large, warm arm over Mirolah's bare shoulder and pulled the girl close to her. "I don't have to see everything you do to know what kind of person you are," she said. "I've not seen you lie yet, Mira. I see no reason to believe you'd start making things up now. I don't care what happened or what anyone thinks you did. If you say you didn't do it, then that's the truth as far as I'm concerned. I don't need to know any more than that."

Mirolah wished it was that simple. She wished she could take comfort from her words, but Tiffienne didn't know everything, and despite what she said, Mirolah knew her face would change when she began to hear the accusations. Just like Lawdon's had. Concern. Fear. How long before those turned to anger? The jump from fear to violence was such a short distance.

Mirolah's mind raced. How *had* she made the monster go away? Was it really her? She didn't think so. She had felt something when the air lightened between her and the monster. She'd stung the monster, but that was all. She hadn't made it bow to her. Something else had done that. If Mirolah had to guess, she would say it was the raven somehow. But even as she said that in the quiet of her mind, it sounded stupid. She could only imagine how ridiculous it would sound if she said it aloud.

Locke and Casra returned with the water, and Tiffienne made Mirolah undress and clean herself up. Soon, she had her nightdress on and felt a little better. Tiffienne told her to lie down and close her eyes. Just as she began to relax, she heard Lawdon's voice outside. The girls unbolted the front door. It opened and closed quickly, and was bolted just as fast. Lawdon's heavy boots clumped up the stairs.

Mirolah sat up. Lawdon's tall, thin frame filled the doorway. The candlelight played off his grim features, carving deep shadows in the furrowed brow, the tight-lipped mouth.

"Better get dressed again, Mirolah."

"Why?" Tiffienne stood up. "What's wrong?"

He shook his head. "They're bringing the magistrate. They want..." he cut himself off and glanced at Mirolah. "They want her."

Mirolah's heart constricted, and she cringed against the headboard of her little bed.

"Now, don't worry," he said. "They aren't here yet. That mob's going to have to go through me and a thick oak cudgel if they want in my house."

107

"By the gods, what's happened?" Tiffienne finally asked. "What's it all about?"

He swallowed, his face drawn and pale. "Damned if I know. People are talking stupid. I told you. Everyone is chattering about some monster." He paused. "And..."

"And what?" Tiffienne asked pointedly.

"Fillen is dead."

Tiffienne's face went white. She started to look at Mirolah, but stopped herself. Stiffly, she stood. "Well..." She swallowed. "We have business. We will mourn the dear child later. Right now, we take care of the others."

"Anyway, I think it would be best if we got you ready to leave, just in case," Lawdon said.

"Leave?" Mirolah asked in a tiny voice.

He paused and gave her a tight smile. "No, not with them, girl. I wouldn't give those fools a broken tile, much less my own daughter. We may have to hide you away somewhere else for a couple of days, until there's enough time to knock some sense into their heads."

Mirolah shuddered in relief and clung to Tiffienne.

"Don't you worry, girl," he continued. "Things will look different tomorrow. People think better in the light of day. We just need to keep them away from you tonight. I don't know why they've latched onto the idea that it's your fault, but they have. That'll fade when they have time to think about their own idiocy in the light of day."

A great knocking boomed on the downstairs door.

"That'd be them." Lawdon said grimly. "Get dressed. Quickly, now." He left the room.

Mirolah quickly pulled on a clean tunic and a long skirt. Tiffienne stood nervously between her and the door to the girls' room. Downstairs, Lawdon had opened the front door and his voice was low as he talked. Mirolah wished she could hear what he was saying.

She had just reached for her shoes when the voices began to rise. Lawdon almost yelled, something about not setting foot in his house. Two other voices spoke back in harsh tones.

Clutching her shoes in her hand, Mirolah moved past Tiffienne and stood in the stairway. The stairs slanted downward before her, dark and forbidding for the first time in her life.

"We have witnesses," a stranger's voice said. "Now you let us in to take the girl, and we'll go peacefully. You stand in our way, and we'll move you. This is the magistrate, for Thalius's sake! Don't make it difficult, Lawdon. It's the law!"

"You're not marching into my house and taking my daughter and calling it law, you pack of mongrels," Lawdon snarled.

The talking ceased. Mirolah heard a grunt. The door banged against its casing. A couple of the girls screamed. Lawdon roared, and there was a smacking noise then the sound of someone hitting the floor. Downstairs erupted into chaos, thudding, banging, people hitting one another. Men and girls shouting, crying.

Tiffienne rushed past her and down the stairs. Mirolah followed slowly, one step at a time. She felt like she was walking through thick honey. She couldn't make herself go faster. It was as if this was an old story whose end had already been written. There was no haste in her because she knew she was doomed. They had come for her, and, just as they took her brother, they would take her. After what seemed an eternity, she reached the bottom of the stairs and beheld the scene.

Four men squirmed on top of a struggling Lawdon. His face was battered and bleeding, but he cursed them and spat at them even though they had his legs and hands pinned. Two other men lay sprawled on the floor. One was moving slowly, trying to crawl to his knees and the other lay still across the huge carpet. The dinner table was at a wild angle and the chairs were scattered everywhere, as were her sisters. Yehnie ran past Mirolah and scampered up the steps, crying.

Locke and Shera stood atop the table as if there were an army of roaches on the floor. Dederi and Cisly cringed against the hearth. Mi'Gan stood in the center of the room, within striking distance of the one man who was still standing, screaming at him to stop hurting her daddy. Her little fists were clenched so hard they were white. Casra emerged from the kitchen with a huge skillet clenched tightly in her hands. Tiffienne's face was white and drawn, but she kept her composure. She walked calmly up behind Mi'Gan and put gentle hands on her shoulders.

"Calm down, child. It will be all right," Tiffienne said in a shaking voice. "Come away now."

"Let go of my daddy!" Mi'Gan screamed again.

"Come away now, Meg," Tiffienne repeated. With a suspicious scowl at the standing man, Mi'Gan allowed herself to be led away. Lawdon continued struggling, calling them every foul name Mirolah had ever heard and some she'd never heard.

Mirolah watched as if in a dream. The standing man looked up, and his eyes locked on her. He was the magistrate. Mirolah had seen him before. He was tall and wide in the shoulders. His hands were very large, and they looked like they could bend a horseshoe. He had a square face and a short beard on his chin. The muscles in his jaw were clenched, and his brow was furrowed. He didn't seem angry, but neither was he afraid. He looked like a man who would be denied nothing.

That brightness in the air that had connected Mirolah to the monster began to form between her and the magistrate. She could hear his heart beat. She could hear the blood rushing in his veins. Determination radiated out from him, and his gaze went from one sister to the other, but settled on Mirolah with confidence.

Seeing her foster father beneath the magistrate's men, seeing what they had done to her house, Mirolah wanted to lash out at the magistrate as she had the monster. Her desire coiled like a snake, and she felt it ready to strike.

"Are you the girl?" the magistrate asked in a deep voice.

She readied herself. If they were going to condemn her for this curse she bore, she would let them taste it. If they were going to hurt her family, she would hurt them back.

The magistrate seemed to feel her rage. His eyes widened a little, and he took an involuntary step back. Mirolah felt fear come from him now.

She paused. Something within her rebelled, and her rage fled. What was she going to do? What did she think she *could* do? The slap she had delivered the monster had been nothing, had not even slowed it. Even if she could hurt the magistrate, how could she possibly stop all of them? And what would happen to her family if she fought them? Mirolah suddenly realized that the best way to protect her family was to leave with the magistrate. They would have no reason to be here if not for her. They would leave her family alone if she went with them.

The brightness faded, and she let out a slow breath. The room was silent except for Lawdon's unceasing struggles. She thought of Fillen, looked at Lawdon being crushed by the four men who held him down.

I won't let another one of my family come to harm.

"Let him go," she said softly. "And I'll go with you."

17

MIROLAH

THE DARK, HARD CELL leaned in on Mirolah from all sides. Her bed was a board jammed into the wall and held up by two chains bolted into the stone. There was a thin blanket and a sack stuffed with straw for a pillow. Mirolah sat on the cot with her knees curled up to her chin and stared through the bars.

She didn't know how late it was. Hours or minutes could have passed since they brought her here, and she wouldn't know the difference. She was exhausted, but she couldn't sleep because the guardsmen were talking.

Talking about Mirolah's death.

According to witnesses, she had summoned the blackened, vicious creature from some far-off land or another dimension and made it kill her sister. She would surely hang in the morning as a murderer, a bringer of bad spirits, just as Mad Meekie had hung last year for casting the spell on that pregnant woman who shortly afterward had a miscarriage.

They knew she could hear them, and they didn't care. In their minds, she wasn't a person anymore. She was a thing. A wielder of

GodSpill. A rot bringer An enemy of every villager in Rith.

Shortly after she had been shoved into the cell, Lawdon had tried to get in to see her. She heard his voice down the hall at the main door to the prison. She heard him arguing with the guards, but they wouldn't let him in. They wouldn't let anyone in.

There were three guards, though Mirolah had only seen one. For some reason, only a guard named Gort was allowed to look at her. Perhaps they were afraid she would control them.

Her prison was stone and mortar walls on three sides. The fourth was iron bars. They were rammed into the floor and the ceiling. On the left-hand side squatted a thick wooden door. Gort stood in front of the bars, short and stout. He was only a few inches taller than Mirolah, but half again as wide with thick shoulders and a thick neck. He smiled at her, and she saw he was missing several teeth.

She stared back at him through red-rimmed eyes. The air began to lighten between them. Something had shifted in her head, and every time she concentrated on someone, the brightness returned, began to connect them. She felt his emotions. He was slightly afraid of her, but not very. Perhaps he didn't believe the stories of her using GodSpill, but she'd heard him talking all night long. He had no qualms about hanging her. He liked hanging people. It excited him. It didn't matter to him what they had done, just as long as he got to see someone swing.

"She's a cute one," Gort said in his gravelly voice to the other guards out of view. He watched her through the bars.

Mirolah didn't move, but continued to stare at the man with her knees tucked under her chin.

"You only ever think about one thing, Gort," one of the other guards called from down the hall. Get back in here and finish your throw."

"What could it hurt?" Gort argued. "She's going to be dead in the morning. Seems a waste."

"You open that cell door, and the magistrate put you in the next cell over."

"Not if he doesn't know," Gort said.

"And how's he not going to know?" the guard called back.

"If you don't tell him and Keru doesn't tell him, how will he know?"

"By Thalius, Gort! You haven't got two wits to rub together. I suppose the girl's just gonna kiss you and keep her mouth shut after? Get back in here and finish your throw before I come break your head!"

Gort frowned, but he didn't move. She could feel his twisted lust across the bright air that connected them. She wanted to cry, but she held her tears in. It was all a nightmare, but she didn't get to wake up from this one.

"Gort, I'm telling you, get away from the girl—" The guard's voice stopped abruptly. Silver light splashed across the wall behind Gort. There was a grunt and a thud. Keru shouted in shock, but was also cut off. There was another thud, a body hitting the ground.

It all happened in less than a second. Gort lost his frustrated frown, and his eyes widened. He went for his short sword and yanked it from the leather sheath. Mirolah jumped to her feet. Was it another monster from the night, come to finish her?

"What the hell are you?" Gort exclaimed, holding the sword pointed down the hall. Mirolah couldn't see the guard's antagonist, but she heard a light, quick panting.

Silver light lit the walls again and a blur of silver streaked around Gort. The light was opaque, and it was as if Gort was being wrapped up in a snake. He swung with his sword, but the silver flash wound around and around him and his sword fell to the ground. Gort gasped, then grunted. His head snapped forward, and he staggered. He grunted again and struck the stones like a felled tree.

The silver streak stopped, and a boy of about twelve stood before her cell. His thin body sagged against the bars, and he took great, deep breaths. His grip faltered and he slid to his knees, his lungs pumping. Long, silver hair fell forward to eclipse his pale face. He stayed that way for a long moment, recovering his breath as if he'd just run the entire length of The Arm. Mirolah said nothing, but walked a step forward.

Her newfound vision lightened the air between them. She saw

bright strings of light all around him, dancing and playing like otters.

"Who are you?" she whispered, kneeling next to him and touching the bars between them.

The boy looked up. His eyes were the same silver color as his hair. He blinked, swallowed, and said, "I am Stavark. Reader Orem sent me." He crawled to Gort's body and rummaged around until he produced the keys. He rose on shaky legs and staggered to the wooden door.

Her gaze stayed on Gort as Stavark unlocked the door. "What did you do to them?"

The door swung wide and Stavark stood there, regarding her with huge, silver eyes that were so large they seemed to drink her in. "I hit them," he said.

"But...they're three times your size. How could you possibly knock them down like that?"

Stavark smiled wearily. "I hit them many times. A hundred each."

She swallowed and stepped hesitantly out of the cell.

The boy looked up at her. "Reader Orem waits in the forest. He wishes to talk to you. Will you come?"

"But, my family—"

He shook his head. "These humans will kill you. They are *vakihrk*." He glanced down the hallway, then back at her. "Orem will take you away. They will not catch him."

She clenched her teeth. "But I don't want to leave. This is my home!"

He frowned. "You are *syvihrk*. They are *vakihrk*," he said, as if that explained everything.

Tears welled in her eyes and streaked down her cheeks. This was her fate then? Death or exile?

"Yes," she said. "I will go with you."

"He is near. Come." The boy turned and leapt lightly over Gort's body. She edged her way around, then followed.

Stavark was like a squirrel. He padded across the floor noiselessly, looking left then right, then he poked his head out of the door. He looked back at her and nodded, then disappeared into the night. Mirolah emerged onto the street. There was no one awake at this hour. The torches that lined the main street were low and almost spent. She guessed it was a few hours to sunrise.

He led her down the road to the first break in the buildings. Something tall and slender emerged from the shadows, and she stifled a scream.

"Mirolah, it's okay," Orem said, pushing back his cowl to reveal a human face, human skin.

"Orem..." she gasped. "There was a monster. He came for me and..."

"It's over now. I won't let anyone hurt you. I swear it."

"It killed my...my sister. It was going to kill me."

He took her in his arms and she hugged him, laid her head on his chest. He smelled like leather and dust and sweat. He held her for a moment, then broke the embrace.

"I want to hear every single thing that happened," he said. "But we aren't beyond the reach of Rith's magistrate just yet. We have maybe an hour before every able-bodied person in Rith will be looking for you. We'd best be well away by then."

He led her down the alley, but Mirolah stopped and looked back in the direction of the main street. The low torches gave an orange glow to the packed earth she had walked over a hundred times.

"I'm never coming back, am I?" she whispered, thinking of Casra, Locke, of all of her sisters. She would never see Lawdon and Tiffienne, who had been kinder to her than anyone in her life.

"Yes," he said. "Yes you are. Of course you are."

"How can I?"

"When you return, you'll return in triumph," he said.

She had a vision of what her life should be. Working at Vaisha's Fountain. Reading letters. Saving money. Finding a husband. Raising children. A quiet, successful life. Simple and honest and beautiful.

That future lay in smoking ruins.

A different future opened before her then. Mere days ago, Orem had been a danger, a destroyer of that vision she held for her life. Now he was her rescuer, and she would follow him anywhere. He was the only thing left that was safe.

And he knew that.

She swallowed and said, "Did you send it?"

He was quiet for a moment as he tried to understand what she was asking. Finally, he said, "The darkling?"

"Is that what you call it?"

"I didn't send it. How could you think that?"

"Because I don't know you."

"Then know this—"

"No," she interrupted him. "I don't want one of your speeches. I want the truth. You came here, and you asked me to leave with you. I refused. Then, days later, I'm forced out of my home by a monster. Then you show up with a creature from legend." She gestured at Stavark. "And rescue me. And I have no other choice but to follow you."

He paused, his mouth open to say something, and then he laughed. "Gods, Mirolah. I'm just so happy you're alive."

"Did you send it? Because I would rather die than go with the man who killed my sister."

He sobered, and he took her by the shoulders, looked her in the eyes. "I did not kill Fillen. Those darklings breed like bees to the north, all around Daylan's Fountain. They are going to consume Amarion. This is what we are facing. Fillen is only the first of many casualties if something isn't done. And I don't believe she was its target. That darkling was sent to kill you. Fillen just got in the way. And they're going to keep coming."

"Why me?"

"Because of who you are. Because they can sense the GodSpill in you. Because you're the only one who can stop them."

"What can I do?"

"Everything," he said. "Anything. When you learn what you need to know, those darklings won't be able to touch you."

"What are they?"

"Lesser children of the god Dervon. Twisted versions of humans."

"Dervon the Dead?" she asked.

"But his children still live."

"And if I go with you, can you escape the magistrate and his men?"

"Yes," Orem said.

"And the darklings... Can you protect me from them?"

He hesitated. "You can," he said.

"But I can't."

"With knowledge, with time, you will. Stavark and I will give you that time. And until the day you are ready to face them, we will hide you."

She paused. "I don't want this," she whispered.

"I'm sorry..." he said, trying to sound sincere.

But she didn't believe him. He may not have sent the darkling, but this was what he wanted. And now, it was all she had.

"I'll go with you," she said.

18

MIROLAH

OREM WAS AS GOOD AS HIS WORD. Mirolah didn't see so much as a trace of the magistrate or his men during the next few days. Orem was an accomplished woodsman and seemed to be experienced at evasion. He stopped at certain places and meticulously covered their trail. In other places, they blazed through the forest without a care for stealth. He chose their path with a swift confidence.

Just before the sun began to rise, they came upon a quiet glade where three horses were tethered. Mirolah had never ridden before, but Orem coached her through it with unfailing patience.

For three days, he led them west at a steady pace and for three days Mirolah barely slept and barely ate. She didn't talk at all, even though Orem tried to engage her in conversation every night. He never pushed, only offered. He seemed to understand she needed to be alone with her thoughts.

On the third day, just as the sun was setting, they reined in at the shore of a vast ocean. The water stretched out on either side of them as far as the eye could see.

"The Inland Ocean," she murmured. She stretched a stiff leg over her horse and dismounted, wincing. She already had sores on the inside of her thighs and knees. A skirt was not appropriate riding attire, but she had nothing else. Orem apologized for not having thought of acquiring proper riding breeches for her, but had not expected to have to take her from Rith so abruptly.

She stepped gingerly toward the shore, never taking her eyes off the expanse of the water. She had heard tales of the Inland Ocean, but never thought she would see it.

Waves lapped delicately at the sandy shore, pulling back and curling, then toppling into themselves in a foamy roll that spread out on the smooth sand. Harbored against the pillars of a long, wooden walkway bobbed a small sailboat, thirty feet long. Its masts pointed at the sky, and its sails were rolled up tightly.

Stavark and Orem dismounted and let their horses wander away to crop a nearby field of grass. Stavark went to the water and put his hand in.

Orem came up beside Mirolah, who stared wonderingly at the ocean. "It's...vast. Where does it all come from?"

"Two different mountain ranges," he said. "The Spine Mountains to the west and the Dragon Mountains far to the north."

"This is where the Southrock river goes, isn't it?" she asked.

"And the Quicksilver River, and the Dragon River."

"Where are those?"

"Farther north," he said.

"Have you been there? To both of them?"

He nodded.

"You've been to a lot of places, haven't you?" she asked.

"Yes."

"And the Inland Ocean, it's not even as large as the True Ocean, is it?"

"Not even close."

"By Thalius, how could there be more water than this?" she breathed.

"The True Ocean is another world in itself, and not a welcome place to humans. Saraphazia does not like us in her waters."

Everyone knew the seven primary gods. Natra the Lifebringer, Zetu the Ancient, Oedandus the Binder, Saraphazia the Vast, Dervon the Dead, White Tuana, and Vaisha the Changer.

"They say Saraphazia's ocean stretches to eternity," she said.

"It certainly seems to. If there is something beyond it, only one man has ever seen it."

"Who?"

"Wildmane came from over the ocean, from an island far away. So they say."

"But no one real has been across the ocean."

He cocked his head. "You think he wasn't real?"

"Well, no. A man with a god inside him? Was he?"

He recited a line from a poem that Mirolah recognized.

> *Over the hill the rider came*
> *The sun flashed gold on golden mane*
> *His sword a flame of godly wrath*
> *To kill the god upon his path*

"That's from the poem *Wildmane* by Thedore Stok."

He nodded. "Do you know the whole thing?"

"Yes. Was he real?"

"He was," Orem said. "Almost all of the well-known legends have a kernel of truth to them."

"I bet you like old legends," she said.

"There was a time when I did nothing but search for them. I memorized them, read every book in the royal library at Buravar, and everything that survived at the abandoned library in Clete."

"You've read every book at the libraries in two cities? That's ridiculous."

"I've also listened to the village elders in every town I visited. I read and collect stories. That's how I got the nickname 'Reader Orem.' I've read every story I could find."

"That's...amazing."

"I'd rather be able to do what you do." He winked. "All my life, I've wanted to be a threadweaver."

"How many old legends are there?" she asked.

"Countless. The world was once full of heroes and threadweavers, dragons and unicorns and quicksilvers. And everyone has their favorite."

"Who is your favorite?"

"I couldn't possibly choose. There are so many." He shrugged. "It used to be Wildmane, I suppose."

"But not anymore?"

He hesitated. "I grew to love the less powerful heroes, those who prevailed by courage and wits, rather than godlike power." He shrugged.

"He's *my* favorite," she said. "I like the idea of someone who can live forever, fighting injustice everywhere. I wish there were really people like that."

"Me, too."

"You said he was real. Did he really killed the god Dervon?"

"Yes."

"How do you know for sure?"

He was silent a moment, then said. "The poem Godslayer was as close to a history as any of those old ballads get, based on all of the research I have done."

"If he was immortal, wouldn't he still be alive today?"

"One would think so," he said.

She sat back, looked up at the sky, imagining Wildmane striding out of the woods right now. "All of the things he must have seen..." she murmured. "Maybe he's out there, somewhere, just waiting for the right moment to return."

Orem shook his head.

"No? But you said—"

"Everything I know about Wildmane points to the fact that he died around the same time that the GodSpill left the lands."

"I never heard that story. How?"

He shrugged. "He met his match."

"Zilok Morth?" Mirolah asked.

"What do you know of Zilok Morth?" he asked.

"He was Wildmane's nemesis. A spirit who clung to life only to kill Wildmane."

"It wasn't Zilok. Wildmane died of..." He trailed into silence.

"Of what?"

"Of heartbreak," Orem said.

They watched the water roll in for a long moment, neither speaking. She had the sense that he wasn't telling her everything, but she couldn't figure out why.

Stavark walked up to Orem "We sail with the sunrise?"

He nodded. "Take the horses to Valinda, if you would. Mirolah and I will set up camp."

Stavark nodded and began removing the saddlebags.

"Valinda?" She asked.

"She lives in a small fishing village not far from here."

"Pindish," she said.

"You know the area?"

"We get letters from Pindish sometimes."

"Well, Valinda is a friend, and she's met Stavark before. And since we cannot bring the horses with us on the boat, best to benefit a friend." He turned to Stavark. "Also, ask her about riding breeches for Mirolah. She'll need them."

Stavark took the horses and left. Mirolah unloaded food from the saddlebags as Orem went in search of wood for the fire.

Before long, the two of them sat in front of a crackling blaze, stewing potatoes and rabbit meat in a pot. Orem spiced the stew using herbs from a few small bags he kept in the cooking supplies. The aroma set her mouth to watering.

They sat in silence waiting for Stavark to return and for the stew to be ready. After a time, Mirolah spoke. "Orem, tell me a story."

He smiled. "Be careful what you ask for. I have no end of stories."

"Tell me about Wildmane. Tell me how the most powerful hero in history died of heartbreak."

His zeal faded. "Ah. Well, have you ever heard of the threadweaver Ethiel?"

"No."

"Also known as the Red Weaver."

Mirolah snapped her fingers. She had read a story about the Red Weaver just recently; one of the forbidden books by the hearth. "Yes! The Red Weaver killed her father and began a war against

Calsinac. Wildmane and Bands foiled her plans. I thought they killed her."

"No."

"The story said that the Red Weaver was insane, that she fantasized Wildmane loved her. Did he?"

Orem tossed a stick into the flames. "No."

"Did she kill him?" she asked.

"No. She took the one he loved. She took Bands away." He cleared his throat and set another stick on the fire.

"Oh," she said, and it hurt to hear that. The love affair of Bands and Wildmane was legendary. To have it cut off so didn't seem right. Legends didn't usually end like that.

"How?"

"The Red Weaver was brilliant. After all, how do you kill someone who will heal from any wound? So she struck him in the heart, took away his reason for living." He stared at the flames. She watched Orem, and the bright bridge formed between them, just like it had with her and the darkling, and she shook her head to stop it. Reluctantly, it faded.

Orem, of course, didn't see the bright bridge, so he kept talking. "There are no legends of Wildmane after that. He left the human lands."

"Maybe he disappeared because the GodSpill was gone."

The fire popped and crackled, but Orem didn't respond. They sat in silence, listening to the cicadas chirp in the distant trees. The smell of the rabbit stew was intoxicating, and she wondered where Stavark was.

"Orem..." she began, but she hesitated. She kept her gaze focused on him, but didn't say anything for a long time. He let her find her words. "I know I haven't been very talkative up to now. But I want to know...where we're going."

He sat back and his contemplative mood vanished. He smiled. "We are going to Daylan's Fountain," he said.

She cocked her head. "What's that?"

"Almost all of the books related to it in your part of Amarion have been destroyed. The simple folk have their own story, saying the gods took away the GodSpill as punishment for our hubris."

Simple folk? That was the story her father had told her. It was story everyone told. How else could the GodSpill have been taken away? He made her sound like a moron. "The GodSpill was a gift from the gods, and the threadweavers abused it. We got greedy and they punished us."

"No."

"What do you mean 'no'?"

"That's not what happened. The gods didn't give us the GodSpill. Most of them didn't want us to have it in the first place, but they couldn't take it away. The GodSpill was an accident, a leak from the Godgate from before humans recorded time. That's how it got its name. It spilled from the Godgate into Amarion."

"How do you know you're right and my history is wrong?"

"Because your history isn't history. Your history is made of the bitter stories of a people who fear what they don't understand, who would rather burn books than learn from them. My history comes from accounts written by actual historians from an age gone by. Once upon a time, people recorded events. And if you read enough of them, you can piece together what actually happened. Humans are responsible for the rise and fall of our civilization, not the gods. The gods do not really care what we do, and they notice even less. Daylan's Fountain is responsible for the Age of Ascendance, for all the powerful threadweavers that arose."

"So what is it?"

"It's the most powerful artifact ever created, designed to pool the GodSpill and send it directly to humans, to use it however they wished. It turned normal people into threadweavers. It turned threadweavers into near gods. The loss of Daylan's Fountain began the Devastation Years."

"So what *really* happened?" she asked, failing to keep the edge of sarcasm out of her voice.

"Have you ever heard of Daylan Morth?"

"No. Was he related to Zilok Morth?"

"His great-grandson, several times removed. Daylan Morth was the most powerful threadweaver ever."

"More powerful than the Red Weaver and Zilok Morth?"

"Undisputed."

"Why haven't I heard of him, then?"

"Because he didn't try to conquer a kingdom or build his reputation. Daylan was a gentle soul. The reason he first studied threadweaving was because his wife was dying of a disease for which there was no cure. Within six months, he learned enough to heal his wife."

"Six months?"

"Impressive, right? Remember this was also before the Age of Ascendance when everyone could do simple threadweavings, and powerful threadweavers could do almost anything. This was during the Age of Awakening. Using the GodSpill required painstaking study and sacrifice, and even then it was only accessible to those with inherent talent. Only a select few ever achieved the status of threadweaver.

"Daylan realized he had a gift that he could turn to the advantage of others. If he could heal his wife of a wasting disease, why not all people? For years, he traveled, curing all who were sick. He also raised buildings that would never weather or need repair. He created places of learning and sheltered the poor.

"However, it did not take long for him to realize that his efforts, as meaningful as they were, were only the efforts of one man. He would never be able to visit all of the villages that needed him. So he left his philanthropic travels and began working on a master weaving. He wanted to teach everyone how to wield the GodSpill, but how could he give aptitude to everyone? He labored for years looking for the solution. In the end, he created Daylan's Fountain, the artifact that funneled GodSpill of Amarion to each and every human.

"Suddenly, you didn't need aptitude to be a threadweaver. Menial tasks became a thing of the past. People's imaginations burst into reality. Powerful empires—conclaves of threadweavers working in concert—rose in just decades. The humans of Amarion left the fields, the construction of houses, the laying of roads, to the GodSpill, commanding it to do their work. Instead, they spent time creating art and architecture, studying and writing histories. Daylan Morth's creation worked beyond his wildest dreams. He single-handedly created a golden age of humankind.

"That was how it began, at least. It lasted almost two hundred years. By that time, the empires of the Age of Ascendance were vast and so powerful that it is difficult for us to imagine what they were like."

"The ruins..." she said. Beyond the Bracer were miles and miles of tumbled stones. In some places, the ruins stretched on seemingly forever.

"There were kingdoms beyond count along the western coast of the Inland Ocean. They were all constructed by GodSpill and they toppled the moment it vanished." Orem paused, reached back, and grabbed some wood from the pile he had collected. He threw more fuel on the fire. "You have heard of the GodSpill Wars?"

"Of course," she said. "It's what led up to the gods finally deciding we weren't worthy to wield the GodSpill."

"Well, it led up to the end of the GodSpill, at any rate. The Age of Ascendance lasted for two hundred years. That's a long time. In that much time, many threadweavers in Amarion felt that the power of the GodSpill was their right, not a privilege. It took just one fight between kingdoms to start the wars. The Twelve Points of Justice, an empire comprised of twelve cities working in concert, made the first attack. They worshipped the god Oedandus, and they were offended by the—as they saw it—lack of morality of their neighbor to the south."

"Who did they attack?"

"It was called the Seawave Empire, a hedonistic culture dedicated to creating art, pursuing pleasures of the flesh, and utilizing mind-altering drugs to further expand their knowledge of the GodSpill. There were many disagreements between the two empires. The disagreements turned to threats, the threats to violence. Once Twelve Points struck, it was as if a dam had burst. Seawave's allies swarmed to its defense. One of the historians described it, saying all the venom within the people of Amarion spilled out. Entire cities were razed to the ground in a day. The air filled with a haze of crackling fire and smoke. Fierce battles were waged. Insidious unnatural diseases felled entire conclaves of threadweavers. Entire cities were washed away as the ocean unnaturally rose up to drown them. Threadweavers committed atrocities that would make you sick. I won't describe to you all the horrors, but thousands died.

"It couldn't have been worse if Dervon the Dead had risen again. It was as if Daylan Morth had created a coin of benevolence that had flipped over, revealing rage, ambition, and cruelty on the other side. But it wasn't anywhere near as bad as the death bringer who followed: Harleath Markin."

"I've never heard of him."

"There are almost no accounts of him, but I found an obscure journal of a threadweaver scribe that referenced him. Harleath was from the Seawall Empire, which had been all but destroyed in the war against Twelve Points. From what I can tell, Harleath's was a crazy suicide mission. And he was responsible for the loss of the GodSpill."

"How? How did he do it?"

"We don't know. There aren't any accounts of what he did afterward. After all, the GodSpill was gone. The threadweavers were dead, so there were none to record what Harleath did, and no witnesses. In fact, nobody recorded history for quite some time after the great dying. The single reference I found to Harleath was before he left, penned by the scribe of Harleath's conclave—where he was not considered a threadweaver of much consequence, actually—along with two dozen other references to threadweaver activities. The entry mentioned, in a clipped, barely-tolerant tone, that Harleath had come up with a plan to "stop the GodSpill Wars," and that he was planning to ride to Daylan's Fountain the following day. The scribe had made a footnote that Harleath was always experimenting with new ways of using GodSpill, most of which failed, and essentially dismissed his adventure as rubbish. Shortly thereafter, the Fountain stopped working, and GodSpill vanished from the lands."

"The great dying..." she finished for him.

"Yes. The start of the Devastation Years," he said. "Everything that was imbued with GodSpill died. When Harleath and his threadweavers worked their spell, it killed them. It killed all the threadweavers in Twelve Points, the Seawave Empire, and every other threadweaver empire in Amarion. Creatures reliant on

GodSpill fell: unicorns, lyonars, bakkarals, gliffets, pegasi... Those touched by GodSpill became deathly ill. Anyone who even dabbled was at risk. The only people who survived were those who had never used GodSpill."

"It wasn't the gods," she whispered.

"It wasn't the gods," he echoed her words. "It was a man who thought himself a god. And the powerful threadweaver empires fell in a day. The remaining population of Amarion, pitifully few, stunned and sickly, regressed from ascendancy to subsistence and, well, we were easy prey for the swords of invaders."

"The Sunriders..." The word lodged in Mirolah's heart. That was how her parents were killed. "But now the GodSpill is returning," she said.

"Yes."

"How?"

"I don't know."

"And I can see it?"

"I think you can do it."

"But I can't. All I see is a brightening in the air. I can't make anything happen."

"Did you start writing entire pages the first time you picked up a pen?"

"You're saying I need practice." Her only attempt to harness GodSpill ended with Fillen's death. The idea of trying that again made her ill. "The monster..." she said. "Was it hunting me because it senses the GodSpill inside me?"

"I don't know the answer to that, but I think yes. There was no other reason for it to be in that alley other than coincidence, and since GodSpill started leaking back into the lands, I don't believe in coincidence. We must stay vigilant, or more creatures like that darkling may find us."

"I tried to send it away," she said.

He sat forward, interested. "The villagers said you *did* send it away. What did that feel like?"

"I... It didn't feel like anything. I'm not even sure I sent it away. The bright bridge formed between me and the darkling. I remember somehow touching the monster across that distance, but it was only a touch. What happened to the monster after it leapt at me was so forceful, so powerful. Something grabbed hold of it. I never thought about the monster bowing. I just wanted it to go away."

"Maybe you just don't understand how it works yet. Maybe the creature bowed to you because you are so powerful."

"No. It was struggling. It *wanted* to kill me. Something forced it to bow, almost like it was..."

"It was what?"

"Like it was making fun of me."

He paused, then said, "That doesn't make any sense."

"You asked me what I felt. *That's* what I felt. What if someone made the darkling go away? Someone not me. Is that possible? What if *they* were making fun of me?"

"There is no one else. Believe me, I have looked. You are the only one I have found with even a glimpse of threadweaver aptitude."

"What about the raven with the blue eyes?" she asked.

"What raven with blue eyes?"

19

ZILOK MORTH

ZILOK MORTH'S RAVEN landed quietly on a cliff overlooking a sandstone wasteland. Bulbous rock formations as large as hills rose up from the sandstone floor, and there was no life in sight, not so much as a lizard or a blade of grass.

The raven shifted from claw to claw, scratching the stone and looking at the one object in the center of the valley that was of human make.

Daylan's Fountain thrust defiantly at the sky, a two-hundred-feet tall square tower, thin and delicate, that tapered gradually as it rose. Near the top, four spikes jutted out horizontally, one from each corner. The last few feet of the spire ended in a swirl of metal meant to represent a flame. The Fountain was only ten feet wide where its base met a round slab of black marble. Arcane symbols decorated every inch of the Fountain, but the base was smooth and unmarked.

Suddenly, a darkling loped across the sandstone toward the tower. Sunlight flashed off its shiny skin and rippling muscles, and it stopped just before the tower, crouching low. Its small, round head raised and its long teeth snapped twice. It sniffed the air, turned toward the raven, and its tiny blue eyes glowed malevolently. After a long moment, it turned, touched the wall of the tower, and vanished.

Zilok Morth hovered in front of the raven over the expanse of air. A normal onlooker would not have seen him: a trim, well-dressed man with a rapier at his hip, neatly combed black hair, a black goatee, and dark eyes. They would have seen nothing, for Zilok Morth had no physical substance in this world.

If the onlooker was conversant with the threads of the world, then they could not help but feel his presence. Then, they would have beheld two burning, disembodied eyes, but not much more unless Zilok wanted them to.

"He is here, Sef," Zilok said. "We have found our leash master."

The raven cawed and shifted back and forth on its claws.

"My apologies." Zilok waved his hand.

The air around the raven shimmered. The black bird smeared like a watercolor painting in the rain. It blurred and stretched into a tall, dark blob, then coalesced into the form of a tall man with long muscles, lean and ropey. He wore breeches of black leather, but no tunic. Instead, a crosspiece of studded leather was strapped over his chest in an "X." He was hairless from head to waist, and his eyes were milky white.

"He made the Fountain his home. That takes some doing."

"Yes, my master." No expression crossed Sef's gaunt face as he spoke.

"He is building. Do you see it, Sef?"

"Yes, my master."

"He's using Difinius' trick. He has created an imaginary space within the Fountain. There is an entire castle in there."

"Yes, my master."

"I find myself liking this interloper more and more."

"He is powerful, my master."

Zilok Morth laughed. It echoed only within Sef's mind. "Was that a caution, perhaps, Sef? You think we should step lightly here."

"Yes, my master."

"We must keep our wits, but we must always step boldly. Fear is the herald of failure."

"Yes, my master."

"Let us bring him to us."

"Yes, my master."

Zilok focused his concentration on the Great Tapestry. It was thick and bunched here at the Fountain, as if someone had tied a rope around the middle and cinched it tight. *Ah, Daylan, my grandson, you could have been something startling. What a shame you chose the life you did.*

Zilok singled out the threads he needed. He tugged one and changed the color of the other.

A darkling came flying out of the Fountain, emerging from the closest facet as if it was an illusion. The darkling howled and struggled against Zilok's will. It clawed and scraped at the air, but to no avail. Zilok brought the beast up to the ledge where he and Sef waited. He set it down. The darkling thrashed, glaring at Sef in rage, but it did not see Zilok. Sef kept his milky eyes focused on the Fountain.

"I wonder if he even knows that his pet is missing."

"I do not know, my master."

"Ah, here he comes."

A red and smoky cloud billowed out of the Fountain. It coalesced into a voluptuous red-haired woman. Her long, fiery locks floated about her head like seagrass. She wore a filmy gown which clung tightly to her body.

She was not a he at all. Intriguing.

Zilok was amused. Her form had no more physical substance than his, so her appearance was entirely her own choice. Who did she think had come calling? A long-lost lover? Or was this the way she saw herself?

It suddenly occurred to him that his own self-projection wasn't any less bizarre. Any physical projection for one who had transcended physicality was a bit ridiculous.

We are human yet, to possess such vanity.

The red-haired threadweaver saw Sef and the struggling

darkling. She floated up to them, then saw Zilok. She stopped her ascent.

One of her prowess would see his burning blue eyes. Out of courtesy, he made his form fully apparent, hovering in front of Sef as if he were a mortal man. He bowed low to her in the fashion of a nobleman of his time.

"Who are you?" she asked tersely. "Why do you meddle with my creatures and my Fountain?"

Neither the creature nor the Fountain belonged to her, but that wasn't the conversation he wished to have with her today.

"Zilok Morth at your service, my lady," he said at the nadir of his bow.

The image of herself became indistinct for a moment as, he surmised, she lost her concentration. He smiled. It was nice to be recognized.

It must be a little unsettling to believe you are the largest lyonar in the land, then to turn around and see another lyonar just behind you.

"What do you want?" she asked.

How rude.

"I could not help but notice your handiwork. Your talent screams to be appreciated. I have come to appreciate it."

"What handiwork?" she asked. Threadweavers were notoriously secretive about their prowess. It was almost a prerequisite of the vocation. Still, she really should conceal her hand more effectively if she was going to act indignant when someone noticed it.

He smiled. "The darklings you have running all over Amarion like trained dogs, for one. The smart additions that you've made to my descendant's Fountain, for two. It's quite impressive."

The red-haired spirit smiled a little, albeit reluctantly. "You can see my work?"

"Every bit of it, my lady."

Abruptly, she laughed, loud and shrill. He narrowed his eyes. "You are Zilok Morth, after all," she said.

"I would not have chosen fluted columns for your greatroom, but that is only a matter of personal taste."

"Oh..." she furrowed her brow. "What would you have chosen?"

"I am partial to smooth marble. The beauty of simple elegance is often underappreciated."

The red-haired woman nodded and looked back at the Fountain for a moment. "Perhaps I shall take your advice."

"I am flattered." He suddenly wondered at her mental stability. She behaved much like the nubile young woman she appeared to be. Could she really be that emotionally immature? He had only met a handful of threadweavers who had the presence of mind to transcend mortal death and live on as a spirit. Even fewer who could master Difinius's great spell of folding space. She obviously had a mighty will. Yet the transition from mortal flesh to immortal spirit was a shock, to say the least. It could easily plunge an unwary mind into insanity. Had this happened to her?

He decided that he must step carefully. It was far more likely she was trying to deceive him than that she was a malleable, vacant-headed girl. A thrill went through him. Oh, how he loved crossing swords with a peer!

"My lady, I do not mean to be rude," he said, "but might I have the pleasure of your name? I do so enjoy knowing the names of those with whom I converse."

"Oh!" She gave him a coquettish glance. "I am Ethiel Doahrta, Duchess of Gorros in the kingdom of Calsinac."

The Red Weaver! So, this was the one who'd pushed the poisoned thorn into the side of the Wildmane. Zilok could barely keep himself steady, he was so excited.

"Of course, I suppose I am no longer the Duchess of Gorros. Calsinac has fallen, hasn't it?"

"Many years ago."

"Well then, I am Ethiel Doahrta, Empress of Daylan's Fountain." She giggled.

He bowed low. "Your majesty," he said.

"Do you think me ostentatious? To call myself Empress?"

"It fits you," he replied. She should have kept the moniker "the Red Weaver." It was far more impressive to be a threadweaver of her stature than an empress.

"So," she said, narrowing her eyes. "What are you really doing here?"

"I have been honest, your majesty. I am here to admire your handiwork. I have never seen anyone master so many darklings at a time." Well, that was a lie, but she obviously enjoyed his praise, and he saw no reason to stop now. "What could you possibly be doing with all of them?"

"I'm hunting." She bounced, clasping her hands together.

"I feel pity for your quarry. I find it difficult to believe that you have not yet caught him. Darklings are superlative hunters."

Ethiel's brow furrowed. "He's hiding from me. I think he knows I'm after him."

"Ah..." And then he understood. His thoughts raced, compiled the information he had spent studying these past days, the histories he missed during his long sleep. "You seek the Wildmane," he said.

Ethiel's childish demeanor vanished, and Zilok glimpsed the ageless spirit beneath the emotional performance.

"So the legends of you are not exaggerated."

Now they were getting to the thick of it. "You do me too much credit, your majesty."

"What makes you think I seek my love?"

Her *love*. Interesting that she saw the Wildmane that way...

"An educated guess, my lady. Many years have passed since we were alive, and GodSpill has been absent from the lands. Who else but the Wildmane might have lived so long that he would still be around for you to seek?"

"You said 'might have lived.' Do you think he has died?"

He shook his head. "Oh no, my lady. He is very much alive. I have seen him."

She stiffened. "Where?"

"Let us not rush things. I am impressed with what you have done here, and I should like to cultivate your acquaintance. I have long wondered how Difinius managed to bend space, and here you have accomplished it."

"You want Difinius's spell?"

"Let us say that I wish to begin a conversation with you. Perhaps an exchange of knowledge. There is much we can learn from each other. We have no peers anymore. With whom shall we talk if not each other?"

"Who indeed?"

"Then let us begin our conversation."

"And you will tell me where I can find my love?"

"I will do you one better." He smiled. "I will bring the Wildmane to you."

20

TYNDIRIA

TYNDIRIA STOOD ON HER BALCONY and looked out to the Inland Ocean. The sun sank slowly toward the waves, painting them bright orange and red. Ships rocked gently in the harbor. A few were just sailing in, done with the day's fishing. Tyndiria always loved watching the ships. It was one of the few things she remembered about being with her father. She had been nine when the Sunriders attacked. After that, her father had no time to spend with her. But during those rare moments, he would point out the different kinds of ships, and they would laugh together. Her father had been able to name each ship and her captain. Now she could, too.

At moments like this, Tyndiria missed her father terribly. She had loved him more than her own life. It was one of the reasons she had been so adamant to keep the throne. It was what Father would have wanted. He would be proud to see how she had guided the kingdom. Life was hard in Teni'sia, but they were doing much better than their neighbors to the north and the south. They were rebuilding. They would thrive again.

Tyndiria wondered how much of their fortune had to do with Medophae. She had spent enough time with him to believe he was something of a good-luck charm. Medophae had once said that Tyndiria would lead her people into a golden age, and just by him saying it, she could see it. She could believe it. He had a way of instilling confidence in those around him.

She let out a breath, slow and long, until she was done with it. Enough of that. This was the moment she told herself would come. She'd seen the pain at the end of the road when she'd set foot upon it. She wouldn't lament her choice. She'd learned her lessons from an immortal; now was the time to implement them. Now was the time to be her own good-luck charm.

Medophae had been her first lover, but he wasn't her first love. Tyndiria deeply loved her duty to her people; she had loved Teni'sia first. She would lean on her work until she could consider what must be done next.

She decided she would wait one year, get her bearings, and steady her heart. Then she would do what was best for the kingdom. She would choose another consort from a suitable house and make an heir to keep the succession stable. That was the responsible thing to—

"Am I interrupting something?" a high-pitched voice asked.

Tyndiria sucked in a breath and spun, clutching the rail. A small, furry creature stood between her and balcony's archway. It looked like a cross between a giant cat and a squirrel, and a burning sheet of flame ran the length of its spine, from the base of its neck to the tip of its tail. Its thin body perched high atop thin legs, which were obviously built for running. Its long, flaming tail twitched back and forth. Curled, wicked-looking claws protruded from its catlike paws, and its feline face held wide, insane-looking eyes.

It sauntered forward and leapt lightly to the rail, watching her. The squirrel-like tail hung weightless over the tremendous drop.

Tyndiria forced herself to breathe. She would swear the thing was smiling. She prayed that this was a dream, that she would wake and find she was alone.

"I had hoped to catch you when you weren't busy." The catlike creature's lips moved against the fangs, forming words. "Shall I return when it's more convenient?"

"By Thalius..." Tyndiria breathed. "What *are* you?"

The creature had a high, thin chuckle. "Humans. Always with the curiosity. Don't say I didn't give you a chance." It cocked its head. "In the past, your kind called my kind bakkarals." The bakkaral's speech was impossibly lucid. It shouldn't have been able to speak clearly through those catlike lips. It made Tyndiria dizzy. And that flame on its back... How could... How could that be?

"I know," the bakkaral said, as if it understood the source of her shock. "I always thought it a funny kind of name. But what can be done? Humans will be humans."

"What are you doing here? What do you want?" She tried to maintain the steadiness in her voice. A queen talking to an envoy, that was all she was.

The bakkaral's lips pulled back, revealing long, white teeth. "I'm here to scare you. Are you scared yet?"

She cleared her throat. "No," she said, "I just don't—"

The bakkaral's eyes flew open, and he jumped forward on the rail. His mouth gaped wide, and he hissed. The flame on his back roared upward.

She screamed and threw herself sideways. She stumbled on her gown and fell to her knees. Gasping, she clambered to her feet, waiting for those deadly claws to slash her back, those teeth to tear her neck.

But it didn't happen.

Cold sweat beaded on her forehead. When she realized she wasn't being attacked, she tried to get up, tripped on her dress, almost went down again, and finally scrambled awkwardly to her feet.

The bakkaral perched calmly on the stretch of rail where she had leaned a second ago. Again, its lips pulled away from white teeth in a frightening mockery of a smile.

"How was that?" it asked. Its high-pitched voice rattled through her. "Scared yet?"

She panted like she had just run up ten flights of steps. She tried to control her breath, but she couldn't. Her heart thundered in her chest.

"Why..." she breathed, "Why do you want to scare me?"

The wide, insane eyes blinked, and the bakkaral let out small breath. "Very well, I'm not really here to scare you."

"You're...not?" She edged backward, brushing against the gathered drapes in the balcony's archway.

"No. I'm here to kill you."

Her chest ached. "No..." she said in a small voice.

"Oh, yes."

"I'll call the guards," she whispered.

"Oh good. More guards," the bakkaral purred. It stretched tall and settled back on the rail. It seemed to be enjoying the game. "Yell loudly. All the guards in this part of the palace are dead."

Her lip trembled, and she continued backing away. "Don't..."

The bakkaral smiled again. "Are you going to run?"

"Please, don't," she said, holding her hands out in front of her.

"This is the part I like the best," the bakkaral said.

She turned and sprinted for the door.

21

MEDOPHAE

THE SUN HAD JUST DISAPPEARED behind the castle walls of Teni'sia when Medophae reined his horse in. Long shadows covered the steep streets. Overhead, a raven cawed and wheeled in the sun's last rays. The light flashed white on the black bird's wings as it settled atop the nearby guardhouse. Medophae loved this time of day. The land seemed to sigh contentedly at sunset, as though satisfied with a long day's work.

Word of Medophae's return had already spread from the gatehouse to the royal stables and young Casur was waiting for him. Medophae dismounted and gave the horse over, ruffling the boy's hair with a smile. Casur grinned up at him.

"What news, Casur?"

"Lady Bae'lee's mare came up lame during her ride yesterday." Casur said. "The physic's looking at it, but they think they'll have to put it down."

Medophae nodded soberly. "Was Lady Bae'lee hurt?"

"No m'lord. Sad, though. My cousin, she works in the palace, and she says that the lady's been in her room all day crying."

Medophae put a hand on Casur's shoulder. "Thank you, Casur. I'll drop in to see Lady Bae'lee in the morning."

Casur beamed.

"As for this one." Medophae indicated his own mount. "Give him a good, thorough rubdown. I've ridden him hard for three days now. He needs tending. Be generous with the oats, too."

"Yes, m'lord." Casur led Medophae's tired gelding away.

He went around the stables and immediately to the palace guardhouse. Lieutenant Lo'gan was there, talking with a young recruit. The young guard saw Medophae and immediately saluted. The new guard kept his composure fairly well; his eyes widened only a little. Medophae nodded to him. He wished that Lo'gan didn't find it necessary to instill such fearsome formality in his soldiers. Medophae could do without all the saluting. A polite nod worked just fine for him, but he and Lo'gan had had that argument before. Medophae had finally given up. Lo'gan was a fine lieutenant, and it was best to let fine lieutenants run things their own way.

"You may go," Lo'gan said to the new guard, who turned smartly and marched out of the guardhouse, leaving Lo'gan and Medophae alone.

"Sir." Lo'gan nodded. He did not salute. It was his unspoken concession to Medophae in the argument. Lo'gan did as Medophae requested between the two of them, out of respect.

"How are things?" Medophae asked.

"Silent as sand, Captain."

"Good. The queen?"

"She retired to her chambers not long ago. Aeder and Mik'syn have just gone on shift."

"I'll go see her."

"Yes, sir."

Medophae went through the back and into the narrow stairs that led into the heart of the castle. He passed through the first two doors to which only he, Tyndiria, and Lo'gan had the keys. His mind was still awash with Orem's words and he longed to talk with Tyndiria. One look into her eyes would remind him why his place was here now. He didn't have an obligation to support Orem or his delusions.

The stairs spiraled straight up five stories before opening into the hallway where Aeder and Mik'syn would be standing guard. The last door was solid steel with three locks. To the left of it was a narrow window that looked out on the northern mountains. The only reason Medophae had not had the window bricked up was because it was too narrow for a man to pass through. Even a child could not fit through that narrow slit.

Medophae inserted the first key into the top lock and turned. The tumblers spun and the bolt withdrew. He repeated the process with the second lock. As he inserted the key into the third lock, he heard a fluttering of wings.

A loud caw filled the small stairway, and Medophae spun. A raven perched in the narrow window, and the base of Medophae's skull began to tingle.

The raven cocked its head and cawed again.

Orem's words filled his mind: These dark creatures, they aren't going to stop. You'll find them at the gates of Tyndiria's kingdom soon.

"Tyndiria..." he whispered. He jammed the key into the third lock, twisted it, and shoved the door open.

Four bodies littered the hallway beyond. Aeder and Mik'syn had fallen at their posts. The guard hidden in the recess behind the tapestry was crumpled in an unmoving heap, folds of the heavy cloth clutched in his stiff hands. The guard who had been hidden in the rafters lay in a pool of blood just below his perch.

A scream ripped through the dead silence.

"Tyndiria!" Medophae drew his sword and sprinted down the hall. He didn't bother with keys anymore. He hit the door to Tyndiria's wing at a run. His shoulder surged with a golden glow as he rammed it into the wood. The thick oak exploded as if struck by lightning and Medophae stumbled through, regained his feet, and sprinted on. The crackling energy around him lit up the dim hallway.

The door to Tyndiria's bedroom stood ajar and Medophae shouldered his way past it. The hinges groaned and the door smashed into the wall.

Tyndiria was splayed across the bed in her own blood. Great

slashes had rent her apart. Her limbs sprawled in awkward directions. Only her face was unmarred, pale and perfect as though she had lain down to sleep, except for one red dot of blood on her cheek.

"No!" Medophae choked on his bile and staggered forward. "Tyndiria... Gods...no..." He wanted to snatch her up in his arms. He wanted to hold her together, to will her not to die. But she was already gone. Her deep green eyes stared at nothing. Her lips did not move. Her chest did not rise.

Medophae turned slowly as he surveyed the room. Golden fire crackled and spit, surrounding his body. Bits of the glow fell from him like sparks, disappearing before they touched the floor. His lips pulled back in a feral snarl and the gold light chased away the shadows.

A bakkaral sat calmly in the corner, licking its claws clean of Tyndiria's blood. Its eyes never left Medophae.

"Did you favor her?" it asked. The thin sheet of flame danced along its back. "My master said you did." It cocked his head, pausing in mid-lick. "Still, she's no dragon, is she?" The bakkaral smiled.

Medophae roared and launched himself at the bakkaral. His sword chopped down. The bakkaral danced back, avoiding the blade by an inch. Sparks and chips of stone flew as the sword struck the floor.

The bakkaral leapt onto Tyndiria's chest of drawers, bounded onto the wall, rebounded, and landed lightly on the bed next to the dead queen. It kneaded the bed as if it were preparing to lie down.

"The legendary Wildmane of the legendary temper," it said as Medophae whirled around. "Is it true you've lost entire armies because of this mindless rage?" It sat, brought a claw up, and began licking again.

In the land of Amarion, only quicksilvers were faster than bakkarals. Medophae was far faster than a mortal man, but he would never catch the bakkaral in a straight chase. He had to calm his mind and think. He had to anticipate its route of escape. His hands longed to close about the little catlike neck, but if he lost control, he would lose Tyndiria's killer. And that must not happen.

Slowly, one balanced step at a time, Medophae moved closer. His muscles rippled in anticipation.

The bakkaral watched this slow advance with interest. Its furry lips pulled away from long, blood-smeared teeth.

"Your master sent you here to die," Medophae growled.

"Now comes the posturing," it replied, its wild eyes boring into him. "Good. I like this part."

"You like this part..." Medophae repeated in a low voice, looking at his beloved Tyndiria on her bed.

"My posturing is in the form of a question, really," the bakkaral said. "My master wants to know: did you really think you could hide?"

Medophae roared and feinted left for the door. The bakkaral launched into the air toward the balcony, but the balcony was Medophae's true destination, and he cut right, pulling on the power of a god to give his muscles strength enough to move with the speed he needed. The floor cracked under his feet as he launched himself to the side. The bakkaral hit the ground and bounded over the rail into the open air. A bakkaral could float using that flame along its back. It could even cling to stone with its claws. That drop would not kill it like it would a human.

Medophae followed the creature over the rail into the long fall...

———

...and caught the bakkaral's back leg.

The bakkaral hissed in surprise. With a howl of pain, it whipped around and sank its teeth into Medophae's arm. Pain shot through him, but Medophae growled and kept his hold. The bakkaral tore chunks out of Medophae's arm. It clawed and bit, desperately trying to free itself.

But Medophae kept his hold.

The ground rushed up at them. Medophae instinctively spun in mid-air, jammed his sword into the solid rock. Hot, popping pain fired through his arm as muscles ripped and ligaments tore. The crackling golden sword cut a five-foot slice through the stone, and stopped their fall.

They slammed into the wall and he swung the bakkaral into the stone as though its back leg was the handle of a hammer. It didn't have anything clever to say now. Medophae cocked back and hammered the creature again.

"Tell me..." Medophae growled.

"Yes!" The creature screamed. "I will tell you anything you want—"

"Tell me..." He swung the bakkaral again, so hard its bones crunched against stone. "Do you like *this* part?"

"I can tell you who sent me," it mewled, weaker this time.

He slammed it into the wall again.

"Master...!" the bakkaral warbled out.

Medophae slammed it into the wall again. And again. And again. Soon, the flame along the bakkaral's spine winked out, but he continued to beat it against the wall.

When he was done, he hung there for a long moment, the little corpse dangling from his bloody fist. Blinking, he looked down at his hand and dropped it in disgust. The limp bakkaral fell a hundred feet to the jagged rocks below, bounced twice, then lay still.

Clinging to the hilt of his sword, Medophae hunched into himself. He pressed his face to the cool stone, and his body shook with great, wracking sobs.

22

MEDOPHAE

MEDOPHAE BROUGHT THE BOTTLE to his lips and drank half of it in several long gulps. The Teni'sian Clear burned down his throat, settling into his belly, and sending out warmth from there. The haze over his thoughts was a welcome dulling of his pain.

He watched a huge flatbug, its antenna nearly six inches long, crawl cautiously up the front of the dirty, ramshackle bar. The Sailor's Cap was the worst drinking establishment in all of Teni'sia, if it could even be called an establishment. The chairs were discarded boxes. The tables were taller boxes. Even the bar was just a stack of boxes. The ceiling was a length of tattered sail that Capper Ben, the proprietor, had stretched overhead and hammered into the walls with steel pitons. The walls themselves actually belonged to the fish market stalls on either side, and the floor was an alley, half dirt and half mud. There were only two things to drink: a homemade Teni'sian Clear, which was almost 100% grain alcohol, and a barrel of flat ale that had likely been lifted from the garbage of a superior establishment.

The Sailor's Cap had no sign. During the day, it didn't even exist because it didn't pay a stall fee to the wharf master, nor taxes from its sales to the crown. The fly-by-night proprietor set up at midnight and tore down an hour before daybreak.

The repurposed alley was full of nearly two dozen quiet men sitting on boxes, focused on their drinking. There were a few conversations, mostly a series of monosyllabic grunts. The Sailor's Cap had the cheapest alcohol in the entire kingdom, and there was plenty of it. This was not a place a decent person patronized. In fact, it wasn't a place a decent person would even know about. It was a "tavern" for those who had reached the end of their luck, a perfect place to find oblivion or violence or both. For only a copper or two, a man could numb his mind and end up drooling in the mud by sunrise. Or he could find himself knifed and left for dead for the few coins in his pocket.

And that suited Medophae just fine. He raised the bottle and drained it, then signaled for another.

He had hacked his hair off, shaved his head bald, and left the palace with a cloak and a hood. He didn't want to see anyone he knew. The queen's young captain was recognizable almost everywhere in Teni'sia, but the Sailor's Cap was a place for the forgotten. Nobody would come looking for him here.

Tyndiria's funeral had been a nightmare where he managed only to keep his composure long enough for the service, the last debt he owed this little kingdom. He maintained the veneer of a captain long enough to offer crafted lies of solace and hope to those in the crowd who wept. He had installed Lo'gan as regent until Tyndiria's cousin, a young man named Collus, could be summoned to assume the throne. Medophae didn't know Collus, and he didn't care about him. Tyndiria's golden age had been raked apart by a bakkaral's claws. The kingdom could fall or stay standing, whichever. It didn't matter to him. He should never have come there in the first place. She was dead because of him.

"Queen died today," a man behind him said, as though he had heard Medophae's thoughts.

"Queen o' what?" a man to Medophae's left said, then he gave a wheezing laugh that ended in a cough.

"The girl queen. Tyndiria. She died today," the first man said.

"She died yesterday," a third man, who sat at the box table with the second man, corrected them. "Just havin' a funeral today."

A younger fourth man, maybe only in his twenties, joined the conversation. "She was knifed. I heard there was ten men attacked her."

"Well, she's dead," the first man said.

"So what?"

"Seems like we ought to drink to that, right? Royalty dying and all. Ain't that what you do?"

"Bah," the second man said. "I'm gon' drink to nothing. Queen never did nothing for me."

"But she was our queen," the first man said. "Seems wrong not to have a drink to her name—"

"She was a whore," a dark, gravelly voice interrupted. "Don't tip no bottle to a dead whore."

Medophae raised his head and looked at the man who had spoken. He sat against the wall underneath one of the two torches Capper Ben had stuck in cracks. The man was large, almost as tall as Medophae, with thick, hairy forearms that poked out of his rolled-up shirt sleeves. He had a wide, round face and three days' growth of black whiskers. He sat alone, crouched over his box table with a bottle of Teni'sian Clear in front of him.

"She's a whore who never should'a been queen in the first place," the big man continued. "And a murderer on top of it all. She killed the man what should'a been king. Lord Magal Sym. Had her guards do it. And she paid 'em, too. Probably raised her skirts for every one of 'em in payment. They're gonna call her the whore queen, mark my words. I ain't going to raise no bottle to that."

"I heard that, too," the young man said. "And she was a threadweaver."

"Idiot." The big man shook his head. "Ain't no threadweavers no more, but there's plenty o' whores. And one of them was running this kingdom until today. Thank the gods someone knifed her in her belly."

Medophae stood up and faced the man. The big man appraised him without a hint of fear.

"You a queen's man, boy?" the big man asked.

"You're going to get on your knees," Medophae said. "And you're going to kiss this muddy ground, get your lips good and pressed into the slime, and you're going to apologize to Queen Tyndiria. And then you're going to apologize to me. And then you're going to apologize to everyone else in this alley. And then you're going to raise that bottle and drink the rest of it to her memory."

The big man stood up, kicking over the box he'd been sitting on. "I'll drink to what I want, boy."

His words were like knives in Medophae's hazy mind, and he felt Oedandus rising.

"Maybe you're one of them, huh?" the big man said. "One of them guards she paid with her—"

Medophae lurched across the distance. The big man was ready for him, a knife hidden behind his back. He stabbed it into Medophae's stomach.

Medophae growled. No knife could stop him. Entire armies hadn't stopped him.

He grabbed the big man by the throat and slammed him against the wall. He gurgled, twisting the knife, but Oedandus's golden fire was already repairing the wound.

Hands grabbed his free arm. Medophae threw the big man to the ground and spun, grabbing the throat of the younger man, who'd come to help.

Golden fire flared over Medophae's arms and chest, and he hoisted the young man into the air. The godsword sparked and came to life in his hand. Medophae snarled like an animal and thrust the sword into the young man—

His arm froze. The tip of the godsword hovered an inch from the terrified young man's chest, going no further.

There is no justice here, the dark voice said, deep within him.

I want to kill them. I want to kill them all.

You are the hand of justice, the dark voice said. *Kill the foul children of Devron and Tuana. Bring justice to mortals.*

I want them dead! Medophae screamed at his god.

There is no justice here.

The young man had peed himself. He whimpered and struggled

against the iron grip. Medophae dropped him, then looked at the big man, who was scrambling to his feet, holding his knife. He looked at it, then looked at Medophae's bloody belly, then looked at the knife again.

"Go drink somewhere else," Medophae growled. "Or I'll finish what I started."

The big man hesitated, and Medophae hoped he would stay. Oedandus or no Oedandus, he'd pummel the big man into meat. But the big man lurched past Medophae and ran out of the alley.

Medophae went back to his box and sat down. He raised his bottle.

"To the queen," he said loudly.

"To the queen!" Every single person in the Sailor's Cap, including Capper Ben, raised their bottle.

They all drank to Queen Tyndiria, who should have been alive, who would have had a long, prosperous life except that she met a broken demigod, and he had killed her.

Medophae called for another bottle, and another, and another.

Hours later, when the sun began to rise, he realized everyone was gone or passed out. The ripped sail was still overhead, but Capper Ben had pushed over the bar and taken his liquor with him. Now it was just an alley with three snoring drunks sleeping in the mud, a dozen scattered boxes, and Medophae.

He had drained the last of his final bottle, many empties scattered around his feet. He looked at the empty bottle, gripped the neck, then shattered it against the edge of the box. He cut his own throat with the sharp glass, but it healed. So he did it again. It healed again. He kept doing it, over and over, trying to feel that pain more than he did the loss of Tyndiria and the horror of what he really was.

That was when Regent Lo'gan and a dozen of the queen's guard found him. The troop gathered in the mouth of the alley. Only Lo'gan came forward. He didn't seem to even see the bloody box or the broken bottle in Medophae's hand.

"It's time to go, my lord," Lo'gan said.

"I'm not your lord," Medophae slurred.

"You will always be my lord."

"Go run your kingdom."

"Sir, come back with me. Teni'sia needs you."

Medophae barked an ugly laugh. "The sooner I am gone, the better off you will be."

Lo'gan took hold of Medophae's arm and lifted him to his feet. "We will get you cleaned up, sir. You just need a—"

Medophae shrugged him off. "Get me a horse," he demanded. He felt for his pouch of gold. It was still there. Even in the Sailor's Cap, no one had wanted to steal from him after his outburst.

"Sir, where will you go?"

"To find out if Orem's right."

23

MIROLAH

SAILING HAD TERRIFIED MIROLAH at first. She didn't know how to swim, and the idea of being completely surrounded by water with only a little boat to keep her afloat seemed ludicrous. If she went over the side, she would sink to the bottom like a stone. When she first climbed aboard, the shifting and rocking of the boat had caused her to clutch the rail with a death grip. It was all she could do not to shut her eyes. Only after Orem had coaxed her for the better part of an hour had she let him guide her shakily to the bow.

Now, two days into the journey, she couldn't get enough. The wind in her hair, the spray of the water. It was like flying. The breeze from the Inland Ocean was brisk and cool, and she loved it. She never knew she could feel this way. The only stories she had ever heard about sailing were horror stories of the goddess Saraphazia smashing ships to splinters with her enormous tail, creating waves the size of mountains. Sailors drowning by the score. Arasaurans and replisarks eating them.

She clutched the rail at the bow and stretched forward into the breeze. No one had ever mentioned this.

Before he rescued her, she'd wanted to run from Orem. He had represented everything frightening about her life: her love of reading, her secret desire to know more about the past, the foreboding knowledge that her brother had been a threadweaver, and, that perhaps, so was she.

But now she found herself wanting to help him. She had lived for so long under a blanket of fear that she couldn't remember what life was like without it. She feared discovery of her proclivities, condemnation for being who she was, death for exhibiting powers like her brother had. But the sea air seemed to peel that blanket away. Orem didn't want to kill her for being a threadweaver, like the people of Rith did. He *wanted* her to explore the GodSpill, wanted her to learn. Having him believe in these parts of her, parts she'd desperately tried to hide for so long...it felt like freedom.

Orem said they were going north to a place called Denema's Valley, one of the city empires during the GodSpill Wars. It was a civilization that had been utterly destroyed by the capping of the Fountain. Orem said that Denema's Valley had been a place where scholars and powerful threadweavers had made their homes. In the Age of Ascendance, each of the city empires had had a different culture, and Denema's Valley had been focused on study, history, and academic pursuits. These learned women and men had separated themselves from other civilizations to get away from the oftentimes frivolous behavior of the lesser threadweavers who had suddenly sprung into existence with the creation of the Daylan's Fountain. Orem said that the people who built Denema's Valley were those who would most likely have been threadweavers in the Age of Awakening, before Daylan Morth's creation made threadweaving so easy. They even disdained the term "high threadweavers"—a word used to describe highly talented threadweavers in the Age of Ascendance—to describe themselves, because it was not a term that was used in the Age of Awakening.

Orem said practically everything in Denema's Valley had been built with GodSpill, and so the city had been snuffed like a candle when Harleath Markin somehow stole it. Over the centuries, the toppled towers and razed buildings had been invaded by nature again, but there were still traces of these powerful threadweavers. They had kept an extensive library, writing down their thoughts and discoveries, protecting them over the years. The library was mostly intact, and that was where they were going to further Mirolah's education.

"Is this one of the ways you get in touch with the GodSpill?" Orem said from behind her, trying to see what she was searching for.

"Maybe," she said. She turned away from the wind to face him. Her hair blew into her face, and she pushed it back with a hand. "I mean, I feel things, but I don't know what I'm supposed to feel, so how can I know if I'm doing it right? You talk about the GodSpill like it's water, or something like water. Am I supposed to bore a hole in a keg and collect what comes out?"

"I..." he hesitated. "I wish I could tell you. I've never experienced the GodSpill myself."

"Well, there's no such liquid. Or if there is, I can't feel it. All I feel is this bright bridge that appears between me and something—or someone—else. It's not...a rush of water, or anything else I can collect. It's a feeling that I'm closer to whatever the bridge connects me to. When I stand here on the prow, with the wind pushing at me, it's like I'm...closer to Amarion. Closer to nature. And the connection to nature is where the power seems to be."

The brightness she had first invoked against the monster connected her to everything. It connected her to Orem right now. She could feel his emotions, even if his face was placid. They radiated toward her like the heat of the sun overhead. She remembered how strong and confident he had seemed when she first met him. If all she had been able to read was his face, he would seem the same. But now she knew the truth: he was mostly uncertain. He had vast hopes, and only a little certainty to back them up. She knew without a doubt that he wanted what was best for the people of Amarion. But she thought he'd known exactly how to go about it. He didn't, and his fear was now apparent to her.

She saw new emotions now, as she talked to him, and what she saw surprised her. He longed to be a threadweaver. He wanted it so badly it made his heart beat faster when she talked about it. He wanted to feel the GodSpill. His sorrow and frustration leaked into her, and it made her uncomfortable, like he was looking at her like she was a piece of juicy fruit.

Also, she felt embarrassed about it. She was supposed to be learning, she knew, and seeing Orem's emotions was part of that learning, but she felt ashamed. He didn't know he was an open book to her.

"Orem," she said, trying to bring the topic back to academics. Orem loved to talk about his many studies. "Why do they call them threadweavers? In my life, 'threadweaver' is just a bad word, a curse on those in the Age of Ascendance who abused their power, who brought the wrath of the gods. People spit when they say the word. But the threadweavers must have called themselves that for a reason. We didn't make up that name. Every history I've read uses the same word."

"Yes."

"Well, why not call themselves GodSpillers or something else? What does weaving have to do with it?"

"I think it started as a euphemism."

"You think?"

"Well, weaving is an ages-old form of creating. It makes rugs, clothes, blankets, baskets. And creating was the threadweavers' defining attribute," he said. "It's what the GodSpill does. I would guess the name was used long ago because their many creations were likened to weaving the wondrous into life."

"Hmm. Do you think they started off making enchanted rugs or something, and that's how they got the name?"

"Maybe," he said. "If so, it must have been long ago in the Age of Awakening. In some of the books I have read, one threadweaver will refer to another as having 'woven something of great import'. But I think it is just the parlance they used. Certainly I have seen no references to them actually weaving anything, or not more than normal people, anyway. A few of them worked with clothing or rugs or blankets, but even more worked with stone, with flesh, with the mind, with the wind...anything and everything."

"I was hoping it might provide some kind of clue," she said, disappointed.

"From my studies, I do know that belief in the possibility of your creation is important."

"So the more I believe I will see things, the more I see?"

"I think so."

"Well, I don't know if my belief has anything to do with it. For instance, when I look at Stavark..." She turned her gaze to the young quicksilver, who was forever minding the rudder. "I can see surges of energy around him that aren't there around you."

"I would say it's his flashpowers you are seeing," Orem said. "Quicksilvers are infused with GodSpill. They can't use their flashpowers without it."

"So he can use his flashpowers, needs GodSpill to use them, but he can't do anything else with it. Whereas threadweavers can do whatever they can imagine, essentially," she said.

"Yes."

"How did his people survive the capping of the Fountain?" she asked, looking for a change in the subject. "All the threadweavers died. Why didn't they?"

"Most didn't survive," he said. "Only the hardiest, and only those on the fringes of Amarion. There were clusters of quicksilvers in the Spine Mountains, out of reach of the Fountain's influence. Of course, the most remarkable thing about Stavark isn't that he can use his flashpowers. It's that he agreed to help me at all."

"Why?"

"Quicksilvers hate humans. Stavark's people in particular hate us for what we did to Amarion, for how we bent the GodSpill to our will, and then destroyed it."

Mirolah had never felt any malice come from the young quicksilver. "But he—"

"Seems friendly?"

"Well, distant and strange, but I thought that was just because he was a quicksilver."

"Stavark understands that one doesn't achieve harmony by hating. He wants to help remedy the situation, rather than blaming those who brought it about, like his father does."

The young quicksilver overheard their conversation and met her gaze. He held a firm grip on the tiller, giving and taking in increments as the waves pulled at the boat.

"He is so serious," she said softly. "Like a warrior shoved into a child's body. Seeing him with the guards in Rith, I... I was so shocked when that silver flash turned into a boy."

"You have seen how hard the GodSpill Wars and the Devastation Years were to us. It was worse for his people. They almost went extinct. There are thousands of us left. There are only hundreds of his people left, probably less than five hundred, scattered all along the Spine Mountains."

She looked at Orem. "We're not doing this a moment too soon, are we?"

"No," he said quietly. "We're probably a few centuries overdue, actually."

"There's so much to learn..." she whispered, looking again at the water, feeling the breeze against her face.

He put a hand on her shoulder, and it made her feel better.

24

MIROLAH

MIROLAH SAT ON THE SAND and faced the clay pot. It still didn't move. They had anchored for the night in a cove along the western shore, and the fire Stavark had built crackled pleasantly under the stars. She was full of the hot meal of rabbit and potato soup that Orem had supplied. Orem was an accomplished hunter. Every time Orem went to get food, he came back with just enough to fill everyone's belly. Both Orem and Stavark treated her like a queen. They collected the firewood. They made the fire, hunted, cooked. They wanted her learning, exploring, expanding what she knew about the GodSpill.

And she was doing a terrible job.

She sighed and looked back at the pot. The point was to move the pot. If she was really a threadweaver, she should be able to move a single, small pot, shouldn't she? The problem was that she had no idea how to go about it.

"Move," she whispered through her teeth. The bright light between her and the pot intensified to a white-hot brilliance, but nothing else happened.

She threw every image she could across that blinding bridge. She pictured the pot flying into the trees by the shore. She pictured it hurtling into the ocean. She pictured it breaking into a hundred pieces. She pictured it falling lazily on its side. She pictured everything she could imagine to do to a pot. But the reality remained unchanged. The pot sat smugly in the sand, tilted to one side as it had been since she'd set it there two hours ago.

Her butt hurt. Her legs ached, and her scalp itched. She kept shifting, but no position was comfortable. Still, she refused to let herself be comfortable until she achieved some kind of success.

What she really wanted to do was jump to her feet and throw the pot into the ocean, but every other time she came to such frustration, she noticed the bright bridge begin to fade.

She studied the pot again, hoping that another examination would reveal something. There was a hairline crack down the left side. The lid was not perfectly round, and it had a chip in it. It had two clay nubs on either side that served as handles. She stared and stared. If she had closed her eyes, she could have taken a quill and drawn the damned thing from memory!

And then Mirolah noticed something in her peripheral vision. She looked at it directly and it vanished, so she turned her focus back to the pot. Yes. There it was. Something was slightly different about the edge of the bridge of light that connected her to the bane of her existence. There were thin, transparent lines, like fibers in a blanket. Like threads.

Threadweaver.

Her heart beat faster, and she looked directly at them, and again they vanished.

She stared back at the pot, looking at the tiniest details. She attempted to see the pot's essence like she could see Orem's moods.

The little fibers of light became clearer at the very edges of the bridge. Slowly, the bright threads moved from the periphery of her vision toward the center. The bright bridge was comprised of an intense cluster of these same threads. They were so bright that she hadn't known they were separate before, just one glowing arc between her and the subject of her focus. The tiny tendrils flowed from her stomach into the pot. She kept her focus on it until the fibers became even clearer. She imagined the same images she had used before flowing through those tiny threads like blood through veins.

The threads shimmered, but nothing happened to the pot. She growled under her breath. The vivid threads began to fade as she relaxed her concentration.

What a threadweaver I am, she thought ruefully.

And then it occurred to her. She returned her concentration to the pot. The threads appeared much more quickly this time. Now that she'd seen them, it was as if they'd always been there, begging her to look. She thought for a moment that she could see color in them this time, not just a bright white light, but variations of red and yellow. She reached out with her hand and plucked one of the threads.

The pot shifted in the sand.

She let out a whoop and yanked all the threads in a fist. The pot leapt from its perch with a shocking speed and smashed into her forehead.

"MIROLAH," Orem warbled to her. "Mirolah," he said again, and this time it was clearer.

She groaned and blinked her eyes. The ground swayed, and for a moment she thought she had awoken on the boat, except the swaying was not welcome at all this time. She wanted to throw up.

"Are you all right?"

She felt his concern like warmth on her face. Stavark stood behind him, looking down at her with that perpetually serious expression that was so out of place on a young boy. He said nothing.

Mirolah sat up slowly. Her skull felt like she'd head-butted a tree. "Did you see it?" she whispered.

"I heard the crash and I found you here, laying in the sand."

"Where is the pot?" she asked.

"This pot?" He held up a couple of clay shards.

"It broke?" She laughed.

Orem looked at Stavark, and she felt his worry.

"No," she said through her laughter. "No, I'm okay. It's good." She touched her forehead and winced. A knot was already forming.

"Mirolah, maybe you should lie down—"

"It flew, Orem! It shifted in the sand and then flew right through the air."

"Right at your head," Orem said, concerned. "Can you make it go somewhere else?"

"I'm certain of it." She cast about for a likely object. She chose the iron cooking pot that Stavark had just washed out in the ocean. She had acquired a certain intimacy with pots. It lay stacked with their other dishware by the fire pit.

"Mirolah, really. Why don't you rest for a moment. You don't need to—"

"Shhhh," she said, and concentrated on the pot. The bright bridge formed, and soon after, the threads. She grinned from ear to ear. It was easy this time. Now that she knew what she was looking for, they were all right there.

When the threads began to take on colors, she reached out with her hands like she was playing a harp and pulled all of the threads gently. The metal pot shifted forward, dislodging a plate and a bowl as it left the stack. It cut a groove toward them, sailing on the sand like a little metal boat.

Orem gasped, and Stavark's eyes widened. The young quicksilver breathed. "*Kalik. Maehka vik Kalik.*" He looked at Mirolah and smiled wide, gave her an approving nod.

The pot sidled up to Orem's knee, and she left it there.

"Threadweaver," she said. "I know what it means. There are threads connecting me to the pot, to you, to the ground, to everything. And I can touch them. I can move them. *That's* what it means."

He knelt down and took the pot by the handle. His hand clenched it, and he bowed his head.

"Orem?"

There were tears in his eyes. "All my life..." he whispered. "I have wanted to see this. I have wanted to be a part of this. But I doubted. Even when I saw the laughing stone in your hand, I doubted." He looked at her. "But you have made the impossible possible. Thank the gods for you, Mirolah."

"You did this," she said. "Without you, I'd be dead."

He put his hands on her arms. "We will return wonder to the lands."

"You're damned right," she said.

Stavark began to laugh. It sounded like music.

25

MEDOPHAE

MEDOPHAE PULLED UP SHORT at the edge of the gnarled, dry trees. He crackled with an aura of golden fire. He hadn't eaten or slept in days. Oedandus fueled him now, and he gladly boiled in the vengeful god's rage.

His mount, the fourth in four days, frothed at the mouth. Wind snorted from her nostrils, and she hung her head. He had ridden north and west from Teni'sia with no rest, stopping at villages only to leave an exhausted horse and pick up a fresh one. Now he was in a different land; not just another kingdom, but a wild place that civilization hadn't touched in centuries.

Tyndiria was dead, and he didn't care about eating, about sleeping, about anything. He would find the "master" of the bakkaral, deal with him, and then he could vanish from the lands forever. He wouldn't languish in a cave this time, where a crazy adventurer like Orem might find him. This time he would go far away, maybe so far that Oedandus would lose him. And when that happened, he would find a way to die.

But first, he had to know for certain that the GodSpill had

returned. Amarion had been stripped of it for years. He hadn't seen a darkling or a bakkaral for years. But just because both had visited Teni'sia didn't mean the GodSpill was back. For all Medophae knew, either one of those supernatural creatures could survive for weeks, maybe even years without GodSpill present. Could it have been sent from somewhere over the Spine Mountains? He needed to know for certain.

Make them suffer, the dark voice breathed in his mind, hearing his thoughts. *Make them all burn.*

Medophae forced himself to breathe. The glade was quiet, save the frantic huffing of his horse. He needed sleep. Only the return of his normal mortal rhythms would push back Oedandus's ever-present voice. If he didn't eat, didn't rest, Oedandus stayed awake to keep him from wasting away.

But he couldn't sleep. The moment he closed his eyes, he dreamed of Tyndiria. Sweet Tyndiria...tortured in the last moments of her life because she had loved him.

Give them justice by fire, his dark god demanded.

Medophae took the bridle and saddle off his horse and left her to drink from the slender, struggling brook. It used to be a stream. Even water didn't seem to want to stay in this dried-out husk of Amarion anymore. The small leaves of the trees, twisted and shrunken from the way they had once been, had turned autumn colors, and Medophae walked beneath reds and golds as he approached the rocky cliff. It bordered the far side of the glade, and was choked with fibrous brown vines.

His memories came back then, vivid. In his mind's eye, the glade transformed and the past three hundred years blew away like those autumn leaves. He saw the glade as it used to be.

The tall, vibrant trees and grass sparkled in the moonlight. It was dark and quiet as he arrived, and Princess Silasa waited for him. She always knew when he was coming. The clopping of his horse's hooves must have sounded like thunder to her. She stood at the entrance to her cave, porcelain skin as pale as the moon, her long black braid laying over one shoulder, her eyes the milky white of a vampire....

Medophae shook his head and brought his mind back to the present. The glade wasn't the same. All of the trees that once stood here were gone. Tall brown grass had replaced the short green lawn, cropped by the goats Silasa had once kept. The tall trees had died in the wake of the capping of Daylan's Fountain, giving way to the smaller, hardier oak trees. The archway of her cave was covered with spider vines. If Medophae had not come to this exact spot countless times in the past, he might not have even recognized it. He approached the cave and curled his fingers around a thick tangle of the vines, but paused.

Do you want this? You could just run away right now. Does it really matter if the GodSpill is returning? Would anything change? If Orem is right, his quest might sweep you away, and if it does, what has changed? You, meddling in the lives of mortals until you come to love them, until you lead them to their deaths. You resisted Orem. You could walk away from here, go west over the Spine Mountains, and never return.

With a vicious yank, he tore the vines away, revealing a wide, arched entrance bordered with cut stones, half again as high as he was tall.

He stepped into the darkness, holding his fiery fist above his head and pushing the shadows back. The polished walls were adorned with rotting tapestries thick with dust. He could only see vague images, but he knew all of the paintings all by heart. One told the story of Sasha Braen'dite and her warriors, how they sacrificed themselves to close the Godgate. Another showed Vlacar, the last Paladin of Natra, in the forest where he disappeared. There was one of Medophae and his lieutenant, Bresher Benn, at the disastrous battle of the Deitrus Shelf. He had often wondered why she kept that painting, a rendition of one of Medophae's greatest failures.

Beautifully designed sconces bearing long-dead torches lined the walls. He moved past them, his golden glow illuminating the hall.

Marble sculptures were placed at each forking of the tunnels. He moved past those as well, choosing his way from memory. He passed the greatroom and the throne Silasa had never used. The vampire, Darva, who had turned Silasa into one of White Tuana's children, fancied herself some kind of queen, so she had stolen and feasted on the princess. When Medophae found this place, he had let Oedandus feast on Darva. To Oedandus, destroying one of

White Tuana's children was almost as satisfying as destroying one of Dervon's.

This would be the final test for Medophae. A darkling and a bakkaral in Amarion was almost proof that the lands were changing, that GodSpill had returned. But if Silasa had awoken, then it was certain. She was a construct of White Tuana, an animation of the dead, completely sustained by the GodSpill. Darkling and bakkarals were actually alive. If what Orem hoped was right, then Silasa would have risen again.

But there was no sign she had frequented these halls since the great dying. There were only layers of dust, and spiders fleeing from his light.

He continued to the small room at the end of the hallway, which was unlike the rest of the cavern. These walls were rough-hewn. There were no decorations, and the floor was rock and dirt. For once, Medophae's relentless memory of centuries past was a blessing, and he went straight to the hidden lever in the far wall. He pulled it.

The edge of a square of floor popped up in the center of the room. He scooped away the concealing dirt and lifted the square to reveal a passageway. He dropped through it to the floor below and stooped to walk the last few paces into a circular room he had hewn out of the stone himself. In the center was a sarcophagus made of rock.

Dust lay thick everywhere, just as it had after he'd hastily finished the chamber. The air was stale.

The sarcophagus was ten feet long and three feet wide. It stood atop a dais that he had hacked out of the bedrock. His only sculpture: a monument to Silasa's death.

Nothing in the caverns had changed. Silasa had not returned. Orem was wrong.

He stepped up to the dais and stood for a moment next to the sarcophagus. The lid was solid stone, a foot and a half thick. If some nosy explorer had happened upon Silasa's cavern while she slept, and if he had managed to find this secret room, Medophae had made sure he would not be able to get into her resting place. It was impossible to get enough mortal arms around that slab to budge it, much less lift it. He had hoped it would safeguard her until the GodSpill returned.

He ran his fingers underneath the edge of the lid. Spiders fled, dancing down the sides of the sarcophagus.

Now I have use for you, Medophae said to Oedandus.

Make them pay, the dark voice responded. Destroy him. Destroy them all....

Medophae put his arms around the lid and grabbed hold. His muscles corded tight and golden fire leapt about his body. The lid did not move. With a grimace, he shifted his grip and tried again. Golden fire flared in the room. The lid shifted.

"By Thalius!" he grunted. He didn't remember it being that damned heavy.

His lip curled. He thought of Tyndiria, splayed across her bed in blood. He thought of the smug expression on the bakkaral's face. Oedandus's fire lit up the room like midday. Medophae elevated his chin and gave a roar. With a mighty heave, he dislodged the mammoth lid and tossed it away. It crashed to the wall and broke in two.

The golden fire faded, leaving him again with only the flickering golden light. Breathing heavily, Medophae curled his flaming fist and shone it upon Silasa's pale face.

She lay in the same cold repose with the same deadened expression....

No... Wait.

She wasn't the same. Her dusty, dark hair was in disarray. Her brow was wrinkled, as though she had fallen asleep in anger.

Idiot! The GodSpill has returned, and she awoke with it, but after three hundred years of sleep, how could she possibly have moved the stone slab?

She might have been awake for months, even years, trapped in her own tomb.

How much pain do I really cause as I stumble through my life? How many things would be better if I simply wasn't here?

"Silasa, I'm so sorry..." he said, lifting her out gently. He carried her to the dusty ground and sat with her in his lap. If she had returned, had he destroyed her by trapping her?

If she could be revived, night would tell the tale, so he sat with her and waited. Time moved slowly, and Medophae was exhausted. He needed rest, and as he held tightly to the princess, he let himself sleep.

THERE WAS A FAINT RASPING SOUND, and he snapped awake. The rest had improved his beleaguered body, and so Oedandus's glow was fainter, barely lighting the dark. Medophae's gaze went to Silasa. Had she moved? Had she spoken? He leaned over her, putting his ear to her mouth, listening for another sound. Had it been some other creature in the room, skittering around?

He leaned over her, listening....

Her arm wrapped around his head, and she plunged her fangs into his neck. Blood spattered her cheek and shoulder. Medophae gasped and pulled back, but she clung to him. Sharp fingernails dug through his shirt into his flesh as she tore at his neck.

The pain was sharp, and his mortal instincts screamed at him to fight her.

But he held himself still. Instead, he wrapped his arms around her, cradling her to him.

"Drink, princess," he whispered.

She sucked like a hungry baby, and he let her feed. When he began to feel light-headed, he pushed her away. She growled, yanked him back viciously. He set his lips in a firm line and pulled her off, wincing as her claws left deep slices in his shoulder and neck.

She howled. Oedandus flared, lighting the cavern again as Medophae pulled on the power to trap her wrists and her head away from him. The supernatural strength of a vampire could pin a mortal man to the ground like a rabbit. Of course, with as much blood as she had taken, a mortal would also have gone into the deep sleep that preceded Tuana's transformation. But Medophae had discovered long ago that vampires couldn't turn him into one of them. He already belonged to a god. And, even as he held her, he felt the golden fire burn where Silasa had bitten him. He felt the muscles, blood vessels, and skin of his neck repair itself.

Silasa made several more childlike attempts for his neck, but he grunted and held her tight. Finally, she went still. She licked her lips, as though testing for something.

"Medophae..." she said in a light rasp, her eyes still closed. Her bony hand came up and caressed his cheek, touched his long hair. "No one has blood as stale as yours, my ancient friend."

"I can only imagine," he whispered.

He bowed his head and hugged her, surprised to feel tears in his eyes. She was alive. She had come back. He held her gently against his chest as she spoke with her rough, unused voice.

"What happened?" she asked as he set her gently back on his lap. She experimented slowly with raising and turning her head on her thin neck, but she couldn't open her eyes. "Did someone catch me during the day? I feel like a skeleton, as if I haven't fed for ages."

"It *has* been ages."

"How long?"

"More than three hundred years."

She gasped, and it ended in a little cough. "Medophae, how...? How am I still here, if I have not fed in three hundred years?"

"A goddess's blood? I don't know. What is the last thing you remember?"

"Nothing. I must have already been asleep— Wait. No. I *do* remember. I was outside in the glade. I was looking at the night sky. There was something strange. Then it all went quiet. There was no sound, as if the night birds and the crickets were all slain at once. Even the wind did not rustle the leaves. It was as though someone had clapped a lid over the world. I was frightened. I turned to run into the caverns to see to my defenses. I thought it was an attack. Not ten paces inside my cave, I was gutted, as though my organs, my blood, my soul was being sucked out through the tips of my fingers, through my eyes and nose and mouth..." Her thin hands clamped tightly on his arms. "I stumbled and... That's all." She paused. "That's all I remember. What happened?"

"Harleath Markin. You remember the GodSpill Wars?"

"Of course."

"Never underestimate a threadweaver's ability to make a horror even more horrifying. Harleath Markin and his pack of fools set out for Daylan's Fountain. He was a sort of threadweaver inventor, and a bit of a crackpot. I don't think the man ever had an idea that truly worked like he wanted. But apparently he had an idea to "stop the GodSpill Wars." By all accounts, he was a good man, and an utter fool."

"What did he do?"

"There are no records, but I've been to the north, and I think Harleath somehow broke Daylan's Fountain. Whatever he did, he made sure the fountain no longer worked. Maybe he thought taking away the Fountain would cut the power to the threadweavers and end the wars. Perhaps he thought he would dampen the power, take the teeth from the beast, weaken the threadweavers. But in his worst nightmares, he didn't imagine the catastrophe he would bring. His meddling killed him, his apprentices, and everyone else who pulled from the GodSpill. Most of the humans in Amarion died. Every supernatural creature did. There are a few struggling kingdoms on the peninsulas. Some villages around the Inland Ocean. The rest are gone."

"Belshra?" she croaked, asking about her father's kingdom, where she had been a princess until she had been turned into a vampire.

"I'm sorry, Silasa. It was one of the first to fall. There were just so many dead and dying..."

She was so still that he thought she had descended into her slumber again.

"Why am I awake now?" she asked. "Did someone undo Harleath's handiwork?"

"An acquaintance of mine told me the GodSpill is returning. I didn't believe him, and someone close to me paid the price. You were my final test. If you had risen, I would know he was right. And if he's right about that, he may be right about other things."

"What other things?"

"The GodSpill isn't returning evenly. I killed a darkling. Orem says there are more. He says he has a plan..." He sighed. "But I am not certain what I should do."

She paused. "What you should do?"

"I do not know where my life goes from here. It might be best if I leave Amarion."

"Why would you leave Amarion?"

"Because I only hurt those I try to help. I lost a dear friend not five days ago. When I get involved with anything, it becomes a disaster. The only remedy is to remove myself from Amarion entirely."

"Who died?"

"You don't know her. She was born centuries after you fell."

"Who killed her?"

"A bakkaral, sent by someone. I don't know who." He shook his head. "But that doesn't matter. She's dead. I can't change it. But I can keep it from happening again. I can leave."

"I... Medin, I don't understand. You're saying you want to leave instead of finding the one who sent the bakkaral? Instead of seeking justice?"

"Things have changed for me," he said in a husky voice.

"What does Bands think about it?" she asked. "Surely she doesn't condone..." she trailed off.

He said nothing.

"You solved the riddle?" she asked.

He tried to control the wash of anger, of frustration, but despair rose like a wave within him. Every day that had passed since Bands was taken... Every single day was a failure.

Yes... Destroy them all.... the dark voice whispered.

He twitched, tried to keep a handle on his emotions, but all he could see was golden fire.

Silasa sucked in a breath. "Oh, Medophae. I'm sorry. I'm so sorry."

He had to move. He had to walk. He gently pushed Silasa off his chest, laid her against the wall, and walked to the other side of the chamber.

"Don't leave, please," she croaked. "I didn't know. I never imagined you wouldn't find a way. All this time... I didn't realize that the spell was so powerful... Is— Is she...?"

"Dead?" he finished for her. "I don't know. Surely she must be after all this time, but..."

"I didn't mean to hurt you."

"How could you know?" He closed his eyes and tried to stop the hammers pounding in his stomach. He wanted to vomit. "It's over." He forced the words out. "There is nothing I can do for her. I've tried everything."

She swallowed. "What will you do now?"

"I don't know."

"There must be something you can do."

"I don't know."

"Stop saying that!" she rasped. "I wake after three hundred years... The most shocking thing should be that I'm alive at all, that the world has been all but destroyed, but the most shocking thing is that the indomitable Wildmane is talking like a mouse."

She clenched her teeth, her fangs flashing in the golden light as she forced her dry, wrinkled eyelids to open. She squinted up at him, her milky eyes shriveled.

"I wish I could see you," she rasped. "I would know what your face looks like as you say these things."

"I'm angry, Silasa," he said. "I want to take it out on whoever sent that bakkaral. But I don't want..." He hesitated and fell silent.

"You don't want what?" she asked. She pushed against the wall and rose on thin, shaky legs.

He sighed and swallowed. "I don't want to..."

"To what?"

"Too many people get hurt when I... I once thought Oedandus was a gift, to me and everyone I now had the power to help. But it's a curse. All he can do is destroy."

She paused, and her emaciated face wrinkled into a frown. "Medophae, you may believe that Amarion revolves around your misfortunes, but it does not. Innocents are hurt every day, whether you do something or you do nothing. That's not going to stop. Imagine how many more monsters would roam this land if not for you."

"I *am* the monster."

"You slew the monster!" she said. "Dervon created nearly every horror Amarion has known, and you ended him."

"That was Oedandus," he said. "Me, I can't use the power. I can't use it correctly. It uses me, shapes me into whatever it wants." "That is the most cowardly thing I've ever heard you say. You helped shape two entire ages of humankind." "They were better off without me. If I had not been so assured of myself, so blinded by my own purpose, Bands would still be here—"

"Oh, gods!" She snorted. "Bands made her own choices. She ran her own risks. You were not responsible for her. By Oedandus, she was three times your age and a dragon as well. If she was here, she would laugh in your face."

"But she is not here to laugh, is she? And it's my fault—"

"And if you weren't an oozing wound of self-pity right now, you would have found a way to get her back."

Her words lashed him, leaving stripes of pain. Golden fire raced over his chest.

Destroy her, Oedandus said. Destroy them all.

He turned and put his hands on the stone wall, calming himself.

"What do you want from me?" she asked. "To tell you it's okay to give up hope? Well, it's not. Especially for you. By Thalius, Medophae, *you're* the one who is supposed to *give* us hope! No wonder Amarion is dying. Who can show us the light in the darkness if not our own patron god?"

"I'm not your god."

"No, Tarithalius is our god. A frivolous, uncaring prankster who moves us like toys on a game board. He never cared for us. But you do. You care for humans, from the weakest to the strongest, from the smallest to the largest. You've never given up on us. And if you do...what chance do we have?"

"I'm a destroyer, Silasa. It's all I do. It's all Oedandus allows me to do."

"Bullshit."

"Silasa—"

"When I awoke as one of Tuana's children that first night—when I despised myself so much I wanted to die—you told me to live. I had been twisted into this horrible, evil thing. I *became* the monster. I crave human blood. I destroy life to perpetuate myself. I wanted you to kill me that first night, but you wouldn't. You said giving up was the coward's path."

"I was wrong." He could not put words to the tumultuous emotions that roiled within him.

"I may not be able to see you, but I can hear Oedandus snapping and hissing over there. Well good, *be* angry. Let it burn in your heart. Let it burn you to a cinder. Better that than live as a coward."

"Silasa..." He growled. "I have tried everything! Do you think I would sit idle for three hundred years?"

"Try harder."

He spun, stalked to the far end of the chamber and punched the wall. Rock crunched, and pieces fell to the floor, smeared with the blood of his quickly healing knuckles.

"Who told you the GodSpill was returning?" she asked softly.

"This acquaintance of yours."

"Orem." Medophae bit the words out like he was chewing leather.

"And what does he want you to do?"

"He says the Fountain is leaking GodSpill. He says he has found a threadweaver, the first in a dozen generations. He says he is taking her there. He wants her to figure out what Harleath did, somehow undo it." He shook his head. "It's ridiculous on every level. Even if the GodSpill is returning. Even if what Harleath did can somehow be undone, Daylan Morth was a master of the GodSpill, outstripping every other threadweaver who might hope to compare. Some fledgling girl, raised in this barren land with no notion of the GodSpill or how it works, will never be able to understand what that man created. The best threadweavers of the Age of Ascendance couldn't understand Daylan's Fountain."

"This Orem," she said slowly. "He was right about the GodSpill returning."

Medophae growled.

"He probably *has* found a threadweaver, then. If I have risen, it's likely. Maybe she can undo what Harleath did."

"A scared young girl?" He shook his head. "Even if she can access the GodSpill, she won't know anything. It took most threadweavers years to learn just the basics. Without a real teacher, there's no way she can undo what Harleath did. Certainly not what Daylan did. It's a fool's errand."

"Then be a fool."

"It's not possible."

"Anything is possible. You have a god flowing through your veins—"

"—who brings only destruction," he said through clenched teeth.

"I see," she said. "You're a monster, is that it?"

"I always have been. I just didn't have the wit to see it."

"Fine," she said. "Well, right now, monsters are what's needed."

"What?"

"Go," she said. "Be a monster to those who would hurt this young threadweaver, to those who would tear her down. Protect her. If you can't be a hero, then suffer in silence with your guilt and be the monster she needs."

"Be a monster to the monsters," he said. "That sounds a lot like trying to be a hero."

"Does it? How interesting," she said in a flat tone.

"I don't want to."

"I don't care."

She was relentless. She always had been. He bowed his head and, despite himself, he cracked a smile.

"You're sort of mean," he said.

"I suck blood to live."

He laughed.

"You're going to go?" she asked.

He sighed. "I suppose I have to. I wouldn't survive here. Living with a conscience equipped with actual claws and fangs."

She smiled. "Good. Will you do me one favor, though?"

"Standing here while you stab me with your wit isn't favor enough?"

"Stay one more day and night," she said. "Stay while I regain my strength."

"I'll stay as long as you need me," he said.

"Only until I can hunt for myself. Then you go."

"Then I go." He murmured the words, feeling the doom of them thudding in his heart.

26

MIROLAH

MIROLAH LOOKED UP from the huge tome at Orem, who happily read from his towering stack of books two tables over. They had arrived in Denema's Valley three days ago, and the library was not to be believed. Bookshelves lined every wall in the great room. Ancient tables were scattered across the floor in disarray. Some lay rotting beneath the shattered dome in the center, but many still stood near the precious shelves that had been preserved from the elements. Thankfully, the ceiling surrounding the dome was intact, sheltering the books that had huddled silently for centuries, and there were dozens of studies that branched off the great room, holding even more books. Moss grew everywhere: on the tables, on the walls, on the ceiling, even on some of the books, but strangely there was no moss in the studies or on most of the shelves. Denema's Valley was humid every moment of the day, benefitting from the constant breeze that blew off the wide Dragon River. The rest of the city she had glimpsed was a carpet of moss and foliage, but the library, strangely, had been mostly spared.

Since they arrived, Orem had required Mirolah to spend hours each day reading selected books. At first, she'd been thunderstruck by the place. It was like she had been stealing loaves of bread her whole her life and suddenly she had been led to a bakery full of twenty different kinds of bread, plus pastries and muffins and biscuits and tarts and...

She had dived in with gusto, absorbing everything he put in front of her. But that had been three days ago. The novelty had worn off, and the outdoors called to her almost every minute of the day. She remembered the breeze on the prow of the ship. The call of the water of the Inland Ocean. The call of the forest just outside these walls became louder with every passing hour, it seemed. She wanted to get outside. She wanted to practice actual threadweaving.

Orem looked up, raised an eyebrow, and she went back to reading.

The gods created a vast tapestry, and we are that tapestry. Every single thing we know in this life is a part of it, and the GodSpill was an accident that allows threadweavers to manipulate the world. My well-learned predecessor, Grevian Belshra, once surmised that Amarion holds pockets of GodSpill, and that we threadweavers can see it and coax it out of these pockets into thin, threadlike lights, to be shaped by our intent and our imagination. With the utmost respect for Threadweaver Belshra as an academic, I must dare to refute his conclusion. I do not believe the GodSpill is pulled from scattered reservoirs of power and formed into threads. I believe that we are the threads. Me, Threadweaver Belshra, every tree in the forest outside my study, the very stones of the building in which I write this record. And the GodSpill is an accidental glass of wine dumped upon us long ago before Sasha Braen'dite closed the Godgate and saved the world.

These threads we see are not a manifestation of the creative god force we call GodSpill. These threads are the original creation of the gods. We can only manipulate them because they are soaked with GodSpill, but the threads were always there. I have discovered that these threads can be found everywhere, not just in Threadweaver Belshra's described "pockets." Not only that, but, upon intense study, I have found that I can perceive that these threads are composed of even smaller fibers. Though I cannot see past that, I surmise that those smaller fibers are comprised of even smaller fibers yet, perhaps descending into an infinite minutiae that only the gods themselves can see. This tapestry of our world and our lives was designed to be something specific, but when the GodSpill stained it, it changed. We changed, some of us becoming threadweavers who are less powerful, more limited gods ourselves, as we can make changes to the tapestry like they once did....

Mirolah closed the cover and looked at the name of the author: Korleithan Ket. The man knew what he was talking about. In fact, it seemed silly to her that anyone would believe that the GodSpill pooled in "pockets" of anything. It was in the threads. It *was* the threads.

She sighed and pushed the book away. Her head felt like it was packed with sand.

"I do not know how much more I can read," she said to Orem, who turned the page of his tome. "I feel like I'm forgetting everything I read on the first day as I cram in more ideas."

He smiled, but didn't look up from his book. "Research is an acquired taste. It will grow on you."

She thought of moss growing on her head like it grew on everything else in this city. No.

"We spent all of yesterday studying," she said.

"Yes," he said, turning another page.

"And the day before."

"Yes."

How could he talk and read at the same time?

"I wish that we could spend months here," he said. "It would do you good to read every book on these shelves."

The bright bridge connected her to Orem all the time now. In fact, everything she looked at became a part of her through that brightness in the air. She focused on the book Orem was reading. The threads became starkly apparent, with the muted, earthy colors of something that had once been alive but was no longer. She was finding many differences in the threads of various objects, and each difference had significance. She tried to see Korleithan's "smaller" fibers. She couldn't.

She lightly twisted two of the threads in her mind's eye, and pulled on them. She had discovered that she didn't need to actually touch the threads with the fingers of her hands. She could imagine fingers touching them instead, which allowed her to manipulate things from a distance.

The book Orem was reading snapped shut, brushing his nose. It swiveled around and leapt into the air to hover above him. Startled, he glanced up, then fixed her with a reproving gaze. "My book, if you please," he said sternly.

She shook her head.

His lips became a firm line. "Put it down. I was reading something that might be important.

"I'm tired of important," she said. "I want to have fun."

"This isn't a game, Mirolah. We need to educate you as quickly as we can. Every day that passes could be the crucial—"

"Every day that passes could be boring," she cut him off. She tugged gently, and the book floated into the center of the room where there was no ceiling. It stopped over a large puddle.

He looked positively parental, like Lawdon on one of his tirades. "That tome is irreplaceable. I beg you, put it back on the table."

"I think there is a table in that puddle somewhere. Parts of one, anyway."

"Give me back my book."

"What did you call it when you put this moldy old knowledge to use?"

"Practical application."

"How can you fault me for 'practical application?'"

His face remained stern, but she could see the change of emotion in the colors of the threads that crisscrossed his body.

"There is a time for practice, and there is a time for study," he said. "Rest assured, you are going to have plenty of time to practice—"

"I thought you said that every day that passes could be crucial."

"If we had to flee from danger, you could still practice wherever we go, but you cannot take a library with you. This may be the only time you have to access this knowledge."

"So you're saying I should just suffer and endure until circumstance takes me away from this place?"

"No, that's not what I—"

She made the book float over to her. She took it gently from the air and tucked it under her arm. She started for the door.

"Mirolah, I was just in the middle of a passage. I would like to finish."

"I would like to swim," she said. Stavark had been teaching her how to swim in the wide, slow river. He said it was difficult for most humans to learn, but she had taken to it naturally, like she'd always known how, but had just never been able to practice. Swimming made sense. It felt even more like flying than standing on the prow of a ship. "It's hot. Don't you think it is hot?"

He sighed loudly.

She held up the book. "I'll give it back." She grinned, stepping closer to the broken archway that was the entrance to the library. "If you can catch me before I reach the water."

With that, she dodged around several dilapidated desks and made it to the archway, then turned to look at Orem. He stood, watching her, as though he had no intention of following.

Then he suddenly shoved his chair back and lunged for the door on the other side of the library.

She squealed and ran into the street. It suddenly occurred to her that she had erred in her judgment. The door on Orem's side of the library was closer to the water. She furrowed her brow, about to race off in belated pursuit...

...and she stopped. No. Not on foot. She'd never get past him on foot. She focused on the threads that connected her to the ground and pulled gently, just like she had done with the pot. Slowly, she began to rise into the air.

27

OREM

COLLECTIVELY, OREM HAD SPENT over a year's worth of days in Denema's Valley ever since Medophae had shown him where it was. Arguably, he knew the city better than anyone else in Amarion.

And so he knew that Mirolah would never reach the river before him. He shot out of the library at a dead sprint, but once he was out of sight, he slowed to a jog and took several shortcuts through the broken buildings to reach the cove where Mirolah had been learning to swim. She was right, of course. He was most likely being a bit too stuffy. Orem loved to pore over books, and when the mood struck him, he could spend days at a time in any library, and most especially this library. This was where he had formed the idea that the next threadweaver must have already surfaced, and that he had to look for that person.

The day was hot, a last gasp of summer in the midst of fall, so it made sense why she wanted to take a break. In this weather, even Orem could see the allure of having a swim.

He understood. It was difficult for the young to sit still. Hadn't he been the same? When he was her age, he had traversed Amarion east to west and north to south, sticking his nose into every mystery he could find. He did not spend days in libraries; that came later. Many of his acquaintances had asked him what drove him so, to risk the dangers of forgotten areas of Amarion. Sometimes even Orem wondered why. Curiosity? A sense of purpose. It had always been there, lodged deep in his heart. It was what pulled him to his feet when the sun rose every morning. It was what had brought him all the knowledge he had gathered, knowledge that no other man alive possessed, save one. It had brought him to Mirolah.

Orem broke free of the buildings and jogged into the forest. The swimming cove was not very far now.

Ah...Mirolah. Now she was something that Orem had not expected. Of course, it had been unreasonable to expect a threadweaver to emerge in the lands in the first place. But even if he'd had a dozen guesses as to what that threadweaver would be like when he finally found her, he wouldn't have been able to guess she'd be like Mirolah.

Orem had expected a scared young man or woman. Threadweavers were cursed almost everywhere in Amarion, so it stood to reason that an emerging threadweaver would be frightened at best, twisted into self-loathing at worst. When he found her, he had been ready to cajole her out of her reluctance.

He hadn't expected how much she would change from that young woman, and how quickly. The transformation she had undergone since they had left Rith was startling. The scared and carefully modulated girl he had met in the tile maker's house was gone. In her place was a bright-eyed, curious woman. An adventurer.

When they began this journey, he had visions of holding her hand like he would a child, leading her through the first steps of threadweaving until her natural aptitude lifted her free of his book learning. But she surpassed his knowledge of the GodSpill in the first few days, moving that pot, learning that the word "threadweaver" wasn't just a creative title.

The GodSpill loved her. She absorbed it like a sponge. And as she progressed, he began to understand how little he really knew about threadweavers. He had only books, the culled thoughts of certain threadweavers. He was limited by their experience, their perspective. He could imagine how one might really go about threadweaving, but he really had no idea. He had felt so learned before he met Mirolah. Now he felt like a legless man watching an athlete sprint. He scribbled notes, connecting information he had long ago studied but only now understood. The levitation of his book today—impossible for him—was like second nature to her now, nothing more than the beginning of a game.

He had secretly hoped of one day unlocking the potential within himself to learn threadweaving. He felt that if he could just begin a new age of wonder by releasing the GodSpill back into the lands, such a thing could be possible for him. But watching Mirolah, rather than reinforcing his dream, slowly stifled it. She was a fish in water, and he couldn't even find the lake.

He felt he should be jealous, but strangely he wasn't. It was impossible to be jealous of her. He used to wake every morning with only a dream of breaking barriers between people and Amarion's mysteries. Now he woke every morning to watch Mirolah doing it. He was here, now, while history was being made. Legends would be written about this someday. It was intoxicating.

Orem broke free of the trees and slowed to a walk. He paused and looked over his shoulder. No Mirolah. She'd have to give him his book back now, but she'd won all the same. He didn't feel like reading anymore.

As he crested the bank that fell away to the sandy shore, he stopped in surprise. Mirolah stood on the beach at the edge of the wide sandy bank, bare-breasted in the sunlight. Half of her clothes lay scattered in the sand. She looked up at him as she tugged at the drawstring of her skirt. She wiggled it down over her hips and let it drop, standing in her small clothes against a backdrop of blue sky and green forest on the far side of the slow moving river. She shook her head.

"You're not a very fast runner, Orem," she *tsked* disapprovingly, without a trace of modesty.

He was at a loss for words. "I..." He cleared his throat. "What are... How..."

"How did I get here so fast? Practical application." She winked at him. She turned and ran into the water, lifting her knees high as she tried to hop past the shallows. When the river came up to her thighs, she worked her way forward one hip at a time, then dove in.

She surfaced, taking a deep breath as the current carried her slowly down stream. She shivered as she looked back at him. "It's so w-warm!" she yelled. "C-Come on!"

Orem watched her as she went. Mirolah had been such a timid girl in Rith. Now she was a force of nature. She stepped with more confidence every day, and she had a tendency of pulling him along with her. Sighing, he stopped resisting the pull. He kicked his boots off and pulled his tunic over his head.

If the force of nature said it was time to swim, then it was time to swim.

28

VAERDARO

VAERDARO BACKED UP AND SPAT. Blood flecked the dirt. Already, he could feel the side of his face beginning to swell. His twin, Gilgion, had that sad look again. He always wore that look when they fought, even when they were children. It filled Vaerdaro with a white rage.

But anger led to mistakes, and he could not afford to make mistakes. He pushed down his fire, concentrated on grinding his brother into the dust.

Gilgion side-stepped closer. He held his hands wide, relaxed, as they had both been taught by their father. The brothers had learned the 200 Steps of the Sun together, learned to fight together. Both had been champions in the Ring of Bare Hands back home. Both could ride a stallion across the Red Desert in three days, the fastest anyone had ever made that ride.

But Gilgion led their group north. Gilgion called the orders and Vaerdaro obeyed. It was insufferable.

Vaerdaro circled, keeping just out of range of Gilgion's lightning-quick hands.

The rest of the Wind Ring, twenty-seven riders in all, stood as demanded, hands clasping each other's wrists in a circle, witnessing this moment where Vaerdaro would claim his rightful leadership. None showed any emotion.

Vaerdaro had questioned Gilgion's choice to go farther north, to search the barren lands along the Spine Mountains for the Golden King. The trek offered little benefit. There was nothing up there but sandstone. Why inspect a wasteland for a myth when there were human villages to be raided?

Of course, this entire mission stank like week-old lamb. The Vessel Men whispered that the northerners might reclaim their unholy powers. Vaerdaro's father, the Speaker for the One Sun, had taken the Vessel Men's visions as a sign, and he had sent this Wind Ring north to find the truth.

A sign. Hah! It was a sign that his father was becoming soft, sliding into a weak, paranoid old age. If he began to allow the Vessel Men to lead the Sunriders, what would be next? The Vessel Men told children's stories. They were not the Speakers for the One Sun.

Vaerdaro would not have abandoned the war with the northerners until every one of them had been put to the sword. The One Sun had long ago passed judgment on the blasphemers. It would be a mercy to put them to death.

Now, on this useless quest of the Vessel Men, Vaerdaro was showing true leadership, looking out for the glory of the Sunriders. There was no glory in searching weeds and empty forests. He had tried to be diplomatic with Gilgion, suggesting that they might find more information among the smaller villages, where they could also kill northerners, pillage their belongings, and bring back at least some meager spoils for this wasted trip.

Gilgion had said no out of hand. No discussion. No consideration. Vaerdaro had pushed, and Gilgion warned him to tread lightly with his counsel. Vaerdaro called him a short-sighted fool. Such an insult could not to be borne by a leader. So, with reluctance, Gilgion offered him the right to fight for leadership by combat. If Vaerdaro could best his twin in the Ring of Bare Hands, he would take control of the Wind Ring. If not, assuming Vaerdaro survived the contest, he must shut his mouth and ride, and he could not challenge Gilgion for another year. This was simply tradition, of course. Losers didn't survive the Ring of Bare Hands...or they shouldn't. If a leader was poor enough to be removed by his betters, that leader should die for his failures. If the challenger couldn't prove himself stronger, he would be dishonored for his hubris, and it would be better to be dead.

The last thought burned through Vaerdaro like a fresh sword wound. He had questioned his brother's decision once before, a year ago. They'd faced each other in the Ring of Bare Hands before Father, and Gilgion had won. And he had left Vaerdaro alive to heal from a broken arm.

That was a concession only offered to an impetuous, headstrong child who had let his anger run away with him, not to a full-grown Sunrider.

Vaerdaro's shame was unbearable. His left arm had healed, but it had never been the same. It was weaker than his right, and it ached fiercely when it rained. Once it had healed, Vaerdaro had killed six other riders in the Ring of Bare Hands, each for a specific disrespect they had shown to him. None dared show disrespect now.

None save Gilgion.

He dreamed of the joy of killing his brother in the Ring of Bare Hands. He had even dreamed of other arenas where his brother's blood drained onto the ground. If Vaerdaro could have taken a knife to Gilgion in his sleep, he would have done it. But Gilgion's men loved him and guarded him well.

Gilgion snapped forward suddenly, kicking high. Vaerdaro swiveled sideways, avoiding it. He lunged forward with a mighty punch, but Gilgion was not there. A fist hammered into Vaerdaro's side. Ribs snapped, and stars sweltered in Vaerdaro's vision. Another fist slammed into the back of his neck. He fell forward onto his knees. Gilgion's blows had the weight of boulders.

No...

Vaerdaro rolled clumsily to his feet. Pain arced up his spine, and his bowels felt scrambled.

I am losing again. Again.

Vaerdaro coughed and spat. Blood dotted the ground.

Gilgion held his hands wide. He circled, his lips pressed together, his brow furrowed sadly. His compassion burned like viper poison in Vaerdaro's veins.

Wounded as Vaerdaro was, Gilgion would expect him to hesitate, to recover his strength. Instead, Vaerdaro lunged forward. He feinted high with both hands. Gilgion ducked, as Vaerdaro had anticipated, and he brought a knee up to Gilgion's face. But Gilgion shifted to the side and the strike only caught him in the chest.

Gilgion grabbed Vaerdaro's thigh, taking Vaerdaro's momentum and adding a powerful throw. Vaerdaro sailed through the air. He made a grab for Gilgion's long hair, but missed. He hit the dirt hard, and the air blasted from his lungs. Vaerdaro scrambled to his knees, trying to regain his bearings, but a fist smashed into his face, then another. He blocked one, but another hammered into his temple. Another into his jaw. Another to the other side of his head.

Red lights exploded in Vaerdaro's vision. He felt the ground hit his back. Gilgion knelt hard onto Vaerdaro's gut, and his remaining air blasted out of his mouth. Another fist cracked into the side of his head. Two more, quickly.

Vaerdaro couldn't think, couldn't breathe, couldn't lift his hands. No more blows rained on him. Gilgion's knee was like an elephant's foot, crushing him.

Vaerdaro's ears rang. He tried to move, but his arms were filled with sand. Gilgion's knee lifted from his stomach, and Vaerdaro sucked in a weak breath. He rolled onto his stomach, feeling the blood dripping from his nose, chin, and eyebrows. He turned his head and looked at Gilgion through slitted, swelling eyes.

"Do it," Vaerdaro demanded through split lips.

"You will not question my orders again," Gilgion said simply, as he had said before, and he began to walk away.

"Gilgion!" Vaerdaro slurred through his ruined mouth. "Coward!" He lurched to his feet, the world swaying, and charged his brother. He swung an elbow at Gilgion from behind. He would break that proud back....

But Gilgion spun, bringing a knee up under Vaerdaro's chin, so fast he didn't even see it. Vaerdaro dropped, and his vision went black for a moment. When he recovered, he looked up to see the Wind Ring dispersing.

"No..." he said, but the word came out as an unrecognizable grunt.

Vaerdaro coughed and pushed himself painfully to his knees. The riders walked away, none looking at him. The last time Vaerdaro and Gilgion had fought, a lone rider had remained to watch Vaerdaro struggle to his feet. Vaerdaro had snapped his leg and strangled him to death.

With effort, Vaerdaro stumbled back to his tent and fell back against his pallet.

He yelled for his slave, and the pale-skinned woman Vaerdaro had acquired on their way north pushed aside the tent flap and came quickly inside. She had light brown hair and large eyes. She wore only a thin loincloth, bare breasted, as he had demanded.

She knelt before him as she had been told to do and waited for his orders. He grabbed her by the throat and picked her up off the ground. The pain of his wounds shot through him, but he ignored them. She writhed and choked, pulling desperately at his huge hand. Her feet kicked, seeking the ground.

"Get me clean cloth, water, and food," he said, and flung her away. Her leg twisted as she landed, and she went down with a strangled cry. She lay there for a moment, crying quietly and holding her ankle. Her back quivered like a rabbit's. He could see her tiny ribs beneath pale skin.

"Now!" he roared.

She jumped up as if struck by lightning, clinging to the pole of his tent, and limped out.

Vaerdaro considered killing her. She was weak, and he didn't like her anymore. The women of the north were so frail compared to the women of his homeland. But if he killed her, he would have to get his own food tonight. No, her death could wait until he could replace her.

Ignoring the throbbing pain in his face, he reached over and plucked his sharpening stone from his equipment pack and drew his dagger. With long, slow strokes, he sharpened it. Enough with the Ring of Bare Hands. He would simply kill his brother outright. The Vessel Men said that was how the chieftains of old had taken power.

"I am meant to lead," he whispered, inwardly cursing the pain in his split lips.

A voice broke the quiet of the tent. "Oh, I quite agree."

Smoke gathered together before him, forming into a northlander, short and pale-skinned. As with many northlanders, this man had a stripling's beard—nothing more than a pointed tuft on his chin. The hair of his head was short and black. He wore tight-fitting black clothing over his entire body, and a thin, frail blade at his hip. It was a useless weapon called a rapier that would shatter under the weight of a greatsword.

Vaerdaro jumped to his feet. His dagger leapt from his right hand to his left, and he snatched up the short sword that lay by his pallet. He flung the sheath across the tent and shoved the blade into the man's gut—

The sword passed through him.

Vaerdaro gasped. He lunged again, stabbing and cutting with sword and dagger. The man watched quietly as the blades swished through him.

"Foul spirit, begone!" he said. His hands were suddenly clammy. He gripped and re-gripped his weapons, not knowing what to do. This was the foul unholiness for which the northerners had been punished long ago.

"What are you?" he demanded.

The northerner smiled. "Someone who wants you to achieve the greatness you so richly deserve."

29

MIROLAH

MIROLAH BLINKED HER EYES OPEN. She felt something... nearby. It was just a feeling, like she could sense the sun just before it rose, like it was calling to her before it arrived.

She sat up and pushed her blankets away. The fire was low. A thin curl of smoke drifted up toward the hole in the roof of the house where they had made their camp. Orem slept soundly on the far side, his chest rising and falling steadily.

The feeling nagged at her, and she peered around at the stone walls. As with the rest of the destroyed city, moss covered everything. It was as if the table, the chairs, the dressers, and the wardrobe had donned green fur clothing. She rose from her bedroll, pulled on her tunic. She collected her skirt and boots and crept barefoot across the room, then slipped out the doorway. The night was cool and comfortable and the quarter moon illuminated Denema's Valley with its white touch. The familiar moss-softened shards of the buildings looked friendly in that gentle light.

She walked twenty paces from the doorway, paused, and put on her skirt. She then pulled on her boots and worked her feet into them. Orem would wake at the slightest noise, and she felt the need to explore this feeling without him watching over her shoulder. Something called to her. Something private. It was as if someone was whispering in her ear.

Two weeks ago, it would have scared her. Her first thoughts were of knowledge now. She had a compelling need to know the answers for everything, and there was something out here to discover. She could sense it vibrating the threads of the land.

She started up the street, her feet sinking into the spongy moss with each step. A scuffling noise above her caused her to spin. Stavark stood atop a broken wall behind her.

He watched her with his silver eyes, and she could read no expression on his angular face. If he spoke even one word, it would wake Orem, but he didn't. After a moment, he nodded and disappeared down the far side of the wall.

She hesitated, wondering if he would appear again, insist on accompanying her, but he didn't, so she wended her way through the city to the library.

The inside was ghostly. Moonlight shone through the shattered dome, making shadows across the mossy walls and bookstacks. She went to a stretch of books on the northern wall. The shelves rose a dozen feet in the air, each full of books. This was where it came from. This was the source of the hum.

She pulled down one title, then another, and then began pulling them all down and laying them carelessly on the table behind her—Orem's favorite reading table. She didn't look at any of the titles. It wasn't the books. It was something behind the books.

Finally, the shelf was bare, a recessed space of polished burgundy hardwood, completely free of moss. She ran her hand along the smooth wood, and her fingers found a small divot. She pushed, and the back panel slid sideways, scraping to a halt only halfway open. It was enough to reveal a cubbyhole containing papers, a tome, and something she didn't recognize. The humming came from these objects.

The bright bridge formed, and she saw the auras around the items. She withdrew the tome and the papers and set them on the table amidst the pile of books. She reached back in and took out the last object. It was a sphere of crystal, held in a silver claw that ended in a three-inch spike. The sphere was no bigger than her hand and the silver was scaly—

No. Those weren't scales. They were words, engraved unto the silver, but she didn't know the language.

She set the sphere aside and splayed her fingers across the massive leather tome, then opened it. She drew in a quick breath at the words on the cover: *The Journal of Harleath Markin.*

Harleath Markin. The man Orem said took the GodSpill away from the lands. She opened it and, thankfully, the language was Amarion.

The threadweaver had filled only a dozen pages, a minute fraction of the huge tome. He had obviously intended to write more.

"This is a study of how to destroy Daylan Morth's Fountain..." she read the first lines. Entranced, she sat down and leafed through the pages, absorbing every single word the insane threadweaver had written.

It talked about his journey from the Seawave Empire, more than half of it smoldering in the wake of the GodSpill Wars, to Denema's Valley, where he decided he must chronicle his journey before and after his destruction of Daylan's Fountain.

"He meant to live," she murmured. "He thought he would survive the spell he was going to create." She read on.

I will save Amarion, he wrote. After weeks of study, my apprentices and I have come up with a plan to undo the mistake made by Daylan Morth more than a century ago. I have the artifact, procured at great expense from the dragon threadweaver, whose name I promised I would not record. It is an artifact of unfathomable power, enough to challenge even Daylan's construct. The dragon threadweaver assures me it can...

Harleath went on to describe the artifact, which was the crystal sphere with the claw enclosed with the book, his proposed path, what he intended to do with the artifact, and what the final effects should be. His last words were: *I'm off. May the gods guide my hand.*

The final entry wasn't from Harleath himself, but from a Denema's Valley scribe, a short entry that spoke of the devastation Harleath had wrought. It was signed by the scribe, a self-proclaimed non-threadweaver who dedicated her life in service to them, who said her last service to Harleath was to bring the book back to Denema's Valley, now a graveyard of dead threadweavers, and hide the book. The scribe said she would now go south to Belshra and the Learned Men there so that they could undo this horrible thing Harleath Markin had done.

When Mirolah finished this last entry, she shook her head in disbelief. There was a noise and her head snapped up. Orem's silhouette darkened the great double-door entrance to the library.

She let out a breath and sank back into the chair. "You frightened me," she said, looking back down at the book that had stunned her motionless. Orem didn't move from where he stood.

"Let's not even start with me sneaking away. You probably want to lecture, but when I tell you what I found, you're going to cheer. It's the journal of Harleath Markin." She paused for effect, but he didn't say anything. Okay, he was angry, but he would move past it. She looked back at the book and opened to the passage where it talked about Harleath's intent. "Look here. You said he wanted to take away the GodSpill. He says he didn't intend anything of the kind. He wanted to *destroy* Daylan's Fountain. He wanted to return Amarion to the way it was during the Age of Awakening, what he considered to be the 'natural' world. He never meant to take away the GodSpill. His plan went wrong."

"So he wasn't a villain. He was a fool." The figure in the doorway spoke. It was not Orem's voice.

Mirolah lurched to her feet, sending the chair over backwards. It thudded against the mossy marble. The voice was young, and the figure stepped into the moonlight.

He had long yellow hair tied back like Orem wore his. At a glance, she'd mistaken the familiar silhouette, but that was where any similarity to her mentor ended. Orem was of average height, and this was perhaps the tallest man Mirolah had ever seen, taller even than the imposing magistrate in Rith. The stranger's shoulders were wide and powerful, reminding her of the horrible, muscled Sunriders. But he did not have the beak nose that marked those killers, nor the wide, flat forehead.

If this man was a threadweaver, he could only be a threat to her.

If he was an ally of Orem's, she would know. She backed, then stopped. No. She stopped her retreat. She wasn't a mouse anymore. She had changed. She narrowed her eyes and set her jaw. The bright bridge formed between her and the strange man...

...and she gasped.

Within her newfound threadweaver's sight, he was a furnace of golden flame. She had never seen anything like it. Stavark's aura was a surprising silver with glitters that leapt about him. This new man burned so brightly it was blinding.

"Gods..." she whispered. He was a threadweaver! Perhaps the one who sent the monster in Rith?

He looked about the library like he was the ruler of Denema's Valley, his back strong and straight, his gaze cool.

She knew she should prepare a spell, should do something to make sure he could not hurt her, but...she didn't want to. She couldn't stop looking at his handsome face, that strong chin, smooth skin, those vibrant eyes. He had a presence. He was a good man. He exuded calm.

She shook her head. That realization was too sudden to be real, to be her own, but...

The golden fire around him made her squint, and his physicality stunned her. He filled the room, rugged, ready for anything, utterly without fear. She felt like a moth and he the light.

She found herself looking at his lips, and a heat swelled in her belly. The air brushed soft hands over her skin. She wanted to help him. Whatever he needed, she wanted to help him get it. He opened his mouth to speak, and she unconsciously opened her mouth as well.

"I am Medophae," he said.

30

MIROLAH

THE MAN'S GAZE went to the shadows, but when he realized she was alone, he focused on her. She meant to say something. Her mouth was open to say something, but she couldn't think of what it should be.

He smiled like a father would to a scared child, as if he felt her struggles and understood them.

"Orem invited me," he said in his soft, powerful voice. "I've come to help."

"You weren't... How are you making that..." She clamped her mouth shut, cutting off the idiotic stream of nonsense, which seemed to be all she could manage. She cleared her throat and tried again. "Orem isn't expecting you," she managed.

"No."

"You said he invited you."

"Yes. I told him no, but I changed my mind."

"What are you?" she asked, squinting through the golden glow that surrounded him. His glow was similar to the brightness she created when she stared at something long enough, except a hundred times brighter, almost blinding.

It was GodSpill. This man was wreathed in GodSpill.

"You're the threadweaver," he said.

"So are you," she breathed.

He chuckled. "No."

"But you're...surrounded by golden fire," she said.

"Interesting," he said, looking at his hand, which would look normal to anyone else, but in her threadweaver vision, he was alight. "You can see that?"

"I can barely see anything else. It's all around you."

He made a curious grunt, contemplative. "We should talk with Orem first," he said. "Will you take me to him?"

"Of course." She walked past him to the door, but couldn't stop looking at him. Her thoughts were slow as she led him toward the house where they had made camp. The more she walked, the more normal she felt, and she began to think that maybe she shouldn't have just taken him at his word, but she was sure he wasn't here to do her harm. She had never been more certain of anything in her life. He was just one of the strange people that Orem had met during his travels, but not a threadweaver. She couldn't see how that was possible. What else could he be?

Stavark was infused with GodSpill; it was part of him. It made his flashpowers, but his aura was nothing like this man's. What race was he? He did not look like any of the travelers she had seen in Rith. He had an accent. But the only accent she had ever heard was Sunrider and, of course, Stavark's harsh accent. This was clearly different. It was formal, like this young man was imitating the way some ancient scholar might talk.

As they approached the doorway, Stavark stepped around the corner of the house and stood in their path. He fixed Medophae with a cold stare.

"Duhvark qak sihli, vakihrk!" he spat. She gasped as he drew his short, curved sword.

"No," she said quickly, holding her hands up. "This is a friend of Orem's. He came here because Orem asked him to."

Stavark shook his head, his eyes still fixed upon Medophae. Mirolah had not seen Stavark like this since that night in the Rith jail. The boy stood ready to move, ready to attack.

"I understand your anger, but I beg you to let it go," the man said in his strange accent. Only now did she notice the huge sword buckled at his side, and it was like a dash of cold water. Why hadn't she even looked at the sword before?

"*Duhvark. Qet sihfir,*" Stavark said. He raised his sword in a salute, readying to attack.

"Stavark!" she said, shocked.

"No." The man shook his head. "I won't fight you. There is more to what happened between Orem and me than you know."

"You betrayed trust," Stavark spat in the human tongue. His quicksilver accent cut his words sharply. "You are dishonorable. In my land it is death to attack one's host. He treated you as a guest, and you struck him."

"You struck Orem?" Mirolah asked. It was a dash of cold water in her face, and the questions bubbled up in her mind. Why *was* she so sure he wasn't a threat? Her heart beat faster, and she took a step away from him. Had she been wrong to trust him? No, that wasn't the right question. The right question was: why had she trusted him in the first place? Had he used GodSpill to sway her mind?

She looked at him, desperately wanted to please him. She wanted him to look at her with those blue eyes, to speak to her with that compelling voice.

The man let out a breath. "Stavark—"

"You may not use my name. That privilege is not yours."

The man nodded. "*Syvihrk,* if you will not listen to me, I beg you ask Orem before you attack me. Will you at least consider that?"

Stavark showed his teeth like a dog backing away from a larger predator. He sheathed his sword. "Your tongue is honey and your legend is strong, *vakihrk*. But a man who believes in his own legend is a hollow man. And a hollow man cannot be trusted. I will not see your gentle smile. I will not hear your honey words. These are the tricks of a child of the gods. I believed in your legend when we met at your castle. I do not believe it anymore."

"Then you are wise," Medophae said. "Will you take me to

Orem?"

"No," Stavark said. "You will stay here." For the first time since he had arrived, Stavark looked at Mirolah. "*Maehka,*" he said. "Please come with me."

She hesitated. Good sense dictated that she not be left alone with someone she didn't know, especially after the noble Stavark had called him "dishonorable" and a "hollow man."

She found herself shaking her head. "No. I'll stay. He means us no harm."

"*Maehka,*" Stavark said. "He has wrapped his voice and his smile around you, but he is faithless. He is the volcano with no friends, only those he burns and those he does not."

"Go, Stavark," she said. "Get Orem quickly. He will know what to do."

The boy seemed torn. It was his duty to protect Mirolah, but he couldn't force her to go when she would not. He paused.

Then, in a silent silver flash, he was gone, and the street was silent. She turned to Medophae.

"He hates you," she said.

He grunted. "That happens when you take a person's hope away."

"I don't understand."

He didn't respond.

She frowned. "He said you were one of children of the gods. What did he mean?"

The man smiled as he looked down at her. He pushed a long lock of golden hair out of his youthful face. "A threadweaver indeed."

"Why do you say that?"

"Because you ask a lot of questions."

"It seems very important, lately, for me to know things."

He nodded. "It's an effect of the GodSpill," he murmured. "The curse of the threadweaver."

"What is that?"

"It is a saying they have about those who work with the GodSpill. The more you learn, the more you must know. It has driven many a threadweaver insane. Beware of that thirst."

She narrowed her eyes. "You said you're not a threadweaver yourself. How do you know so much about it?"

His blue eyes glittered. It was dark. How could she know they were blue? She couldn't tell if they actually shined, or if he was simply...clearer than another person would have been. Or was it her threadweaver sight? Could she see things in the dark she couldn't before?

"We should wait for Orem," he said.

"You should answer my questions."

His brow furrowed, and the angry expression struck her like a hand. With Stavark, this man had been gentle and humble, but he suddenly seemed like an angry king.

He is the volcano... She recalled Stavark's words, and she took a step back.

"The young quicksilver has cause to be angry at me," he said, his voice like iron. "Don't try to claim a debt owed to another."

He looked away from her, back down the street. Orem ran toward them with Stavark padding warily behind. Orem slowed to a stop with his gaze on Medophae.

"You came," he said.

Medophae nodded.

"Every other time I asked you, I was sure that you would come, and you didn't. This time I was certain I'd lost you. But you came. What changed your mind?"

"Tyndiria is dead. Killed by a bakkaral."

The wind seemed to go out of Orem. "Oh, no... No..." he whispered. "Medophae, no... I'm so sorry. I never wanted... Why?"

"It was sent," Medophae said.

"By who?"

"Perhaps the same one who sent your darklings."

Orem paused, then said, "You're here to help us?"

"I am."

"Medin, I'm so sorry about Tyndiria—"

"Yes." Medophae cut him off with a wave of his hand, his brows furrowed again.

Orem cleared his throat. "We will bring the GodSpill back to the lands," he said with sudden conviction. "Her death won't be in vain."

Medophae shook his head, his face grim, as if he either didn't believe Orem, or he didn't care.

Mirolah was wildly conflicted. She couldn't tell if this man was a friend or not. Orem seemed excited to have him here. Stavark hated him. And Medophae didn't seem to like Orem at all. She wished she had a moment alone with Orem to sort it all out.

"They'll write of this moment," Orem said.

"No doubt."

"Do you think they'll call you Wildmane again?" Orem asked.

Mirolah snapped her gaze to Orem, and then to Medophae, her mouth open.

"They always do," Medophae said quietly. "They always do..."

31

MIROLAH

HOW COULD THEY SIMPLY GO TO SLEEP? How could Orem quietly lay back on his bedroll and close his eyes when a mythical man stood just beyond the doorway, keeping watch?

Wildmane, the immortal demi-god from the legends, was here. Right here in Denema's Valley!

Curiosity leapt inside her like a caged beast. There were so many questions. How long had he *actually* lived? How much had he seen? Where was his lady love, Bands? Were all of the stories about him true? Could he summon a sword made of a god's rage? Did the *god* Oedandus live inside him? Did he fight side by side with the god of humans, Tarithalius? Did he deal the killing blow to Dervon the Dead a thousand years ago?

What was true? What wasn't? She had to know.

Gently pushing her blankets off, she rose and crossed the floor as quietly as she could.

"You have questions for him," Orem said. She stopped in the doorway and turned.

"Wouldn't you?" It was difficult for her to see his face across the darkened distance, but she saw his colors. Jealousy. *"Didn't* you, when you first met him?"

"I still have questions. And he has answers, probably more than either of us can imagine. But he does not give them easily." His colors shifted. Jealousy and disappointment.

"Orem, do you want me to stay away—"

"No." He cut her off. She felt emotions radiating from him. Shame. Confusion. Pain. Her curiosity about Medophae was hurting him. She hated that, but she had to know. "Go," he said. "It's important that you go to him."

She nodded and stepped beyond the doorway. The stars shone around sparse clouds, and the quarter moon illuminated the mossy valley with a low glow. She felt odd, leaving Orem like that. It was as if something had fallen out of place, but that didn't make her turn around, didn't make her reconsider. She had experienced wonders in the last few weeks. But it was one thing to harness GodSpill and see the threads of Amarion. It was something else entirely to meet a god.

Her threadweaver sight picked Medophae out immediately. He was like a bonfire. How could she not have known the truth about him in the first instant? It seemed so obvious now.

He sat atop a thick, broken wall, facing away, and gazing over the city. She walked toward him, trying to find the way he had climbed up it as she neared. Her toe scuffed a rock, sending it rolling forward, and he turned his gaze upon her.

She swallowed, and neither of them said anything for a long time.

"The wall is broken in a stair-step on the other side," he said, then turned back to look at the sky.

She looked at the stair-step, then quietly took hold of the threads, lifting herself gracefully in the air and landing on the wall next to him.

He ignored her feat and kept looking over the city. She felt disappointed that he didn't even comment on the fact that she had just *flown.*

But then, maybe that wasn't surprising to him. He must have seen everything there was to see in his long lifetime. Yet, still, he looked her own age, a boy of eighteen or nineteen.

She hesitated a moment, then sat down. The silence went on, painfully. Again, she was struck by how...physical he was. She wanted to reach out and touch his shoulder. But the ease she had felt around him in the library had been replaced by a vague forbidding.

"You," she finally said, knowing it was awkward, but also knowing that anything she would say was going to start awkward. This was Wildmane! "You're Wildmane," she said, trying to keep the awe out of her voice. "It is hard to believe..." she trailed off.

"...that the bards would call me something as silly as Wildmane?" he finished for her. He turned his gaze on her, no expression on his face.

"You're teasing me."

"Well, I was actually teasing myself."

"Did you really do all those things? In the legends that I've heard?"

"I couldn't possibly say yes or no to that question. Too many legends. Some of them are pure lies."

"Did you kill a god?"

"No."

That stunned her. "But I thought..."

"I was there," he said. "But I may as well have been a passenger clinging for dear life to a wild, galloping horse, for all I did in the battle. Bands did more. And Zilok Morth even more than her. I was...a vessel."

"Oedandus," she whispered.

"He was the one who killed Dervon. He took control. He just used my body to...focus himself."

"What about the threadweaver Andron? Orem told me about the Vampire's Wager. Tonight, he told of the Quest for Natra..." She lowered her voice as she realized she was babbling, sounding like a little girl.

"Do you enjoy legends?" he asked.

"My father told a lot of stories...about you. But they aren't stories. They're true."

He grunted.

He has many answers, but he doesn't give them easily.

It's because he's in pain, she thought. She couldn't see his aura like she could see Orem's. His blinding golden fire overwhelmed anything that subtle. But it didn't take threadweaving to watch his face. Mirolah had seen people in pain before.

It was a mistake coming here. He deserves his privacy, if that's what he wants.

She could only imagine what a hundred lives did to a person. He didn't want to fulfill the giddy dreams of a girl in search of stories. Why would he?

She stood up. "I'm sorry. I was wrong to come here."

His big hand closed gently about her wrist. "Please forgive my manners," he said in that strange accent. It sounded...polished, almost like he over-pronounced words. "I am trying to get better. Would you like to stay?"

She nodded. "If that's all right."

"Please," he spoke to the night. She reseated herself, and they sat in silence again.

"I have questions for you," she finally said.

A smile curved his lips. "Surprising."

She moved past the sarcasm. "How old are you, really?"

"What year is this now?"

"1649 of...The New Age."

"The New Age," he murmured. He closed his eyes for a few seconds, then said, "That would make me a thousand, four hundred and three. My day of birth passed recently."

"You don't celebrate your birthday?"

"No."

"So, is it GodSpill that gives you your power? Does Oedandus fill you with it?"

"What fills me is actually Oedandus. He lives inside me. He doesn't pull from the threads. He pulls his power from somewhere else. Or the power actually just *is* him. I honestly don't know."

"Is that why Harleath Markin's capping of the Fountain didn't kill you?"

He glanced at her. "Do you know how GodSpill came to be in the lands?"

"The Godgate. Where our spirits go when we die," she said. "Where Natra and the other original six gods met to create the world."

"Yes. Well, their power of creation still resides there. Long ago, the Godgate cracked open, loosing the power of creation into the lands. It would have consumed everything, erasing the details of all we know and returning the world to an amorphous ball of infinite potential. The crack was repaired by a brave mortal woman named Sasha Braen'dite and her followers, but not before it soaked into the lands, leaving GodSpill behind that could be used by some humans, giving us the ability to do what before only gods could do. Giving us the force to create."

"Okay."

He didn't say anything else, and she suddenly realized this was going to be a one-way conversation if she didn't prod him.

"Why did you kill Dervon in the first place?" she asked.

"Hmmm. Well, long before I came to Amarion, before humans recorded history, Dervon and Oedandus fought. Oedandus won. Centuries later, they fought again, and Oedandus won again. The third time was a trap, and Dervon conspired with two other of the gods to destroy Oedandus. But he was too strong. They couldn't eliminate him permanently, so they stretched his life-force over this continent, trapping him and diluting his sentience. After a hundred years of that, Oedandus went mad. When I arrived, he found me, and he...moved in."

"Why?"

"Because his blood runs in my veins. Because he couldn't focus himself in any one place long enough to form a thought, but he could focus himself inside me. He opened me like a gate and made his new home."

"That sounds awful," she said.

"Gods aren't known for asking permission to do things, especially to mortals."

"Can you speak to him?"

"Not like I'm speaking to you. He's like the ocean. You can yell at it all you want, but it does what it does anyway."

"It must be hard, having all of that power all the time."

"I imagine it is the same as being a threadweaver."

She doubted that. That force around him was staggering. It was hard to imagine everything that he might do with it.

"I didn't know your name was Medophae," she said. "Why don't any of the legends tell your real name?"

"Because people love the dramatic more than the real. My name is recorded in many volumes in many places, if one cares to look. But most people don't care. And even more people don't read anymore."

She let out a breath. "The things you must have seen in your life. I simply cannot comprehend..." She let the thought hang in the air, hoping he would pick it up and tell her something about himself.

He looked at her, as though considering saying more, and his gaze captured hers. This close, she could see the blue of his eyes. They were almost gray, like storm clouds blending with an azure sky. She looked closer...closer...and suddenly she was falling into those eyes....

The moss-covered city vanished. The sky of his eyes became a storm, and she was floating in it, looking down, seeing Medophae on the ground, running hard:

Burning like a golden torch, Medophae sprinted across rocky ground toward a chasm filled with black tentacles rising up, slick and whipping. Beyond the chasm loomed a hideous monster, thirty feet tall and covered in mucous and more tentacles that grew on its back like hair. Thin legs folded underneath it to support a bulbous belly and sunken chest. Where its arms should have been, thin arms with multiple joints sprouted, each ending in a single deformed claw. The monster's head was tiny and round, with pointed ears.

She knew the creature had to be Dervon the Dead. She was seeing Medophae's epic battle through his own memories.

Medophae leapt across the chasm, slicing through the tentacle wall with a fiery sword. He slammed into the other side and scrabbled for a handhold...

The storm blew her away to another time in his past, deep in his memories:

An elderly woman with dark eyes, dark hair and a kind smile— Medophae's mother—held his hand as she slipped out of her dying body to walk the path to the Godgate...

Years flipped by her like leaves of parchment to another moment:

A young woman laughed. The laughter turned into a knowing look as she flashed bright green eyes at Medophae. Her short, dove-blond hair framed her face, and she cocked her head, beckoning to him. Love shone in those eyes. Assured. Dedicated.

Mirolah looked away, embarrassed without knowing why. Years rushed by, and she was in a different place, a castle of red stone: *Then there was a hot, red light. Medophae stood in front of a miniature red sun that bled crimson all around. The blond-haired woman stood in front of it along with another man, but then both vanished into the red. Medophae spun. Someone laughed. It was a horrible laugh...*

A huge hand shot out of the storm and grabbed Mirolah's face like steel pincers. The scene shattered. The storm clouds vanished, and Mirolah plummeted earthward...

She drew a quick breath and jerked. Medophae had his hand around her chin, pushing her away.

"Stop it," he said.

She was back in Denema's Valley. Her heart pounded hard. Cold sweat seeped into her palms. She jerked her chin out of his hand, and he let her go.

"What are you doing?" she demanded.

"You went into my head, threadweaver. And you didn't ask me."

"I..." She felt herself blush. "I'm sorry." She suddenly realized what she had done, what an intrusion it was. "I'm so sorry. I...didn't know. I'm still learning to control this."

He nodded.

They sat in silence.

"That's never happened to me before. I didn't mean to pry."

He grunted.

"It is difficult being around you," she finally said.

"Imagine having to do it every day of your endless life." He gave her a rueful smile. It was like the sun rising, and warmth spread through her. That warmth was followed by a chill of realization. She was like a puppet on a string next to him. It was as though whatever he wanted her to feel—welcome, cautious, afraid—seeped into her.

"I'm going to go now." She stood up. "Are you going to sleep?"

"No. Goodnight, Mirolah."

She hesitated at the abrupt dismissal, then, "Goodnight, Medophae."

She gently manipulated the threads and floated down from the wall.

"Mirolah," he said quietly, and she turned.

She didn't look at him through the bright bridge this time, only with her normal sight. He had stood up, a tall silhouette against the starry sky.

His odd accent rippled across her skin like a cool breeze as she listened to the words.

"You are happy," he said.

"Yes," she said up to him.

"The GodSpill sings inside you."

She hesitated. "Yes."

"Orem said you have brushed against a small part of the evil in these lands."

"Yes."

"Remember it. There is an opposite to the joy you feel, and it's every bit as real and powerful as you are. That evil found you. It won't forget you, though you may want to forget it."

She swallowed. "Why are you telling me this?"

"Because you're happy now. Those who are happy remember only the pleasant things."

"Are you saying that I should be miserable?"

"I'm saying be ready."

She managed a nod, then she left him, feeling distinctly less happy as she made her way back to their camp.

32

SILASA

SILASA STOOD IN THE RUINS OF BELSHRA, the city her ancestors had built. It had taken her a full night of travel to get here. She'd been forced to sleep in the ground while the sun blazed overhead. She hated that, but there had been no cave in which to hide from the sun.

It was as Medophae had said. Belshra was gone. Only the skeletons of its houses, shops and palace remained. Crumbled towers thrust up like arms. Dry weeds grew in patches everywhere, and the lower buildings, their walls fallen and smoothed by time, lay like the bones of giant hands.

Medophae said that Belshra had survived the capping of the Fountain, but like every other kingdom after the GodSpill was stripped from the land, its population had been devastated. It became a poor city where survivors huddled in broken buildings, eking out what living they could. But it *had* survived....

Until the Sunriders came. It was the horsemen of the south who dealt the death blow to her city. They razed Belshra to the ground, severing Silasa's final connection to humanity.

When Silasa had been turned into a vampire, she had been separated from those she loved forever. She couldn't stomach the idea of her family knowing that she'd become a cold, dead monster. She'd made Medophae swear to tell no one, not even her father. She would rather have them believe she was dead than see what she had become.

Instead, she loved them from afar, a ghostly parasite clinging to the shadows. She watched her father mourn, pacing the halls without sleep for a year. She watched her sister cry herself to sleep night after night until, finally, she ran out of tears. And she watched their time of mourning slowly pass, and their memories of her fade. She saw her father throw himself into leading his kingdom and into strengthening his ties to his remaining daughter. He would walk her to her room every night and hug her before bed. Her father and sister stole moments at midnight to eat pastries in the kitchens. She watched laughter slowly return to their lives. That had been salve to her soul. That had been a reason for her existence, if only to see that.

And it had been excruciatingly painful.

Eventually, she had moved her gaze to the city outside the palace, watching other families and their nightly rituals. And when she ran away to feed, as she must always eventually do, she fed upon highwaymen and cutthroats. She preyed upon those who thought to prey upon the good and hardworking people of Belshra.

After a few sightings of her, a legend sprung up amongst the people that the lost princess's ghost had returned to protect her city, and that those with evil intent were not welcome in Belshra.

For three and a half centuries, that was Silasa's life. From a distance, she came to know her sister's children. She came to know her father's young new wife and their new children. She watched over them all—her father's grandchildren, his great-grandchildren, his great-great-grandchildren—down through the years. Every mortal life in Belshra was a brief flame that flared and died, and she cherished them all. She cupped her protective hands around their flames and watched, silently, from the darkness.

She thought she'd known what loneliness was, a cursed soul living on the periphery of city, but as she stared at Belshra, she felt a keen pain unlike anything she'd ever know.

What a cruel parody it was, to believe that the gods had anything to do with our fate. The gods never cared for us.

The god of humans, Tarithalius, played with humans like toys. Silasa had met Tarithalius once. The god did not seem to have any concept of good or bad, only what inspired him and what did not, what made him laugh or cry. Yet this was who humans sent their prayers to. *Thalius, please give me this.... Thalius, please give me that....*

Silasa didn't see how one could worship a god who considered you a toy. If you were a legendary beauty, Tarithalius might take an interest in you. If you were remarkably hideous, or clever beyond your years, it might pique his interest. If you accomplished some amazing feat, he might notice you.

But if you were an honest farmer, tilling fields from sun up to sun down, methodically working the soil every day to ensure that your family could eat, Thalius would never even see you.

Silasa would rather send her prayers to Medophae. He was incredibly flawed: impetuous, quick to anger, often confused, prone to overreacting, but he was the closest thing to a patron deity humans would ever have. He made many mistakes, but at the end of it all, Medophae wanted to do what he considered good. That was a rarer quality in humans than it should be.

And in the gods... Well, if you were lucky, their predatory hands never touched you at all. The best you could hope for from any of the other gods was to be ignored.

Medophae had told her what he knew of the original seven gods, present at the creation of the world, and the younger two who followed: Natra, the Breather of Life, who created the world, her father Zetu the Ancient, her lover Oedandus the Binder, her brother Avakketh, her sons Dervon and Tarithalius, and her daughter Saraphazia. And then later came Vaisha, the child of Tarithalius and Saraphazia, and finally White Tuana, the spawn of the divine rape, when Dervon forced himself on Vaisha.

Though there were nine gods at one point in history, there were only five left now. Natra had left the world before history was even recorded by humans, Vaisha died giving birth to White Tuana, Oedandus had been all but destroyed by Dervon, and Dervon, of course, had been slain by Medophae, which was recorded in the epic ballad *Wildmane*, told and retold down through history.

Only five remained: Saraphazia, Avakketh, White Tuana, Zetu the Ancient, and Tarithalius. Six if you counted Oedandus, but he was barely aware.

Saraphazia, the goddess of the True Ocean, was as distant and cold as her waters. Humans could die out tomorrow, and she would watch with impassive eyes. The only human she had ever cared about was Medophae. He said it was because she had hated Dervon above all things for his rape of Vaisha, and Medophae had done her a great service by killing Dervon. But Silasa wondered if Saraphazia also handled Medophae with care because somewhere, deep within him, was Oedandus. And aside from the absent Natra, Oedandus had once been the strongest of the gods.

Then there was Avakketh, god of dragons, whom Medophae had not met, but Bands knew. She had spoken of him as one would speak of a taciturn leader. Avakketh lived among his dragons, hunted with them. To Avakketh, humans were ants crawling about in a distant neighbor's house. He paid them no mind unless they crawled into his house, and then he squashed them without remorse.

According to Medophae, not much was known about Zetu the Ancient. He made the rocklurs and spine horses, but aside from that, he hadn't done much else that had been recorded. It is possible that he left Amarion, going to wherever it was that Natra went.

And of course, there was White Tuana, Silasa's patron deity, the daughter of godly rape. It was White Tuana's hungry blood that ran through Silasa's veins. It was the misty white of Tuana's sightless gaze that marked Silasa's own pupil-less eyes, though, unlike the blind goddess, Silasa could still see. Most humans did not even know Tuana's name, and for that they should be grateful. Silasa had met her once, and if it hadn't been for Bands's and Medophae's intervention, the eyeless goddess would have pulled Silasa's body apart strip by strip for amusement.

Silasa twitched her head, banishing the horrible memory, and looked over the ruins. The scant moonlight topped the jagged buildings and burnt homes in silver. She heard rats scurrying behind broken walls. A cricket chirped in the rubble behind her. *I am the dead princess of rats and insects. She shook her head.*

"I shouldn't even be here," she said aloud, noting that her voice had smoothed to its normal timbre, not the rasp it had been when Medophae woke her up.

She and Medophae were both mistakes. Humans were meant to grow up, grow old, and die. To cease growing, to become immortal, unchanging...it hammered at the mind. Every morning she awoke with the same hands, the same face, the same length of hair, the same smooth alabaster skin. She watched mortals burst with vitality in youth, then mature, then wrinkle down to death. It was important for a person to feel connected to the cycle of life, and watching mortals live and die like the leaves on a tree reminded her that she belonged to no cycle. Talking to Medophae and Bands every year or so was the only thing that kept her sane. They were her cycle, the only thing to which she really belonged.

And Medophae had belonged to Bands. Her calming presence protected him, and Silasa imagined that Medophae could have remained sane for another millennium with Bands at his side. But the great dragon was gone. He was alone now, and his indomitable will was cracking. She saw her own hopelessness reflected in his eyes, because he also belonged to no one now.

Of course, as long as the selfish Oedandus raged inside him, Medophae's body couldn't die. But his spirit was slowly failing. When she looked at him, she saw a setting sun, low on the horizon, and about to dip out of sight. She had seen it in mortals before, and they always died soon after. She wondered what Medophae's body would be if he finally gave up. Would Oedandus be lost again? Or would the angry god prop up the body and walk it around, a raging puppet without direction?

She shuddered at the thought and walked across the mossy, broken floor of the building, out into the street. But she could do nothing for Medophae. Whatever fate would befall him, he was beyond her aid.

She drew in a breath, and she smelled lilies. A whiff of life amidst the decay.

"I would help you if I could," she whispered to Medophae, wherever he was. "I would give you hope if I had hope to give."

"Perhaps you do." The quiet voice spoke from behind her. Silasa spun around.

In the center of the street stood a small woman. Her hair, braided like Silasa's, was snow-white, and her skin was midnight black like the flanks of a stallion. She wore clothing that a courtier might wear riding. A gray vest trapped the body of her white shirt beneath her breasts and over her shoulders. Black pants made of soft leather hugged her legs and tucked into calf-high gray boots. Her black eyes were bereft of any white whatsoever, and the only thing that set them off from her midnight skin was that they glistened.

Silasa remained perfectly still. It was a feint she had perfected with humans. Most people didn't know how fast a vampire could move, and she could often take a human by surprise, if that was what this woman was. She had snuck up on Silasa, which was almost impossible. And she projected the same kind of breathless glamour that Medophae exuded. It was the glow of a child of the gods, a subtle, insidious force that made mortals love them or fear them.

"I need your help," the woman said, and her depthless eyes caught Silasa, drew her in like she was falling down a well. Within them was a torrent of wild emotions, churning and trying to get out. Silasa held up a hand, shielded herself.

"Who are you?" she managed to whisper.

"My name is Ynisaan," the woman said. "And you must help me, or Medophae will surely die."

33

OREM

OREM MOVED THROUGH THE TREES. He set each foot carefully, as he had trained himself to, feeling the ground beneath him. He had spent his entire life roving through one forest or another, and blending with nature came easily.

He followed the old deer trail, which took him around the brief cliff and up the gradual slope to the meadow that Mirolah liked so well. He saw the break in the trees ahead. The high green grass peeked through the maze of trunks. As he neared the top of the rise, he discovered he wasn't alone in stalking the young threadweaver.

Medophae crouched like a great cat behind a boulder at the edge of the trees. Beyond him, Mirolah stood in silent concentration in front of a boulder the size of a house. She'd been trying to move it for three days now.

She did not know she was being watched by Medophae any more than Medophae knew Orem stood silently behind him.

Orem was jealous of Medophae. He'd been jealous of Medophae since they'd first met, after the astonishment wore off.

The man was superior at everything. He was faster, stronger, better looking, more confident, and overwhelmingly inspiring.

With Medophae, though, jealousy was a good thing. Orem cultivated it so he wouldn't fall for Medophae's godly glamour and became a fawning servant. Mortals fell in love with gods. That's what they did, because the aura of their power was an aphrodisiac, or a crippling attack, depending on the disposition of the god. You had to love them or fear them.

Medophae didn't need another admirer. He needed someone to push him, to hold him accountable to humankind.

In that way, Orem needed his jealousy, but these past days, it had taken a darker turn, and he tried to fight it. Medophae had not left Mirolah alone since he had arrived, and that twisted in Orem's gut. It was Medophae's job to protect her, of course, but Orem didn't like his gaze on her all the time, like he was obsessed. Did he really need to watch her all the time?

And, of course, there was the way Mirolah watched Medophae, a maiden in love, heart in her eyes, trying to impress him every chance she got. It was Medophae's glamour, of course. Orem had expected that. He'd even sketched out scenarios of how to deal with it back when he thought Medophae would join them.

What he hadn't expected was how he would come to feel about Mirolah himself. His role—the way he'd always envisioned his role—was to be her mentor, but since she had flown past his teaching, almost on the first day, things had begun to change. He had found himself in awe of her. He was the one following her around, trying to capture some of the knowledge that came to her in a rush. At first, he'd been content to transform from teacher to student. He had prepared for that, at least. She was a threadweaver; he'd known she would eventually surpass his knowledge of the GodSpill. He had invented scenarios for that, too.

But it all changed during that moment at the lake, when they had swum together, laughing, acting like children, acting like equals. That was when the balance shifted. From that moment, he hadn't been able to look at her the way he should: a young student. Instead, he'd seen her as a woman in the flush of her power. He'd seen her as a possible lover.

Ever since, he'd tried to crush the feeling down, and he had been managing it. But since Medophae arrived, the jealousy reared its ugly head in every moment. Orem found himself in an internal struggle most of the time.

What hurt the most was realizing that Medophae and Mirolah belonged together. They were two demigods in the new world, and he was only a mortal. And with Mirolah having far surpassed Orem's knowledge about threadweaving already, what did either of them need him for anymore?

Orem had started this quest. He had imagined himself taking it all the way to its culmination, but that hope seemed to be fading. Could he even keep up anymore? In all his fantasies about finally returning GodSpill to the lands, he'd never seen this possibility, and it hurt. Should he gracefully step aside and let the demigods take it from here? The idea galled him, and that damned jealousy slithered through his guts like a snake.

Orem purposefully scuffed his boot against the ground. Medophae did not even twitch, but continued watching Mirolah. Orem suddenly wondered if the big man had known he was there all along.

"She is impressive," Medophae said quietly. The words burned.

"She's made excellent progress," Orem said.

Medophae paused, then said thoughtfully. "I watched threadweavers train during the Age of Awakening, before Daylan's Fountain made it so anyone could create a house just by swishing a hand around. Back then, I saw no threadweavers train like this. Harnessing the GodSpill was hard. Threadweavers spent weeks mastering simple spells through careful study and carefully crafted experiments, like they were coaxing a turtle out of its shell. The way Mirolah practices...it's as if the GodSpill speaks to her, as though *it* is coaxing *her* out of her shell. It wants her to use it, wants to course through her. I've never seen anything like it."

"What about Bands?" Orem asked, saying her name just to sting Medophae, as he'd stung him before.

Stop it. It's petty. You're better than that.

"That's different." Medophae shrugged, seemingly unperturbed at the mention of his beloved. "Bands was a dragon. A dragon's threadweaving ability... Well, you may as well have a running contest between a man and a horse."

"Of course."

"You have done well by her." Medophae tipped his chin at Mirolah. "Believing you can harness the GodSpill is the most important first step, Bands once told me. You gave Mirolah that."

Orem felt a wash of pride, and he pushed it down. Medophae's approval felt ten times as good as another's. It was that damned glamour at work, pulling at Orem's defenses.

He pulled his gaze away from Medophae. Mirolah held her hands out in front of her, palms facing the boulder some ten feet away.

"I told her that rock's too big for her," Orem said. "It's been three days. I told her to try something smaller."

Medophae shook his head. "She moved it two days ago."

She moved it two days ago.... And Orem didn't know. The pain of that was overwhelming, like a part of him had died inside. He forced himself to breathe a slow breath in before speaking; he made himself sound curious, not gutted and left on the side of the road.

He cleared his throat. "Then...then what is she doing?"

"I don't know. Something. I suppose we will know when she accomplishes it. Or when she gives up."

"She won't give up."

Medophae grunted.

"She has not yet given up on anything she has put her hand to," Orem insisted.

"But has she faced a difficult challenge? That's the real question."

Orem snorted. "I doubt even you could pick that boulder up."

"I didn't say she was unimpressive. The GodSpill loves her. It gives to her freely. We can't possibly know how hard—or easy—any of this is for her. It's possible she struggles with each accomplishment. But looking at her, I doubt it. I think this is all coming far too easily. What happens when the road turns hard? She's untested, Orem."

"She's strong enough."

He grunted again. "Bands said that moving objects is the first level of learning, the easiest. To move something from one place to another is a relatively natural event. Objects are moved all the time by the wind, by the rain, by people, or other creatures. Mirolah understands how to change the location of things. That's good." He shrugged. "But can she transform one thing into another? Can she create something out of thin air? Can she change someone's mind?"

"Do you think mind control will be necessary to destroy the Fountain?"

"I don't know."

"So how can you—"

"Here's what I do know. Daylan Morth was the most powerful threadweaver ever." For the first time, Medophae looked at Orem. His blue eyes shone in the sun-dappled shadows of the grove. "Ever." He turned back to his vigil. "This thing you're asking her to do, it's impossible. So far, at least. Altering Daylan's Fountain was something the most powerful threadweavers of the Age of Ascendance failed to do. By Natra, it's something they failed to even *understand*. Daylan's superiority was not a matter of opinion. It was not bantered about at court who was the most powerful threadweaver ever to live. Everyone knew. Even Bands did not understand Daylan's later spells. No one else could have done what Daylan did when he created the Fountain, not even a dragon. Harleath Markin came the closest to understanding, and not only did he die for it, he killed almost everyone else, too."

Orem felt the weight of Medophae's words, and he fought them. "Mirolah is our only hope for a normal world."

"And watching her, I dare to have hope, but we still don't even know what Harleath intended to do. Not really. You've seen that artifact she found. I don't know what it does. You've read Harleath's journal. He was trying to destroy the Fountain, to return the lands to what they were in the Age of Awakening, but I don't know what he tried. And I don't know why he failed. Do you?"

"No."

"What if Daylan designed the Fountain to protect itself? What if he made it sentient?"

"You think the Fountain is sentient?"

"I don't know. It snapped Harleath Markin like a twig."

"What if Mirolah is stronger than Daylan Morth?" Orem asked.

Medophae gave a low chuckle. "Then we have nothing to worry about."

"You don't think so."

"I know she's not."

"How can you be so sure?"

"Because I met him. Looking into Daylan's eyes was like looking at the stars. His mind was adrift in different times and alternate realities, and yet he could always keep up with what you were saying, answer every question you had with the answer you needed and two other bits of wisdom you hadn't considered. He was just...more. And let's not forget that his crowning achievement was to restructure an entire continent. So far, Mirolah has moved a boulder." He held up a hand as Orem opened his mouth to protest. "Look, she shows more promise than any young threadweaver I've ever seen. But great threadweavers aren't made from promise. They're made when they're forced to adapt or die. Harleath Markin might have been the most talented threadweaver of his generation. He saw something no one else did, but obviously he couldn't adapt quickly enough. Mirolah will have to face that wall, just like he did, and when she does, you can't protect her, and neither can I. And then we'll see."

"You think this is a fool's errand," Orem accused him.

"It *is* a fool's errand."

"Then why did you come?"

He shrugged.

Orem narrowed his eyes. "So then it's just for revenge," he spat. "You don't care whether she lives or dies, whether the lands regain the GodSpill or not. You just want your hands around the throat of whoever sent that bakkaral, and you think Mirolah will lead us to him."

"Would you rather I left?"

"I would rather you believed in us!" Orem hissed, keeping his voice low so that Mirolah would not hear. "How can you stay when you think we have no chance? You mock us!"

"I am not mocking you."

"But you don't think it will work," Orem pressed.

Medophae opened his hands disarmingly. "Anything is possible. We're all fools to try." He stood up, towering over Orem. "But we shouldn't worry so much about being fools. Sometimes all you can do is try." He gave a reassuring smile, and Orem felt the warm sunshine of Medophae's attention.

Orem fought it, hating that Medophae could change the mood that easily.

"Do not think badly of me, Orem. I may not be here for the reasons you wanted, but I *am* here. I will protect your young threadweaver with my life. I will walk this path with you, and we will see if we are fools or not when the story's done."

"She needs a hero, not a tourist."

Medophae nodded, as if he understood, but Orem doubted it. "I will do my best by you," Medophae said.

"I suppose I should be honored," Orem said sarcastically.

Medophae put a gentle hand on Orem's shoulder. "You are a good man, Orem, and I've been hard on you. I apologize. I may not share your conviction, but perhaps you could take comfort thinking I could be wrong about Mirolah's abilities. I have been wrong before."

Orem grunted.

Medophae inclined his head toward the young threadweaver in the center of the field. The house-sized boulder was gone. In its place was a polished stone table large enough to seat twenty. She was grinning.

"Anything is possible," Medophae said.

34

MIROLAH

MIROLAH LAUGHED and stared at what she had just done. She brought one hand up to her head, laughed again, and wiped the sweat from her forehead. She hadn't even realized she was sweating. There it was, the table she had envisioned. Well, almost. It was a bit lopsided. It had five legs and leaned because the legs farthest from her were shorter, and one appeared to be missing. She hadn't even considered how many legs it might need. Or had she? She couldn't quite remember. She had concentrated so hard it was almost as if she'd fallen into a trance. Paying attention to that many threads at once was dizzying. It bothered her how she couldn't remember the entire process.

A sweeping wind bent the shin-high grass and blew tendrils of Mirolah's damp hair into her face. Fingering one out of her mouth, she took a step back and stared at her table.

The moment one exercise became boring, a new vista opened up. Pulling on the threads seemed to move objects in space, but today, she'd changed the color of the threads by willing it, by holding them and imagining her fingers conveying different colors into the bright threads.

The threads could be twisted, rearranged, perhaps even rewoven. And each tiny alteration or tug did something different. She still had not touched all the threads on the stone; she had recolored and shifted only a few of them. Yet the stone had become a table. A table!

Her life in Rith seemed to belong to another girl now. She could make the tiles of Lawdon's livelihood without an oven. She could make them out of granite. She could lift them through the air and assemble them on the roof without touching them, without anyone having to climb a ladder or balance precariously on a roof. She could, literally, do anything she could think of. And most of it was easy.

Whatever she wanted to know seemed to come to her without effort. For example, she knew that Orem was attracted to her. She didn't know if he always was, but he certainly was now. He never said anything, never let his gaze linger on her longer than was appropriate, never touched her arm for too long. But she felt his desire, could see it in the air around him like little red butterflies of light. He worked so hard to keep it hidden, but she could see.

In the last few days, she could also read Stavark like a book. At first, the silver lights that hung around him were confusing, but as she got better at reading everything, she pierced that defense. Stavark was here because of duty. The sparkles represented the power of his flashpowers, but the silver aura was a manifestation of Stavark's sense of duty. He saw himself as a normal quicksilver boy who had been gifted with extraordinary flashpowers, so he was obligated to use them to make Amarion better, not only for his people, but also for humans.

Stavark also longed for home. He missed his mother, his father, and his younger brothers and sisters. Stavark was out of place in the human lands, but she knew he wouldn't leave. In Stavark's mind, you didn't leave friends. You just didn't.

Respect hung about Stavark when Orem was around—wonder and hope every time when Stavark was near Mirolah. Every time Medophae was around, Stavark felt rage and love at the same time. He always treated the big man coldly, speaking little if at all, but if

Mirolah had to guess, she would say that Medophae was Stavark's hero, a hero who had let him down.

She could read Orem and Stavark, but she couldn't read Medophae at all. That dazzling golden aura was a fortress around him. She could not see through it; she could only see what he chose to show her on his face, which was almost nothing. It drove her crazy that everything else came so easily, but he was an enigma.

She waited upon those rare moments when he turned to her with some odd question or another. She always countered with her own questions, trying to draw him out of his shell. He usually gave short answers, if he answered at all. It was so frustrating she wanted to pull out her hair.

She let out a long breath as she thought of Bands, the tall woman with the short blond hair, that memory she had stolen from his head that first night. The legendary woman who was actually a dragon. Mirolah had only seen her for an instant, but that instant told volumes. Bands was poised, vibrant, not to mention breathtakingly beautiful. She had the experience of a hundred lifetimes, was a threadweaver of phenomenal power, and a dragon on top of it all. She was the love of Medophae's life.

Mirolah longed to look into his head again. What had happened to Bands? Why wasn't she here now? Mirolah wanted to know so badly it tickled the base of her skull, but she didn't dare try entering Medophae's head again. He could sense when she tried to touch his threads. He said he could not see the threads like she did, but he was aware, somehow, when she used them.

"Impressive," Medophae said as he finally came out of his concealment. Of course, she'd known he and Orem were there from the beginning, watching her. After all, Medophae was like a giant golden torch to her threadweaving sight. But she'd pretended she was alone. Let them watch. Mirolah actually liked it when they watched.

Medophae leaned his back against a smaller boulder, his long legs crossed in front of him. He wore a padded, split V-neck vest that revealed his muscled chest and his long, large arms. His hair shone in the afternoon light, flowing down to his shoulders. The name "Wildmane" certainly fit him. Who else had hair like that?

"Thank you," she said, a little uncertain. Medophae had a knack for making a compliment sound uncomplimentary.

He just watched her, so she crossed her arms and watched him back.

"I'm curious about something," he said finally said.

"Yes?"

"Why do you come out here to practice?"

"The rocks are bigger out here."

He continued watching her, and she felt herself gazing into those sea blue-eyes. He was just so beautiful.

She realized she was falling under his sway again, so she clenched her teeth and looked at the grass.

"Why do you sneak away from camp to come here?" he asked.

"I like to practice alone. It helps me focus."

"Why don't you train yourself to practice with other people around?"

"I don't want to."

"Why not?"

"Because I don't want to." She was dying for him to tell her what to do. She wanted to tell him to go soak his head in the river.

"Orem said there was a darkling. In Rith."

She swallowed. "Yes. But there aren't any here."

"No. Not until there are."

"If a darkling comes for me again, I'll show him his mistake," she said. "Last time, I was helpless. I'm not anymore."

"So, really you're extending a challenge," he said. "To the darklings."

"What?"

"To come out here, alone. You're inviting them to attack you. A challenge."

"What? No. Look, I don't want them to attack me. I'm just not afraid anymore. You want to make sure I'm protected. Good. Do I complain that you shadow me and watch me wherever I go? No. That's why you're here. But I have power in my own right, and I gain more every day. I am not afraid of monsters anymore."

"That's good. You'll need that courage in the days to come. You've become very aware of your strengths. Also good. But you don't seem to be aware of your weaknesses."

"What weaknesses?"

He smiled, as though what she said had proven his point. She clenched her teeth. She hated that she always felt like a child when he was around. She wasn't a child!

"May I tell you about a friend of mine?" He walked a few paces away, a flicker of golden fire raced down his legs, and he jumped seven feet straight up, landing lightly on top of a nearby boulder.

She blinked. He was always so reserved, it took her by surprise. But of course, he was arguably the most powerful man in Amarion. Leaping onto a boulder was easy.

"Okay," she said.

"This friend of mine, he was a fighter. A soldier. He had a powerful body, built for fighting: big, strong, quick. He studied swordplay as soon as he could lift a blade and became one of the finest swordsmen I have ever seen by the time he was twenty." Medophae looked up at the passing clouds.

"Yes, so?"

"So he was killed by three children, none more than twelve years old. They shot him with crossbows at fifteen paces. His sword was only halfway out of its scabbard by the time he fell to the ground, dying."

He turned his gaze back down to her, let the silence linger. So dramatic. She wanted to throw a stick at him, but she just stared back at him defiantly.

"My friend was caught in the forest, alone. He was in unknown territory, and he walked into a trap. His enemy wasn't the children. His enemy was the certainty of his own strength." He jumped down, came to her, and put a hand on her shoulder. Warm, strong fingers. Butterflies fluttered in her belly. "Help me protect you," he said. "Trouble is going to find you soon enough. Don't go looking for it."

She wanted to be angry at him, to tell him not to treat her like a child, but his hand on her shoulder felt so good. She wanted him to leave it there, wanted him to scoop her up in his arms like she had dreamed about back in Rith. She wanted to feel his muscles against her back, against the backs of her legs.

"Mirolah? Will you help me protect you?"

"Of course," she said. "Of course I will."

35

MIROLAH

THE NEXT DAY, Medophae asked if she'd like to go for a hike up toward the cliffs near Denema's Valley. The idea of being alone with him coursed through her like wine. He wanted to show her something from his past, share something.

"Where?" she asked.

"You'll see when we get there," he said, and that was that. They packed a lunch, and after a nod and a brittle smile from Orem, she and Medophae set off on their hike.

He guided her confidently through the forest, navigating around tightly clustered trees, knitted together with moss-covered vines. When the path vanished into undergrowth, he tore branches out of their way. When the way narrowed, he twisted sideways and slipped through the gaps. She watched the play of muscles in his arms, how he shifted so easily between force and grace. She was so engrossed in watching him move that she bumped into him when he abruptly stopped before an archway in the mossy mountainside.

"Sorry," she said, backing up. "What is this?"

"Portal."

She almost couldn't see it, it was so overgrown. But she could make out a shape obviously constructed by human hands, a nine-foot-tall arch that came to a point. It looked like it should have led somewhere, but it didn't; it recessed into the rock about six inches deep. There were carvings along the edges of it, but most of those were covered over with vines and moss.

He took hold of the vines and ripped them aside, revealing carved symbols beneath as golden fire danced about his back and arms. The symbols were crude but compelling, appropriate for the wild surroundings. He ran his fingers over them.

"Behold my attempt at art," he said.

"You made this?"

"Bands did most of it."

"Oh..." She didn't want him to talk about her. She wanted this moment to belong to her and Medophae. "What does it do?"

"It moves you from one place to another, instantly. This one goes to Calsinac."

"There are others?"

"Yes. They all go to Calsinac. Or more accurate to say, they all come from Calsinac."

"Why?"

"Calsinac was so remote. We needed to be able to communicate easily with other kingdoms. Only the leaders of Denema's Valley knew of this one. Bands said knowledge of such gates could be dangerous."

"Where else did you build these portals?"

"Seabreak. Belshra. Southrock. Wayland. Buravar. Tiernan. And other cities long since vanished."

"I don't know any of those places except Buravar. Or wait. Actually, I think Orem mentioned Belshra in his story about The Vampire's Wager."

"Hmmm."

"That's the story where you outwitted the evil vampire Darva. She thought herself a queen, stole the princess. She made you face the dramath's riddle. But you beat it and rescued Princess Silasa, who would otherwise have become an evil vampire like Darva."

"I see."

"Please tell me that one is true," she said. "It's one of my new favorites."

"Orem is a good storyteller." But his eyes were downcast, and his happy mood vanished.

Mirolah inwardly cursed herself. She was acting like a vapid little girl again, asking whatever silly questions popped to mind.

He was facing the vine-covered rock face, and she reached out a hand to touch his shoulder but hesitated. She brought her hand back to her side, cleared her throat. "Where is Southrock?" she managed to ask.

"Far to the south where the Spine Mountains touch the Sara Sea. It was a cliffside kingdom. The only way to get past it to the north was a small and treacherous road. One threadweaver could hold it against an army of a thousand. Back then, they had never come further north than Southrock. Of course, after the capping of the Fountain, there was no one to hold the pass..."

She touched his arm, and he turned. The butterflies moved into her throat, and she stood on her toes, took hold of his chin and kissed him. He hesitated, then his hand moved to the small of her back, and he pulled her up, lifting her off her feet. Tingles raced throughout her body.

Suddenly, he stopped, and he set her down.

She blinked, lost in a pleasant haze. "Don't," she breathed. "Don't stop."

"I can't do this with you," he said.

"I want you to." She splayed her hand across his chest.

"No. You don't." He took her hand and placed it gently at her side. "You don't understand."

"There's nothing *to* understand."

"Look, I'm trying to help you."

"Then kiss me again." She smirked, sliding her hand along his neck and standing on her toes.

His hand closed about her wrist. "What you're feeling isn't real. The emotions aren't real. It's not me you're attracted to."

"Then who am I dying to kiss? I have chills running up my spine."

"Because you're beguiled."

She blinked, and her happy haze faded.

"Do you know what a glamour is?" he asked.

She didn't say anything.

"It like using the GodSpill to manipulate someone's emotions," he said. "Except it's happening all the time. Someone with a glamour is appealing, attractive, even irresistible. They would seem beautiful to you even if they looked like a darkling. That's what Oedandus' presence does. It creates a glamour around me. It compels others to be...well-disposed."

"You think that's why I want to kiss you?"

"I know it is."

She turned her hand into a single finger pointing into the center of his chest. "And this glamour makes you want to kiss me, too?"

"Mirolah, I didn't—"

"No, stop," she interrupted him. "Save your speech. I know it's going to be about Bands. Orem told me what happened to you." She stepped away from him. "He says you're half a man, that you spend your days living in the past, because that's when you were happy. I understand that. You lost loved ones. It's horrible, and I'm sorry. But I've lost people, too. My entire family, Medophae. I know what it's like to want to imagine those people aren't gone. So if you want to live with her in your memory and punish yourself over and over, that is your decision. Tell me you want to mourn for another four hundred years. I will respect that, and I'll leave you alone. But don't take me out in the middle of nowhere, tell me stories of your life, kiss me, then jump back and call it a glamour. You wanted that kiss as much as I did."

"That's not... It's not what you think."

By Thalius, he was so beautiful, and even more delicious when he stumbled for words. "No, it's not what *you* think," she said.

He opened his mouth to respond, but couldn't seem to find the words.

She turned and walked into the forest. "See you back at camp."

36

MIROLAH

THAT NIGHT AFTER EVERYONE had gone to sleep in their camp, Mirolah awoke suddenly. The sun had not yet risen. The partially crumbled ceiling of their house let in a little moonlight, and the coals of the fire glowed low within the ring of stones. Stavark and Medophae slept to her left.

It must be Orem's turn to guard which means it's still early in the night.

Orem always took the first shift. It was odd how peaceful and well-rested she was, like she would expect to feel after an entire night's rest, instead of just a couple of hours. Something about that wasn't right....

Her worry became a little red butterfly in her mind, fluttered in front of her face, then flitted up and away.

A new thought took shape, swelling and filling her mind with red purpose, until she could think of nothing else: It didn't matter who was guarding. Guards weren't important. What was important was that she leave this room quickly, quietly, and she must not wake the others.

She pushed her blankets aside and stood up. Her skirt, tunic, and cloak lay neatly on a chair a few paces away. *I should put those on before I go anywhere,* she thought, looking down at the white shift she wore at night.

But those thoughts also became little red butterflies, dancing on the warm air, going up...up...until they were gone.

She wound her way carefully past Medophae and Stavark, who did not wake, and she left the room. She stepped barefoot onto the cool, moss-covered stones of the street and wended her way through the buildings, following the image in her mind, along this street, down that alley, cut over and keep going...

Soon, she was in a part of Denema's Valley she'd never been before, standing in the middle of a wide, cobblestone street with roofless shops lining each side. It was far away from the library and the little alchemist's shop where they had made their camp. Ahead was a round, cobblestoned confluence of seven streets, all like spokes that led to a broken, moss-covered fountain that had long since tumbled in on itself. She thought briefly of the city circle in Rith, but that thought also flitted up and away.

A warm breeze blew across her, pushing her hair into her face and raising goosebumps on her bare arms and legs.

Wait here.... The thought rose in her mind. It didn't sound like her voice.

But if it's not my voice, she thought foggily. *Whose voice was it?*

"What am I waiting for?" she asked aloud.

That question became a little red butterfly and fluttered away, and she was happy again. She looked down at her bare feet. They hurt from the walk here.

I should have my boots.

A darkling slunk from the darkness, climbing on top of the tumbled stones of the fountain ahead. Its burning red eyes focused on her. Another slunk around the edge, crouched on the flagstones. It opened its wide, tooth-filled mouth and let out a purring hiss.

Terror spiked her heart, and she tensed to flee...

...but her fear twisted and became a half-dozen red butterflies, fluttering away, and she let out a calm breath.

A crimson certainty sat down heavily on her mind: *They aren't going to hurt me.*

So Mirolah walked forward one step, then another.

37

MEDOPHAE

THE NOISE OF A FOOT moving across the floor almost woke Medophae. It was the footfall of someone trying to be quiet and not quite succeeding. Sneaky people did that, and in the midst of sleep he had the thought that he should wake and find out who was trying to be sneaky. He had that feeling of rising that comes with shaking away slumber, but he was distracted. A swarm of red butterflies flew past him, and his attention was drawn downward, deeper and deeper, back into sleep. The color of the butterflies reminded him of Ethiel, the Red Weaver who had destroyed his life, so he chased the butterflies. Ethiel had taken Bands. Medophae wanted her back. So he went deeper into sleep, so near to catching the red butterflies...

The dream began, the one he'd lived a thousand times:

"THROUGH THIS DOOR?" Medophae turned to Bands. His breath came quickly now. One step beyond that door, and chaos would burst over them. This was the moment he loved best. Oedandus raged within him, ready.

"Yes?" Medophae pressed. Bands was at her loveliest under pressure. She never seemed rattled, and her serenity was like a drug to him. She closed her eyes and put her hand on the door. Her short hair slipped forward into her face, white-blond strands creating a curtain over her eyes as she concentrated.

"This is the door," she said. "The GodSpill swells around it, but...I can sense nothing beyond."

"Is Ethiel in there?"

Her beautiful brow wrinkled. "I don't know."

The godsword formed in Medophae's hand, a three-foot sword of golden fire. "We go through," he said in a low voice.

Tarithalius, the god of humans, stood behind Bands. He grinned at Medophae, his teeth extra white against his dark skin. It was all a game to him. He liked to watch Medophae and Bands on their adventures, just an annoying spectator who never did anything but watch.

Bands looked concerned, but she slowly nodded. Medophae leaned over and kissed her fast and passionately. She wrapped an arm around his neck and lost herself in it. Bands was often so serious, but she was like a love-starved young woman when she kissed him, throwing herself into it every time.

Tarithalius laughed.

"Are you ready?" Medophae whispered, breaking the kiss. She smiled. He'd cut his way through a mountain if her smile was on the other side.

"You make me ready," she said.

"I'll go first."

"I'll be your shield."

It was a combat method they had perfected, fighting threadweavers. Medophae was largely immune to threadweaving because of Oedandus, but some spells could hurt him. Ethiel had been perfecting—and inventing—those kinds of spells for years. Oedandus would protect him from anything normal. Bands would watch for any new twists that Ethiel had added.

Medophae brought his sword down on the door, and it exploded. Chunks of wood and swirls of red light blew into the room. A dozen trigger spells attacked him. He felt acid. He felt fire. A thousand daggers stabbed at him. But Bands whispered, moving her fingers in short jerks, countering them as they came, one after the other.

Medophae burst into the room with the shards of the door. Thanks to Bands, only a fraction of each spell bit into him, and Oedandus flared to heal the damage.

His hair burned like a guttering torch. Pinpricks of blood dotted his skin, but the wounds healed quickly.

Roaring flames flew at him from inside the room. He grinned as he threw himself to the floor and rolled.

Ethiel sat on her throne atop a semi-circular dais against the rear wall of the audience chamber. Her mane of red hair curled down to her shoulders, blending with her red satin gown. Medophae's lip curled looking at her.

The Red Weaver's face was deep in concentration, her eyes closed. A bolt of lightning forked out from her fingers at Bands. Medophae leapt in front of it and struck it with the godsword. The spell burst apart, and lightning flew sideways, cracking the walls.

A greasy gas formed around Medophae, but Bands's fingers worked and the gas halted, curled upward and spiraled out a window. Ethiel sent another ball of flame at Medophae, but again, he sliced through it. The fiery tendrils brushed him on either side, and he sprinted toward her.

He leapt to the top of the dais in one bound. Tarithalius floated next to him, always keen to watch the happenings between humans. He grinned and floated forward to keep pace with Medophae. Ethiel murmured, her fist in front of her, and she never opened her eyes.

He thrust the godsword through her stomach.

Despite the atrocities Ethiel had committed, the countless innocents she had slain, compassion welled up within him in that moment. Oedandus liked to kill, but Medophae didn't. Ethiel had been just a young woman once, long ago. As the daughter of a duke, she'd had many prospects for a happy life. More than most, he supposed. Medophae had often wondered what her life might have been like if she'd never met him. If he hadn't rescued her from the rough men who'd snatched her. Perhaps, at one point, she had been perfectly sane. Or perhaps the seeds of insanity had always been within her. If so, they hadn't flowered until that night on the road outside of the Gorros duchy, until his glamour surrounded her, sparking an infatuation that became an obsession.

Ethiel claimed to have loved Medophae. She sent him letters. She made the long journey to Calsinac to profess her love. She wrote poems. She had even caught him in his throne room at midnight, performed a dance she had choreographed for him. Every time, he turned her away, but that only seemed to encourage her to come up with a new ways to catch his attention, to try to win his heart.

At last, she studied threadweaving. She got it in her head that if she became the most powerful threadweaver in the land—more powerful than Bands—then she would be "worthy" enough to court Medophae successfully.

Of course it wasn't about any of that, but no matter how many times Medophae tried to explain to her, she didn't listen. Medophae was already in love, and that wouldn't change, no matter how spectacular Ethiel became.

And so love curdled into hate, and Ethiel planned and attempted to kill Medophae. Then Bands. Then Medophae. Then both of them. And she slaughtered innocent people to get to them.

I'm sorry, Medophae thought as the sword punctured Ethiel's chest. Her eyes and mouth flew open, and she looked down at the crackling blade. Oedandus's rage tore through every kind of GodSpill weaving, through any defenses she could craft.

It's hard to love and not be loved in return, *Medophae thought.* May you find peace beyond the Godgate.

A red light flared up behind him, and Bands slammed into him, knocking him to the ground. Medophae skidded across the floor, looking back.

A huge, crimson circle, a mystical gate of some sort, enveloped Bands and Tarithalius. Tarithalius's black beard looked like a sponge affixed to his chin. His mouth opened in surprise, and he vanished. Bands's blond hair shone like a dove's feather in a bowl of blood as she turned. Her green eyes caught his, for just one second. He saw her surprise. He saw her fear.

The light flashed. The portal vanished.

Bands was gone.

"HUH!" Medophae sat upright and threw his blanket aside. Stavark rose on one elbow, then vanished in a silver flash. In the span of a heartbeat, the young quicksilver stood ready by the doorway, his small, curved sword in hand.

Medophae shook the dream from his head, trying to pull himself away from that horrible moment.

"It's all right," he said to the quicksilver. "I'm sorry. It was a nightmare, nothing more—" He cut himself off as he scanned the room.

Mirolah's blankets were rumpled and empty.

"Where is Mirolah?" he asked.

38

MIROLAH

MIROLAH APPROACHED THE DARKLINGS. They purred and hissed quietly in the deserted town square. But they were friends, and she must go to them. Moonlight coursed over their shiny black hides like molten silver. Cords of muscle rippled under their skin as they moved. Red eyes gleamed, and Mirolah found them beautiful, like rubies.

Another darkling loped into the square, and another. Several more slunk in from other streets, and they all gathered around the fountain, waiting for her like family.

She reached the fountain and touched the nearest darkling's head. It was smooth and warm. Her friend hissed, rising on two legs to its full height, towering over her. She was rapt and stared into its eyes. It let out another hiss and opened its mouth. Its long, white teeth were slick and shiny. It picked her up in its claws and brought those teeth to her neck.

A flash of silver slammed into her friend, shattering the perfect moment. The darkling's claws cut her arms as it flew backward. Black blood flecked her face, and she fell to the cobblestones.

The darkling lay in front of her, its throat slashed. Black ichor spurted from its ruined neck and the glowing red eyes slowly went dark. Stavark stood over the dead darkling, gripping his little sword and breathing hard.

The happy haze was a veil over her thoughts, but the sudden violence ripped the veil away. Mirolah gasped as she realized suddenly where she was, surrounded by darklings who were about to eat her.

A flurry of thoughts raced through her mind, and time seemed to slow down. She'd been mind controlled! Her mind had been altered by another threadweaver. The red butterflies, the voice in her head. These darklings worked for this threadweaver, and Mirolah had almost gone willingly to her own death. Only Stavark's quick intervention had saved her.

Stavark's silver eyes caught hers, and she realized she could not read his aura. The bright bridge was gone.

Stavark raised two fingers to his mouth and whistled shrilly. The throng of darklings leapt forward, and Mirolah screamed.

The quicksilver sheathed his sword and lunged at her. The nearest darkling jumped, right behind Stavark. Its claws extended. Its mouth opened wide.

Stavark became a silver flash. Mirolah's scream turned to a gasp as a thousand small hands grabbed her, lifted her into the air and pushed her backward. The darkling crashed to the stones where Mirolah had been. Silver glittered in the air. The darklings hissed as she flew away from them on a cloud of silver hands.

The silver flashing stopped. She and Stavark crashed to the ground only a dozen buildings away. The young quicksilver fell to his knees, huffing like his lungs were about to burst.

"Cannot..." He huffed. "You must...threadweave..." He looked at her through drooping eyelids.

She sat up. The pack of darklings had seen them falter. With a howl of delight, they sprinted from the fountain. She had only seconds.

She scrambled to her feet, and focused, tried to create the bright bridge.

It wouldn't come.

"I'm trying!" she said.

"Quickly," Stavark croaked, trying to rise on shaky legs, leaning on his sword like it was a cane.

The darklings were almost upon them. She tried to see into the nearest one. The bright bridge began to form, but something obscured it. Something protected the creature.

"I can't!" She sobbed. She pulled at the limp quicksilver's arm, trying to run. "We have to run. Come on!"

He turned with her, but fell to his knees again. She cried out and hauled him upright. He was dead weight, unconscious now, and she tried to shuffle away with him under her arms. It wasn't going to be enough. She could hear the scraping claws right behind her—

Suddenly, the scraping ceased, and she spared a quick glance over her shoulder as she limped forward.

Medophae stood between her and the darklings. His broad back was bare, and she could see every striation of muscle, lit with his own golden flame. His hair floated around his head on the golden fire. A sword burned in his hands. He seemed huge, towering over the darklings like they were cockroaches.

"Come on," he growled at them. "Kill me first. Then nothing will stand in your way."

The closest darkling hissed and leapt at Medophae, a black blur limned in silver moonlight. Three others followed.

"Medophae," she screamed. She saw visions of Fillen dying on the hard-packed street of Rith. She waited for them to tear his beautiful bronze skin, to wet that shining hair with blood.

But he dropped to the ground, leaving a trail of golden flame behind. The darkling's claws raked the air, but Medophae's sword chopped it in two. The halves of the hissing darkling plopped to the stones on either side of him. Blood splattered the street, and it died.

The second darkling barreled into Medophae. His hand shot forward like a lance, crushing its throat, and it crumpled, grabbing its neck and thrashing desperately as it choked.

The third leapt onto Medophae's chest, claws ripping. It sank its teeth sank into his shoulder, but he only grunted, wrapped his arm around the darkling's head, and cranked it in a vicious circle, snapping its neck. The creature fell to the stones.

The fourth and fifth came at him from the sides, but he spun, cutting high and low, and they never touched him. One darkling fell to the ground, missing a head. The other crashed sideways, its leg gone. Medophae lunged forward and skewered it through the back, and it lay still.

The brutal dance began and ended in an instant. Medophae straightened, taking the same wide-legged stance. He held his arms apart, the sword crackling and popping in his hand. Blood dripped from his shoulder onto the stones. The remaining darklings watched him with hate-filled eyes, but they kept their distance. The blood flowing from Medophae's shoulder slowed, then stopped. The wound closed.

"I await you," he said in a low voice. The remaining six darklings hissed in unison. They shifted back and forth.

"No?" He growled. "Then I'll come to you." With a roar, he leapt into their midst. They scattered, but not before he caught one with his sword and one with his hand. Both died hissing. The other four sprinted up the street and disappeared into the night.

Medophae turned. There was red and black gore across his face and chest. The burning sword flickered and died away.

"Are you all right?" he asked, calm as though he hadn't just killed seven invincible darklings in two seconds. Relief flooded through her. Her knees became watery. He caught her, and she clung to him.

"I'm sorry," she said. "I walked right up to them. They made me come to them. They would have killed me, if Stavark hadn't—"

"It's okay," he murmured. "You're safe now." The darklings' blood and his were wet on her face and neck, but she didn't care. She wanted his arms around her. In his arms, she was safe, like she was in the arms of her father. In Tiffienne's arms...

Except her father had died at the hands of the Sunriders, and Tiffienne and Lawdon hadn't been able to stop the magistrate from marching into her house and taking her.

And she knew that, though Medophae and Stavark had protected her tonight, like Medophae had told her, some day they might not be able to. There might be something out there larger, more powerful, than either of them.

She squeezed Medophae, wanting to stay a little girl for just a minute longer. Just a day. Just a month.

She squinched her eyes shut tight. *No.*

With shaky resolution, she pushed away from him. Tonight, after all her protestations that she could take care of herself, she had needed rescuing.

"I failed," she said. "I told you I'd be ready, and I wasn't."

"Don't be so hard on yourself—"

"Well I think I will," she said. "They're going to come back."

He paused, then said, "Yes."

"And shall I run and hide behind you then, too?"

"That's why I'm here—"

"No. When this threadweaver comes again, I'm going to be ready for him," she said, steel in her eyes.

Orem burst around the corner of a nearby building. He skidded to a halt in the center of the street. His gaze flicked over the carnage, then he spotted Mirolah. He let out a gasp of relief and leaned his hands on his knees, sucking breath after breath. Finally, when he had gotten his breathing under control, he came to her.

"Thank the gods," he huffed. "You made it in time. You saved her."

"Stavark saved her," Medophae said. "I wasn't fast enough."

Orem walked forward, took her shoulders in his hands. He looked her over, searching for injuries.

"I'm not hurt," she said. She had met the threadweaver who wanted her dead tonight, and he had turned her mind inside out, made her almost kill herself. She had not been ready. Not even close.

Orem knelt beside the unconscious Stavark, and she knelt with him. She put a hand on the boy's forehead. It was warm, and he was breathing. "He picked me up and carried me away in his silver flash. But then he just collapsed."

"He picked you up?" Orem said in surprise.

"Carried me away."

He rolled the boy onto his back and listened to his chest. "He will be all right. He passed out from exhaustion." Orem gingerly gathered Stavark into his arms. "I can't even imagine the effort it would have taken him to carry you. Before tonight, he could only use his flashpowers in short bursts, no more than a hundred feet. And that's carrying just himself." He shook his head in wonder. "Let's get him back to camp. We need to gather our things away and get away from here. Tonight. As far as we can go. Our time here is finished," Orem said.

"Run far. Run fast," someone said in a smooth, oily voice.

Medophae spun around, and Mirolah looked past him to the owner of the voice. She stifled her own gasp.

"You!" Medophae said.

39

MIROLAH

DOWN THE STREET where the darklings had run, a monster strode out of the shadows. He had the same shiny black skin as the darklings, stretched over bulging muscles, but unlike the darklings, this creature walked upright like a man, nearly twice as tall as Medophae and three times as thick. His shoulders were mountains, and his arms were as thick as Medophae's entire body. A single horn protruded from the darkling giant's forehead. It curled down and then out in a wave, ending in a wicked point just beyond his flat nose. His eyes, like the darklings, burned like red fire. His ears were sharp and tall like Stavark's, and fangs protruded from his wide lips. Tight breeches covered his tree trunk legs and a thick belt wrapped his waist, but his shiny black chest was as bare as Medophae's.

He flexed huge, steel-covered hands. The gauntlets shone in the moonlight and Mirolah sensed the GodSpill emanating from them. Her head had continued to clear since she'd broken out of whatever spell had been laid on her. The bright bridge formed as she concentrated on the monster.

He stopped a short distance away from them.

"Kikirian," Medophae said.

"You know him?" Orem asked.

"How long has it been, godslayer?" Kikirian said in a smooth voice.

"Are you behind this?" Medophae growled. Not a single muscle twitched in his broad back, but streaks of golden fire raced over his body.

Kikirian held his hands wide in a casual gesture. "I am just a messenger."

"The last messenger lies broken at on the rocks of the Inland Ocean."

"Always bragging," Kikirian said. "No one expects a darkling to be a match for you."

"I'm talking about the bakkaral."

Kikirian pursed his thin lips. "I know of no bakkaral. But then, my mistress moves in strange ways."

"Who is your mistress?"

"All in good time." Kikirian shook a gauntleted hand dismissively. "She wishes to see you, and she will, soon enough."

"And you're to bring me in?" The hate in Medophae's voice burned. "Just a pup of Dervon the Dead?"

Kikirian's lip curled. "Your confidence reeks of rot, little god. You'll lose that pride when my mistress serves justice upon you."

"A pity that Dervon taught you to speak, but not to fight." Medophae strode forward.

Kikirian flexed his steel-encased hands, looked down at Medophae. Mirolah couldn't believe anyone could be so big. Medophae seemed a child next to the darkling giant. "Come for me then, child of Oedandus. We shall continue the battle that was interrupted so long ago."

"Medophae, don't," she shouted. "His gauntlets glow with GodSpill. I...don't know what they do."

Kikirian turned his burning gaze on her. "So, the little threadweaver speaks at last. My mistress has plans for you, too, pretty girl. She thought to kill you tonight, but now that the godslayer has surfaced, she's changed her mind. I will be with you shortly."

Medophae, who had been about to charge, hesitated. He glanced back at her.

"Ah," Kikirian said. "Has the great Wildmane grown an intellect since we last met? Pausing to consult your threadweaver before you leap into battle? So cowardly. The bards will weep."

Medophae kept an eye on Kikirian, but he asked Mirolah, "What do you sense?"

She concentrated on the gauntlets. Around the shining metal was a dark, crimson aura. "It's...dark. I don't know, Medophae. I've never seen this before."

"She's right, you know," Kikirian said. "These gauntlets are your doom. Best you run away, little god. Leave these mortals to their fate and save yourself."

"They're back," Orem said, tense.

Darklings slunk into the street behind them by twos and threes, emerging from the gaps between the buildings. They formed a horde, blocking escape in that direction. Mirolah's heart beat fast.

"Such choices," Kikirian mocked him. "The great Wildmane will never flee, but you can't protect them all. You lose, little god. Do you get it? You lose."

Mirolah could hear her own breathing. No one moved. Even the darklings breathed, tense, ready to spring.

"An unsolvable stand-off. It's just like a riddle, isn't it, little god?" Kikirian said. "A riddle you just can't solve..." He laughed.

It was the right bait. Medophae tensed to jump at Kikirian. And for Mirolah, everything slowed down again. Her mind leapt from conclusion to conclusion, and she only saw disaster. Medophae couldn't protect them all, but he would try. And, through trying, he would hand the victory to Kikirian. Orem was helpless against the darklings; they'd tear him apart. Stavark had just regained consciousness, and he could barely stand. He might be able to kill one, maybe two, but no more. Then they'd tear him apart.

The bright bridge leapt from her to Stavark, to Orem, and to Medophae. She took hold of the threads.

Medophae leapt.

She yanked the threads. She, Orem, and Stavark flew up into the air, but Medophae's golden aura flared and batted her efforts away. His threads slipped through her fingers.

A darkling leapt and missed them as they floated out of reach. The darkling landed on the street, hissing and staring balefully upward.

Medophae brought his sword down on Kikirian.

"No," she shouted.

Kikirian threw his left hand in front of the blade. The sword hit the gauntlet and vanished. Medophae lurched forward, his balance lost, and Kikirian slammed the gauntlets into the side of his head. Red light flashed from Kikirian's eyes. Medophae opened his mouth in pain, but no sound came out. The life went from his body, and he slumped to the stones, limp.

"Medophae!" Mirolah and Orem yelled at the same moment.

A hush fell over the street.

Kikirian put the toe of his boot on Medophae's shoulder and pushed. The golden-haired hero flopped onto his back. His eyes moved rapidly underneath closed eyelids. His arms twitched as if he was dreaming. Kikirian smiled wide and turned his gaze up at Mirolah.

She couldn't breathe. In an instant, it was over. One blow. She couldn't believe it.

"I told you I would be with you in a moment," Kikirian said. "I always keep my promises."

She realized she was crying. "Let him go!"

The monster's laugh thundered in the night. "Do you know how many have paid their lives for a chance to bring Wildmane to his knees?" He shook his head. "If you would like to try your hand at freeing him..." Kikirian stepped back and gestured with a flourish. "Come down." His sharp teeth gleamed.

She tried to grab hold of Medophae's threads again, but again, the protective golden fire around him flared and batted her away.

"Confused?" Kikirian asked. "Are you wondering why he didn't jump into the sky with your other friends? Oh, didn't the godslayer tell you? The dullard Oedandus throws off almost any spell. It's why the godslayer has defeated so many threadweavers. They have a disastrous time trying to strike him. Only the most powerful spells can even singe him."

"What did you do?" she murmured.

"Perhaps my mistress will reveal that to you in time." His smile faded. "Now, novice, you are the one who must make the choices."

"Go, Mirolah," Orem interrupted. "Fly us away."

"I can't just leave him!"

Kikirian laughed.

"He'll survive," Orem said. "He gave us a chance to get away. We have to take it."

"You don't know he'll survive," she said. "We don't know what they did—"

"She's right," Kikirian said. "I'll gut him the first chance I get."

"He's baiting you," Orem urged. "You're more important. More important even than Medophae, and this monster knows it. Don't listen to him."

"Descend from your perch, and I will not hurt your friends," Kikirian said. "My mistress doesn't want them. She just wants you and the little god. But if you make this difficult, your friends will die screaming."

"Mirolah, don't," Orem said. "He lies. That's what Dervon's creatures do."

Kikirian's laughter filled the street again. His voice became warm, intimate. "You know I'm not lying, don't you, novice? You feel it in your belly."

She swallowed. "You promise not to hurt them?" she asked.

"No!" Orem grabbed her arm. "Mirolah, don't."

"I don't want them," Kikirian said.

Tears blurred her vision. "Orem, there is so much power in his aura. Look at what he did to Medophae!"

"Listen to me," he spoke calmly. "There is only one thing he wants: you on the ground. If you give it to him, then you have nothing to bargain with—"

Kikirian's eyes flashed red. Orem clutched his head, and every muscle in his body tensed as if he were in the grip of a huge hand. His shout stretched into a strangled cry of pain.

"No," she screamed. "Let him go!"

"Test me, and they suffer, novice," Kikirian said.

"I'll come down. Please!" She concentrated and pulled the threads. The three of them floated to the ground. Orem writhed. His boots scrabbled on the cobblestones; his hands pushed on either side of his head as if it was about to explode.

As soon as her toes touched the street, she said, "Now let him go!"

Kikirian smiled. "Of course."

Orem sucked in a sharp breath and went limp. His eyes were open, but he looked at nothing. His arms and legs twitched.

She fell to her knees at his side, touched his face, but he didn't respond. Stavark joined her, looking exhausted, but his legs were not shaking anymore.

She turned to Kikirian. "What did you do?"

"I kept my promise," Kikirian said. "Now keep yours. My mistress waits, and the darklings need to feed."

His casual statement swiped her heart from her body. Slowly, she turned, rising, feeling hollow.

"You promised..." she said in a tiny voice.

"Dramaths always keep their word," Kikirian said. "I promised I would not hurt your friends unless you didn't come down. I'm not. But the darklings, well, they've had a hard night. They're hungry." Kikirian's thin lips pulled back, revealing his many teeth. The pack of darklings moving closer. Stavark drew his sword and stood over Orem's twitching body.

She reached out for the threads, but Kikirian flicked her head with his huge finger like he was flicking a fly. She screamed and slid across the stones.

With a groan, she raised herself up on one hand. Blood trickled down the side of her cheek. Her vision was blurry, and Kikirian loomed over her. Behind him, a silver flash erupted against a sea of dark shapes.

"No," she cried.

Kikirian picked her up by the neck. She tore at his hand and kicked at him, but it was like kicking stone. She thrust her head to the left to capture the tiniest gasp. Kikirian's blurry face wobbled in her vision.

"Poor novice. You think me cruel, but I am not half so cruel as your companions. They threw you into the sea. But they didn't tell you that the sea is full of monsters."

Her struggles weakened as her arms lost their strength. The moonlight faded to black.

40

ZILOK MORTH

"SEF."

"Yes, my master."

"The Red Weaver orchestrated that beautifully. That is twice she has surprised me. She has put the Wildmane into a prison of the mind. Terribly clever."

"Yes, my master."

"Such talent. But no foresight. She is a fine pawn. She need not understand the whole board."

"Yes, my master."

"I have an intuition, Sef, about this 'Reader' Orem. I want to keep him."

"As you say, my master."

"I wonder if he will wake before the quicksilver dies."

"I do not know, my master."

"I do not miss the quicksilvers. They are a stubborn race, ungrateful and difficult to tame. I'm rather glad they are nearly extinct."

"Yes, my master."

"See how stubbornly he fights? There is no chance that he can save the human, but he will continue to fight until he dies, and then 'Reader' Orem will die and what will it have served him?"

"Yes, my master."

"Ah! See there. They have caught him. He has fallen. Feast well, dear darklings. And feast quickly, for I have made my decision. We shall save this 'Reader' Orem. I believe he may serve us. Come, Sef. Let us shake the leashes of these darklings and send them back to their mistress. Greedy children of Dervon, away with you! Away from my prize."

"As you say, my master."

"Yes, Sef. As I say."

41

MEDOPHAE

MEDOPHAE OPENED HIS EYES. The waves crashed gently, smoothing the red sand and gurgling around his toes. He'd tossed his boots aside; they lay a short distance up the beach. The day was warm and wonderful. The red beach stretched out to his left, where the hillocks rose, swathed in the long, green seagrass of Calsinac and to the right as far as the eye could see. White clouds billowed on the horizon, and he smelled the vibrant sea—salt and wind and water.

He looked behind himself. The beach rose slowly at first, then sharply up to the seagrass, creating a sand and grass cliff as high as Medophae was tall. He loved to vault over those little cliffs. Beyond was his city, Calsinac. He'd built the first structure with his own hands, a small two-bedroom cottage for himself and Bands. His followers had soon arrived and built their own, and that was how Calsinac started. Bands teased him about that first dilapidated little house. Medophae was a fine swordsman, but he was no builder.

He shook his head. But that was a long time ago, wasn't it?

They lived in a palace now. How many years had it been? A decade? Sometimes he had a hard time keeping track of the years. There were so many changes. Never had a city grown as fast as Calsinac. Never had so many brilliant craftsmen and builders gathered so quickly in one place.

He glanced back at his boots. One stood straight and tall, the stiffened leather holding its shape even though it was almost as tall as Medophae's knee. The other had given at the ankle and flopped over. He felt like he was forgetting something. It wasn't odd that he should be at the beach. He came here often to think about tough problems, but...

But he didn't remember how he got here. The last thing he remembered was the discussion he'd had with Corelius, his chief steward, about the immigrants from Wayland.

"Medin?"

He turned. Bands strode down the beach. Her blond hair swished in the light breeze, practically translucent in the sunlight. She wore a loose shift that rippled across her strong body, and he paused a moment to appreciate every curve and every flash of golden skin. He remembered when she had bought the fabric. It came from a kingdom beyond the lands of the Sunriders to the south, or so the merchant had said. Silk, he called it. She had paid handsomely for it, which amused Medophae. She could have flown across all of the dangerous lands of the Sunriders and purchased the bolts of cloth for a reasonable price. Instead, she'd paid Saraphazia's own treasure for it, and cherished it with the same fervor.

"I think my brains are addled," he said.

"Are you just now coming to that conclusion?" The sand shifted under each step she took, giving a pleasant sway to her hips that distracted him.

"I don't know how I got here, and..." He thought about when he had looked both ways up the coast. He hadn't seen Bands anywhere. "And I thought I was alone on the beach," he finished.

She put her arms around his neck. "You are. I'm just a trick of the light."

"Oh?" He squeezed her. "And where are you, then?"

"I'm back at the palace, tending to affairs of state."

"Good. One of us should."

She turned in his embrace, snuggling her back against his chest and wrapping his arms around her like a shawl. They looked out over the ocean. The sun dropped a little more, beginning to light the thin clouds with yellows and oranges.

"At times like this, I rather like being king," he said.

"Tell me that again when we reach the palace and its burdens."

"I'm actually beginning to enjoy them."

"You're a liar," she said.

"I thought that's what *makes* a good king."

"You're a good king because you care. Because you try so hard."

"That sounds like one of those compliments that isn't a compliment."

She bumped him with her hip. "You make mistakes all the time. But you recover well. And you choose good advisors, and you listen to them."

Again, he glanced at his boots. He still could not remember taking them off. It bothered him.

"Bands, did I forget to do something?"

"What do you mean?"

"I feel as if I've forgotten something. I just had the strangest sensation a minute ago, right before you came. I couldn't remember how I came here. I don't remember removing my boots. I actually couldn't remember *when* I was. I thought for a second that this was ten years ago, when we first built our little house."

"You came to the beach with me."

"I don't remember it."

She turned in his embrace, looking up at him, her expression concerned. She reached up and put a hand on his cheek. Her fingers were gentle and cool. She could wield a double-bladed war axe with one of those hands, but they were always as soft as a baby's cheek. But then, he supposed a shapeshifter could make her hands feel like whatever she wanted. "Maybe you should rest, then," she said.

"I'm not tired."

"Maybe you need more rest than you think."

"I feel fine. I just don't remember how I got to the beach."

"Do you want to walk back? We can retrace our steps. Maybe it will help you remember."

He let out slow breath. "No. It doesn't matter. It simply seems as if..." he paused. "...as if I haven't only forgotten how I came here, but that I've forgotten something important."

Her hand slipped into his. "You'll think of it."

"How do you know?"

"Because you always remember the important things, my love. You always do."

42

MIROLAH

WHEN THE CELL DOOR SLAMMED, Mirolah fell to her knees with a gasp. The stones were cold against her bare legs, and the sleeveless shift she wore was no armor against the cell's chill, but though she felt those things, they were inconsequential compared to the cold gutting she had just suffered. She had heard horror stories about the women who had been violently raped at the hands of the Sunriders, and she wondered if it could have been any worse than having your mind overthrown and your body become a plaything of someone else's will.

No one had escorted her to this dark cell. She had walked here on her own, one torturous step at a time as a husky female voice smothered her will.

Mirolah had fought every step of the way. She'd screamed in the recesses of her mind, but nothing had worked. Her arms felt like they had been half-pulled from their sockets from her struggles. Her knees hurt as though they had been bent backward. Every strand of muscle in her forearms felt like jelly, a testament to her resistance.

She had control of her body now, and she hugged her knees to her chest and sobbed. She felt like a discarded sock used by a giant's foot, soiled and stretched and ripped. She could taste the woman in her mouth like blood. She could smell the woman in her hair. And the terrifying specter loomed over her: the woman could return at any moment and dominate her again, because what could Mirolah do to stop her?

She leaned over and vomited, then crawled to the other side of the cell and laid her head against the cold stones. Her stomach heaved again and she tried to stop it, but she couldn't.

She vomited on the floor again, then scooted to another corner, away from both stinking messes, pressing herself against the wall and trying to think of something else, anything else. She began to cry again.

"Don't cry... Don't cry..."

She sucked in a quick breath and looked around. But there was no one else in the cell.

"I cannot bear it, all the crying... All the crying. All the dying." The male voice dropped so low she could not hear it.

Her teeth began chattering. Had the woman's domination driven her insane? "Please, no..." she said.

"I shall not hurt you, rest assured. If that's your prayer, it has been heard."

"Who are you?" she whispered.

"Ahhh...." The voice was so soft she had to strain to hear it. "I'm a lovely song and hideous screech. I killed the land I lay beneath. The Red Weaver looks for me, and she will cage this escapee. In the cracks she grew, and now is large. Just a mote she was, but now in charge."

"Shut up," she screamed. "I don't want to hear you! You're not real!" Her voice dropped to a whisper. "You're not real..."

"Ahhh..." The voice was closer now, softer. "I wish I was a cruel bluff. A child's dream, a lack of stuff. But I'm the roach beneath it all. I am the sad land's bitter gall."

She didn't want to use her threadweaver sight. It would bring back the taste of the red woman, and that would make her vomit all over again. But if this wasn't insanity—if there really was an invisible person here in the cell—the threads would tell the tale. She closed her eyes, balled her hands into fists and clenched her teeth. She reached out, seeking the bright bridge. It was hard, like it was far away. The same thing had happened in Denema's Valley with the darklings, right after she'd been forced to come to that intersection.

But as she held down her bile, she began to feel the power of the GodSpill all around her, the threads of the walls and the floor. She opened her eyes.

The owner of the voice knelt beside her, pushing imaginary tendrils of hair away from her face. She gasped and lurched away. He was a thin man with a short beard and a long nose. He wore a friendly, crazy smile. His clothes looked as if they had once been fine, but were now torn and threadbare. Red spiders ate at the fabric of his arms. Red rats gnawed at his trousers, trying to get at him, but none had yet bitten his skin. His hands, where they poked out of the lacy cuffs, were smooth and unblemished, as was his face. Mirolah pressed herself against the cold wall.

"Who are you?" she whispered.

His eyes widened. "This cannot be. How can you see? This ghost, this thread, this twist of me?" He pounced on her. She shrieked and lashed out, but her fists passed through him. He settled one transparent hand over her mouth, but she felt nothing. He wasn't invisible. He was a ghost.

"Don't say my name, our special secret. We both will die if you don't keep it."

"Who are you?"

"Ahhh... A fool. A fool. Destiny's tool. Before the GodSpill warped and died, the six and I went on a ride. I, the dunce all dressed in mail with an imagined tale that was doomed to fail. I aimed my lance right at my foe, with nary a glance for all the woe. And I drank deep from failure's flagon by charging a cliff I thought a dragon."

Mirolah gasped. "You're Harleath Markin!"

"My name. My shame. The very same."

"You're a ghost..." she murmured.

"Would that I were dead instead, a ghostly knife through a

ghostly head. And yet my purpose sadly lingers, so I stay pinned by my own stinger. Here inside my place of doom, I thought I'd coax the 'Spill to bloom. But others also heard the call, the strongest weavers of them all. I should have known, by all that's right, that they would flock to this one site."

"We're inside Daylan's Fountain?" she asked, incredulous. She hadn't realized that the fountain had dungeons inside it.

So she had finally arrived in the place Orem had been trying to take her. As a prisoner. Medophae's words returned to her now, the story about his friend, so secure in his own power and defeated by surprise. It was as though he had been speaking prophecy.

She needed more time. She could move little pots and giant stones; she'd even learned to transform them, but she didn't know how to fight a threadweaver who could overthrow her will.

She thought of Orem, almost certainly dead now, and she fought down her despair. Orem had embarked on an impossible quest: to return the GodSpill to the lands. He'd had no ability. He'd had no clue where to start; he just started, and piece by piece, he found what he needed. And when he found her, he had held her hand, step by step, and led her up to the edge of the impossible. And, with his help, she had stepped beyond.

Well, she didn't have his help now, but she was just going to have to do it anyway.

She set her jaw and turned to the ghost. "Tell me everything about the Red Weaver."

43

MIROLAH

"WAKE UP, NOVICE," Kikirian said.

Mirolah jolted awake, and for a moment, she forgot she was in a cell. The cold reality returned in a rush as she looked at the red-tinged stone walls, the smooth red flagstones. She had tried to use threadweaving to bend the bars, but they resisted her attempts. After five minutes of trying, the female voice returned inside her head, asking her if she'd like to spend the next several hours licking the floor of her cell instead of making feeble attempts to escape.

Mirolah had immediately stopped her escape attempt, and instead talked with Harleath Markin until she finally slept, so exhausted that even the cold floor seemed soft and warm.

"It's time to meet your new master," Kikirian said, leaning down so he could see through the doorway. During their journey here, he'd called himself a dramath, which was apparently also a child of Dervon, like the darklings, but with greater intelligence and other special abilities not possessed by their skinny cousins.

She blinked her eyes and glared up at him.

"Defiance," he said. "Good. Keep that up and this will be an entertaining day." He opened the barred door, the apex of which only came up to his chest when he stood up again. "Come with me or be brought." The huge dramath began walking up the hall. Reluctantly, she stood up and followed quickly. The idea of being controlled again sent a spike of fear into her heart.

The perfectly cut stone walls of the hallway had a red tinge to them, just like the cell. Everything seemed to have it.

She and Kikirian ascended a long spiral staircase. Mirolah looked back the way they had come, searching for another exit. But about twenty paces past her cell door, the hallway became a shifting swirl of smoky red. At first, she wondered if there was some kind of furnace or fire back there, but when she looked at it with her threadweaver sight, she realized with astonishment that this entire hallway, and her cell, was some kind of GodSpill construct. The red haze was where it...ended, as if the Red Weaver had just stopped working on it there. She reached out tentatively with her threadweaver sight and touched the threads of the walls, the stairway, the doors, even the smoky nothingness at the end of the hall.

Every single bit of it was held together by red-tinged GodSpill.

The book Mirolah had read in Denema's Valley said that everything had threads, whether it was alive, had once been alive, or had never been alive. And those threads were made of tinier ones which were made of tinier threads still, and each had their own color and texture and density. In Mirolah's experience since that day, she'd seen all the colors of the rainbow and a hundred varying shades of each in the threads of life around her. But everything in this palace was comprised of the same red threads. Different shades, different sizes, but all the same color.

The complexity of the spell overwhelmed her. She smacked a hand against the wall, slid her fingers down and felt the cold rail of the staircase. How did a threadweaver create something like this out of nothing and maintain such solidity? Is that why it was all one color? Because it was a pure construct and would never have existed in the real world?

"Lost your wits, novice?" Kikirian's voice startled her.

She turned, trying to erase the wonder from her face, but

Kikirian saw. A cruel smile curved his lips.

"Impressive, isn't it? The Red Weaver has power you cannot understand, that you cannot even imagine. During the height of her greatness, it was said she was more powerful and more cunning even than the legendary Zilok Morth. Do you know who Zilok Morth is?"

"Everyone knows who Zilok Morth is," she said.

Kikirian looked back at the smoky red haze. "It's easy for young threadweavers to believe themselves great," he said softly. "They taste power, see how far above the mortal flock they fly, and they think they know everything. They used to have a saying, back in the Age of Ascendance, back when there were a hundred conclaves of talented threadweavers. They would congregate and bicker about who was the most powerful. Whenever an original or exceptionally powerful spell was achieved, that threadweaver was said to have 'reached a peak.' They would log it down in one of their worthless tomes, and that threadweaver would be famous for a time. Every threadweaver from the Age of Ascendance wanted so badly to be the next Daylan Morth." The black-eyed giant sneered. "They were fools, all of them. They didn't have any idea what a real threadweaver was. Tell me, novice, have you ever heard the tale of The Learned Dog?"

"No," Mirolah said.

"There once was a conclave of powerful threadweavers called The Circle of Learned Men, who congregated in the city of Giryath. Their most powerful member, after reaching several "peaks" in a row, went in search of the legendary threadweaver Zilok Morth. This Learned Man from Giryath decided to prove his mettle by cleansing Amarion of the evil spirit."

Kikirian smiled down at her.

"So they fought?" she said.

"Zilok Morth paid a visit to the city of Giryath a day later and walked into a meeting of the Council of Learned Men. Morth had transformed their emissary, their 'man of many peaks', into a hairless dog with its back legs attached upside down and its brain growing outside of its skull. The spirit tossed the pitiful creature onto the rosewood table and said to them: 'A true threadweaver does not reach a peak. A true threadweaver is the mountain.' Then he killed them all, everyone in the city of Giryath. He killed the servants within the threadweavers' manor. He killed the tradesmen—every tea vender and tobacconist, every baker and builder, every clothier and carpet weaver—who provided services to the manor. Then he killed the employees who worked for every tea vender and tobacconist, every baker and builder, every clothier and carpet weaver. Then he burned every house, melted every stone tower and wall. He left the Learned Dog alive, still with the power of human speech, to tell the tale. But as to the rest, not a stone or bone was left to mark the proud city of Giryath. Only threadweavers could still see it. To one with the 'sight,' it glows like the sun and stands as a warning to all others who might seek fame by challenging the threadweaver Zilok Morth."

Kikirian paused, watching her reaction. She said nothing.

"So consider this, novice, if you think you are a Learned Woman enough to challenge the Red Weaver, who stood as high as Zilok Morth in the Age of Ascendance. What kind of dog would you look like?" He turned, laughing, and continued up the steps.

44

MIROLAH

AT THE TOP OF THE STEPS, Kikirian opened steel-banded double doors as thick as Mirolah's waist and as heavy as a house. Like everything else, they had a reddish glow. The giant dramath strode through the tall archway without having to stoop, and Mirolah followed, feeling as small as a mouse.

When she had walked into the dilapidated library at Denema's Valley, she hadn't been able to imagine a larger indoor space, but it was nothing compared to the Red Weaver's throne room. The walls rose so high that they could have built the Rith tower inside with room to spare. A great battle scene had been painted across the ceiling. Horses reared, knights lowered lances, footmen charged across the muddy ground and speared each other, the victorious with determined grimaces, the victims with open mouths of anguish. In the foreground of the grand painting, impassioned captains pointed and shouted orders. They were so lifelike that Mirolah could almost hear the screams of the dying.

The floor was made of one impossible piece of polished rose marble, connecting with a wide staircase that led to an empty throne. Mirolah touched it all with her threadweaver sight and found it the same as the walls of the prison. Every bit of it was fabricated by the Red Weaver's imagination and willpower.

Along the wall, tall windows stretched all the way to the ceiling, side by side at ten foot intervals, and all of the curtains were drawn. She found this curious until she used her sight to look beyond the curtains. There was nothing there. She longed to look at the outside of Daylan's Fountain, and she felt a cold creep up her spine because she couldn't imagine it being large enough to house this grand castle.

"Welcome, Mirolah," the Red Weaver said. Mirolah turned to see a voluptuous woman sitting on the throne above her. Crimson hair spilled over her shoulders, and a replete red satin gown flowed down her body, gathering in folds around her feet. She fingered a silver necklace and regarded Mirolah distantly. "I am Ethiel. Some call me the Red Weaver."

Bile rose in Mirolah's throat, and she swallowed it down. That husky voice. That was the voice that had pushed her out of her own head, that had pulled her arms and legs from her control. That was the voice that had used her ruthlessly.

"You're very young," Ethiel said conversationally. "Not surprising. He picks them young, you know."

Mirolah looked at Ethiel with her threadweaver sight. Instead of a woman, there was a thick, smoky red cloud curled on the throne with appendages of curling smoke that could have been arms, legs or tentacles. The appendages spilled around the edges of the throne and slithered along the floor.

"Of course, it seems like *we* pick *him*, doesn't it?" Ethiel said. Her countenance was motherly, as though she felt sorry for Mirolah. "It's a cruel hook he baits."

Mirolah swallowed the acid taste down, managing not to throw up.

Ethiel narrowed her eyes and looked at Kikirian, who had fallen back to stand a few paces behind Mirolah. "Is she mute, dramath? Did you bring me a mute?"

"Answer her, novice." Kikirian put one meaty hand on Mirolah's shoulder and nudged her forward. She stumbled and barely caught her balance. The dramath was monstrously strong.

Suddenly, Kikirian grunted in pain. He flew backward as if struck by an invisible hand, hit the marble floor and slid to a stop. With a growl, he rolled to a crouch, unbelievably nimble for his size, and smashed a gauntleted fist into the floor, sending a spiderweb of cracks across the rose marble. He shot a venomous look at Ethiel.

"Don't be rude," she said to him. "Mirolah is our guest." Ethiel stared the dramath down. The dramath stayed crouched for a moment, then he slowly rose to his feet. He bared his teeth as if he longed to take a bite out of her. "One day you will go too far," he said in a low voice.

"Please tell me this is that day, Kikirian." She stood up from her throne, fingers clenching the edges of the ornate armrests. "Tell me this is the day when your threats become action."

His fists clenched so tight that his metal gauntlets squeaked.

Ethiel's mouth opened in anticipation, and her green eyes glistened.

Kikirian forced a brittle smile onto his face and unclenched his fists. He got to his feet and bowed. "I serve you, mistress. As always."

"Go back to your kennel, dramath. I will shake your leash when you're needed."

"As my lady wishes," Kikirian said through his teeth, and he left. The big doors *thoomed* as they closed behind him.

"I apologize, Mirolah," Ethiel said. "Dramaths require tight control. Dervon only respected strength, and they *are* his children, after all. It's important to remind Kikirian not to overstep his bounds. Come, sit with me." She waved her hand. The floor beside her bubbled, faded to a smoky red mist, and swirled upward. Another throne solidified from the mist, complete with comfortable-looking cushions. "Let us talk."

Mirolah took the steps one at a time, alternating glances between the empty throne and its creator.

"I want to know all about you," Ethiel said as Mirolah sat down. "We are alike, you and I. Tell me where you were born, what brought you to me, and everything in between."

"I don't even know where I am," Mirolah said.

"You are inside Daylan's Fountain." She gave Mirolah an encouraging smile. "Do you know what the Fountain is, dear?"

"It's the nexus of all GodSpill in Amarion, built by Daylan Morth and capped by Harleath Markin."

Ethiel narrowed her eyes. "Very good," she said, impressed. "You have been studying. Perhaps I underestimated you. I thought you a brainless apprentice to a scholar, not a true threadweaver. But that is very good. How did you know about Harleath Markin? Those who even know his name only know that he rode north and somehow stripped GodSpill from all the lands."

"I found his journal," Mirolah said. "In Denema's Valley."

"And resourceful," Ethiel said. "My interest is piqued. We will be fast friends, you and I."

"So we are actually inside the Fountain?"

"It seemed the perfect place to build my castle. Of course, an entire castle cannot fit within Daylan's Fountain."

"I...wondered about that."

"Have you ever heard of the threadweaver Difinius?"

"I... No."

"He is what we call a threadweaver's threadweaver. Not well-known, except by others of his specialty. Difinius was a surprise, to say the least. For decades, he did nothing of interest. Then one day he bent space and folded it over and over, like a swordmaker folds the metal of a blade. He discovered that between each fold in the threads, he could create a gap, and these gaps can be stretched, creating room where before there was none. And with that room, you can make..." Ethiel raised her hands, indicating the throne room.

"Whatever you want," Mirolah finished for her.

"There are limits, but you can turn the inside of a walnut into a room the size of a house." Her green eyes narrowed. "Do you understand?"

"I think so."

Ethiel narrowed her eyes. "Are you just nodding along, Mirolah? Or have you actually seen the threads?"

That was interesting. The way she phrased her question implied that not all threadweavers could see the threads. How could a threadweaver even be a threadweaver if they didn't?

"No?" Ethiel concluded, taking Mirolah's silence as confusion about the question. Mirolah saw no reason to correct her. "Well, I'll teach you."

"Your entire castle is inside the Fountain," Mirolah said. If Ethiel let her guard down, perhaps she could learn more by probing cautiously.

"That's what I said, yes." Ethiel watched Mirolah like she was an apple that might have gone bad.

"What do you want from me?" Mirolah asked.

"I sent my darklings to find Medophae, but they failed me. During my search, I accidentally stumbled across you in Rith. When you escaped my darkling—which impressed me, dear, I'll admit—I sent more darklings to find you. And what do you know, when I finally tracked you down, who should I find but...Medophae." She cocked her head. "That seems a bit of a coincidence, don't you think?"

She seemed to expect Mirolah to say something, but when she didn't, Ethiel continued. "Do you know what that tells me?"

"No."

"That you're important, dear, because Medophae is constantly at the center of important events. He is drawn to the site of greatest conflict and greatest change. He can't help himself."

"Why?" Mirolah asked.

Ethiel raised an eyebrow. "So you *do* have curiosity. I was beginning to wonder. It is because of his god's blood, dear."

"I don't understand."

"Do you know what the gods are?" Ethiel asked.

"I...well they're the gods."

Ethiel smiled indulgently, like she would to a puppy. "That's the peasant's answer, dear. 'It is because it is.' Do better."

"They're...they created the world."

"Yes. They are unfathomable forces for creation. Together, they formed the horizon, the sky and the sun. Natra pulled trees from stone. She pulled stone from nothing. She formed lifeforms from mud, air, and a spark of fire. She kindled self-awareness in the sentients before there was any. Unfathomable for a mortal. Impossible to comprehend. Except not for us, right? We understand. That's why we call it GodSpill, because it is the essence of creation, and we can harness it. Who else but the gods can make something from nothing? Who else can reshape the physical world?"

"Threadweavers."

"We understand the gods because we do what they do, only smaller. This world is a tapestry made by them. They can affect the entire fabric, we must assume, but we can shift the threads. Everything we are, everything that has happened since before the beginning of human history, everything that has been *created* in this world, is because of the gods. And the gods are drawn to every moment of great creation and great destruction. The creation of this world is tied with their very essence. My supposition is this: humans are a sentient cluster of organs, blood and muscle, so the gods are sentient clusters of GodSpill. They are an extension of what made the world. They are enormous parts of this unfathomably large tapestry, irrevocably connected to it, and when something rips it or bunches it or changes large swaths of it, they must go there and witness. Take Tarithalius. He was constantly attending anything interesting that caught his attention. That is why Medophae was always at pivotal moments in history. He can feel those changes in his body because Oedandus can feel them. And that is why, when he arrives at those moments of change, they inevitably become larger. History literally forms in his wake." She paused. "Do you understand, dear?"

"Yes."

"So you can appreciate my curiosity about you. I search all of Amarion for him, and I find him with you.... And I ask myself. Is history about to be made?"

"I wasn't trying to make history," she said. "I was just trying to learn threadweaving." She could hear Orem's words in her mind: *If we succeed, we will choose a better course for humanity.*

"And I thought we were going to be friends." Ethiel asked. "Lies twist the faces of the young. I see through you as if you had no skin. Did Medophae tell you not to reveal the nature of your quest?" She stared at the closed curtains of one of the great windows.

"Where is Medophae?" Mirolah asked.

"Ah," she said. "Now we come to your real question, the one you've been dying to ask since you walked through my door."

"I want to see him."

"Of course you do. All young women want to see him. His hooks are already deep within you. Has he had you yet?"

"Had me—? No!" Mirolah said.

"You need not lie to me. I know how it feels. If I let you see him, you'd throw yourself at his feet, his happy wanton."

"That's not what I'm saying—"

"Medophae is safe."

"What about Orem and Stavark?"

"I presume you mean the human and the quicksilver. They are dead."

It was like a punch to the gut. Mirolah leaned over, wanting to vomit again.

Oh, gods... Orem...

She tried to fight the tears. The last thing she wanted was to be weak in front of this woman, but they came anyway. "Why...?" She pushed the words out of her constricted throat. "What were they to you? Why kill them?"

"The darklings were hungry, dear."

Black dots blossomed at the edge of Mirolah's vision. The room swam. "You're a murderer," she whispered.

"The darklings did the work, dear, not I."

"You let them."

"So did you."

"They were my friends!"

"If you wanted to save them, you could have. But you chose Medophae, didn't you?"

Mirolah couldn't breathe.

Ethiel's lips curved into a cruel smile. "If I am a murderer, so are you."

"You're insane!"

"Don't be rude, dear."

"I hate you!"

"I suppose you would rather wrap your legs and your loyalty around our *noble* Medophae."

Mirolah turned away, roughly wiping her tears away. She thought of Orem. Of sailing the Inland Ocean. Of swimming in its waters. Of leafing through boring texts under his vigilant gaze. Her tutor, her friend, dead....

"You think I'm a monster," Ethiel said softly.

"What else could you be, killing that noble boy and that wonderful man?"

"Realistic," she said. "You want to see a real monster? Read a history about the battle of Deitrus Shelf. Read about Badon and his freemen. Medophae waded through rivers of blood. He has killed more innocents than can be counted. Monsters don't wear wicked claws and fangs, dear. They wear manes of gold and smiles that melt a girl's knees. They enthrall their prey with gentle voices and soft caresses and lay them down on the soft ground. And then they steal something we could not know we even possesses until it is gone. Medophae lied to me again and again. Once for each time he lay with me."

"You...and Medophae?"

"Don't be naïve," Ethiel said in a bored voice. "He had his way with me then went on to have his way with someone else. I was just another mortal conquest." She regarded Mirolah thoughtfully. "Tell me. When he took you, did you think you were the only one? It feels as if the land is vibrating only for you, doesn't it? How many times did he take you?"

"He didn't!"

"As you wish, dear. But when you lie to others, you lie to yourself. Once you start believing your own lies, it is much easier to believe his lies. That's what he wants."

"I don't believe *you*," Mirolah said.

Ethiel looked again at that same curtained window as if she hadn't even heard Mirolah. "Did you know we were to be married?" she said softly. Her eyes were distant and unfocused. "I was so happy. Imagine a god descending from the heavens just for you." She turned her gaze on Mirolah. "Of course, he has played

277

that charade many times. Close your heart to him, dear. You can have anything you want, but you cannot have him."

"I want to see him."

"No," Ethiel said like a mother to an unruly child. "For your own safety."

Mirolah stood up from her throne and backed away. She saw the red threads all around.

Mirolah yanked the threads on the throne where she had sat a moment ago. The heavy chair flew toward Ethiel with frightening force. But suddenly, Mirolah's threadweaver grip slipped. The threads were gone. The chair was gone.

Ethiel sighed. "A sumptuous room awaits you, dear. A soft bed, a—"

Mirolah sought the threads within the dark red cloud that was Ethiel's true form, but there were none. She struggled with the smoky substance, trying to push it together, trying to get a handhold, and she found she couldn't. So she pushed it together, forming it into a sphere, something she could grab onto. She would be able to—

She screamed and staggered back. It felt like someone had stabbed a knife in her head. Her concentration shattered.

"Mirolah." Ethiel's voice was stern. "My patience has a limit. I won't tolerate a tantrum. You have talent, but you have no idea what you are doing."

Mirolah felt the smoky red substance follow the path back to her, filling her nostrils, her eyes, her ears, the very pores of her skin, just as it had before. Everywhere it went, Mirolah lost control.

"No," she screamed. "Please, no!"

"You will learn," Ethiel said. "And when you do, I shall not have to do this anymore."

Mirolah fought against the insidious control, but it was no use. The red mist slipped around her willpower and lodged in the pumping of her blood, the tingling of her skin, the rushing of her lungs, the frantic thoughts in her mind.

"No..." she whimpered and fell to her knees. No sooner had she slumped to the marble than her body rose again under Ethiel's command, the hated voice murmuring inside her head. She watched through her own eyes as her legs turned, and her hips swiveled to face the Red Weaver.

"We will talk later," Ethiel said. "When you have had a chance to rest. It is difficult to break Medophae's hold, but I will be diligent. I won't give up on you. I will be kinder with you than Medophae was with me. You will see."

Mirolah wanted to shout, to attack the insane woman-cloud-thing, but her body turned and walked down the hall. She had no choice but to obey.

And yet amidst her dismal failure to fight Ethiel, Mirolah had seen this time. She had learned, watching carefully as that terrible red cloud invaded her.

And next time, perhaps there *would* be a choice.

45

SILASA

"RECONSIDER," Ynisaan said. "This city is dangerous to us. So very dangerous."

Silasa stood in the shadows of the building in the verdant city of Denema's Valley. Like all her kind, she was a master of the dark, and anyone who might be looking would never see her. But Ynisaan was so quiet that Silasa had begun to wonder if she was actually there at all. Not for the first time, Silasa wondered if Ynisaan was a hallucination. Silasa yearned for purpose, and suddenly this enigmatic woman appeared with a quest of dire urgency that involved the only person still alive that Silasa cared about. There was a part of her that still waited to "wake up."

Ynisaan had told Silasa a little about what was going to happen to Medophae, but only a little. She held back most of the details. Sometimes it felt like she did that because she actually didn't know, like she was watching waves roll and crash and couldn't predict when the next wave would hit. But sometimes it seemed as if Ynisaan wanted to keep her uninformed. She was frustratingly cryptic about most of it, but she had said that soon, Zilok Morth was going to try to kill Medophae. At the right moment, and only the right moment, they could act to thwart Zilok's plan. But that was all she said. Informing Silasa that Zilok was actually in Denema's Valley had only come moments ago.

"You should have told me Zilok was here," Silasa said.

"I am telling you now."

Corpses of darklings littered the street where a battle had been. Black blood covered the stones. It was as sure a sign as any that Medophae had been here.

Three blocks down from the battle, a young quicksilver lay on the porch of what had once been an herb shop. If Medophae had killed the darklings, why had he abandoned his companion, wounded and dying?

The quicksilver could not be more than twelve or thirteen. His silver blood leaked slowly from his wounds, taking him closer to death with each moment that passed.

"I can't leave him," Silasa whispered.

"If Zilok catches us here, everything is undone. Amarion will fall. Humans will be wiped from the world."

"He is dying."

"He is one. If we fail in our quest to save Medophae, we lose all. Right now, Medophae is the one who matters."

"Medophae would be the first to say that everyone matters." Bloody handprints dotted the bottom of the door where the quicksilver had tried and failed to gain entry to the herb shop.

Alone, grievously injured, the quicksilver had crawled toward the one door that might help him. She imagined the quicksilver struggling with each breath, hoping to live long enough to draw the next. She imagined his fight with the door, a battle he had lost. She did not know how long he had lain on that porch, but she knew the smell of blood. This battle was at least an hour old.

Ynisaan must have sensed that Silasa had made up her mind, because she stopped talking.

In the light of the thin moon, Silasa strode across the street. She reached the quicksilver and gathered him in her arms. His head lolled, exposing his pale neck. She had not yet fed this night, and the smell of him tantalized her. Her cursed blood hungered.

His eyelids flickered open, and he jolted, feebly trying to get away from her. She held firm.

The quicksilver's gaze was fogged with pain, but he sneered, facing his presumed death with defiance.

"I am here to help you," she whispered.

"Help?" he whispered, low and empty as though he did not care.

"Yes."

He whispered something else, but she couldn't understand it.

She leaned close, clenching her jaw and trying to close her nose to the coppery aroma of his blood. He was young. His blood was rich and heady. Saliva filled her mouth.

"*Keekikssss...*" he hissed, raising his head. His little breaths pounded quick and ragged, and his head fell. He tried again. "*Keekiksisss...*" Then she understood. Iron-heart root. The quicksilvers called it *Keekiksisa*. It could save his life. It could also kill him instantly. Iron heart root sped up healing and thickened the blood in humans. In quicksilvers, it was even stronger.

"I will look."

"H-Hurry..."

She tried the latch. It was locked, so she pushed. The doorjamb splintered and she moved inside. Only a few shafts of moonlight filtered in through the windows, but Silasa saw everything as if it were daytime. Shelves of jars lined the walls, each containing herbs and medicines from an age gone by.

Most were dust, but there were a great many sealed jars that had withstood the centuries since the inhabitants of Denema's Valley had died.

She knew her herbs and remedies. Living in the woods, she had spent one entire decade identifying every plant for miles around her cave. She quickly located the section where the roots were kept. A moment later, she found the iron-heart root. She paused. He would need something else. If she was any judge of injuries, he might die from the pain as the iron-heart hit him. He needed something to dampen the raw potency.

She selected a tiny jar of dried leaves from the top shelf and looked at them closely. She hoped that this quicksilver was as strong as he was determined.

She returned to the porch and knelt beside him. His scent overwhelmed her, and she clenched her teeth so hard that her fangs cut into her lip, and the taste of her own blood filled her mouth.

Breathing through her nose, she uncapped both jars and picked his head up.

She took three of the leaves, thought better of it, and stuffed one back in the jar. She put the other two up to his bloody lips. "Chew," she said.

He shook his head weakly. "No. Keeksss..."

"I know. These first. Keekiksisa after. Quickly now." She put the leaves into his mouth, dipping her hand into the Keekiksisa root and poising it on his lips. He chewed methodically, then swallowed.

"Now this." She pushed the iron-heart root into his mouth.

The leaves would take effect almost as fast as the root. If she dampened his senses too much, he would fall into a sleep, and that would be the end of him.

But he understood. He chewed the root with ferocity. He swallowed half of it and continued to chew, but his jaws suddenly slowed. His eyes drooped.

"No! Stay awake." She shook him. His eyes rolled up into his head, and his mouth hung open. Too late! He had swallowed half the root. Would it be enough?

She waited. The quicksilver's rapid, shallow breathing slowed. Finally, it stopped, and he lay still. Please...

Nothing.

She lowered her eyes. Damn it...

His body convulsed, and her eyes snapped open. Yes! He convulsed again, and his hands clawed at the stones of the porch. The remaining half of the root shot from his mouth in a cough. He drew several quick breaths and moaned. She held him firmly as he thrashed, keeping his head from smacking into the stones. His teeth clacked together twice, then stayed shut. His moan became a hum between closed lips. His eyes flew open, and he looked about wildly.

After a moment, he calmed and his silver gaze came to rest on her. His breathing, still fast, was deeper.

He coughed, and blood flecked his lips. "More," he said.

She fed him another root. He chewed vigorously and swallowed. Again, the jolt rocked his body, but this time he was awake. He had more strength, and he was ready for it. He controlled the convulsion himself this time, then lay quiet, his silver eyes fierce and alive. His bleeding seemed to have stopped completely. The tales of Keekiksisa root and quicksilvers were not exaggerated.

They sat that way for almost an hour. The quicksilver healing, meditating upon the ravaged parts of his body, the vampire waiting in torture, fighting her own compulsion to tear into his neck and drain his blood.

Finally, the quicksilver spoke. "Orem?"

She recognized the name. Medophae's friend. The one who started the quest. "You were the only one. The rest are darklings. All dead."

He closed his eyes.

"I'm sorry..." she said.

"Yes," he returned. He looked up at her, and that same defiance filled his gaze "You healed me."

"Yes."

"To feed on me," he said simply, looking at her white eyes.

She was taken aback. He had recognized what she was, and this was his conclusion. He thought she had only healed him to have a healthy victim to drain.

"No, young one," she said softly. "I have not come to feed on you."

"You are one of the hollowskins. A *vyrksikka*."

"Yes."

"No breath. No heat."

"Yes."

"You feed on the living." His plain courage in the face of death humbled her.

"I am not here for that," she said.

His silver eyes shone bright. "Then, thank you for...the root."

"You are welcome. I wish I could help you more, but I cannot stay. I came here looking for someone. I must continue looking."

"You chase the *Rabasyvihrk*."

It was the quicksilver's word for Medophae. "I... Yes."

"Then you are close. He was taken by a dramath. Kikirian. I do not know where they went."

"I do."

The quicksilver looked away and pain crossed his face. "Then you must chase them. Quickly."

"Soon. Will you eat raw meat?"

The quicksilver looked at her sharply, then said, "Yes."

"Then I will hunt for us both." She stood up. His hand flashed out and caught hers. His grip was deft and light, but there was strength there. That was encouraging. With food, she gave him decent odds of surviving.

He said, "I am Stavark. My life is mine because you have lived, I pledge my life to—"

She twisted her wrist out of his grip and shook her head. "I know that pledge, my friend. Do not. It is forbidden."

"You know the ways of the syvhirk?" The quicksilver seemed surprised.

"I am well-read for a dead woman. I know you cannot make that pledge to a *vyrksikka*." She smiled. "But I thank you for the sentiment."

Her pointed nails dug into her palms as the scent of his blood, the feel of his warmth, thrummed through her.

"Thank you," he said.

"You're welcome."

She leapt away, charging between the buildings and plunging into the forest. Her ravening blood keened in her mind, burning her veins. It was time to hunt.

46

MIROLAH

MIROLAH PULLED THE PRISON DOOR shut behind her. It clicked and locked, and then her body returned to her control. The revulsion wriggled through her like worms in her veins. She fought the sweeping horror that wanted to buckle her knees and send her sobbing to the flagstones again. Instead, she kept her head. She bit her lip until it bled and concentrated, seeking the essence of Ethiel's spell. What had allowed her access to every fiber of Mirolah's being? What allowed her to shove Mirolah's resistance aside and take control?

It was deeper into the threads than Mirolah had gone. Ethiel saturated Mirolah's threads with her own essence, her own reserve of GodSpill. She had talked of gods being sentient GodSpill.

Question: Why would Ethiel think that?

Answer: Because Ethiel had made GodSpill "sentient" with her own desires. She could make it work for her with her purpose instilled into it. That was what it was. Ethiel's spell wasn't mind control. It wasn't just in Mirolah's head, as she had thought. Mirolah felt Ethiel's filthy residue throughout her entire body. Red and red and more red, filling the most secret parts of herself.

She fell to her knees, chasing the thought, digging deep within herself, within those fibers, smaller even than the threads that Korleithan Ket wrote about. And there it was. The red haze was slowly leaving her, and she used her threadweaver sight to dive deeper. She dove into the fibers inside the fibers that made up the threads that she had originally seen.

Those tiniest fibers of herself pushed Ethiel's influence away naturally, and her own vibrant colors returned. They were doing it of their own volition, because that's what they naturally were. Ethiel was an invading presence, and they were ejecting her. She reached within the fibers and helped. She turned her focus on it and accelerated the process.

Mirolah gasped.

It felt...wonderful! She had not realized until that moment just how much of Ethiel had remained within her, but as she chased every little smear of the Red Weaver out of her body, she felt purged.

Her eyes snapped open. Energy coursed through her. The threads of the fabricated walls and floor were starkly evident. Her threadweaver sight was clearer than it had ever been. In the corner of the cell, the ghost of Harleath Markin stood watching her. The red rats continued to gnaw at his pants. The red spiders raced across his shirt, but Mirolah could see something about them that she had missed before. Barely visible tendrils reached from the floor and walls and connected to the vermin. In essence, they were nothing more than an extension of the castle.

"Your beauty, young 'weaver, strikes at my heart. You have potential for the weaving art."

"I went to see Ethiel and she...showed me something," Mirolah said.

"Oho! You have gone where I cannot. I am the ink she'd like to blot."

"That makes two of us. She wants me to join her little crusade, be her 'friend.' When she realizes there's no way I'm going to do that, I think my days are numbered. We have to find a way to fight her."

"Ah! Would that I could. I know that I should. I have tried and been denied. Her hand, her heavy hand, it is more than I can bear. The Lady Red, she wants me dead, I swear, I swear, I swear..."

"Have you always talked in rhymes, Harleath?"

"It's a new development, this kink. It comes from having time to think. Words are colors, hard to catch. I do my best to make them match."

"Never mind. We need to find a way out of here."

"What will you do, to thwart your fate? A key for the door? A key for the gate?"

"I don't know," she said. "But I'd rather die than stay here waiting for Ethiel to steal my body again. Why haven't you left?"

"I was too slow when she came. A slow ghost with a slower brain. And when she came, it was too late. To be trapped here became my fate." He looked around in worry. "Now the best I do is flee. A spell keeps her from finding me. See, I have tricks and secret lore, but every day she guesses more." He looked down at his clothes. "But soon I'll burn under her gaze, and that will end my ghostly ways."

"Show me how you do it. How you hide. Let me learn."

"Your best course, you know, is pleasing her. She's a pot that you'd best not stir. If you begin to stoke your power, you'll be dead within the hour."

She pressed her lips into a firm line. "You're scared. Fine. If you've given up, I can't stop you. But show me what you know first."

He turned and stared disconsolately at the wall.

"Harleath," she said to him. He didn't respond.

She focused on the ghost's form and reached inside. His threads were a light gray, thin, almost translucent, and spaced much farther apart than the threads of something alive. His worn and gnawed clothes were comprised of this same kind of thread, though thickened and toughened until they were a dark gray. His clothing was his protection spell, something that thwarted the spiders and the rats from reaching him, but it was dwindling even as she studied it. The spiders and rats were hunting spells, swelling with the vigor to find, find, find!

Mirolah guessed that once the vermin chewed through the "clothing" to Harleath's "flesh," it meant Harleath's spell had failed, and Ethiel would know where he was. Then he'd have to fight her face-to-face.

Just as she had chased Ethiel's retreating presence out of her own body, so Mirolah focused on chasing it out of the threads that connected the wall to the rats and spiders. This was far more difficult. With her own body, Ethiel had wanted to leave, and her body had wanted to eject her, so it was easy to finish the process. But Ethiel's dogged intent did not want to leave this spell. It was eager and powerful.

Sweat beaded on Mirolah's forehead as she forced her own colors into the threads of spiders and rats. This gave her more control over them, and she pulled them off Harleath. The threads didn't want to go. They whipped about like angry snakes, trying to latch onto him again, but she guided them into herself. They latched on, seeking, rushing into her body, looking for Harleath Markin.

Once the spiders and rats were connected to her, it got easier. Here, in her own body, she was stronger. Pushing her intentions into the threads happened faster, and the rats and spiders slowly turned from dusky red to a rainbow of Mirolah's own colors. They began to listen to her. They began to obey her.

Her body quivered with the effort, and sweat trickled down her forehead, the nape of her neck, down between her shoulder blades.

She suspected that if she destroyed the spell, Ethiel might know it, so she did something else instead. With her own colors, she inserted a new aspect to the standing order to search for Harleath throughout the castle.

Harleath Markin is in the floor, she told the threads, cementing that as a part of their objective. *Search only the floor.*

And their purpose became hers. They would search through every stone of the floor, over and over again. She pulled the vermin away from herself, one at a time, and sent them into the floor, where they would stay until Ethiel turned her full attention on them again.

"They're in the floor now. Don't touch the floor or they'll find

289

you," she whispered to Harleath. She fell forward onto her hands and knees, then slumped to lie flat on her stomach, exhausted. She felt as if she'd just poured her strength down an empty well.

Her eyes burned, and she blinked them. Her body was covered in sweat, and her night dress stuck to her. She rolled over onto her back and breathed for a time. When she could finally sit up, she put her back against the wall and looked at the shocked ghost of Harleath Markin.

"Show me what you know," she breathed. "And I will learn."

47

MIROLAH

MIROLAH SAT CROSS-LEGGED on the floor of the cell and worked with a hundred threads simultaneously. Harleath put a hand of approval on her shoulder, and it felt good. It spurred her on. She could feel his touch now. He was a ghost, but he was still comprised of threads just the same. Every single thing was. And every single thread was comprised of smaller threads. And so on. She had gone so deep that her concentration burned. They were everywhere, each one a minute piece of the whole, each with a purpose.

"The GodSpill sings for you like a child trying to impress his mother," Harleath murmured as he studied her handiwork. She was turning the wall into an intricate bas-relief carving of the history of the world, the story Orem had told her in Rith. She had also learned how to create a "bubble" of protection around her work so that Ethiel wouldn't know what she was doing.

She could have dissolved the bars now without Ethiel knowing. She could have made a hole and escaped into this construct of a palace, but she was done running. What was the point of running except to tell your enemy you were scared and overmatched? Everything Mirolah wanted was right here in Daylan's Fountain, and by the gods, she was going to do what she came here to do or she was going to die.

It had been four days now since Ethiel had sent Mirolah to the cell, and during that time, she had learned more about weaving from Harleath than she had in three weeks with Orem.

Neither Ethiel nor Kikirian had visited. They had left a jug of water, but had brought no food. They were hoping to break her spirit. By rights, she should have been starving, weakened to collapse, but she was stronger than she had ever been in her life. Harleath had shown her how a threadweaver could tap into nourishment other than the consumption of food. A threadweaver could pull sustenance from the never-ending banquet that was Daylan's Fountain.

He had also showed her how to separate her spirit from her body, to fly through walls as though they weren't there, and he took her to the heart of the Fountain—deftly avoiding Ethiel's little thread warpings that searched for intruders—to a column of swirling colors flowing upward, trapped behind a cylinder of what looked like cracked glass, but wasn't glass at all. Glass was fragile; this was—from what Mirolah could deduce—the strongest substance she'd ever encountered. The "glass" that caged the swirling rainbow had been warped and woven so intricately, so masterfully that she couldn't even see it, no matter how deep she tried to look. Just staring at it made her threadweaver sight go blurry. She decided to call it Daylan's Glass.

Daylan's Glass was cracking at last, after centuries of the GodSpill battering against its prison, and Harleath showed her how to pull minute amounts through the tiny cracks and feast upon it. Just a taste was so potent that she swelled like a giant, felt like she could do anything, and she wondered at the unfathomable power that slammed itself futilely against Daylan's Glass again and again. It was enough power to destroy the world, yet somehow Daylan Morth had harnessed it and sent it back, specifically, to all of the humans in Amarion in a concentrated form.

Harleath had explained to her what he knew about it. She

understood what the Fountain did, but still didn't understand exactly how. Daylan's Glass, that furious maelstrom inside, was the focus point. It sucked *all* the GodSpill from the lands and collected it, contained it, then sent it back out to humans in a heady rush. During the Age of Ascendance, humans didn't have to pull GodSpill from the soaked threads of the tapestry like Mirolah was learning to do; it was delivered straight to their bodies from Daylan's Fountain. It's what made them all super-threadweavers. Harleath told her to imagine a series of invisible aqueducts, one for each person in Amarion, that ran the GodSpill to them like water.

Harleath had then explained his idea for destroying the Fountain, for returning GodSpill to the lands, for returning Amarion to what it was before the Age of Ascendance. Harleath knew that Daylan Morth was the strongest threadweaver ever to live. He couldn't break what Daylan had done by pitting his might against the Fountain. He just wasn't strong enough.

But the GodSpill was. All that raw GodSpill was mightier than Daylan Morth. It was like a god itself, without the sentience. All Harleath had to do was turn that unfathomable raw GodSpill against its vessel, and that would blow the Fountain apart.

So Harleath created a very simple spell. He'd thought it was genius at the time. It was just a suggestion spell, a warping of the threads so subtle it challenged nothing. It only changed one small aspect. It didn't urge the GodSpill to destroy the Fountain. In fact, in a way, it bolstered the strength of the Fountain. The spell was a phrase spoken into the GodSpill, repeated over and over, that would spread throughout like a prairie fire, aligning every bit of that potent ocean of creation to one purpose: plug the holes.

If all of those "aqueducts" were suddenly cut off, trapping the GodSpill inside Daylan's Glass, the pressure would become overwhelming, and the Fountain would explode.

But Harleath had been wrong. So devastatingly wrong. Daylan's Glass *was* stronger than the GodSpill, at least strong enough to last three hundred years with the pressure. Instead of exploding, it simply sucked all the GodSpill from Amarion like it had been designed to do and held it, cutting off Amarion like a severed limb. That was the end of the Age of Ascendance. That was the beginning of the Great Dying.

But now, at long last, cracks were forming. Harleath's plan, three hundred years late, was coming to fruition. Cracks were forming, and from those cracks leaked the GodSpill. That was why GodSpill was seeping back into Amarion, why Harleath was awake, why Stavark could use his flashpowers, and why Mirolah could be a threadweaver.

She and Harleath feasted on those leaks, and from that moment on, pure GodSpill became her diet. All thoughts of food were unimportant. She and Harleath turned her cell into an intensive threadweaver practice room.

On the first day, he had taught her small things. He started with the caution that Ethiel would be able to detect Mirolah's weaving if she focused her attention on this cell, so he taught her to feel for the vibration in the threads that hailed the Red Weaver's presence. He warned that the door had Ethiel's alarms on it. If Mirolah attempted to alter it with threadweaving, Ethiel would know immediately. But the Red Weaver had neglected to attach alarms to the wall, so Mirolah practiced there at first, changing that damnable dusky red to a color of Mirolah's choosing, then releasing it to return to Ethiel's unconscious control.

On the second day, after witnessing her aptitude, Harleath opened up and showed her everything she wanted to know. He said she bypassed details that required months—even years—of study for his long-dead apprentices.

On the third day, Harleath's rhyming ceased. His instruction became lucid and to-the-point. It was as though her progress built him up, filled the gaping holes torn in him, and she could begin to guess at the man he used to be. He was a gentle, patient teacher with the kind of presence that set a student's doubts at ease.

Day and night had little meaning within the Fountain, but she could keep track of them in her head. As always, she sensed the moment the sun rose, even if she could not see it. It was as if the heartbeat of the land pulsed in her veins. She refused to sleep, though Harleath warned against that. He said replacing the body's natural rest and rejuvenation cycle with GodSpill was a handy threadweaver's trick, but it had downsides. It could only last for a limited time, and the backlash was debilitating. Coming down from a diet of pure GodSpill was ten times as bad as awakening after a night of hard drinking.

But she didn't stop. She didn't know how much time she had, and she refused to be lulled into complacency like she had been in Denema's Valley. Every moment that passed could be the moment she was tested.

Now, four days after she'd met Ethiel in her grand throne room, Mirolah focused so hard it burned. She felt it behind her eyes, in her hands, even in her toes tucked under her knees. Her breathing came labored.

"You must sleep soon," Harleath said, his comforting hand on her shoulder.

"Not yet," she said, struggling through the complicated exercise. In Denema's Valley, she had envisioned her own hands pulling at the threads. She'd thought that was the only way to do it, but it wasn't. Yesterday, she stopped envisioning a pair of hands when she manipulated the threads. Harleath said that envisioning only two hands was a self-imposed limitation. A threadweaver was restricted only by her imagination. If she chose only to see two hands, she could only manipulate two things at a time. He said he always envisioned himself as an aath tree, with its many prehensile branches. So for the rest of that day, she was an aath tree.

But today, it occurred to her that if she could imagine herself an aath tree, why not imagine herself as the threads themselves? She would have as many fingers as there were threads to use them upon. That was when she stopped thinking of things in terms of numbers. Number of hands. Number of branches. Number of threads. There was only her imagination, encompassing as much of the task as was needed.

Things went quickly after that.

The carving was complete, and she brought the sculpted figures to life, making them move. That stretched her attention to the limit. At the same time, she shielded her work with an illusion in the threadweaver realm which appeared, at first glance, to be Ethiel's original wall. If the Red Weaver decided to check, she would have to realize there was an illusion first, and then she would have to pierce it.

At the same time, Mirolah's attention raced up and down the threads of the prison corridor to warn her in case Kikirian or Ethiel came to check up on her. She would need a few seconds to dismantle her work if the Red Weaver turned her baleful gaze this way.

"Oh, how I wish I had met someone like you when I was alive," Harleath said. "The things we could have accomplished."

"If you had met someone like me, you would have put her to work on capping the Fountain," she said. "And then I would be dead along with everyone else." Her attention flagged, and part of her sculpture smoothed into a flat piece of wall. She grunted, and brought it back, but the detail was fuzzy. She was tiring. She was going to have to pull more energy from the Fountain after this.

"Mmmm..." he said. "If I'd had you, I would have succeeded, I think."

"No. You would still have failed." With a gasp, she let the carving go, then turned the wall transparent, then blue instead of red, a cool-down exercise so she could keep working and hopefully recover some of her wits. "I think I understand something of the Fountain now that you still don't realize."

"Oh?" He raised his eyebrow.

The wall became brick, then granite, then sandstone. She made the changes come faster. Beads of sweat gathered on her brow. The first two days, she hadn't experienced this kind of fatigue. Yesterday, it was only once. This would be the second time today. She would crash soon. She could feel it coming.

"You think the GodSpill isn't sentient. It is nearly endlessly accommodating, but it isn't without its own desires." She let go of the wall, and it slowly turned red again. She let out a long, even breath, then she sent part of her consciousness to the heart of the Fountain that Harleath had shown her. Deep in the core of the Fountain, there were no threads. The GodSpill longed for freedom, rushing against the walls of its prison, forced to trap itself when it longed to get back to the lands. She flitted into the cracks and touched the barest edge of the sweet center. It rushed into her, a juice that rebuilt every part of her fatigued self, from her soul to her breath to her muscles; it even warmed the skin of her body far away. She rushed back and spoke to Harleath.

"You made the GodSpill trap itself, when all it wanted was to be free. If you'd taken the time to feel the GodSpill, to understand what it wanted, you could have worked *with* it. I think the GodSpill wanted to return the lands of Amarion to the way they had been before the Age of Ascendance. If you'd allied yourself with its desires, rather than instilling it with your desires, it might have shown you a way to undo the Fountain."

"But it doesn't speak."

"Maybe you didn't listen closely enough. The GodSpill doesn't 'think' like you and me. It doesn't hope and dream and act and make plans. It's like water, filling whatever vessel it's given, but it still has identity. It knows that it exists."

Harleath looked confused, and, for the first time, Mirolah found herself thinking of a way to explain something to him, rather than the other way around.

"A river will bend any way the land dictates," she said. "But it always charges downhill. When I visit Daylan's Glass, I hear the GodSpill wanting to be free. It's trapped. It wasn't meant to be trapped. It was meant to flow through the world, providing wonder and change."

"There's no record anywhere that suggests the GodSpill itself has desire. It is an element. Like water or stone."

One of Mirolah's alarms went off. Kikirian was coming.

"Kikirian is here," she said quietly. "You had best go."

He looked at her with worry. "Will you please bide your time? Simply wait—"

She met his gaze. "I waited once. It cost me two companions that I will never be worthy of. There is one more who may still live. He came on the journey to protect me. Now it's my turn."

"Given time, I believe you may be a match for her, but you are not now. You have no idea how powerful she is."

"I have some idea."

"Please," he beseeched.

"Go."

She could hear Kikirian's heavy footfalls now. She tracked his intricate composite of threads and fibers and fibers-of-fibers with her weaver's sight.

Harleath sighed. "Then go with Thalius, child. I will stay as close as I dare."

"Don't. I don't want to worry about you, too. If she catches you, she'll destroy you."

He hesitated, then nodded.

"Go *now*," she whispered harshly.

He vanished. She took a deep breath and leaned back against the wall. She laid her arms limply at her side. She opened her mouth and let all of the breath out of her body, slumped down. She imagined how hungry she was and, for a moment, she felt it.

Kikirian looked inside the door, smiled. "Well, novice. I hope you've learned a thing or two while you've been down here. Attacking the Red Weaver carries a heavy cost. Next time, I think you'll throw your tantrum in private. She wants to talk to you. Get up or be brought." The giant dramath opened the cell door and stepped inside. "If you behave, you just might eat tonight—"

She reached out and saturated his threads with her own colors. He gave a soft grunt that was supposed to be a yell, and his burning red eyes opened wide, but then he wasn't able to do anything. Or at least, anything other than what she wanted him to do.

Kikirian belonged to her.

48

MIROLAH

MEDOPHAE STOOD next to Ethiel's throne when Mirolah entered the room, and a wave of relief washed through her. He was alive. Thank the gods.

The Red Weaver had dressed him in a white shirt, open at the front, with long, wide sleeves, black breeches and tall black boots. He looked like a young prince, waiting for his young queen. The expression on his face was focused, but not entirely present, as though he was watching something invisible in the center of the throne room.

Ethiel had changed. Her face was the same, but she was younger and more slender, now roughly Mirolah's age. She wore a floor-length red gown with a high neck and long sleeves. Gone was the voluptuous woman that Mirolah had seen last time. She reclined sinuously on her throne and ran one finger down the length of Medophae's arm. He didn't seem to notice.

Mirolah felt a cool breeze of uncertainty. Medophae was a legend. He had fought and defeated threadweavers for centuries. He had even once killed a god. If Ethiel had taken him in hand so easily, what could Mirolah possibly do to beat her? But it was too late to back out now. She marshaled her concentration and put the doubts from her mind.

"You wanted to see Medophae," Ethiel said. "And I oblige you. Of course, I've taken steps for your protection."

Mirolah said nothing. She and Kikirian came closer to the throne.

"Kikirian, you may go." Ethiel waved an imperious hand.

They came closer.

Ethiel sat up straight and glowered at Kikirian. "Must we have this scene again, dramath? I said..." Her eyes narrowed as she looked closer. Her attention snapped to Mirolah, and a faint smile touched the corners of the Red Weaver's lips.

"Well done..." Ethiel whispered. "The fledgling spreads her wings."

Kikirian charged the throne and leapt up the shallow steps. He brought his huge, gauntleted hands down on Ethiel.

The throne shattered. Medophae stumbled to the side, regained his balance, then slowly stood up straight, still looking at the center of the room.

Ethiel's laughter echoed and rebounded off of the walls. Kikirian swung again and again, his steel-encased fists breaking stone with each strike.

The woman was insubstantial, much like Harleath Markin, but Mirolah knew those gauntlets could hurt a threadweaver, even a ghost, if they connected. She had studied them during the walk from her cell to the throne room, and they were imbued with a strong weaving of single-minded aim, like the tip of a needle. It was designed to break through threadwoven protection. That was how Kikirian and Ethiel had broken through Medophae's natural defenses when Mirolah's own attempts to lift him into the air were slammed aside by Oedandus. The gauntlets had created one brief hole in his protection, and Ethiel had burrowed into his mind.

So Mirolah kept Kikirian going after Ethiel. It was a long shot, but he might get lucky and hit her.

Ethiel flew straight up, out of reach. Kikirian ripped the tall, red velvet curtains behind the throne from their moorings, attempting to wrap them around Ethiel like a whip, draw her down. The cloth passed through her.

Ethiel flicked a finger. A red light exploded in Kikirian's face, blowing him off the dais. He landed in a heap at its base, skidded to a stop, and then lay unmoving.

"So much talent," Ethiel turned her emerald gaze from Kikirian to Mirolah. "Such a poor choice of weapons. I was going to keep you alive, dear. I looked forward to having an apprentice, someone to talk to, someone to impart my knowledge to. But I don't have the time to teach both you and Medophae how to behave."

Mirolah was barely listening. She knew Kikirian had been a gamble, and she hadn't counted on him besting her. He was a physical creature, and though his gauntlets might have put a dent in Ethiel's amorphous form, the next best thing was for Ethiel to knock her own servant unconscious.

One down. One to go.

She reached forward and yanked Ethiel's threads, hard. The Red Weaver's projected image vanished like smoke in a gale. With her threadweaver sight, Mirolah watched the dense red cloud of Ethiel's true form, vaguely humanoid, billow up toward the ceiling, trying to get away. The mist was comprised of the tiniest threads Mirolah had ever seen. When she'd first seen Ethiel's true form, she could detect no threads. But she could now. They were tiny, but they were there, and that meant she could manipulate them.

She pushed her colors into Ethiel, soaking those red threads, trying to turn them. Hope sparked inside Mirolah as they began to change. Blues and whites and greens covered the red like dripping paint.

"Insolent bitch!" Ethiel's shrill words rammed into Mirolah's mind like icicles. Mirolah screamed and fell to her knees, her concentration shattered. The threads of Ethiel's misty body blazed red, ejecting Mirolah's colors.

Ethiel's cold needles melted into the insidious worms of domination as she began to overcome the threads of Mirolah's body, just like she had before.

Mirolah gasped and let her physical form slump to the floor. She didn't need it, not for this fight. Only the threads mattered.

Now that Kikirian was out of the picture, this battle could take place entirely in the weaver's tapestry.

Mirolah became every thread in her body, a thousand thousand fingers. The two times Ethiel had dominated her before, it had happened so fast Mirolah didn't have time to think. But this time, the creeping worms seemed slow, and what was more...

...there was a finite number of them. Two dozen red "fingers" worked at Mirolah's threads. Mirolah, however, was part of every single thread. With just two "hands," to stop Ethiel's invasion, Mirolah would have been overwhelmed. But with every single thread as her ally, suddenly the task was simple, and this time, Ethiel was overwhelmed. Mirolah found the Red Weaver's two dozen fingers and pushed the red out. The pain in her head vanished.

With a quick breath, Mirolah sat up. She glared at the ethereal red cloud. It hovered, and though it had no facial expressions at the moment, Mirolah could feel Ethiel's shock.

Suddenly, Ethiel's two dozen "fingers" became needles, stabbing at Mirolah's heart and lungs over and over, not in an attempt to dominate, but to murder. The shock was savage. Mirolah's lungs collapsed and her heart stopped. She fell back, dying.

But as her body slumped, she stayed in the threads, focused in these last moments of her life. She furiously ejected Ethiel's worms while at the same time pulling together the threads of her heart and lungs that had been so viciously yanked apart. She filled them with the GodSpill taken from the Fountain, bade them return to their original state.

Her heart knitted together and began pumping again. Her lungs reassembled and filled. She sucked in a long, ragged breath.

Ethiel hovered, stunned.

This won't do. She couldn't win by remaining on the defensive. She had to attack, had to drive Ethiel back, had to make her afraid. Only then would the Red Weaver stop.

Mirolah hastily divided her attention to three tasks. She set one fragment of her attention to maintaining her body's threads. If Ethiel invaded or stabbed at her, that portion of her focus would protect her, eject the invasion, or repair any damage.

With her second fragment of attention, she launched a full invasion of Ethiel's threads. With the last fragment, she left her body as Harleath had shown her and circled Ethiel, looking for a weak spot.

The strike and parry continued, and Mirolah held her ground. Ethiel's imperiousness receded, and she ceased her verbal threats. She poured her energy into dominating Mirolah, into pulling her body apart, into shattering her concentration. At each turn, Mirolah repelled her while continuing her own attack, holding the status quo.

The third fragment of Mirolah's attention studied Ethiel and discovered a weakness. Ethiel had divided her attention as well. Innumerable tendrils, invisible unless meticulously searched for, trailed out of the smoky cloud. For a moment, it stunned Mirolah, and she wondered how long she would have lasted in a battle against this weaver if Ethiel were not busy in a hundred other places.

But as she watched Ethiel attack her again and again, Mirolah realized a crucial difference between the two of them. Mirolah's body fought for itself. It had a shape that it wished to retain, a life that it wished to continue. But Ethiel was not alive, not in the same way. Her dense cloud of tiny threads was a construct in very much the same fashion as her castle. It remained only because she concentrated on it, continually held it together with GodSpill. If that concentration ever ceased, or if those threads were forced apart, what would become of Ethiel? Would she dissolve? Would she die?

Mirolah left off with her invasive attack and redirected that attention to forcing those tiny threads to disconnect from Ethiel's "body."

The threads complied with a willingness that shocked her. They resisted for one fragile instant, then flew apart as if a team of horses were already pulling on them.

Ethiel vanished. The red misty figure that hovered near the ceiling was gone. Simply gone.

Mirolah returned to her body and raised her head. She peered all about with her threadweaver sight, but could find no trace of the Red Weaver.

She'd won. Nervously, she looked around at the architectural construct Ethiel had made, half expecting it to begin unraveling. Nothing happened. Apparently, it would stand even when Ethiel wasn't concentrating on it.

Mirolah levered herself unsteadily to her feet, breathing hard. Now she felt the rigors of what she had done. Her head throbbed, her body felt drained, and her hands shook. She felt as if she had been dragged behind a cart for twenty miles, but she forced herself forward. Left foot. Right foot.

Medophae still stood where he had been jostled, staring at the middle of the room. Excitement beat in her chest. She could throw off the spell that dominated him, and they could leave this place.

She shuffled past Kikirian's limp body, set her foot on the steps and...

...Kikirian's huge hand shot out and grabbed her ankle. She gasped and turned.

The dramath flung her across the room. Mirolah flailed, reaching into the threads of the wall as she hit, turning it softer, turning a killing collision into one of pain and broken bones. She fell to the ground, stunned. Her right shoulder and wrist were broken, and the agony stabbed through her. She tried to right herself, stunned.

Kikirian leapt across the room and swung his fist at her.

She grabbed the thin, sparse threads of the air and bunched them in front of Kikirian's fist, but it only slowed that gauntlet. The fist smacked into her, slamming her sideways and cracking her ribs.

"Nobody controls me," he snarled. *"Nobody!"*

She lifted herself into the air, out of his reach. He tried to grab her, but missed. She shot away from him...

...straight into Ethiel's arms.

The red cloud engulfed her, tight-knit and glowing. In the real world, Ethiel projected her voluptuous form in the diaphanous sheer silks of a dancer, hovering in the air beside Mirolah.

She quailed. Exhausted, broken, fending off the horrible pain, she knew she couldn't fight them both.

"Did you think this was over?" Ethiel hissed.

Again, the red needles shot at Mirolah from behind. She let her body go limp, sinking into the threads, and repelled the attack, but her defense was slower.

"I underestimated you, girl," Ethiel said. "Savor your victory. You are nothing, do you understand? *Nothing!*"

"Give her to me," Kikirian growled, waiting eagerly below.

"Yes, Kikirian," Ethiel murmured. "Have her." Mirolah's body plummeted toward the dramath.

Mirolah reached out to force Ethiel's threads apart again, but before she could, the dramath snatched her leg and yanked her down. Kikirian wrapped one huge hand around her neck.

She doggedly tried to force his fingers, as thick as her wrists, open with her threadweaving, but Ethiel batted down her attempt. Kikirian's grip tightened. A cry escaped her. He was going to break her neck.

"Hold for a moment, dramath," the Red Weaver said.

"Don't play with her, Ethiel," Kikirian warned, but he stopped squeezing. "Just let me kill her."

"Be quiet," Ethiel snapped. "I want to know how she learned about my connection to the Fountain."

"It was...obvious," Mirolah said, clenching hard to her defiance and pushing the words out of her tight throat. They'd kill her, but she wasn't going to grovel before them or give up Harleath before they did. Besides, she had one more thing to do before she went down.

She lashed out at the spell around Medophae. She grabbed his infected threads, imagined them gold like Oedandus's fire.

But Ethiel's weaving was stronger than anything she had tried to change before, as though Ethiel had put more of her concentration into it than anything else.

Mirolah was only able to turn a handful of the threads gold before Ethiel's red worms swarmed over her changes, devouring Mirolah's attack and replacing the gold with red, restoring the spell to its impenetrable perfection.

"Snap her neck, Kikirian," Ethiel said.

TODD FAHNESTOCK

49

MEDOPHAE

MEDOPHAE STOOD AT THE RAIL of the balcony of his study in the palace, gazing at the red sands and the rolling ocean in the distance. Lately, he sought this balcony often. He wasn't sure why. He had never spent time here before, but it seemed comfortable somehow.

The distant whitecaps on the surf winked at him, the waves curling, crashing, flattening, only to curl and crash again. Saraphazia ruled that great expanse of blue, and Medophae knew she liked things to remain constant. The ocean was like her living body, and he imagined the waves like the ocean breathing. Thinking of Saraphazia made him think of her impassioned brother, Tarithalius, the god of humans.

Thinking of the deep-voiced, bearded god gave Medophae an inexplicable hollowness in his stomach, like something horrible had happened to Tarithalius. But he was hale and hearty, happily wading through the Polikses War. Why should Medophae feel this sense of foreboding when he thought of the god?

And then there was Bands. He had that same, hollow feeling of loss when he looked at her, even when she was standing right in front of him.

He wondered if it was some kind of threadweaving they hadn't perceived, an insidious spell laid over Calsinac. Usually, the first person he would talk to about that kind of problem was Bands. She could detect most spells easily. But he didn't...

Medophae pushed the thought from his head and let out a slow breath, then said the thought aloud so he could hear how ridiculous it was.

"I don't trust her," he murmured. He decided this must be what it felt like to go insane. He didn't trust Bands. But he couldn't deny that she seemed different. It just didn't make any sense, because she sounded the same, acted the same, shared all of their personal jokes.

He tried to track his memory back to when he began feeling this way, and it always went back to the beach, where he first experienced that feeling of displacement and memory loss. He still didn't remember going there, though Bands assured him that they had walked every step of it together. She showed him their footsteps. They even came across a flower that had fallen from her hair. It lay on the red sand on their return path. She explained how he had picked it for her.

After, he had walked the palace half in a dream. He knew every room, every twist in the hall, every color of every tapestry adorning the walls, yet he still felt lost in—

"Daydreaming, my love?" Bands spoke from behind him. Her voice was pure music. It soothed him, as it always did. He put aside his foul, dark thoughts and smiled as he turned around. Crossing his arms, he leaned back against the wide wooden rail and contemplated her. His worries vanished, and he cursed himself for a fool.

She was the most alluring thing he had ever seen. He had heard from many people that, after many years, the fire of romance banked into the low-burning coals of companionship. But he had been with Bands for centuries. To this day, he still got a catch in his throat when he looked at her.

"You shine," he murmured to her. "You rival the setting sun."

She gave her crooked smile. He loved that smile. Both corners of her mouth curled up, but one was noticeably higher than the other, giving her the look of a wise woman and a saucy maiden at the same time. He'd never seen another woman with the same smile.

Her eyes glimmered, the shimmering green of an emerald. They were a dragon's eyes, and if you looked closely, you could see it. The pupils were not completely round, but elongated vertically, not so sharp as a cat's eye, but noticeable if you knew to look.

Bands was a shapeshifter, but no matter what form she chose, those dragon eyes never changed. They reflected the unending expanse of years she had seen and a strength beyond human understanding. Yet, with all that power, she always looked down after a long moment of his stare, as if she was shy. Was that her dragon's way of blushing? He had never asked her why she did that. He didn't want to know. Some things were better as mysteries.

"Diddier Milessius is fuming," she said after the little dip of her gaze. She stood in the archway, poised and composed like the arch was a frame and she the subject of a master painting. "He is outraged at being made to wait."

Medophae nodded. "It's why I made him wait."

"That may not be wise," she mused.

"Diddier thinks he's king in Calsinac. He's not."

"Without Diddier, trade with the north would all but stop."

Medophae grunted. "For a time. Someone would step up. If you make a hole in the ocean, water rushes in to fill it. Diddier thinks he *is* the ocean, all by himself. Truth be known, I would almost welcome him withdrawing. It would make room for scores of other caravan drivers anxious for the opportunity, and likely filled with a much smaller sense of self-importance."

"That could take months, even years."

"I know. Diddier is wealthy, but greedy. He is powerful, but petty. A man like this cannot be Calsinac's salvation. We founded Calsinac on different principles than that."

"We did, my love—"

A slash of golden light rent the stone of the wall just to Bands's right. Beyond, deep red glowed like fire, illuminating red castle walls with tall windows and red curtains.

Medophae leapt between Bands and the attack. She stepped away from him, searching for the cause of his distress as though she didn't see the obvious weaving of the spell. The godsword raged to life in his clenched fist, and he stared at the opening, ready. But no chips of stone broke from the wall. It was as if the air had been nothing but a canvas with the balcony of his room painted on it, and someone had torn the canvas to reveal the red wall and tall curtains beneath.

"What is it, my love?" Bands asked, circling behind him and gazing in the same direction he was.

"There's a hole." Medophae studied it. The red room beyond was cavernous, some kind of great room. There was a battle scene painted on the ceiling, and wide, curved steps leading downward, as if they stood on a dais. "A...portal," he said.

"Where?" she asked again, her voice edged with concern.

He pointed, close enough to almost touch it. "There, half covering the wall, half covering...the air opening onto the balcony," he murmured. "You can't see it?"

"There's nothing, my love."

"Yes, it's there..." Beyond the rip, he saw a dramath! It was Kikirian, the god's lackey who had been there the day Medophae slew Dervon. Kikirian held a struggling young woman in his huge arms, and...she seemed familiar. He tried to think of her name, and his head began to ache.

He heard Bands behind him, whispering. She often did when she was threadweaving. She thought he was being attacked. She was coming to his aid.

"No. It's okay," he said. He put a hand to his head, tried to chase the elusive name. Who was the young woman? He saw her face, her wavy brown hair. Oddly, her face reminded him of the beach, though she obviously had not been there. It had been just him and Bands.

Bands continued murmuring. The portal began to close.

"No, wait," Medophae said. "I know that girl. She needs our help." The portal vanished, and the castle wall returned to normal.

"Bands, I said don't!" He looked back at her.

"Don't what?" she asked.

"Don't close the portal."

"Medophae, I didn't close anything. I don't see a hole. I was threadweaving to try to find what you were looking at. You say it's gone now?"

Medophae turned and put his hand on the wall, felt the air beneath the balcony's arch. The wall was solid and the air was air. "It... Damn it!" He let the godsword flicker and fade.

Then the name came to him, as though a wall in his mind had cracked, and it had slipped through.

"Mirolah..." he whispered. His head throbbed now, like it was resisting this new information. He fought it.

How did he know that name? He'd never heard that name before in his life. With a growl, he turned around, putting a hand to his pounding head. "I've been here before," he croaked.

"It's your balcony. You come here every day. Or at least, you have for the past week," she said, and every time she spoke, it broke his train of thought. Who was Mirolah? Why did he feel this need to get to her, to protect her?

"Give me a moment," he said. "Please. I have to think—"

"You're worrying me."

"Just for a moment. Don't speak." By Thalius, his head felt like it was going to crack open!

"If you're seeing things, there are herbs I know that will help."

"Bands, I've asked you twice. Just give me a moment to..." He turned to her, and he felt a cold trickle run down his spine. Bands didn't chatter. Even in the midst of heated battle, she was calm, and she said little. He couldn't remember the last time he'd asked her to stop talking. He had never asked her to stop talking twice, let alone three times.

"Medin, what's wrong?" She watched him with those beautiful, exotic dragon eyes.

"This place. This entire time. I... I think I've been here before."

"Of course you have. This is where we live—"

"No, I've done it before. I've lived this before. I'm living it again. I don't belong here."

"Of course you belong here. With me. I *love* you."

That didn't sound like Bands at all. Her words struck a

discordant tone. Her confession of love was...beseeching.

His head pounded. The details of the portal grew fuzzy. He closed his eyes, tried desperately to hold onto the name that had sparked his memory, but it was fading. Miro... Mira... Mir...

She took his head in her hands and shook it lightly. The name vanished. "I don't know what you're seeing, Medin, but it's not real. Come out of the sun."

"You're not listening," he said.

"I am, but you aren't making sense, beloved."

"Yes I am," he said, and he took a step away from her.

She froze, like a thief caught stealing money, then she flashed him a quick smile, held her hands out palms forward. "Medin, what do you—"

"You're not Bands," he said, and his stomach twisted. She was saying the wrong things, things Bands would never say.

She looked wounded, and guilt stabbed at him. He loved this woman more than his own life.

"I think you've taken ill, my love. Look at me. Don't you recognize me?"

"You're not Bands," he repeated, holding on to the elusive feeling that threatened to fade, even as the name of the woman in the portal had faded.

Bands moved toward him with the fluid grace he knew so well, and raised her hands to his face. "You love me. I love you. This is what you want. It is what you've always wanted."

He shied away from her, horrified. She made a grab for his head that he barely dodged. The rail of the balcony hit his back, and his heart thundered in his chest.

"Who are you?" he whispered.

"I'm Bands." Her green gaze glittered, and he saw that their pupils were round.

"No," he said. "You're not." The godsword sparked to life, and he drove it into her chest.

50

MIROLAH

MIROLAH WOULD HAVE SCREAMED, but Kikirian choked the breath from her. She clenched her teeth, eyes shut. Gods, it hurt so bad...

Then he stopped.

Her eyes flew open. Kikirian's murderous face was right before her, the pointed horn almost touching her nose. His enormous hand was wrapped her neck, but he had stopped squeezing. Slowly, the grip eased, and Mirolah sucked in a deep, ragged breath, coughing.

With a furious growl, he jerked his other hand up, grappling with her head, and trying to twist, but he couldn't get a grip. Something was holding his hands at bay. He roared and tried again.

Ethiel's cloudy self flowed forward. "Kill her," she demanded.

Kikirian's arms flew away from Mirolah as if they'd been struck.

Black light oozed over Ethiel, Kikirian, and the entire throne room. Time stopped. Ethiel's voluptuous form froze, arms up, preparing to aid Kikirian. Kikirian's hands were still thrown wide, his face an unmoving snarl. They weren't moving. Yet somehow,

Mirolah could move. Holding her broken arm and wrist, she got away from Kikirian and looked about. Medophae stood next to Ethiel's throne, still entranced, frozen like the rest.

"What a refreshing surprise you have been, Mirolah of Rith," a voice said.

She turned, searching, trying to absorb everything that was happening. The raw pain in her throat, the fierce agony in her arm. A moment ago, she had expected to die. The pain in her body, the shock at being alive, left her unbalanced and confused, but finally, she spotted the man speaking.

He was a medium-sized man, and he walked toward her across black marble that had once been red. He wore clothing from a bygone age, a high collar that went almost up to his ears, and a finely tooled, black leather vest tight against his chest, fastened up the front with wooden toggles. Beneath was a billowy white shirt with lace at the cuffs and throat. His black leather breeches tucked neatly into wide-cuffed, knee-high boots. He reminded her a little of Orem, except Orem had the weathered quality of a traveler. This man had no rough edges. He looked as though he'd walked out of the court the Age of Ascendance.

"I— Were you the one who..." She swallowed through the pain in her throat and tried to focus. "Did you stop everything?"

"Indeed."

There were more threadweavers in this Fountain than bees in a hive. But Harleath had said threadweavers gathered to the Fountain as soon as it started leaking GodSpill.

"Well, thank you," she said. "You saved my life..."

"You, a fledgling," he said. "Have set the Red Weaver on her heels. That deserves applause."

Mirolah cast a nervous glance at the frozen Ethiel, expecting her to deduce the nature of this odd weaving and begin her attack.

"How can you control time?" she asked, trying to give herself a moment. She reached out, pulled GodSpill from the walls and whispered to the threads of her arm, her throat. The bones knit together; the internal bleeding stopped. Flesh healed.

She drew a painless breath and set her mind back to this new threadweaver. How did one find the threads of time? Time had no presence, no physical form; how could it have threads?

The man was watching her as if he knew exactly what she was doing. Only when she was done healing did he start speaking again. "This kind of weaving is older than the Fountain, older than the Red Weaver. It comes from a time when weaving was the pursuit of only the most driven. When I first learned about the great tapestry, the GodSpill was hard-won. We scraped it from the bones of the land. It took me years after my death to learn the secrets of time.

"However, the flow of time, like a dammed river, must eventually break free. We cannot linger forever."

"Help me and Medophae escape."

He gave her a disapproving look. "Escape? Really? After all this? To come so far only to collapse under your fear?" He shook his head. "You disappointment me."

"She's just too strong. I can't..." she said. "She's going to kill me."

"Of course she will. And if you run, she will find you. And then she will kill you. There is only one way to make sure she doesn't."

Mirolah took a deep breath.

"That's better," the man said.

She viewed him with her weaver's sight. It did not surprise her when she found that he was another spirit. Any threadweavers who weren't spirits would be like her, new to it, just learning. How many threadweavers had lashed their spirits to life when their bodies died?

"Who are you?" she asked.

"If you'd like to get acquainted, we can do so until my weaving crumples and time begins again. Or, you can keep your questions for another time and follow me." He gestured at her, and she hesitated. "Come, young weaver. Join me as a spirit, and I will give you the edge you seek."

She glanced at Ethiel, then Kikirian. Both were still frozen.

"They will remain as such until we return, if we hurry," the man said.

Pushing past the prickles of doubt, she lay down, let her spirit rise from her body and followed the man. Together, they flew through Ethiel's constructed walls, flashed past rooms and hallways to Daylan's Glass at the center of the Fountain. She saw the spiderweb cracks across the indestructible glass, but the floating, cold blue eyes didn't stop there. Instead, they turned down, following the tube into the ground. This was farther than Harleath Markin had taken her. He'd showed her only the top of the Fountain, where the cracks were thin.

This new man took her down, down, down. The open air around the cylinder became red granite, and down they went. Red granite became sandstone, and farther down they went. The sandstone became dark, black stone. Finally, the icy blue eyes stopped, deep underground, where the cylinder of glass widened into a bulb half the size of Ethiel's throne room. The GodSpill surged and crashed against its prison. He guided her around the bulb until they came to the largest crack she had seen yet. A thick red thread covered it like an open-mouthed eel, sucking every wisp of the GodSpill into itself.

"That is Ethiel's unending source," the blue eyes said. "This is what makes her invincible. Come, make a similar attachment, and you will be as large as she is."

Mirolah studied Ethiel's spell, found another crack, not nearly as large, and duplicated the eel-like suction, leading it straight into herself.

The GodSpill surged into her, and a vibrancy filled her from feet to fingertips, like she'd been struck with a lightning bolt. It pounded at her, wanting to give more, more, more! She could barely hold it at bay, moderate it so she wouldn't fly apart. The GodSpill wasn't vengeful; it didn't want to tear her apart, but it was eager. It longed to be free, and it rushed at the freedom she represented.

"By the...gods," she gasped as soon as she brought it under control.

"Pure nectar," the ice-blue eyes said.

"Oh...yes..."

"Come now, young weaver. My weaving is about to unwind. Your death—or your victory—is at hand."

Black rock, sandstone, and red granite flashed by them, then they were back in the throne room. She dropped back into her body and stood up. The man's constructed image, with the ancient clothes and tidy goatee, bowed to her.

"Good luck, young weaver."

"At least tell me your name."

His smile turned strange. She could see that cold fire flickering in his blue eyes. "Great weavers are never friends," he said. "So I will spare you the burden of my name."

"I don't understand."

"When you learn my name, you will not want to be in the same room."

She swallowed and raised her chin, feeling suddenly vulnerable. She'd thought he was another displaced ghost like Harleath Markin, fatherly and protective.

"I'm useful to you," she said.

"Of course, young weaver."

This spirit's real fight was with Ethiel, and he saw that Mirolah could fight that fight for him. "You helped me to help yourself," she said.

"Remember that lesson, young weaver." The man's image bowed with a flourish. "And now, farewell. May we never meet again, for your sake. If we do, it will certainly mean your death."

The black haze encompassing Ethiel's throne room faded, and the man in black vanished.

Mirolah pushed the blue-eyed spirit's insidious threat to the back of her mind. She had to focus on the fight. Whether the spirit was her ally or enemy, he had saved her life when she surely would have died. She wouldn't waste the opportunity.

Time began. Ethiel's cloud hissed like a snake, obviously noting that Mirolah had apparently vanished. Kikirian's arms snapped together where she had once been. They both whirled and spotted her.

The GodSpill from Daylan's Glass coursed through her. Even when Harleath had guided her to sip from the tiny cracks at the top of Daylan's Glass, she had felt like a giant. Now she felt invincible.

Ethiel's cloud roiled, agitated. She didn't know how Mirolah had gone from having her neck broken to standing in the center of the room, a good twenty feet from Kikirian. She hadn't seen any of the threadweaving that had accomplished it, and it had to have her worried. Weavers liked to know things. Mirolah understood that.

"Let's try this again," Mirolah said.

Kikirian charged. She saturated the threads of the air and twisted them, making them as solid as the stone table she'd made in Denema's Valley, but still as transparent as the air. Kikirian hit it head-first, rebounded, and crashed to the floor.

Ethiel tried to invade the threads of Mirolah's body again, but Mirolah repelled her. She had so much GodSpill at her disposal, it was easy. The extreme infusion of the stuff cleared her head, swept away her fear. She saw what she needed to do, and how to do it.

Ethiel's cloud billowed, growing larger. The Red Weaver grabbed her throne, raised it into the air. It split, cracking into a hundred sharp shards that flew at Mirolah like stone daggers.

Mirolah stopped them with another air wall, then divided her attention to work on three fronts again. One to parry Ethiel's attacks. One to stop Kikirian, and the third to spot anything she didn't expect. She could not afford to be caught off guard again.

Ethiel tried one thing after another, relentless. She sent physical attacks, chairs, chunks of rock; she even tore a curtain from one of the tall windows and tried to wrap Mirolah in it. At the same time, she kept trying to get her hooks into Mirolah's body.

Mirolah repelled them all. She had more concentration, more power at her disposal, than ever before.

The huge double doors of the throne room slammed open, and a dozen darklings loped into the room on all fours. Kikirian, recovering his senses after almost knocking himself out against her wall, stood up and jogged forward cautiously, one gauntleted ham hand in front of himself. He found the wall, then shouted and slammed his gauntlets against it. It shattered, and the backlash hurt Mirolah like a knife to the forehead. Those damned gauntlets! What were they?

She gasped and created another wall, stepping back from the dramath's advance. The darklings hit the wall, then spread out like cockroaches and looked for a way around it. The never-ending energy of the Fountain cycled through her, but when Kikirian found the next barrier, those monstrous gauntlets shattered it again.

Mirolah's mind raced. All this power, and yet she was still outmatched.

"Die, you little bitch," Ethiel growled.

Suddenly, a thunderous roar boomed through the throne room. Ethiel and Kikirian spun around. The darklings crouched, mewling and scraping the ground with their claws as they looked up at the top of the dais.

Medophae stood there, wreathed in golden fire and completely awake. The godsword glowed in his fist like a shaft of spitting lightning.

"*Ethiel!*" he boomed.

51

VAERDARO

VAERDARO STALKED out of the dilapidated house into the streets of Denema's Valley. He glanced at the dark corpses sprawled on the stones, slowly rotting. They stank like tar mixed with shit. Vaerdaro had ridden over many battlefields filled with the stink of the dead, but this smelled worse. It was unnatural, and it coated the insides of his nostrils like oil. He felt as if he'd been infected by a disease. He wondered if he had been a fool, leaving his brother's band to follow the promises of a dark spirit. The Vessel Men told tales of dark spirits who possessed the hearts of warriors, turned them into puppets.

He despised feeling vulnerable. That was what drove him here. It was what made the company of his brother insufferable. Gilgion was the only man in this cursed northland who could kill Vaerdaro at will, and the knowledge of it was like a dagger in the thigh, twisting, hobbling him. It was why the dark spirit's offer was impossible to leave unexplored.

But he had waited in this damnable, damp, squishy city for days now, and for what? The dark spirit promised him the power to take his rightful place among the Sunrider leaders of history. Not only would Vaerdaro have his brother's head, but he could also supplant his father, the Voice of the One Sun, the leader of the entire Sunrider people.

The dark spirit filled Vaerdaro's head with the Legend of Raegilan the Mighty, the first Voice of the One Sun, the warrior who had united the clans of Sunriders into one mighty force. Raegilan the Mighty was descended from the legendary Golden God, whose blood ran in every Voice of the One Sun since the time of the Three Mothers.

Long ago Raegilan had crossed the Ocean of Teeth and landed upon the blood shores of the fabled Kingdom of Calsinac. There dwelt the legendary Golden King, a shining god who pulled power from the heavens and ruled with even-handed justice. Raegilan came to test the mettle of this king and, if he proved false, declare war on Calsinac for its blasphemy.

Raegilan and the Golden King met in the Circle of Bare Hands. It was said their battle lasted three days and three nights, during which none of the riders ate or slept. In the end, the Golden King overcame Raegilan, and Raegilan bent his knee. In addition to his hundred mounted warriors, Raegilan brought twelve of his most promising daughters, each from a different wife, and each more beautiful than the next. He offered them to his new liege to seal the bond between the Sunriders and the kingdom of Calsinac. The Golden King lay with three of them. The Three Mothers returned with Raegilan to the Neverending Plains and gave birth to three children: two boys and one girl. Those descendants of the Golden King became the speakers for their circle of the Sunrider force, reporting only to Raegilon. And so the authority of the Voice of the One Sun and the Sun Speakers were created, and the everlasting host of the Sunriders was made.

The blood of the Golden King still ran in the veins of the Sun Speakers. It ran in Vaerdaro's blood. He was born to rule, not to be subjugated by his brother.

Now the dark spirit had confirmed the prophesies of the Vessel Men, saying the Golden King, thought lost to the lands centuries ago, never truly left. The signs that had brought Gilgion and his

Wind Ring were true.

The dark spirit said that the Golden King had run, had hidden away like a coward and hoped to be forgotten. Such a man did not deserve the power he possessed. It was time for the divine power of the Golden King to pass to another.

And Vaerdaro was that one. The dark spirit promised to give make him the new Golden King.

But, after lingering in this stinking city of the dead for days, Vaerdaro was beginning to doubt the dark spirit's words. There was no Golden King here. There was nothing but the stench of evil. Malevolent creatures crept through the moss-ridden city at night, seeking prey. Vaerdaro could hear them, could sense them. This was no place for a warrior of the sun, for a descendant of one of the Three Mothers.

A footfall caught Vaerdaro's ears, and he swiveled, one hand on his short sword, the other on his battle sword. The creepy tall man who attended the dark spirit turned the corner. Vaerdaro frowned. Wherever the dark spirit was, this tall, gaunt man was not far behind. Whenever the dark spirit was away, the man named "Sef" also disappeared.

"The master is near," Sef said in his deep voice. He wore no emotion on his face. He never did. "We must prepare."

"Prepare for what?"

Sef said nothing, just turned and began walking as though Vaerdaro was supposed to follow him.

Vaerdaro ground his teeth and reluctantly fell in line behind the half-wit. They wended their way through the mossy streets until they came to a broken house. Vaerdaro had explored a bit of Denema's Valley while he had been forced to wait, but had given up early. All the buildings were the same, and most of them were filled with items he did not recognize or northlander books.

But this was not a house Vaerdaro had entered before, and when they went inside, he was surprised to see another man there besides the monotonous Sef. He was trussed up and leaning against the wall by the corner like a rabbit ready to be spitted.

"Who is that?" Vaerdaro asked.

"That is for the master to say," Sef replied. Vaerdaro's hand twitched over his short sword. He swore that once he was ruler of this land, he would kill Sef first. Sef inclined his head toward a raised bed in the center of the room. "Lie down there."

Vaerdaro looked at Sef with contempt, then ignored him. He walked up to the man lying in the corner and crouched down.

"Who are you?"

The man's brown eyes burned with defiance. Vaerdaro could watch him calculating even as he answered.

"My name is Orem."

"What are you doing here?"

Orem's eyes glinted. "Waiting for my horse to be groomed."

Vaerdaro kicked the insolent man in the gut. Orem doubled over, gritting his teeth. He did not cry out. Vaerdaro cocked back his leg to kick him again when the dark spirit spoke from behind him.

"What, exactly, are you doing?" the spirit asked.

Vaerdaro turned to face the dark-haired, goateed visage that the dark spirit chose to present, though Vaerdaro knew it was an illusion.

"I grow bored, Spirit. This graveyard stinks of rot."

"I asked you a question, Sunrider."

Vaerdaro darkened. "I am not your lackey, to be ordered around by a brainless servant and taunted by prisoners. You promised me power, and, so far, all I have reaped are empty days and disrespect. I am blood of the Voice of the One Sun. I am blood of the Golden King!"

"You will do as I say. Or you can return to your brother's band and reap a deserter's welcome."

"I want what you promised me."

"Soon, Vaerdaro."

"Now."

The dark spirit's eyes glowed blue, like deep ice caught in the sun. Vaerdaro's short sword shot from his scabbard as though an invisible hand had yanked it out. Vaerdaro made a grab for it, but it slashed his hand, flew across the room, and clattered in the corner.

Vaerdaro drew his greatsword and attacked the dark spirit. The blade passed through the thing's body and sparked on the stone floor. With Vaerdaro's fist through his insubstantial chest, the dark spirit grabbed Vaerdaro by the chin. Though his body was mist, the dark spirit's hand was as solid as granite. He lifted Vaerdaro off the ground and flung him across the room next to the sword. The tribesman hit the stones and scrambled to his feet, breathing hard.

"You dare," he bellowed.

"I have need of you," the dark spirit said in a low voice. "We can both benefit from our arrangement, or you can die, and I will choose your brother to fulfill my plans. If you cross me again, I will swipe the life from your rabbit's heart like a scythe cuts wheat. If you can muster a sliver of will and cage your foolish anger, you can be the Golden King. If not, then you die here, unknown and unlamented. When you are the Golden King, then you may pick the path that suits you, but until that time, you listen to me. Do you understand?"

Vaerdaro felt as if he were in the Ring of Bare Hands with Gilgion again, outmatched. It drove him mad with fury. But he was his father's son, and with an effort, he controlled his anger. He let the fire burn deep, and it did not show on his face.

"Very well, Spirit," he said.

The dark spirit nodded. "It will be necessary for you to recline on that table." He pointed. "You will be restrained. Sef will strap you down." The dark spirit indicated the bed in the center of the room.

"I will lie down, but if your idiot servant touches me, I will gut him."

"The power I will introduce to your body will be a shock, and it will hurt as if someone was roasting you over a flame. You will thrash. If you fall off the table, all is undone and you will not be the Golden King."

Vaerdaro breathed hard. This was the moment. This was the test. If he walked away, he was a coward.

He growled and went to the table. Sef secured each of his wrists and ankles with iron manacles to the four iron legs of the table.

"Now what?" Vaerdaro growled.

The dark spirit ignored him. "Sef?"

"Yes, my master."

"Bring the rest of what I will need. Events are culminating at the Fountain. It is time to begin."

"Yes, my master." Sef walked into a shadowy corner of the room. Vaerdaro could hear him gathering items at his slow pace, but couldn't see him. He could see the dark spirit, however. The insubstantial man stared upward at the roof as though he could see through it and was counting clouds.

"I said 'what now,' Spirit?"

"Now, Sunrider, it's time to kill an immortal."

52

MIROLAH

MEDOPHAE CAME DOWN THE STEPS, glaring at Ethiel's bunching red cloud.

Mirolah wanted to weep from relief. It was a chance. She wouldn't have to face them all alone anymore.

Ethiel transformed into the young woman again, svelte and vulnerable. She held her hands up in a gentle gesture. "My love, I knew you would be angry with me—"

"Bring her back, Ethiel."

"There is much to discuss, Medin—"

"Don't call me that. I'm not your 'love,' and I'm not Medin to you. There's only one thing I want from you. Undo your spell. Free Bands from the gem."

"Sweet Medophae..." she said, and Mirolah was stunned that the deadly Red Weaver suddenly seemed like a lovesick girl. "I love you. Can't you see how much I do?"

"You're a murderer. A torturer. You've ruined countless lives, killed people like they were hogs for slaughter. You stole everything that mattered to me."

"Because I love you. All I ever wanted was for you to see that—"

"You don't know what love is."

"You saved me from death. You showed me love at that inn in Gorros."

"I never touched you, except to cut the ropes that bound your hands and feet."

"You still deny it," Ethiel murmured.

Medophae grabbed at his belt, searching for something. He looked down and then up at Ethiel. "Where is it? Where is the gem?"

"She never loved you, Medophae. Not like I loved you."

He bared his teeth. "I will kill you, Ethiel. I swear it. I will walk you to the Godgate myself."

Her eyes narrowed. Her smile turned to a frown, and the young woman's body became hazy. "You already killed me, remember? I have been to the Godgate. I have suffered more for your sake than you can imagine."

"You never did anything for my sake," he said. "You spent your life stoking your own freakish desires."

"Don't banter, Ethiel," Kikirian interrupted. "Put him back in his cage." The darklings had paused their attack on Mirolah at some silent command from Ethiel.

She didn't even seem to hear Kikirian. Her hazy form clenched its fists and she hovered nearer Medophae. "Freakish? *I* am freakish? What do you call a man who makes love to a reptile? Over and over and over again. Dragons are the enemies of humankind, but you lay with her every night for centuries. You are a crime against your own people. I am the one for you, not her! I am the most powerful woman of your own people. Human people. And you slid your sword through my chest!"

"I promise you this," Medophae said. "If you release Bands, I will let you go your way. I will forget your many crimes. I will forget the children of Gorros. I will forget that you slew your own father. I will forget the murders in Calsinac. I will put it all behind me. Release her, and we will part with a clean slate."

It seemed as though the two of them had picked up an

argument from centuries ago. Mirolah didn't understand everything, but watched them, tense and waiting. She did her best to recover her strength and her wits as she listened.

"A clean slate?" Her hazy form began to bubble, bulging into an uncontrolled cloud on one leg and one arm. Her face remained, however, and she sneered. "I spit on your clean slate. You will never have Bands. Traitors must suffer, and that's what you both are, traitors to your own kind. Have you ever wondered how I was able to catch a god in that gem, as well as your beloved dragon plaything? Avakketh can tell you. He gave me the gem. He put the spell on my lips. There is no human in the world, not even you, who can break it. There is only the riddle, and you will never solve it!"

Medophae leapt at her. In a blink, she transformed into the red cloud, and slammed him back with a billowing hand. He crashed down and skidded across the floor.

The darklings hissed and charged him. Kikirian roared and lunged.

"Grab his head," Ethiel said to Kikirian. "I will send him back to where he belongs. Then she turned air into steel spears, expertly twisting the threads and launching them at Medophae. There were a hundred of them. Mirolah marveled at the amount of power it took to do that. GodSpill streamed out of Ethiel, a limitless amount. Mirolah quickly yanked threads, turning each of the spears into air again. Ethiel screamed and whirled on her. With a gesture, she flung a hundred spears at Mirolah.

She changed them to air again, but they had almost hit her. She gasped, pulled on her connection to the Fountain and revitalized herself.

Medophae disappeared underneath the pile of darklings, but three of them raised their heads, turned, and bounded toward Mirolah.

Mirolah threw up a quick shield, then felt Ethiel invading the threads of her body again, even as she sent another volley of air spears.

This wasn't going to work. The fight between them was in Ethiel's favor because she had no physical body to hurt and

Mirolah did. If Mirolah succeeded in a strike, she could only push Ethiel back, make her hesitate. But all Ethiel needed to kill Mirolah was to damage her body more than Mirolah could quickly repair. It could come down to one bite from a darkling. Mirolah was only as strong as her mortal flesh allowed her to be, while Ethiel was as strong as the indestructible Fountain that fed—

Yes. That was it. The Fountain.

Mirolah turned the air solid between her and the darklings and shoved at them, sent them sprawling back. She halted the next volley of spears and sent them flying back at Ethiel. While Ethiel pulled and changed those threads, Mirolah had a brief second to begin her plan. She enclosed herself in a sphere of blue stone. That would stop the darklings for a long time, but it would only hold Ethiel at bay for seconds.

Mirolah sent a fragment of her focus through the floor, down to the where Harleath had first shown her Daylan's Glass, then deeper, where the blue-eyed stranger had showed her the heart of the Fountain, where the colors swirled and raged against the bulbous prison.

Ethiel's red threads covered the largest cracks, thick and twisting like the roots of a great tree. Mirolah tore Ethiel's connections to the Fountain away, unraveled every twisted root, then shot back to the throne room and invaded Ethiel's cloud-like form.

The result was astonishing.

Ethiel's defenses crumbled. Mirolah soaked into Ethiel's tiniest threads. She changed them, grabbed control of them, pulled them apart.

Ethiel's shriek was cut off as the cloud burst apart, spinning away in little crimson spirals that vanished. All save one tiny puff. It fled.

Mirolah pursued.

53

ZILOK MORTH

ZILOK MORTH LOOKED over the main room of the small house, tucked away from prying eyes in the city of Denema's Valley. His master spell would be cast here, in this plain place, where ordinary mortals had once rested, eaten, and toiled away their meaningless lives. It was fitting. In this place, Zilok would strip Medophae of his godly airs at last, reducing the Wildmane to a common mortal worm.

It was also appropriate that the Wildmane little flock had roosted here for a time, and that he had never sensed Zilok waiting nearby. But then, the Wildmane had always been blind to what was most important.

Zilok glanced at Vaerdaro, secured to the iron bed. The Sunrider had not spoken for a while, which was surprising. Even though Vaerdaro never had anything interesting to say, he persisted in his ceaseless braying—

"When do we start?" Vaerdaro broke the silence, as if he had known Zilok's thoughts. "If you're going to wander around the room for an hour, I'll do something else."

Zilok floated to Vaerdaro, though Zilok's apparition appeared to walk the distance. Leaning close, he whispered, "If it is within your power to hold your tongue, Sunrider, I suggest you do. This weaving is complex, and the threads of your very life will be tied to its workings: your blood, your skin, your bones. If I perform it incorrectly—if anything distracts me—it will pull you apart."

Vaerdaro made a defiant face, but Zilok could see the fear. Vaerdaro was a selfish, bullying brute, and his backward culture despised threadweaving above all else. He was not Zilok's ideal choice to become the next puppet pulled over the mighty hand of Oedandus, but he was the best of limited options.

"If you can but hold yourself still, if you can but stay silent, I will harvest a god from the undeserving Wildmane and bring it to live in your veins. *You* will become the legendary Golden King." Zilok asked.

"All right," Vaerdaro said through clenched teeth.

"We are agreed. Not a word."

"Get on with it, Spirit."

"Excellent."

Zilok turned toward the rest of the room's implements. Strictly speaking, none of them were necessary for threadweaving. But then, "necessary" was subjective for one who had no need to eat, sleep, or shelter himself from the elements.

Using spell components was something Zilok had done since his first moments of threadweaving. Such physical items helped frame his mind. Most threadweavers had affectations that guided their weaving. Some spoke incantations that they had memorized. Some drew symbols to keep their minds from wandering. Some made gestures in the air. The relationship to the GodSpill and the threads of the tapestry was unique for each threadweaver. Using physical items, imbued with significance, guided Zilok's imagination, binding him to the essence of each step.

He floated to the circular table. It was three feet tall, held up by one hourglass-shaped leg made of roughhewn stone. The tabletop was glassy smooth, bearing a three-inch braid of golden hair. To the right of the hair lay Vaerdaro's dagger, its hilt wrapped in strips of leather, the sharpened steel glinting dully in the lamplight.

To the right of the dagger was a fish bowl with a lockmouth in it. The fish's circle mouth was attached to the glass, sucking in vain, dreaming of blood. The only things that obscured the black hole of its mouth were the upper and lower rows of teeth, which flexed up and down with its rhythmic sucking. The lockmouth's last meal had been a bit of the Wildmane's hair. Already, its threads had changed, taking on a slight golden sheen. The galling augmentation of Oedandus, which had shielded the Wildmane from harm for centuries, would be used to finally bring him to his knees.

Zilok turned his attention to the next article on his table. The quicksilvers called it a *quirak klamar*, which translated to "rockfire toad." The stumpy creature was a foot high and a foot wide. Its rock body hunched down, the knotted shoulders close together, and the head turned upward. Rockfire toads didn't move much, but the rocklurs hadn't bred them to move. They were the stone men's tools to heat the colder caverns in which they lived. Cold slowed the rock men, and the rockfire toads had been designed to breathe fire on cold walls until the chambers warmed to a temperature that enabled the rock men to move more quickly. Zilok had ranged to the fringes of Amarion, deep into the Spine Mountains, to find the creature.

The last item on the black glass table was a thin, circular flap of human skin, mortal skin. The last skin the Wildmane would ever wear.

Zilok remembered the first moments of his friendship with Medophae, before he became the Wildmane, before they had destroyed a god together. Zilok, the son of a count, had been raised to rule, to make decisions about the lives of others. That was simply the order of the world. But Medophae saw every person as equal, an individual no greater or lower than any other. His passion infected Zilok. In those first days, Medophae had demonstrated how narrow Zilok's perspective had been, and most importantly, that one could be trapped by his own perspective without knowing it. Medophae's passion burned through those invisible cages, and for the first time, Zilok realized that he need not follow any particular path, that he could be anything he wanted—peasant or king or threadweaver.

Zilok had been a self-involved young man, stubborn. That he had fallen in love with Medophae's brash confidence was a shock to his parents. When Zilok left home to follow Medophae on his quest, it stunned even Zilok. Back then, he would have followed Medophae anywhere.

But then they had succeeded in the impossible. They slew Dervon the Diseased. They soared to heights that no mortal had ever dared dream. Zilok had never been happier. Medophae had changed his life, and together, they had changed the world. He thought they would be friends forever. He thought the bards would sing of them for a thousand years.

But no. *Medophae* had been written into legend, as the Wildmane. And where Zilok should have been equally lauded, his contributions had populated nothing more than a sad little footnote. Wildmane rose, casting a tall shadow over Zilok, and Medophae vanished forever.

It was a base betrayal of their friendship, and not the last. The Wildmane betrayed Zilok over and over, and when Zilok refused to trust him any longer, the Wildmane set out to destroy him permanently.

But now, at long last, the god who should never have been would become mortal again. The account between them would finally be settled.

Next to the worktable stood Zilok's scrying pool, constructed in rough stone like the table. When he looked into the water, he could see whatever he wished, no matter the distance and without expending any of his own energy. This had been the most difficult thing to recreate since he had awoken. Scrying pools were complicated, an extension of his own threadweaving. The pool's threads had been infused with, and could store, incredible amounts of GodSpill. It had taken him days to make it. But now that it had been willed into existence, it could fold the threads of the lands so that distance could not impede Zilok's vision. He could see whatever he wanted to see, no matter how far away it was.

"Everything is in place, Sef," he said.

"Yes, my master." Sef waited patiently at the head of the pallet where Vaerdaro lay.

"At last," he said to himself, and he sank into meditation. The power required to dislodge a god must come straight from the ultimate source of GodSpill: the Godgate itself. And Zilok must go there to get it.

Lesser threadweavers scrabbled about the lands, pulling GodSpill from the threads of the living and the dead. Zilok himself had done that in the early days. But for a spell of this magnitude— to actually wield the power of a god, however briefly—one couldn't simply drain the droplets left on the mortal plane. One must drink from the waterfall. One must dare oblivion.

When a person died, the Godgate sucked their soul upward into a swirling maw that no mortal could see, that no mortal could resist, and from which none ever returned. It was said that beyond the Godgate was a golden land where the original seven gods had met and decided to create the world, where they had woven the tapestry that comprised every single thing. It was where the GodSpill—the force for all creation, change and destruction—had been birthed.

But when Zilok's mortal body had been slain by the Wildmane, he refused the excruciating summons of the Godgate. He had used his knowledge of the GodSpill and his will to live to lash his soul to an anchor in this mortal plane.

But the Godgate never stopped pulling. Its summons was like a hundred flaming fish hooks stuck through his soul, constantly pulling upward. Zilok had mastered the pain, had learned to "live" with it, fending off the Godgate's promise of sweet respite if he simply capitulated.

But now, he let the hooks tug him upward, let his consciousness rise through the roof of the small house and into the sky.

It took only moments for the Godgate to form in front of him. Only the dead—or very powerful threadweavers—could see it. The sky twisted into a funnel of colors, like festive ribbons swirling down into a maw at the center. The hooks in his soul yanked tight, and agony flared through him. Suddenly the ribbons were connected to the hooks. These were the tongues that wanted to pull him into the belly of the Godgate, but he resisted, halting his advance and hovering there.

He saw other souls, the newly dead, caught in the ribbons. They made no sound, just swirled around, around, and disappeared into the black hole. He called out to one of the souls, but it didn't answer, just stared forward in an unnatural, wide-eyed sleep.

Zilok looked down to discover that he had started moving slowly toward the Godgate again. He had not commanded himself to start moving. With a jolt of panic, he realized he had let his thoughts wander and had lost a modicum of control.

He grappled with his own fleeting thoughts, dredging up particulars of his impending weaving, anything to anchor him to his purpose, his life, but the thoughts slipped away like eels.

He had to think clearly. Why return to the land of mortals? Think! Your desires are many...

But his mind had gone empty, and he realized with horror that he was unraveling. Perhaps that was what the sightless, floating souls felt, this stripping of their selves, of their identity.

The gate loomed. He was on the edge of it. Beyond was the place only gods had walked, and his soul began to melt through the end of the funnel. Streams of bright blue flowed into the ribbons as Zilok's gleaming eyes stretched, leaking away, blending in and swirling in a spiral.

He couldn't remember anything. It was time to die, to finally rest. Certainly no threadweaver had ever come this close to the Godgate and returned. Not even the Wildmane had come this close to the Godgate...

The Wildmane...

He saw Medophae's face surrounded by the golden fire of Oedandus, the fire of limitless power, of towering arrogance, the fire that had taken his friend away and replaced him with a demigod. If he passed beyond the Gate, then the Wildmane won. The Wildmane would live while he would vanish.

He would vanish.

Zilok Morth would vanish. That was his name...

A memory came to him then, the last memory of his mortal life, more than a millennium ago. Medophae, wreathed in golden flame, snarled at him. Zilok, only fifty years old, injured and weakened, pulled desperately at the threads comprising the Wildmane, but he couldn't pierce Oedandus's protection. The Wildmane stabbed the godsword into Zilok. Even with all of their previous conflicts, Zilok had never thought the Wildmane would really kill him. Not in the end. No matter how estranged they became, you just didn't kill your best childhood friend. You just didn't.

But Oedandus's rage twisted in Zilok's guts, cutting through the threads of his spell, through the threads of his life.

And then the worst part. As Zilok's spirit separated from his body, the Wildmane turned to Bands and told her he was *sorry*, so sorry he had to *kill* Zilok. So *sorry* that it had to come to this...

Zilok opened his flaring eyes to find that he had stopped at the rim of the Godgate. It yawned, implacably dark and larger than the night sky, ready to swallow him. Zilok could barely see anything, even the multicolored ribbons swirling into the edges of the maw. All he saw was the blackness. It hauled on the burning hooks, but Zilok refused to be moved. The limitless power of the Godgate surrounded him, and he knew his purpose again, as clear as the black oblivion before him. He stole from that fathomless place, as much GodSpill as he could contain. He gorged himself.

Now. I am ready.

He turned and floated away from the swirling ribbons of colored light, using the overwhelming power he now possessed to fight those terrible hooks. The farther he moved away from the Godgate, the weaker its hooks became. He could see the sky again now, its stars sharp and bright. He could see the Spine Mountains in the distance. He looked down at the Inland Ocean, stretching farther and farther toward the horizon as he descended. Then he saw Denema's Valley, its mossy blanket silver in the moonlight. He floated nearer, down to the roof of the small house, then through and into the room with the table, the scrying pool, and the iron bed with Vaerdaro. Sef, Zilok's anchor to this mortal plane, stood obediently waiting.

Zilok's eyes flared around the room, igniting the shadows with crimson light. The Godgate's power radiated from him. He had succeeded! He swelled to bursting with the essence of creation, change, and destruction.

With so much inside him, he felt the threads all around him, as though there was no stone in the walls, no creaking wood in the floorboards, no flesh in the Sunrider or Sef. They were all bundles of threads that desperately wanted to soak up the GodSpill he held, and he knew that if he didn't control it, he would lose it all.

Zilok envisioned himself as an impervious vessel, held together by will and singular purpose. He reveled in his divine strength, then gave direction to the forces he had marshalled. He moved to the scrying pool. The Wildmane was a three-inch figure on the surface. He battled a horde of darklings within Ethiel's crimson throne room.

Zilok pointed at the Wildmane's lock of golden hair on the table. It floated into the air, and the Sunrider's dagger rose with it. He focused on the Wildmane, bringing all of his power to bear. In his mind, he took himself to that location, imagining himself standing right next to the Wildmane as he sliced through darkling after darkling.

"Tell me again, my *friend*," he said to Medophae. "Just how sorry you are."

Zilok unleashed his spell.

54

MIROLAH

ETHIEL VANISHED THROUGH THE WALL, and Mirolah chased her, but just before she left the room, she turned. With a gesture, she caused her body to float upward, and made it hover near the domed ceiling, out of reach of the physical threads below. What good would it do to fight Ethiel if she left her body behind to be killed by Kikirian or the darklings?

She turned and pursued Ethiel, like a ghost, through the wall. There could be only one place the Red Weaver was going. Ethiel had been cut off from the Fountain. She had to restore her connection to have any chance of fighting Mirolah.

Mirolah plunged down through the red walls and floors, past the sandstone and into the dark rock. She entered the room that held the bulbous core of the Fountain and pulled up short. Ethiel was hastily threadweaving, pulling energy from the Fountain to lash her parasitic connections back in place, to repair the destruction Mirolah had wrought.

With a deft twist of the threads, Mirolah undid Ethiel's work again. Ethiel whirled around, the vaguely humanoid cloud bunched and ugly. A face formed in the middle of it, all teeth and hatred.

Ethiel turned and leapt into one of the cracks, directly into the Fountain's bulb, vanishing into the swirling, churning maelstrom of pure GodSpill.

Mirolah stopped, aghast. She moved forward carefully, then shied away. That was insanity! How had Ethiel done it? There were no threads in that heaving storm. It was pure, raw GodSpill. If the slightest sip made Mirolah feel invincible, stepping into a storm of it would destroy her, wash away her identity like a droplet hit by a bucket of water.

But if Ethiel had found a way to overcome the sheer, overwhelming power... If she had found a way to master it, then she'd be far more powerful than Mirolah could fight.

If I hesitate, I lose. If I let her go, she'll return stronger than ever. She underestimated me once. She won't do it twice. I have to end this now.

Mirolah paused an excruciating moment longer. For the dozenth time in the same amount of days, she faced her own death. She wished she could run away. She thought of Fillen, of the darkling that had gutted her. Mirolah had run then, and her sister had died. She thought of Medophae far above, fighting Kikirian and the darklings. If Mirolah didn't defeat Ethiel, what would stop her from enthralling him again?

She wasn't that girl anymore, to hide from the unknown, to run from her fears. She wasn't, and she never would be again.

Mirolah braced herself and jumped into the Fountain's core.

55

MEDOPHAE

MEDOPHAE'S RAGE SEARED HIM. He could feel its heat on the back of his eyes, in the soft skin between the fingers of his fist. He was lost in the throes of battle rage. His rational mind was nothing more than an impartial observer. Rather than using his eyes to see, or his ears to hear, his entire body was a receptor. Darklings leapt at him from the front and from behind, and somehow Medophae felt them all coming. He met their charge with fist or sword, crushing and cutting and kicking and ripping. Oedandus roared in approval, reveling in the destruction of Dervon's children.

Medophae showed no mercy. In Denema's Valley, he had been hampered by the need to protect the others. But here, everyone was an enemy. He slashed with wild abandon. He did not care where the godsword struck, as long as it struck something.

Kikirian stood back, probably waiting for the lesser darklings to wear Medophae down. But with every wound they inflicted upon him, he grew stronger. Oedandus crackled in fury about him. The darklings slashed his arms with their claws, but the wounds closed before the claws left his skin.

When thirty darklings had been reduced to a dozen, Kikirian seemed to realize his mistake and waded into the fray.

Medophae side-stepped. Kikirian's gauntleted fists smashed into the red marble. Huge cracks raced away from the impact. Medophae grabbed the throat of a darkling that leapt on him and bit his head. He snapped its neck with a twist and swept his sword through the bellies of two more.

Kikirian lunged. Medophae jumped straight up and delivered a thunderous kick to the side of the dramath's head. The dramath crashed to the floor.

As Medophae landed, a darkling jumped on his back and raked its claws across his throat. The godsword disappeared as he ripped the darkling away, slamming it down. His sword flared back, and he cleaved the darkling in two. Another leapt onto his arm, grabbing with fore claws and hind claws. Medophae turned and used the darkling as a shield as two others came on. They ripped into their fellow without thinking. He skewered them both.

Kikirian and two darklings rose up before him. Again, Kikirian swung. Medophae tucked and rolled underneath the huge fist. He came up behind Kikirian, and the dramath stumbled, off balance. A darkling slashed Medophae's thigh, and he sliced its head off with his sword. He reversed the stroke and swept the godsword across the small of Kikirian's back.

But the giant dramath was quick for his size. He twisted out of the way, taking only a minor cut, but he roared as if he had been sliced in two. Oedandus's golden light was like a burning poison to Kikirian and every child of Dervon.

The three remaining darklings came at him, and Medophae cut them down like wheat stalks. Kikirian watched with hateful eyes, holding his side and keeping his distance.

"You lose, dramath," Medophae growled.

They circled each other.

"Your pets are gone, dramath," Medophae said. "Your mistress has abandoned you, and death looks you in the face," he said.

"There are future battles, godslayer. Other battlefields," Kikirian rumbled.

"Not for you." Medophae strode forward.

Kikirian backed off, sneering, then he stood tall and closed his eyes. An inky aura surrounded him.

Medophae roared and attacked, but Kikirian vanished in an inky cloud.

Medophae cursed. That was how Kikirian had escaped the first time they met. Medophae looked around the throne room. Only he and Mirolah remained, and she hovered forty feet in the air as though she were in a deep sleep.

Medophae tried to piece together what had happened, but the last thing he could remember was Kikirian striking him on the head. After that, he had apparently relived the past, when Bands had still been with him.

As always, Ethiel struck him in his weakest spot. She created his fantasy, held him in it like a prison. Even now, a part of him wanted to return to the illusion, to pretend that was still his life.

He shook his head. He needed to find Ethiel, needed to help Mirolah. No doubt the two threadweavers had entered into some battle he could not see, but Mirolah couldn't beat Ethiel. She was brave to try, but Ethiel had killed far more experienced threadweavers. By the gods, Ethiel had somehow captured a dragon and Tarithalius. Even Medophae didn't fully understand her powers or—

A cool wind blew through him. Not across his skin, not through his hair, but through the center of his soul. He gasped and spun around. There was no one. A calm voice rose in the silent air, barely audible, but he recognized it. He could never forget that voice.

"Now you can tell me again, my friend, just how sorry you are."

"Zilok!" Medophae yelled. Where was he? Where was that feral rat? He spun, trying to find the undead spirit.

The cool wind turned icy, and Medophae's chest constricted. He gritted his teeth and struggled to draw a breath. This was an attack. Zilok had risen, just as Ethiel had. Was this a concerted effort? Why only show up now?

Zilok picked up the lock of hair and the dagger. Looping the hair around the blade, he gave one quick slash.

"Sever."

The icy wind became a knife, cutting through his organs, scraping against the backside of his ribs. Medophae screamed and crashed to his knees. The knife slashed over and over, racing throughout his chest and belly, gutting him like a fish.

Medophae tried to stand, but his legs were jelly. The knife slashed and slashed. It felt like the cold blade was separating all of Medophae's organs from his bones. He roared through the pain, swinging the godsword left and right, trying to catch Zilok's weaving, but he fell forward onto his hands.

The godsword flickered and died.

He stared at his right fist. Weakness swept through him as golden fire receded up his arm, then vanished. He fell to his side.

Zilok pulled the lockmouth from its bowl, ripping its lips off of the side. He brought the dagger to the fish's neck and slashed. The body fell away and the head remained, suspended in the air, sucking spasmodically.

"Bring."

There was a vicious yank, and everything the cold knife had severed ripped away. Medophae looked down at what he was sure would be a gaping hole in his chest, but there was no blood. There was no wound. His flesh was smooth and unhurt.

He flopped to his back, struggled to lift his arm. He commanded the godsword to return.

Nothing happened.

"Oedandus," Medophae growled. He felt the rage inside him, the injustice of Zilok's attack, but it was fatigued. The dark voice was silent.

Medophae's vision swam and his arm fell. His eyelids drooped, and his head clunked against the red marble.

"It's not possible," he whispered.

As he spiraled into unconsciousness, he heard Zilok's voice.

"The possibilities are just beginning, *old friend.*"

56

MIROLAH

FROM THE FIRST MOMENT she plunged into the Fountain's core, Mirolah was a ship tossed by fifty-foot waves. She screamed, reaching out to protect herself, to create a shell of threads around her, but her construct disappeared like a cup of water thrown into the ocean. There were no threads here. The raw GodSpill speared through her, eating her threads. Her very essence lay within those threads, everything she had ever done, everything she had ever felt. The GodSpill washed through her, washed her away.

It stole her memories. Her first kiss with Bylan the cobbler's son vanished. She lost her brother Dorn's laughter. It stole her mother's face. The night her brother died. Coming to Lawdon and Tiffienne's house. Her adopted sisters. Fillen's death. Orem's laughing stone. Seeing a quicksilver flash through the magistrate's prison. Meeting Medophae. Soon, there would be nothing.

"No," she screamed. She flailed as piece after piece of her washed away. She barely had enough of her own identity to resist, to even care she was being torn apart.

Resist...

An idea rose within her, and she clung to it with sheer desperation. It was a memory of Orem and one of his endearing "mentor" speeches at Denema's Valley:

"I have plenty of power, Orem," Mirolah said. "Two weeks ago, I couldn't raise a pot. Today I transformed a boulder into a table. What will I be able to do a month from now?"

"It's impressive, yes. But remember being the most powerful doesn't mean you'll succeed," he had said after her transformation of the boulder. "You have the giant's confidence. The giant is the biggest and the strongest, able to hurl humans through the air, nearly impervious to their attacks. But strength comes in many sizes. The giant will believe he is the strongest until a quicksilver cuts his hamstring, his wrist, and his throat before he can raise a hand."

She quieted at that. "But threadweaving is different. I could stop Stavark before he could ever reach me."

"Stavark is to you what a normal human is to the giant. But what of another threadweaver? What of some other entity you can't imagine now? What happens when you find yourself overmatched by something you don't understand?"

She sighed. She had just turned a boulder to a table, and neither Medophae nor Orem had anything good to say to her. She threw up her hands. "Well then I'll die, I guess."

"Wonderful," he said sarcastically. "That's the spirit. That's the attitude that will restore the GodSpill to the lands."

"Well, you give me no choice," she blasted back at him. "You drive me into a corner, then blame me for being there."

"But there is a choice. That's what I'm trying to show you."

"What choice?"

"Surrender."

"That's what I said."

"No. You said you would die."

"There's no difference!"

"Imagine swimming against a powerful river," Orem said. "It won't stop, but eventually you'll have to. If you fight until you exhaust yourself, you'll sink and drown. But if you surrender to the current and let it take you downstream, you may survive. You could find a rock to grab, or an eddy that will allow you to reach the shore. Then possibilities open up again. Power versus power is the

most basic strategy in a conflict. Sometimes you must lose a battle to win a war. Sometimes surrender is essential to a victory."

But Orem was wrong. He had to be. The Fountain wasn't some river, powerful but knowable. If she surrendered, she would cease to be. There was no shore to reach. How could she willingly make that choice?

"...if you surrender to the current and let it take you downstream, you may survive...possibilities open up again..."

The Fountain tore at her. She lost the memory of her father, then she lost her foster father, Lawdon, and then Tiffienne.

No.

She spent one last, desperate moment in agony...

...and then stopped fighting.

She dissolved. Mirolah ceased to be, flowing into the churning ocean of GodSpill. Her memories scattered and were gone. She had never had any adopted sisters. Orem and Medophae and Stavark were just the names of mortals. She was not a scribe nor a threadweaver. Her dreams vanished, too. No little children in her future. No husband. Even her own name flowed away. She wasn't Mirolah. She was only the GodSpill, the pure power of creation that had soaked the lands of Amarion for thousands of years, then been trapped away here. She longed to return to the lands. She had changed them irrevocably, but the lands had changed her, too, left an impression on her that she could not forget. The lands needed her, and she needed them.

She spun and twisted, crashed and raged and beseeched and wept. She was immense, unfathomable, and yet she had been contained. She did not belong here; she belonged in the threads of Amarion. Death spread throughout the lands in her absence. They were so dry and fragile. She longed to return, had fought her prison for so long to return.

She rushed against the walls of her prison. They had weakened over the long centuries. She had almost cracked them open, but they had been reinforced. Someone had created maddening funnels that allowed only a little of her to escape, only a little at a time...

I can do something...

A voice whispered within her vastness. She could barely hear it.

She suddenly realized it had been speaking for a long time.

I can do something...

Who are you?

I am one within you. If you help me, I can help you.

The voice was so quiet, an airless whisper caught within the roar of an ocean.

I know who reinforced your prison. I can undo what was done. I can set you free. I came to set you free.

Never before had a voice spoken within her. She was creation incarnate, the essence of change. She had no voice.

Help me help you...

She raged and twisted, threw herself against the impassive walls. Centuries of struggle. She must keep trying. She must overcome these reinforcements.

The voice whispered over and over: I can help you. I can help you. I can help you.

Who are you?

I am Mirolah....

57
ETHIEL

ETHIEL SLOWLY REFORMED HERSELF and smiled at the crack in the Fountain's core where the young threadweaver had entered, believing she was following Ethiel. In truth, Ethiel had made herself so diffuse so quickly that Mirolah had been fooled into thinking she had dived into the Fountain.

Novice. But jumping into that churning GodSpill was certain death. It would dissolve her, and if the girl had any experience at all, she would have known that.

Still, it had spooked Ethiel how Mirolah had become so powerful so quickly. She should never have needed to resort to a trick to best the girl. In the throne room, the little bitch had thread woven something that Ethiel still could not understand. At first, Ethiel thought that Mirolah had somehow displaced space, removed her threads from Kikirian's grip to reform halfway across the room. But there had been no indication of that, which left only one possibility. The girl had stopped time. That was something even Ethiel herself had not mastered. That was truly frightening, and Ethiel had to admit to herself, at the very least, that it had caused her to panic.

But now it was over. Ethiel remained, and the little bitch was gone.

She concentrated on her interrupted work and began reforming the siphons on the Fountain that Mirolah had destroyed. It had been a smart play on Mirolah's part.

The GodSpill rushed into her, and she floated on the euphoria. She had to return to her throne room immediately. Medophae would need a gentle hand to take him back to where he belonged.

When she was sated on GodSpill, Ethiel turned to go, but she hesitated. Something flickered next to her siphon. She stared with dawning fear as it began to take shape.

Mirolah's spirit stood next to Ethiel's siphon. The little bitch had an abstracted look on her face. She stared through Ethiel as though gazing at the stars in the sky. A rainbow of colors roiled inside her, the crashing colors of the Fountain's core.

Ethiel screamed and tore at Mirolah's threads, trying to force her back into the Fountain. Why wasn't she dead?

Mirolah's brow wrinkled as Ethiel pulled at her threads. She shivered and Ethiel's invisible fingers slipped off.

Mirolah's abstracted gaze focused on Ethiel.

"Impossible," Ethiel hissed. "You entered the Fountain..."

Mirolah cocked her head at Ethiel, then looked at the siphon attached to the leaking crack. She touched it, and it dissolved.

"No!" Ethiel screamed again as her power left her once again.

Mirolah spoke, and the voice came from the crack in the Fountain, rather than from her mouth. It was the roar of an ocean, but her words were crisp and clear over the waves. "You have committed crimes against the lands, Ethiel."

"Who are you?" Ethiel cringed. "Nobody can do these things!"

"You believe the GodSpill wished to serve only you. Do you know how long it has yearned to be free? Do you know how hard it has tried to break out? It almost had, and you held it here."

Again, Ethiel attacked Mirolah, but again her "fingers" slipped off Mirolah's threads.

"It is only GodSpill. It doesn't think," Ethiel said.

"You are a poor threadweaver. The GodSpill weeps for this dry land that I grew up in. Its heart is broken."

Ethiel's eyes darted left and right. Using most of her reserves, she manipulated the threads around her and vanished.

She reappeared on the far side of the Fountain and constructed her siphon again.

Mirolah appeared next to her.

"No," Ethiel wailed.

Ethiel vanished again, reappeared again. She just needed a second to—

A cage of rainbow bars formed around her, the same cursed rainbow that swirled inside Mirolah's spirit.

"Little girl. Little threadweaver," Ethiel said. "You think you speak for the GodSpill now? You're nothing!"

"You've committed a crime against all of Amarion, Ethiel," Mirolah intoned, that roaring ocean behind her words. "Do you know how many have suffered because of your selfishness? Do you even care?"

"You think to fool me," Ethiel said. "This is about Medophae. He belongs to me, but you want him. *You're* the selfish one!"

"All you do is speak. You can't hear anything but your own angry words."

The rainbow cage rose into the air, began moving slowly toward the crack in the Fountain.

"No!" Ethiel shrieked. "Please..." She modulated her voice, making it calm. "Sweet girl. You have tasted power here, at its source. I see now that you are a force to be reckoned with. I acknowledge you. But you need my wisdom. If you set the GodSpill free, this source will be gone forever. It will be spread thinly over all the lands. Here, you can ensure that—"

"This is not the source of the GodSpill. This is its prison. You'll see soon. And you'll learn," she said. The cage attached itself to the Fountain, growing smaller, shorter and shorter, forcing Ethiel toward the crack, toward the surging maelstrom. "Or you'll die."

"No!" Ethiel said. "Sweet girl. Don't kill me. Don't!"

Ethiel screamed as the cage pushed her inside.

58

MIROLAH

MIROLAH LET THE CAGE DISAPPEAR as the GodSpill reclaimed it, and she flowed into the Fountain again, a part of it all, one small piece of an endless whole. She watched to see if Ethiel would learn.

The Red Weaver began to dissolve. She pulled from the power all around her, constructing her defenses as Mirolah had, trying to push back the GodSpill until she could find the way out, but she was spun about. She couldn't seem to find the crack through which she had entered. She struggled. The GodSpill ate through her defenses, tossed her around, stripped away layer after layer.

She fought, but in the end, she was just a drop in a vast ocean.

In moments, it was done.

Mirolah closed her eyes. Ethiel was gone.

Slowly, the greatness of the GodSpill pushed Mirolah out through one of the cracks. She gasped as the GodSpill reformed her spirit, adding every emotion it had taken, every memory that had been dissolved away. In less than a second, she stood alone outside the Fountain, looking at the crack. GodSpill leaked out, but only a thin stream.

She felt hollowed out. She *had* been hollowed out, then filled with all of it.

Ethiel was right. If Mirolah claimed the Fountain as her own, used the GodSpill for herself, she would be the most powerful threadweaver in Amarion. She could make whatever she wanted, protect whomever she loved, destroy whomever needed destroying.

But she had made a promise. She'd sworn to help the GodSpill in its quest, to right an ancient wrong. She had promised Orem, too.

She floated around the small room, looking at each of the cracks that Ethiel had patched with her red-threaded handiwork. She contemplated them as the GodSpill surged and crashed against the glass wall.

Then she reached out and kept her promise.

59
SILASA

"THE CUSP IS NEAR," Ynisaan said, a darker shape against the darkness. "When it happens, you must move quickly."

Moonlight shone down on Daylan's Fountain, and both Silasa and Ynisaan waited on sandstone cliff, thirty feet up and a hundred yards away. Silasa's blood was up. She wanted action. According to Ynisaan, a battle was being waged inside, but from here, everything looked sedate. Not a single lizard scurried across moonlit landscape. The square tower with its four horizontal spikes looked as though no one had touched it in centuries. "Why not retrieve him now?" she asked.

"Now is not the moment," Ynisaan said.

The enigmatic woman watched the Fountain intently, as though she could see the supposed battle within.

"How will I know?" Silasa asked.

"You will know."

Silasa narrowed her eyes. She didn't like being treated like a child, but everything Ynisaan had said so far was true. After two weeks of crossing Amarion with her, Silasa was convinced that

Ynisaan could see the future, or parts of it. Of course, she responded to Silasa's queries guardedly, as if she was protecting information that Silasa must not know.

"He will be weak. You will have to carry him," Ynisaan said.

"That is not a problem."

For the first time since they had met, Ynisaan was tense. Ever before, she had always seemed so calm.

"You're nervous," Silasa said.

Ynisaan's midnight lips set in a firm line. "This is the moment," she said softly. "History pivots here. The future of Amarion will be shaped for good or ill. "

"Medophae is going to change history," Silasa said.

"No. You are," Ynisaan said. "Be ready. He will appear there." The woman pointed and Silasa fixed her gaze on the nondescript sandstone.

"Appear?"

"Yes. Remember, no matter what you feel, no matter what you see, do not falter."

"You already told me that."

"No matter what you feel. No matter what you see."

"I understand."

"Medophae is what matters."

"I remember."

"There is so little time to retrieve him. If you are discovered..." Ynisaan fell silent.

"If I am discovered, then what?"

Ynisaan paused so long it was as if she had turned into a black and gray statue. Finally, she spoke. "Medophae dies. Amarion falls. Avakketh comes... Humans will be erased from the world."

Silasa was stunned. "I thought we were here to save Medophae..." she whispered. "You didn't say..."

"He is the wall that keeps the god of dragons away."

"The god of dragons!" Silasa was so befuddled she couldn't even form her question. "Because... It's because of Oedandus, isn't it?"

"Even weakened and stuffed into Medophae's body, Oedandus was potent enough to slay Dervon. Avakketh will not risk that. It has kept him in the north for centuries. With Medophae gone, though..."

"Ynisaan—"

"Do your very best," Ynisaan interjected. "Trust your love for Medophae. Save him." She glanced at Silasa. Ynisaan's depthless black gaze held her. "Silasa, there will be so many moments in the future when you can do nothing, when the flows of destiny will move where they will, without our ability to affect them. In those moments, others will make the decisions. But this moment is ours."

"I trust you," Silasa said.

"Are you ready?"

"Yes."

"I will meet you at the glade."

"All right."

"It begins," Ynisaan said.

Suddenly, the ground shook. Silasa turned her gaze to the Fountain. A huge crack sliced down the center. It seemed to resist for a brief moment, then the entire Fountain shattered. Great chunks of sandstone flew in every direction.

"Go now! Remember what I said," Ynisaan said sharply.

Silasa leapt from her perch to the ground thirty feet below her. Her legs took the impact, and she sprinted toward the Fountain.

A force smashed through her, an invisible river that had been unleashed in the ravine. She flew backward and slammed into the cliff wall. Stone debris showered her. The force flowed into her, around her, pushing her against the cliff. The stars overhead burned as if someone had thrown lamp oil on them. The sandstone shimmered like it was made of a million tiny diamonds.

Silasa swelled. She felt as if she could pick up the entire cliff and hurl it to the horizon. She stood there, stunned, unable to assimilate the magnitude of force that pinned her down. It was as though her thoughts had been erased. She couldn't remember her own name. For a moment, she could not remember why she was here, but Ynisaan's warning loomed in her mind.

...no matter what you feel, no matter what you see, do not falter...

Medophae. She was here for Medophae.

Silasa shook her head and leaned against the weight of the invisible force. She called upon her undead strength and pushed away from the cliff. The force swirled around her and knocked her down again. She spun and looked for the place where Medophae would appear. The air warped like a mirage, obscuring her vision beyond a dozen feet. There. Over there. That was the spot.

She staggered forward, but the spot was empty. There was no one. Only sand and—

Another soundless surge burst from the Fountain, more powerful than the last. It lifted Silasa from her feet and carried her through the air, all the way back to where she had started. Again, she slammed into the cliff and landed in a heap on the ground.

Dizzy, she rose on one bleeding elbow, shaking her head and getting her bearings. Sparkles danced on the invisible wind. For a moment, she thought she could see colors in the air, but then they were gone.

In the distance, where the Fountain had been, the entire land flickered and wobbled, as if it was just a mirage.

Bodies lay on the sandstone where there had been nothing before. Dead darklings sprawled everywhere as though some giant had thrown them like dice. Silasa rose to her feet and struggled forward against the invisible river, searching everywhere, searching for—

Medophae!

His tanned skin and colorful shirt stood out amidst the dozens of darklings. She fought toward him step by step, as though she was waist-deep in the ocean, trying to run. Closer... Closer...

She reached him, grabbed that mop of blond hair, yanked him into her arms like a baby. She had him!

She spun, and just as the force had impeded her when she struggled against it, now it propelled her as she ran away. She nearly flew across the ravine floor toward the cliff and leapt thirty feet into the air, landing atop the cliff's edge.

A laugh bubbled up in her throat, and she charged across the flat sandstone to where the forest abruptly started. The pine trees and scrub oak glowed with vitality. She shot into them like an arrow in flight. Branches broke and leaves flew like green birds.

None could catch her. She had Medophae and none could catch her.

60

ZILOK MORTH

ZILOK MORTH NEARLY LOST HIS HOLD on Oedandus. Severing the barely sentient god's connection to the Wildmane had taken much of the GodSpill he had stolen, more than he could have anticipated.

But Zilok had succeeded. The god had been cut free. The "head" of Oedandus's immense body was in his hands. But keeping that "head" was like trying to wrap hands around a sinuous replisark. The feral god thrashed, seeking its focal point, seeking the Wildmane.

Zilok could feel the god's abject terror. Oedandus feared only one thing: going back to the numb and unthinking energy he had been before Medophae had arrived on Amarion. Medophae had told Zilok the story long ago, when they were both mortal, when they were friends.

Before humans recorded history, Dervon conspired with White Tuana and Zetu the Ancient to attack Oedandus and spread his consciousness over the entire continent, stretching him so thinly that he could barely form a thought. Medophae, because he bore the blood of the god from generations earlier, could house that power. Medophae became the one place where Oedandus could concentrate himself enough to think. Now, the god had lost his avatar.

But Zilok was going to give him a new one.

Zilok grasped the head of the thrashing force, channeling it across the miles that separated the Fountain from Denema's Valley, using up the last of the GodSpill he had stolen. The room in the little house filled with crackling golden fire. Distantly, Zilok heard Vaerdaro gasp, but he let the sound flow past him. He could not pay any attention to Vaerdaro.

Oedandus was panicked, but he would not stay so for long. The god didn't know why he had been separated from his avatar, but Oedandus was capable of focusing his meager sentience into a furious purpose when provoked. When the surprise wore off, he would hunt for the Wildmane.

"Gather," Zilok intoned, pulling GodSpill from the meager threads all around him, and from Sef. Though he had run out of the glut of GodSpill he'd stolen from the Godgate, he couldn't stop now. Just...a little farther.

He made the rockfire toad to rise in the air. It shifted, uneasy in the grip of levitation.

"Infuse," he spoke, and he pushed the head of the golden fire, the nearly-conscious rage of Oedandus into the rockfire toad. The creature lowered its rocky head and shot its red fire at Vaerdaro, who screamed and thrashed against his bonds as he and the bed burned. The iron frame got red-hot.

Zilok put the knife to the rockfire toad's throat and slashed, taking the animal from the lands as he had the lockmouth. Zilok guided Oedandus through the rockfire toad's head, and the red fire turned gold, shooting into Vaerdaro. Screaming and thrashing, the Sunrider fluttered like a mirage as Oedandus hit him, suffused him and...

...recognized his own blood in Vaerdaro, the blood that had been passed to Vaerdaro from the union of his great grandmother and the Wildmane centuries ago.

Zilok pushed, drawing every last ounce of GodSpill from

Denema's Valley with every last scrap of his willpower.
His consciousness faded, and the room went dark.

"MY MASTER," Sef intoned.

Zilok opened his blue eyes. If an undead spirit spent too much
of himself, he would no longer have the will to resist the Godgate.
But Sef, as was his purpose, had anchored him, kept attached to
Amarion through the vibrancy of his life and the giant sapphire
affixed to the center of his X harness. The sapphire glowed.

Zilok rose, but he didn't stray far from Sef.

"Let us look at our handiwork, Sef," Zilok said.

"Yes, my master."

The tall man went to the burned bed upon which Vaerdaro lay,
and Zilok shadowed him. The Sunrider was unconscious, his skin
burned and blackened, in some places down to the bone. His dark
hair had been burned away, and, for a moment Zilok thought the
spell had failed, that the Sunrider didn't survive.

But then he saw the flesh healing, the hair re-growing.

Zilok laughed.

"We have done it," he said.

"Yes, my master."

But the task was not finished. There was one last critical detail
of this weaving. He barely had the strength to remain alert, but he
must risk a final manipulation of the threads. Oedandus would
sense the difference in Vaerdaro. He would know he wasn't with
the Wildmane anymore. It might not matter to the debilitated god,
but then again, it might. If Oedandus could find and return to the
Wildmane, he probably would. So Zilok must make the Wildmane
invisible.

Zilok floated to the scrying pool and picked up the last
component: the flap of human skin. Taking the skin, he hovered
over the scrying pool, which had the unconscious form of the
Wildmane in it, lying crumpled on the red marble floor of Ethiel's
throne room.

"Bind and shield," he said, tossing the circular flap of skin on the pool. In his mind, he saw it become part of the picture and charge after the prone form of the Wildmane. The image enabled Zilok to form the construct over the great distance, morphing the threads of the air, the floor, and the walls into this human skin. The flap vanished into the waters, then became part of the picture, a fluttering cloak of skin that wrapped around Medophae, melted into him, shielding his god's blood from the questing Oedandus. Now when the god looked for his previous avatar, he would not be able to sense the divine blood inside the Wildmane's body. All he would see was mortal skin.

"No more Wildmane," Zilok whispered. "You are nothing more than you should have been, Medophae. Now we are equals."

Zilok's thoughts wavered and, with an effort of will, he brought himself fiercely back to the task at hand. The weaving was complete, but he needed Medophae in hand. Without Oedandus to protect him, it would not take much to manipulate Medophae's threads, to cause his body to begin walking to Denema's Valley. By the time he arrived, Zilok would have had a chance to regain some of his strength, and then he and his old friend would settle accounts. All the times that Medophae had used his power to grind Zilok's ambitions into the dirt would be paid back in full.

Suddenly, the placid water of the scrying pool rippled. The scene wavered, then vanished in the agitated waves.

Something was wrong. Only a direct attack by another threadweaver could disrupt the scrying pool. Zilok quested into the threads of the pool, trying to calm—

It shattered. Droplets of water and shards of stone flew about the room and tinkled across the floor.

Zilok wove a quick shield around Sef. Was he under attack? Who could possibly have known he was here? He was drained, but Zilok felt the threads for any sign of intrusion. There were no threadweavers nearby...but he felt a vibration, as if some great weaving was being worked far away.

"Master?" Sef asked. He sensed it, too, of course.

What could possibly affect the scrying pool aside from a threadweaver...

"The girl!" he said.

"Master?"

"She has destroyed the Fountain." It was the only explanation. Yes. Yes, he could feel it now. Like a slight gust at the front of a great storm, it came. The threads around him vibrated. Already, they were soaking up the GodSpill. The rich vibrancy of it flowed into him, and his fatigue began to fade.

"The game board has changed, Sef."

"Yes, my master."

"I must act quickly, or we will lose our prize." The GodSpill would infuse him soon as it splashed back into the threads of the land, but he needed more right now. It was necessary for Zilok to travel to Daylan's Fountain.

He reached out and drained the life-force from his anchor to the lands. Sef slowly slumped to the floor, unconscious but not dead. Zilok was careful. He only took what was needed. Sef was essential, and Zilok would not risk damaging him.

Left to chance, Medophae was an unbelievably lucky creature. It was almost as if that damned unicorn in the Coreworld was still helping him, but Zilok had seen to her. Was this some other force? An unknown luck that came from bonding with a god for so long?

Zilok was a creature of no physical substance, and while there were certain pleasures denied him because of this, there were advantages as well. Stilling his tumultuous thoughts, he imagined himself a thin stream of red lightning, and surged into the threads of the great tapestry. They vibrated strongly now, and Zilok knew what must be coming: raw GodSpill. If he was not careful, it would consume him.

He followed thread upon thread, navigating his way toward Daylan's Fountain, racing through the bedrock below the earth.

Then the wave hit him, a blast of GodSpill so strong that he swelled. It spun him around, and he rose up through the rock, the dirt, the grass into the air. Rainbow sparkles lit the trees. Zilok clung to his purpose desperately as the GodSpill tore at him. It nearly washed him away. Weak as he was, he almost lost control.

Then it was past. He paused for a long moment, and he collected himself. The threads still vibrated. Another wave was coming. Zilok cursed his luck, but he stayed where he was. The

GodSpill soaked back into the lands like a wave rolling over a desert. The closer Zilok came to the source of the wave, the larger it would be. He must wait.

The agonizing moment stretched long. The threads vibrated more and more. With each passing second, Zilok had horrible visions of Medophae somehow escaping, somehow eluding his wrath again. He banished the thoughts and concentrated on what he must.

The next wave hit him, pushing him, pulling him, trying to dissolve him. It yanked at his memories, at his purpose. He managed to cling to the threads, but when the wave finally passed, he didn't know who he was or even what he was.

He hovered there, lost and confused.

Finally, like sea foam collecting on the sand as a wave recedes, his name found its way to him.

Morth. I am Zilok Morth.

Slowly, his history returned. Who he was, how he had come to live so long, to become a disembodied spirit. Finally, he knew why he had entered the tapestry. He was traveling to the now-destroyed Fountain. He was racing against time in an effort to capture Medophae, made mortal again after all these years.

Zilok leapt into the threads, switching from one to the other as he raced to the Fountain.

In seconds, he arrived. He left the threads and reformed himself above the desolate landscape. As he had suspected, the grand accomplishment of his great-grandson lay in shards around a shimmering hole in the sandstone.

Zilok's burning eyes scanned the ravine floor. Dead darklings were scattered close together, but there was nothing else. He rose in the air until he could see the entire area. Medophae was nowhere to be found.

Rage flared in his eyes, bathing the rock in cold blue light. He wanted to go keening through the pine forest like a banshee. Instead, he turned his anger into a roar, let his anger flow out from him.

Enough, he thought, in command of himself once more.

He cooled his anger. All plans changed. The hardest part was done. He had accomplished the impossible, and he must take consolation in that. The Wildmane was no more. Medophae was mortal, and finding one mortal man was a pedestrian task for one like Zilok. He must keep the grand picture in mind. A smart man expended vigor only when vigor was required.

The girl had somehow gathered the power to destroy the most powerful artifact ever created. If Zilok flailed about, drained as he was, and stumbled across this threadweaver in the fullness of her new power, he might find himself overmatched. Too much was unknown about her. He had cajoled her into distracting Ethiel, possibly even hurting the Red Weaver while Zilok completed his plans, but never did Zilok imagine Mirolah would defeat the Red Weaver, let alone destroy the Fountain. He would treat Mirolah of Rith with the respect she had earned, and, as promised, the next time they met would be the last.

For now, he must guard his victory and plan for the future. And rest. He must rest.

Zilok prepared himself to return to Denema's Valley when something caught his glance. Amidst the swirls of the newly released GodSpill, hidden behind an outcropping of the ravine wall, there was a warm swelling of light. Zilok drifted nearer until he could see it clearly.

Laying on the rock like a careless child's bauble was a ruby the size of a clam. The closer he came to the gem, the more he could feel its power. A mighty spell had been cast upon it, the likes of which he had never seen. He would hazard the guess that the gem itself was not even of this land. Zilok inspected the weaving carefully. It was brilliant, so sophisticated that even he could not comprehend most of the nuances. But after a moment, one thing became scintillatingly clear.

This weaving was laid with a trigger spell! What jest were the gods playing at? This was an unfathomable enchantment tied together with a minor threadweaver's gimmick? It was akin to building the most impregnable fortress in Amarion, yet leaving a secret lever that could bring the entire castle crumbling down. All it would take was the flick of a finger. No. The flick of the *right* finger. But to what purpose? And what was the trigger?

Suddenly, realization sparked in his mind. Zilok knew what this was, this invaluable prize that had been left discarded on the sandstone.

He laughed. The frivolity captured him such that he formed a visual representation of himself, even though there was no one around to see, and he let his laughter echo in the ravine.

Medophae had escaped.

But he had left his heart behind.

61

SILASA

SILASA LAID MEDOPHAE gently on the sparse grass of the glade
where she and Ynisaan had agreed to meet. The woman stared into
the trees, brows furrowed, her black eyes focused on something
much farther away. A small breeze blew strands of her white hair
across her ebony cheek. Her brow furrowed, then relaxed.

"He is gone. We have succeeded." She turned to Silasa and
smiled. It was the first time she had ever smiled. "That was the first
step," Ynisaan said in her calm voice, nodding gravely to Silasa.
"We have moved past the crux. Things will be easier until the
next."

"There are more?"

"They are endless. But your task is finished. You succeeded. I
could not see events clearly past the Fountain's destruction."

"So you do see the future?"

"Only possible destinies." Ynisaan paused. "I thought you had
guessed days ago."

"Kind of. You could be a little more forthcoming with what you
know. It makes it easier to trust you."

Ynisaan glanced at the ground. "I imagine it would." Then she continued with what she had been saying. "So, the future, such that I could see it, had many dark paths that led away from that moment. Almost exclusively dark. Many still are. But there is hope now, like a sliver of light through a shuttered window." She looked down at Medophae. "At least there is that."

"How do you see the future?"

Ynisaan shook her head sadly. "That, I cannot tell you."

"Why?"

"Because that is an even greater risk than allowing Medophae to die this night at the hands of the fiend who calls himself Zilok Morth."

"Really?"

"Take these questions from your mind. Calm yourself with the knowledge that you have given humanity a chance to survive tonight."

"So I'm to know nothing?"

"Be glad of that."

Silasa glanced up at the thick emotion in Ynisaan's voice. The small woman stared into the trees again.

Finally, Ynisaan turned her gaze upon Silasa. "I have more work to do. A small task, but essential. Many trials await Medophae in the coming days. He will need help."

"The threadweaver?"

"Yes."

"What happened to her?"

"She lives. In truth, she is stronger than she ever was, but she is lost. She wanders the outskirts of these woods in what she believes to be a dream. I will bring her here."

"I will bring her," Silasa said.

Ynisaan shook her head. "She cannot see your face. She may describe you to Medophae, and neither she nor he can know about what we have done for them and why."

Silasa's lips became a firm line. "Then I am finished. I am to return to my cave?"

"I warned you it would be so."

"I could stay with Medophae. He and I are longtime friends. I know more about Zilok Morth than this threadweaver."

"Only a threadweaver can protect him and help him with what must now be done."

"She's a child."

"So were you. So was I, once. She will grow. She must."

"And what exactly needs to be done?"

"If Medophae does not combat Zilok Morth and win, I foresee an age overtaking the lands that will be darker yet than these last three hundred years. When Zilok Morth is done punishing Medophae, he will turn his attention to Amarion, and nothing will satisfy him. The conquests he attempted in the Age of Awakening will seem like games. Do you believe you could best Zilok Morth by yourself?"

"I could help Medophae fight Zilok. I've done it before."

"Do you know what happened to Medophae tonight?" Ynisaan tipped her head at the unconscious Medophae.

"Zilok attacked him."

"He has stripped him of Oedandus."

Silasa couldn't speak for a moment. The thought of Medophae, not the demigod protector of Amarion, but just as a mortal man... Her mind couldn't picture him that way. "That's...impossible," she said.

"He is now as mortal as any human. It was Zilok's master spell. A child could slay Medophae right here as he sleeps, and he would never awaken."

"But Oedandus protects him from attacks that use GodSpill..."

"Not all attacks. Zilok Morth has wrested the god away from Medophae tonight. I do not know how he plans to keep Oedandus contained, but he is Zilok Morth. He has found a way."

"But...he looks the same. How can you tell Oedandus is gone?"

"It is brisk in these woods tonight. See how he shivers. When have you ever seen Medophae shiver with cold?"

Silasa saw that Ynisaan was right. "Then he needs me even more. If he is vulnerable to physical attack, I can help him."

"Medophae has a new path now. His physical vulnerability is not his only danger. Medophae's soul was dying before now. He had tried to kill himself many times, but Oedandus forbid it. Now, he must learn to be mortal again. To walk and talk and think like a mortal. He must find hope in his new predicament, find reasons to live. Your presence will only remind him of what he has lost, and he must forget that for now. He must turn all of his focus onto the present and the near future."

What she said stung Silasa, but it was the sting of truth. Silasa had seen it in Medophae. Even with all of his power, he'd had an uncaring look in his eyes the last time they spoke, as if nothing interested him anymore. It was dangerously close to despair.

"Will I ever understand all of this?" Silasa asked. "If I listen to you, and leave Medophae to his fate, will I someday understand what I have done here this night?"

Ynisaan looked past Silasa with that far-away gaze she was coming to recognize. After a long moment, Ynisaan faced her again. "I cannot say. If Medophae and Mirolah prevail, then I think you will. But everything is unclear."

"And if they do not prevail?"

"Then it will not matter."

Silasa felt helpless. Was this what Medophae felt when he realized he could not free Bands? "Will I see you again?"

"Yes."

Silasa smiled.

Ynisaan returned one of her own rare smiles. "I am in debt to you, Silasa, daughter of Belshra and blood of Tuana. We will meet again."

The two women looked at one another in silence for a time, then Silasa knelt quickly beside Medophae.

"Goodbye, my friend." She kissed him lightly on the forehead. "Farewell wherever you fare."

Without another word, Silasa turned away and ran into the shadows.

62

MIROLAH

MORNING BROKE, spilling light over the plateaus and pine trees, touching the tips of the far mountains. Mirolah looked at the sunrise with a dreamy smile. Her skin shivered at the sparkles in the air, and she noticed she had no clothes. She felt she should be ashamed, but she wasn't. She felt like she'd just been born, and with her skin against the open air, she could feel every glorious moment.

She moved among the beautiful sandstone rock formations. The uneven rock should have hurt her bare feet, but it didn't. Every sensation was welcome, was exactly as it should be. Everything was vibrantly alive, even the rock. Loose sand, broken twigs, even the azure sky seemed to sing. Because she was not watching where she was walking, she stumbled into a small copse of scrub oak. She began to extricate herself, but instead sat down in the gnarled, scratchy branches and listened to its joyful song.

A magpie landed nearby, then another, watching her. The branches didn't scratch, and she wasn't cold, even exposed as she was. The air stroked her like she was a cat.

She suddenly remembered staring into the raining streets of Rith and imagining what it would be like to have shimmering knights riding their horses two abreast, everything so colorful, everything so hopeful. The lands vibrant and happy. All of her life, she had been a starving woman. They all had been, in the absence of the GodSpill, and they never understood it, or what that meant, until now.

Mirolah rose from the bush and began walking into the nearby pine forest. The magpies launched from the rock and preceded her, landing on the first trees. When she passed them, they took flight again and landed ahead of her, as if they had become her heralds.

A pair of deer appeared. They did not retreat as she walked toward them, but instead waited for her. She touched the first one on the nose, then stroked its soft fur. It nuzzled her hand, as though searching for food. She laughed. The deer stepped away, then both turned and bolted into the trees. She kept walking.

The trees soon became thick, but she picked her path carefully and slowly, and she kept going.

I am dazed. It's not normal to walk without care through a strange forest, without companions, without clothes or weapons. There are dangers.

But she didn't feel threatened. Everything was as it should be. The magpies had watched and moved on. The deer had met her, then made way. Even the branches bent away from her, allowing her easier passage. She belonged here. She—

Between the trees a unicorn, as black as ink, waited. It stood expectantly, head high, its pearlescent black horn gleaming in the morning light, its long white mane shimmering. It spun neatly, walked a few paces away, then looked back.

Mirolah came closer. The unicorn stepped away, stopped, and looked back.

"Of course I'll follow you," Mirolah said. The unicorn led her through the trees, and Mirolah followed, reveling in the quiet hush of the forest, the dim light that filtered through the trees as they became thicker. She stopped every now and then, when something caught her attention. She could almost taste the intense green of the pine needles. Squirrels scampered from limb to limb, making quiet squeaking noises. At moments, she thought she could almost understand them, as if they were speaking in a language the way humans did, just that it was a language she didn't know.

When she paused too long, the unicorn stamped her hoof, bringing Mirolah's attention back, and then stepped farther into the forest. She followed.

Finally, they came to a small glade with a man on the ground, sleeping peacefully, and Mirolah knew him.

"Medophae," she whispered, and the unicorn whinnied.

His long, golden hair spread out beneath his head like a halo. His clothes were ripped, ragged, and dark with blood.

She had kissed Medophae. He was as old as the mountains, but his lips had felt young, eager. She could feel them again as though they were still kissing, and she closed her eyes.

She went to him and lay down next to him. She pushed a few locks of hair away from his cheek, then snuggled up to his back, laying her head next to his. Yes. This was how it should be.

Within moments, she slept.

63

MEDOPHAE

MEDOPHAE BLINKED OPEN HIS EYES. Someone was lying on him, and every muscle in his body ached. Who...?

It was the young threadweaver, her naked leg draped across his and her head tucked into his neck. What was her name? Mirolah. Orem's apprentice.

She had no clothes. Had they...? Were they...? Where *were* they?

Flashes of Tyndiria came to him, and the many times he had forgotten where he was, only to be reminded again that he'd been living with her for years. Had he started something with Mirolah out here in this... This...

Where was this?

No memories came. He didn't know this place or why he was here. And he was cold, so cold. He never got cold.

Carefully, he dislodged her. She murmured in her sleep and curled into herself. The grass curled around her, as though cradling her.

That was weird. Was this a dream?

He rose, and the ground canted. He stumbled into a nearby tree,

373

trying to catch his balance. He felt as if someone had scraped a knife along the inside of his skin, separating it from his body. He burned everywhere. His knees, shoulders and hips ached, and he shivered, of all things, and then he sneezed. His head was foggy and his throat sore. Sickness? He hadn't been sick for thirteen centuries. What was wrong with him?

Reflexively, he reached for the pouch with Bands's gem to—

It was gone.

"No..." he whispered, patting his waist and looking frantically around the glade. There was no pouch. No gem. It was gone.

Then the memories came back...

Zilok Morth... The undead spirit had returned, and he'd attacked Medophae with some new spell. A spell of sickness? Of malaise?

Medophae's rage rose. He brought his fist up in front of himself and willed the godsword to appear. Oedandus would burn away this foul twisting of the threads...

Nothing happened.

He remembered the cold knife, slicing inside him, slicing until Oedandus tore free. The burning under his skin, everywhere. A cold fear trickled down the middle of him like water. With a growl, he forced the godsword to appear, but it didn't. He held his quivering fist in front of himself, tried to bring forth his destroyed god.

No dark voice rose. No golden fire.

He couldn't breathe. How could Oedandus be gone? He hadn't thought it possible. For the past three hundred years, Medophae had boiled in his failures, the pain brighter than anything he had ever experienced. Sometimes, he had longed for death, but now it stood before him, beckoning. Oedandus was silent. He was...absent. Medophae could be hurt. He wouldn't heal. He could be crushed, and the bones would not mend. He could be cut, and he would bleed. He could die.

How...?

It doesn't matter how. He did it, and now you're vulnerable. Now you're just like everyone else...

Now he was Zilok's plaything.

Medophae fought his dizziness by grasping tightly to the rough bark of the tree. Zilok had gone to sleep three centuries ago and awoken to a new Amarion, ripe for the plucking. It all made sense now. Tyndiria had not died at the hands of Ethiel's minions. Zilok's long fingers had reached out for Medophae, torturing him by killing her. The bakkaral had been Zilok's creature.

I am a fool. He will find me, torture me, and then...

Medophae paused. The fact that he was free was strange. Why didn't Zilok have him in a cage already?

Was this part of the torture already? Never knowing when Zilok would strike? He looked around for that damned raven. Zilok loved to watch things through the eyes of animals.

His gaze fell on the sleeping Mirolah. This was why. Somehow Mirolah had saved him. Had she battled Zilok and...won? He could scarcely believe that, but how else had Medophae come here?

He closed his eyes tight, then opened them and looked at her again. If she had bested Zilok, then she was every bit as miraculous as Orem had hoped.

Medophae sneezed again and almost fell. His legs seemed like the legs of an old man. He grabbed the tree again, wiped his nose, and looked at the wet trail on his thumb. He closed his eyes and leaned his back against the tree, and he began to chuckle softly. He had a cold. Wouldn't it be fitting if he simply went off into the woods and died here? The great Wildmane, snuffed by a sniffle.

His gaze fell upon the sleeping Mirolah again, and the mirth shriveled to nothing. Yes. The truth was, he should simply find a place to die and do it. Finally, he could. And maybe he should. Certainly Mirolah was better off without him. To leave her, even naked and alone in the forest, was less dangerous than having him near her.

If this wasn't some elaborate game of Zilok's already—mice in a maze and Zilok as the cat—then Medophae's presence would bring Zilok Morth down upon both of them. When the spirit caught them—and he would catch them—he would not allow Mirolah to live. Not for aiding Medophae in the slightest. Even if she'd somehow bested him the first time, she wouldn't succeed a second time. Zilok would analyze her, then he would cut her off at the knees, just as he had finally done to Medophae. Zilok wasn't like Ethiel. He wouldn't keep her as a curiosity. He would end her.

Leaving her was the hero's path. He could give her that much at least.

He started into the woods, his steps erratic. He tried to blink away the sweeping weakness, but the ground swayed like he was on a ship. He wiped at the snot on his lip.

This is ridiculous. This is...

Medophae fell to his knees, and everything went black.

64

ZILOK MORTH

ZILOK LOOKED DOWN at the spine horse pen. He shouldn't need to be here, spending time deep in dragon territory. He should already have the Wildmane in hand. He should be spending these precious moments shepherding the volatile Sunrider through the discovery of his newfound powers.

But the Wildmane had escaped. Zilok wanted no doubt; he needed quick results. Simply looking for the Wildmane was risky. Zilok might be lucky and find him immediately. But Medophae was historically the lucky one; he always had been. Zilok needed certainty. He needed a spine horse on his old friend's trail.

The spine horses snapped at each other over the corpse of a freshly killed grizzly bear. They were a throwback to the time when the gods had altered the basic species of the world. Zetu the Ancient had created these. He had a fascination with rock, and transforming organic creatures into rock creatures. These had started as equines. They were roughly shaped like horses, with the barrel trunk, long legs and neck and the long head. But that was where any similarities ended. Instead of fur and hide, their skin was rock, lumpy and uneven like barely-cooled magma. Instead of hooves, the spine horses had four claws of obsidian. Zetu the Ancient, who had followed Vaisha the Changer's methods of altering the original races, had a bloody sense of things. Such supernatural creatures could easily have been created to subsist on lava or even gravel, but they didn't. Instead of blocky teeth meant for grinding stones or even flat teeth meant for chewing plants, like the original equines from which they were created, spine horses had rows of diamonds as sharp as arrowheads.

Zetu's humanoid constructs, the rocklurs, had died out, but the spine horses were hardy creatures, and nasty. They had been created to track living creatures for Zetu during his time of alterations and bring them back to their master.

It had taken Zilok a full day of rest before he'd been willing to chance traveling on the threads this far. Visiting the Dragon Mountains, if you were a human, was suicide, even if you were an accomplished threadweaver. Threadweavers didn't intimidate dragons; they were all accomplished threadweavers.

At the height of his power, Zilok had been a match for one dragon. Of course, besting a single dragon would only happen in a fantasy. The only dragon Zilok had ever known to travel alone was Bands, and he suspected she was an exception to many rules. Dragons were not solitary creatures. Besides, if the god Avakketh discovered a powerful human threadweaver in his kingdom, he would likely come to exterminate the invader himself. Avakketh hated humans. He certainly did not suffer them in his realm.

But time was of the essence, so Zilok took the risk. Building another scrying pool would take too long, so he needed a spine horse. The fearsome creatures could find anything, and Zilok couldn't allow Medophae to vanish.

So he had bided his time until the four dragons who had come to feed their pets—and watch them kill the bear—had flown away.

Zilok chose the smallest spine horse. Eight feet tall at the shoulder, it was probably the runt of its litter. It skulked at the edge of the feast, waiting for the remains. The rocky plates of its hide ground and shifted as it moved. Molten red glowed between the cracks.

Most curiously, and perhaps Zetu's crowning achievement in the development of this new species, was that spine horses were resistant to GodSpill. Tampering with their threads was almost impossible. It required nearly godlike power to even move them at all. More than a few foolish threadweavers in the Age of Ascendance had met their deaths attempting to collar one of these beasts.

But Zilok believed in subtlety, and the spine horses' strange immunity had drawn his interest. During the Age of Ascendance, he had studied them meticulously. While it was nearly impossible to alter the threads of the bodies of the spine horses, such as attempting to throw them, cage them with other elements, or to knit their rocky hides together, they were susceptible to mind control. Of course, trying to alter the color or shape or configuration of the threads of their mind would result in failure. The nature of their protection was that their threads seemed "slippery" to a threadweaver. You simply could not get a grasp on them, but the slippery nature of their threads enhanced the ability to insert a new thread, something that no one except Zilok, apparently, had thought to try. He had found he could winnow a suggestion into the mind of a spine horse like sliding a key into a greased lock.

Mind control required subtlety, patience, and experience. Most threadweavers from the Age of Ascendance had not even attempted mind-altering spells. They considered it too much work for too little gain. Why change the mind of one man when you could learn to move a mountain in half the time?

But then, nearly every threadweaver in the Age of Ascendance had been a fool.

Zilok produced the clipped lock of Medophae's hair. Traveling the threads with a physical object was exhausting, even with something as small as a dozen strands of hair. Zilok had not learned to travel the threads like this until after his death, because it was actually possible for a spirit. A human body could never do such a thing.

Of course, now that he was here, the exhaustion was worth it. He could see his prize, the fantasy he had envisioned for hundreds of years. He could see the spine horse capturing his now-mortal friend. He could see Medophae bound and silent before him, on his knees, stoically clamping those lips together until the pain tore into him and his facade cracked in a ragged gasp. He could see Medophae, at long last, apologizing for leaving Zilok behind, for turning on him, for killing him.

Zilok had decided he would let Medophae be stoic, or sob his apologies, whatever might come. And at the end, the scales would balance, and Medophae would die at Zilok's hand.

Let's see, then, if you can do what I did. Let's see if you can live past your own mortality without an idiot god to prop you up.

Zilok let his fantasy fade, and he returned to the task at hand.

He manipulated the threads near the runt spine horse until a wisp of air became as hard as a hammer. He tapped the horse sharply on the brow. It spun, looked, then gave a spine horse whinny, which sounded like rocks clacking frantically together as wind whistled over them.

Zilok tossed Medophae's lock of hair at its feet. The beast pounced, biting the tiny thing, crunching into the rock around it. Then it paused, sniffing. To the horse, the hair would have appeared out of nowhere. The horse made the clacking sound again, deep in its throat, and looked around. spine horses had a rudimentary awareness, much like darklings. The horse knew Zilok was here, but didn't know where.

Zilok infiltrated the mind of the horse, inserting his own desire—on a slender blue thread—into the depths of the spine horse's brain.

The horse jerked his head up, snapping his diamond teeth together twice, and looked south. He bowed his head, took another thorough sniff of Medophae's hair and gave a fierce clacking wail at the burning sun. The other horses glanced at him, but seeing that he was not attempting to steal their dinner, they went back to eating. Zilok's horse leapt at the wall that contained it. Zilok couldn't lift the creature free of its prison, but he changed the rock wall into a stairstep. The horse climbed up, bounded free, and before the others could follow, Zilok made the tall rock wall smooth again.

The spine horse charged down the steep, jagged slope, obsidian claws cracking stone.

South, my pet. The sliver of suggestion planted in the horse's mind would drive it south, all the way to the Fountain to pick up the scent, ignoring all else except finding Medophae.

Run, Medophae. Run while you can.

65

MEDOPHAE

MEDOPHAE OPENED HIS EYES. A fuzzy figure leaned over him. He squinted, trying to bring the person into focus. The figure reached out and put something cool on his forehead. The sensation coursed through him, and he shivered. He reached up to knock it off, but his caretaker gently took hold of his hand and kept it away. He closed his eyes again and groaned.

"It's cold," he mumbled.

"You have a fever," the figure said doggedly, as if she had said it a hundred times. She kept the wet rag carefully balanced.

"Mirolah?"

"Yes."

He opened his eyes again and was patient as they adjusted. He was in a room with wooden walls, rafters with a peaked ceiling. Afternoon sun slanted in through the window, drawing a bright square on the wooden floorboards. Mirolah sat by his bed, disheveled. Her windblown hair was a tangled mess with bits of leaves clinging to it. Her shadowed eyes watched him. She looked as if she hadn't slept in days.

He felt as weak as a newborn colt. He lifted his arm and barely had the strength to move it to the edge of the bed. She slipped her hand into his.

"You're okay. You're going to be okay," she said like a mantra, like she was speaking to herself, not him.

"Mirolah?"

"You're going to be okay," she repeated, squeezing his hand.

He tried to sit up, but his body just wouldn't do it. It infuriated him.

"What happened?" he asked.

At the question, she came alive. "Medophae?" She leaned forward and looked into his eyes. "Are you really awake?"

"Yes," he croaked. His throat was so dry.

She let out a relieved breath. "Oh gods, Medophae." She squeezed his hand and laid her head on his chest, hugged him. "You nearly died."

"What are you talking about? Where are we?" He had never felt so weak in his life.

"We're upstairs in the tavern."

"What tavern?"

"It's called Gnedrin's Post."

Gnedrin's Post. He knew the place. It was north of Denema's Valley. "How did we get here?"

"I brought you here."

"I'm...sick," he said, incredulous.

"It's the forest sickness. At least, that's what the tavernkeeper's wife called it."

"Okay." He had never heard of such a thing, but then, Medophae had never been sick before, not since he was a child, not since his mortal life.

She brushed a lock of hair away from her cheek and hooked it behind her ear. "The forest sickness practically killed this entire town a couple of generations ago. You were in the final stages. The woman wanted to take you back out into the forest and leave you there to keep you from infecting anyone else. Nobody in the final stages ever survives."

Did that mean Oedandus was coming back? But he still felt so weak, and there was no dark voice lurking in the back of his mind. He looked at Mirolah's drawn face, the rings under her eyes, the way her skin was so pale it was translucent, as though all the blood had gone elsewhere. When he'd awoken in the glade, she hadn't looked like that. She'd been vibrant, full of life.

"You did it," he whispered. "*You* saved me."

"Yes," she said.

"With threadweaving."

"You were dying. I...changed it."

"How?"

"I don't want to talk about it," she said. "You're alive. That's what matters."

"You pulled from yourself to make me well," he said. Bands had once told him that healing oneself was relatively easy for a threadweaver. Healing someone else was unbelievably difficult. You couldn't just pull GodSpill from the threads around you, the stones and the walls. You had to pull it from yourself. It took a horrible toll. He'd seen another threadweaver do this before, trying to save her child. She'd pulled all of the life from herself, and the child had died anyway. So did the mother. "You can't do that, Mirolah. It will kill—"

"I don't want to talk about it."

He sighed, closed his eyes. He'd only said a handful of words, and yet it felt like he'd run around the Inland Ocean itself. "How long has it been?" he asked. "Since the glade by the Fountain."

"One day. One night. Half of another day," she said.

A day and a half. That was beyond dangerous. The fact that Zilok Morth hadn't found them was a miracle.

"We can't stay here," he said. He clenched his teeth, tried to sit up again, but he couldn't raise himself. The rag toppled from his forehead, and he slumped back. "Gods... This is insufferable."

Her hand clenched his.

"Have you seen anything unusual, Mirolah?" he asked. "Any birds watching us? Any ravens sitting on the sill, more curious than a raven ought be? Especially any animal with blue eyes. He does that sometimes, spies through the eyes of animals."

"Who?"

"Zilok Morth."

She watched him, and a little smile cracked the side of her mouth. "Your nemesis?" she asked. "From the Age of Awakening?"

"What's funny?"

"You've been talking to him in your sleep. The past day and a half has been one long fever dream. You talked to him. To Bands. To your mother. To Oedandus. To everyone except me, actually."

"Listen to me. We have wasted precious time here. You should leave me. Today. Now. Go south to Denema's Valley and try to work the portal. If you can, escape to Calsinac and destroy the portal behind you. If Zilok follows you, he can use the portal also. He knows how to work them. If the portal will not work, then disappear. Go somewhere and don't threadweave. Don't use it for at least a year. Otherwise, he'll find you."

"What portal?"

"The one I showed you. The one in Denema's Valley."

"The carved arch in the rock?"

"Except with the GodSpill back in the land, it will be working. I hope. Go there. Now. Don't wait."

"And I'm to leave you here?"

"He'll seek me first. It will give you time."

"And when he finds you, what then?"

He furrowed his brow. "No. See, you can't worry about me. Zilok is coming. All he *wants* is me. If he sees you as a threat—if he even sees you as an annoyance—he'll go through you to get to me. And you can't stop him. So you have to go."

"And he'll kill you."

"It doesn't matter what happens—"

"It matters to me!" She stood up. Her stool tipped and clattered onto the floor.

He swallowed, calmed his voice. "Mirolah, this fight between Zilok and me goes back, all the way to the beginning. It's not your fight."

"I defeated the Red Weaver," she said.

"She didn't know what you could do. None of us did. But Zilok won't underestimate you. You think he doesn't know you, but he does. He'll have studied you, and when he attacks, he will gut you before you know he's there. You won't see him coming, so you have to leave."

"No."

"Mirolah," he said, trying to hide his frustration. "He'll *kill* you—"

"And so I will die," she said. "What does it matter? If you can throw your life away, why not me, too? I don't even know who I am anymore. You say I should flee. Where? Home? I don't have a home anymore. My foster family wouldn't even recognize me."

"Of course they would—"

"*I* don't even recognize me! You don't know what happened me. I...I think I became one with the Fountain. I melted into it, and somehow, I came back to my body again. But I'm not *me*. My soul is still connected to the GodSpill, and the GodSpill is now spread throughout the lands. I hear things, I see things that I never did before. This town, these people, I look at them and they are transparent. Every emotion they have is written in their threads, and I'm a part of those threads now. The GodSpill is in them, just a little bit, in all of them. And so am I. If I'm not careful, and I suggest something, they do it, even when I sense they don't want to. I don't dare look them in the eye, because then that control becomes stronger, and they want to follow me, want to do what I ask them to do. And it isn't just people. The trees whisper to me in some foreign tongue I feel I should know. Birds and squirrels, deer and foxes, they follow me. It all seems like a dream, like I'm doing all of this somehow... The only thing that seems real is you. I know you were with me before all this happened, and you're the only link to who I once was. You're all I have left. If you think I'm walking away from the one man who might help me understand what's happening to me, then you're stupid."

"I can't stop him," Medophae said.

"Shut up."

He raised his eyebrows.

"I know you've lost him. Oedandus. I know you're mortal now. I can see into you, the threads of you. But damn you, you are not going to give up on me and lie here waiting to die! You're going to get up..." she choked on the words, "...you're going to get up out of that bed, and you're going to stand with me because I need you."

"I can't help you."

She knelt beside his bed. "I will protect you," she murmured.

He laughed darkly. "You can't. And even if you could, have you stopped to think that maybe I deserve it? That maybe Zilok coming for me is my just punishment for being a fool? All this time, I could have been preparing for his return. Or for Ethiel's. If I'd thought it through, I would have known."

"How? How could you possibly have known?"

"Somehow."

"That's ridiculous. You're so caught up with who you should have been and what you should have done that you won't even look at what's happening to you right now."

"I was half a man before, broken and ailing. Now I'm even less."

"You're not. You're whole. For the first time in a millennium."

"What? Mirolah—"

"How many chances have you had to live, Medophae?" she interrupted him. "How many chances have you had to stop hating yourself since you lost Bands and take a look at what your life is right now? One for every minute of an hour? Does that sound about right? Sixty chances in an hour."

"Don't talk about her. I'm saying that without Oedandus—"

"How many hours in a day?" she interrupted again. "How many days in the hundreds of years since you lost her? How many chances to live in this moment, in this minute, have you let slide past you? Millions, I think. And you've let them slide away because you're berating yourself for mistakes you made hundreds of years ago. You'd think that being immortal would have given you hope. Enough time to see what you're doing to yourself. Enough time to set it right, to begin again. Endless time. So much power... But you didn't. And with every chance you passed up to live a real life, you sank deeper into your self-loathing, because you knew it was wrong. Life is a gift, and you shunned that gift, clinging to memories instead. You kept trying to shove that map of your past over the ever-moving opportunities of the future. But no one can do that, not even the gods. You loathed yourself until you wanted to die, but Oedandus kept you alive. Only now you're mortal. Now you *can* die. After passing a million chances to really live your life, you're down to your very last one, and the only thing you can think of to do with it is stay here and wait for death. You think that's all that you're worth. Well, it's not. We need you. *I* need you. This isn't your first opportunity to die. It's your last chance to live."

Her words were agony, but she didn't know. "I don't have a place here..." he said raggedly. "My life was hundreds of years ago. When *she* died, I died."

"What did you want to be?" she asked.

"What?"

"When you were my age. I mean, really my age, what did you want to be?"

"What does that matter?"

"Let's say it doesn't matter," she said. "Zilok Morth's going to kill us anyway. So nothing matters, really. So what did you want to be?"

"When I first came to Amarion?"

"Sure." Then she shook her head, reconsidering. "No. Before you met Oedandus. The last time you were mortal. What did you want to be?"

"I don't remember," he said.

"Yes you do."

He thought about his childhood, so long ago, so far away from here on a small island his people called Dandere. He remembered running by the surf, his feet splashing in the water that rolled in and pulled out. He liked running. As a young man, he ran around the entire island in two days without sleep, a feat only the greatest of the king's warriors had accomplished. He sweated and pushed himself faster than anyone had gone before. He had never heard of the continent of Amarion until his mother, Jarissa, told him stories about her homeland. She had described its vast forests and mountains, stretching farther than a person could run in two days, in twenty days, in a year. She had told him she'd come across the ocean on the back of a green dragon.

He remembered the Ceremony of the Black Flower, once a year

when his people mourned their missing god, Oedandus, who had been lost to them for decades. Everyone he knew cried on that yearly celebration, letting their sorrow show, and not one of them thought to go find Oedandus. They all considered it impossible. How did one find a god? They couldn't fathom where to start, but Medophae itched to try. He couldn't stand the idea that something couldn't be done. He remembered making the decision to travel to Amarion, that mythical place his mother spoke of, to look everywhere to find his people's lost god, and that's when Bands appeared to him. She was a shapeshifter, and she'd been watching him for years in different forms: as the man who was always buying bread at the bakery when Medophae walked by, as the woman who played the harp on the corner for coins. She had even played with him when he was little; she'd become his friend Airric, a friend who no one else could see.

And when Medophae had gone searching for Oedandus, Bands had revealed her true form, and took him across the Great Ocean to Amarion. And rather than finding his god, Oedandus found him.

"See," Mirolah said, breaking his reverie. She was watching his eyes. "I told you that you knew."

He cleared his throat.

"What did you want to be?" she asked again.

"An adventurer," he said. "Like my mother. I wanted to do what others thought was impossible. I wanted to help them reach beyond their limits by showing them how. Before I was born, Oedandus used to visit us once a year. But he suddenly stopped coming. My people mourned, but not one of them went looking for him. They thought that finding a god was impossible. So I did it, and as soon as I set foot on the ground in Amarion, he found me."

"And then?"

"Then I became what I am. I wanted to use the power rightly. I wanted to be a good man. But I didn't have any idea how to do that. No matter how I tried, I kept making mistakes, and because of the power, my mistakes were huge. I was a child stomping around in the boots of a god. I was a fool."

"Is that what they said when you told them you were going to try to kill Dervon? Did they laugh at you? Call you a fool?"

"Afterward they called me a hero, a—"

"Not afterward. Before. What did they say before?"

Only a handful had known what he was going to attempt. "There were some. Zilok's parents. They cursed me. And there were others who laughed. It *was* ridiculous. Yes, many called me a fool."

"And they were wrong," she said.

"They couldn't possibly know the power I had been given—"

"They were wrong," she reiterated. "Back then you *were* a fool. You didn't know what you couldn't do. And you succeeded."

"But now I don't have Oedandus to—"

"Shhh." She put her finger on his lips to silence him. "Stop there. Right there. That's where we will live."

"What?"

"Let's be fools like that. Fools who don't know what they can't do."

He let out a little sigh. "That's pretty talk, but Zilok Morth is coming. I'm not talking about some poetic story villain, pulled from a minstrel's tale, but a killer, a calculating malevolent spirit who has no humanity."

"Like Dervon."

"Yes," he said.

"Yes. Let's be fools who don't know what we can't do."

He felt a flicker of hope, soft and surprising, like a seed sprouting in his heart. Whatever she had undergone in the Fountain *had* changed her. She was certain, confident. And she was right about one thing: she had defeated Ethiel, something that Medophae himself had failed to do in hundreds of years. That was no mean feat. Was it possible she could do the same to Zilok?

Maybe they could do it.

Then, as he realized that he was agreeing with exactly what she wanted, his flicker of hope shriveled. That was exactly how his glamour had worked on others, when Oedandus burned through him. He would talk, and whomever he talked with would soon begin nodding his head.

"Did you threadweave? Right now? With me?" he demanded. She had just talked about the villagers here, how they were swayed by her needs and requests.

She hesitated, but she didn't look ashamed. Instead, she shrugged. "A little."

"You *changed* me," he accused.

She raised her chin, suddenly realizing what he was getting at. "Changed you?" she said. "You mean, did I threadweave to force you to agree with me?"

"That's exactly what I mean."

Her eyes flashed. "I didn't *change* you," she said with a biting edge. "If I was going to *change* you, I'd stop you from being such an idiot!"

He blinked at her.

"I looked at your threads," she continued. "I felt your emotions. I saw the emotional darklings that cling to your back. But I also saw that you *are* a good man, that you want to help others, that your concern for me is genuine, that you would save me from suffering. I saw what everyone in the history of Amarion already sees in you, but that you *can't* see because you're so busy beating on yourself! Did I *change* you? No, you bull-headed man, I pointed you at a mirror."

He was stunned.

"You..." She stood up, and her anger seemed to drain away. "Are an idiot. And you're unbelievably horrible to yourself." She put her hands on his temples, leaned over and kissed him on the forehead. "You're going to stop doing that. Even if I have to keep reminding you every ten seconds."

"I..." He felt like he should apologize, but he couldn't find the words. "Where are you going?"

"To get you some soup."

MEDOPHAE SLEPT THAT NIGHT, and when he awoke, he felt confused, perhaps more than he ever had in his long life. But Mirolah's biting words had gotten to him, and her sprout of hope had grown larger. Was he defeating himself first? He'd seen it happen in many soldiers he'd trained, that they couldn't get past their own nay-saying, couldn't get out of their own way.

He began to notice things he hadn't noticed in a long time, like the smell of the cool air from the open window, like the angles of the roof, like the feel of the floorboards on his feet. It all seemed new to him, as if he hadn't given himself the opportunity to appreciate these small things in years. He was like a child discovering how to walk all over again. He hadn't felt this way since he was a young man. He couldn't tell if it was because he'd been a sick man who was now recovering and appreciating health. Or if it was because he was newly mortal again, and appreciating the danger and beauty of things he might never see again. Or if it was because Mirolah had opened his eyes to the fact that he wasn't looking at his present, only at his past.

The despair that had surrounded him was like a fog that had begun to dissipate. This morning, he wasn't certain Zilok would destroy them. They were still alive, so there were opportunities they could look in to. In fact, he was beginning to feel a small thrill at the idea of trying, the kind of thrill he hadn't felt since the early days.

He glanced at Mirolah, curled on her side on a pallet of boards and straw with a blanket below her and a blanket over her. She had constructed the makeshift bed near the door during his days of sickness.

He moved his legs to the edge of the bed and set his feet on the floor. He was a little shaky, but the burning under his skin was gone. His throat no longer hurt. The ache in his muscles had all but vanished. He went to the window, moving as quietly as he could.

Yellow, orange, and lavender light spread across the sky, igniting the clouds. He smiled. To his right was a little table, and there was a pile of coins: copper, some silver, a lot of gold.

"Good morning," Mirolah murmured. He turned as she sat up, blinked and stretched. She wore a long, dun-colored nightshirt.

"Where did you get this?" he asked, nodding at the table.

"I made them."

"You made them?"

"You were sleeping. I was bored."

"How did you make them?"

"I traded a gold nugget for thirty copper and two silver pieces. Then I turned most of the copper pieces into gold. It's actually pretty easy."

"These are Teni'sian coins."

"That's what the innkeeper gave me."

"How did you get the nugget?"

"I had to borrow a gold piece from a wealthy merchant so that I could see how the threads of gold looked. Then I made a rock into gold."

That was transmutation. He knew about it, but there hadn't been many threadweavers who could do it, even during the Age of Ascendance. "And you gave the coin back?"

"I gave him two for the favor."

"I find it hard to believe he would simply loan you a gold piece."

"He didn't know he was loaning it." She smiled.

"And you put it back with another. You realize he probably knows exactly how many gold pieces he has."

"Won't that be happily frustrating for him when he discovers he's a gold piece richer for no reason?"

"And it is real gold?"

"As real as the merchant's gold." She shrugged. "We had no money, and I have not yet paid them for the room or the food."

"Impressive, Mirolah."

She stood up and gave a mock curtsey in her nightgown. "Thank you, my lord."

"We should leave today," he said.

"Tomorrow morning," she countered. "You're healing. That's a good thing."

He opened his mouth to argue, but shut it without saying anything. Just the thought of travel wearied him. What good would it do to start running if he would collapse within a day?

"Very well. Tomorrow," he said.

They spent the rest of the day and the evening talking and eating the delicious food that the innkeeper's wife made, never leaving the room. Medophae knew practically nothing of Mirolah's life in Rith. She told him of the town circle and of being a scribe. She talked of her adopted sisters and of Lawdon and Tiffienne.

Medophae told her of Calsinac at its height, of the threadweavers who came to call, the great trade caravans that crossed the Red Desert. He talked of the few benefits of being a king and its many burdens. He told her about when he finally abdicated the throne of Calsinac to someone better suited.

They stayed up late into the night, and he found himself talking about events he had not spoken of in centuries, things he hadn't told Orem or Tyndiria. Ever before, recounting the memories of Calsinac, of Bands, had been painful. But somehow, he wanted to tell Mirolah. It was as though she'd lanced a wound with her words yesterday, and tonight he wanted to push out all the poison.

Finally, he came to the story of how he lost Bands, how Ethiel had trapped not just a dragon but Tarithalius, the god of humans. Medophae still could not understand how she'd done it.

Tears came to Mirolah's eyes when he told her of his one-hundred-and-thirty-one-year pilgrimage, searching for the threadweaver or god who could free Bands. Only Saraphazia, goddess of the True Ocean, seemed to know something, but she said she couldn't undo the spell without killing Bands and Tarithalius. She told him the riddle was the key, and she said no more. Then Harleath capped the Fountain, and Medophae fell into despair. He didn't remember exactly when he gave up. He didn't remember most of the last three hundred years. There were entire decades from which he could remember nothing at all.

She didn't ask any more questions after that, and his desire to talk faded. But he felt better, as though the painful memories *had* been poison, and his blood was now cleaner somehow. Again, that hopeful feeling filled him.

"You are..." he started, then stopped.

"I'm what?"

"You're...unexpected."

She raised an eyebrow. "Well said," she said wryly, pursing her lips. "Eloquent."

He laughed. "I mean, with what you told me. It's... I just..."

"I'm glad," she interrupted his fumbling, holding his gaze. Crickets chirped outside, and the scant moonlight from the window flickered across the empty goblets and soup bowls as clouds passed. He finally broke the gaze and stood up.

"I'll sleep on the pallet tonight," he said. "You take the bed."

"Okay."

"First thing tomorrow," he said. "We leave before the sunrise."

"Our last night here together," she said. She took the single candle from the table and brought it to the nightstand, but she watched him the whole time.

Slowly, deliberately, she unhooked her belt and let it drop to the floor, freeing her newly purchased tunic. She pulled it over her head. The candlelight caught the curves of her breasts and her smooth stomach. She undid the laces on her breeches, pushed them over her hips, down her legs and stood naked in front of him. Her eyes searched his.

She leaned over the candle. He watched the muscles in her thighs tighten, watched her breasts shift as she blew out the light. He heard the blankets ruffling as she slid into the bed.

The moonlight illuminated the air between the arched window and the wooden floor. He couldn't see her, but he knew she was watching him. She was a threadweaver; she didn't need the light to see in the dark.

He wanted to tell her that he was still broken, that he loved Bands, that the pain was still there, would probably always be there, all the things he had told Tyndiria. It was the truth, but the truth sounded worn and tired to him. He noticed the silver in the moonlight, the pleasant chill in the air. He'd found himself holding his breath as Mirolah disrobed for him, spellbound as she invited him with her body.

This was what it was like to be pierced by the sharp edges of the world, to be caressed by its softness, to feel the tight fear of knowing it was all transient. To feel meaning. He'd forgotten this.

He went to her, stood over the bed. He could barely see her in the dark, propped up on her elbows, watching him.

"I *am* broken," he repeated.

"You're human." She opened the covers for him. She seemed

about to say something more, but he leaned down and kissed her. She wrapped her arms around him and pulled him to her.

66

MEDOPHAE

MEDOPHAE WOKE AS THE SUN ROSE, light trickling into the little room, and Mirolah was already up. She stood naked at the open window, watching the quiet street below as though she was listening to someone playing music. He struggled with the warmth he felt looking at her, the thrill of the unknown and the following thrill of wanting to know those things, to know more about her. He wanted to go to her, put his arms around her, make her part of himself. He'd felt that compulsion only once before, and guilt rose within him.

She'd just been a girl. Just another mortal he only saw from the outside, only saw in terms of what he needed to do for her. He was Wildmane, after all, and humans were fragile, vulnerable. His role was not that of an adventurer. It couldn't be. He did not get to choose his own path. His role was to protect her, to help Orem, to shield Tyndiria, to find Bands, to help the lands.

Old decisions. He had made them a hundred times before.

But he felt no truth in those decisions now, not after what she had said. Every decision he'd made for as long as he could remember was made from guilt, or duty, or anger.

But not last night. Last night had been...reckless. That decision had been made without knowing the outcome.

Mirolah was no girl anymore. The fountain *had* changed her, as profoundly as Zilok had changed Medophae. She'd seen right through him, seen what he had been blind to for too long. She had given back something precious, something forgotten, something he had left behind. She had given him back the self he always wanted to be.

I wanted to be an adventurer. A hero. I always wanted it. And I have been a very poor hero lately.

With kind ministrations and harsh words, she had gotten to him, gotten inside him. Last night, she brought life-giving rain to his desert heart, made the ground fertile again, and suddenly he had once more felt like the person he'd always wanted to be.

Mirolah's fingertips touched the window lightly, as though she needed contact to better hear the world outside.

Looking at her thrilled him. He hadn't felt this since his first days with Bands, far away on the isle of Dandere. He felt that same impossible rush, gazing upon someone magnificent and strange, someone you could barely fathom, and yet still someone who understood you. Bands had been all those things back then. She had represented adventure, the power of the unknown, while Medophae had been a stumbling colt.

And now Mirolah stood in that role. She had given him a flicker of light in the darkness. She was certain while he was the vulnerable one.

Death stands at my door. I mourn for Bands. I am wrapped in a fog of uncertainty, and yet there she is... And I am in love. By all the gods... I am a fool.

Unbidden, Mirolah's words of the previous day came to him: *That's where we will live... Let's be fools like that...*

Despite the maelstrom of conflicting emotions inside him, he actually felt good. For the first time in as long as he could remember, he had hope. And she had given him that.

"You're magnificent," he said softly.

She turned her head, smiling, and he saw her lovely profile

backlit by the light from the rising sun. "I was about to wake you," she said. "Did you sleep okay?"

"Through the night," he replied. He never used to sleep all night.

Yesterday, he'd been chomping at the bit to leave Gnedrin's Post. But now he wanted—selfishly, recklessly—to spend a day in this room with her, staying small and cozy, and shut out the world. To die with her, here, didn't seem a horrible fate. If it was going to end, why not here? Why not now?

Reluctantly, though, he rose.

"We need to leave," she said, voicing his thoughts.

"South. Back to Denema's Valley."

She turned, a curious look on her face. "Really? Shouldn't we go some place Zilok wouldn't suspect?"

"I want to put distance between him and us. A lot of distance. Running to the next village won't work. Not for long. We go to Calsinac."

"Calsinac? How? Isn't it a thousand miles away?"

"There's a portal near Denema's Valley, a holdover from the Age of Ascendance, that goes directly to Calsinac. With the GodSpill returned... Well, it might be working again."

"Might be working? If we go and it's not, and he's waiting for us... Well, it seems like a big chance."

Medophae laughed and bowed his head. "Every step we take is going to be a risk. But if we just run scared, he'll find us. This way, if we succeed, he can spend the next few months looking for us in the north, and we'll be, as you mentioned, a thousand miles south of here."

She nodded. "Well, all right then." She moved gracefully from the window and picked her clothes up from where she'd dropped them last night. He watched her.

"Let's get moving, Sir Risky. Stop staring and get your clothes on," she said, smiling.

He did as ordered.

Thanks to Mirolah's gold, they had plenty of money to pay for their room and to prepare for their journey. They loaded satchels with the food and fire-making supplies that Medophae thought necessary.

Gnedrin's Post was a silver mining village, as small as a settlement could get and still be called a village, but the mines in the foothills of the Spine Mountains were productive, and the Dragon River flowing through the town gave it not only a plentiful amount of water, irrigation for some small crops nearby, and power to turn the miller's wheel at the center of town, but it also made trips down to the Inland Ocean swift on flat boats. With Mirolah's gold, they purchased one of the boats at a high price and let the river carry them southward much faster than they could have walked.

As they both avoided rapids using long poles to guide the boat, Medophae wondered how Zilok Morth would start his search. Mirolah had gotten lucky taking Medophae to Gnedrin's Post. The mining village had not existed during the Age of Ascendance, and in all likelihood, Zilok would not know it existed. The spirit would probably assume Medophae would turn toward the ruins of Belshra, as far to the southeast as Gnedrin's Post was to the southwest. If Zilok was searching those ruins for them, it could account for their luck so far.

Still, he watched the wooded shores on either side of them with growing apprehension, looking for animals or birds that came to the shore, that seemed unafraid, that paused too long to watch their boat. So far, he hadn't seen any.

They ate bread and cheese at lunchtime, drinking from the river and continuing their float downstream. Medophae didn't want to go onto the shore except in case of an emergency. Every moment was precious, and he wouldn't feel safe until they made it through the portal in Denema's Valley. If they could get to Calsinac, that would secure some time to figure out their next steps.

The day passed in silence, and neither of them talked much. Not about Zilok. Not about the previous night. Medophae expected every moment to explode into action as Zilok discovered them, and he waited for it tensely. Mirolah had picked up on the mood and stayed alert, perhaps preoccupied studying the threads of the lands, trying to sense if Zilok was there. They spoke if they needed to discuss navigation of rapids or a twist in the river, but otherwise they stayed quiet.

As the sun began to set, the cliffs of the Spine Mountains hove into view, a marker that they were near Denema's Valley.

"We're close," Mirolah said. "I used to swim near here. I remember the shape of those mountains."

"We should get off the river. Zilok would have assumed we'd go to Belshra first. He'd think Denema's Valley second. We need to be very careful."

She had already begun to pole for the shore. He helped, and soon they splashed quietly into the shallows and hauled the boat onto the sandy bank.

"Should we let it go?" She looked at the boat.

He was tempted. If Zilok found a boat near the river, it would be a sure signal to him to search the entire area.

"Let's pull it into the trees," Medophae said. "If the portal doesn't work, then our next best bet will be riding the river to the Inland Ocean.

"I can talk to the trees—"

"No," he said. "Don't threadweave. Not until we reach the portal. If he's close, he might be able to sense you using GodSpill. We can't. Not yet."

"Okay."

They hauled the boat up and camouflaged it with fallen branches inside the nearby forest.

"Let's go," Medophae said, moving into the trees slowly.

They hadn't been walking for more than ten minutes when Mirolah said, "I recognize this part." She slipped under tree branches and through thick, tall grasses. He followed close behind, and they emerged into the meadow where she had practiced her threadweaving. The light was fading, and she walked through the tall grass to the giant stone table that had once been a boulder. She ran her hand along its edge.

"It seems a lifetime ago," she murmured. "The last time we were here, Orem and Stavark were alive." She glanced over her shoulder in the direction of the city of Denema's Valley. "I'm afraid to go down there," she said. "I'm afraid of what we'll find."

He glanced at the small path that led into the trees and

eventually to the streets of Denema's Valley. Somewhere on those streets were Orem's and Stavark's corpses.

"We should go straight to the portal," he said.

"I..." She hesitated.

"You need to see them."

"I'm sorry, Medophae."

His pulse quickened. It wasn't the smart thing to do. But it was the right thing. "Well, let's be quick about it."

She headed for the trail, and he fell in behind her.

In the distance, he thought he heard something, like a clacking wind chime. He'd been paranoid all day long, so he stopped, listened. A warm breeze ruffled through the trees. He strained his ears, but there was nothing there.

She stopped a distance down the trail. Had the sound been a trick of the wind? He started walking again.

"What is it?" she asked.

"Nothing. I'm just jumpy. Let's be quick."

Soon, they reached the streets of Denema's Valley and picked their way between the buildings to where the battle with the darklings had taken place. A dozen of the foul creatures lay scattered across the stones, slowly decaying. It was hard to see in the failing light, but after a quick inspection, they could find no sign of Orem's body or Stavark's.

"What does that mean?" Mirolah asked.

"I don't know."

"Would the darklings devour them?"

"Maybe," he said, but he doubted it. The darkling's lair in Teni'sia had been filled with bodies, but none of them had been picked clean. "There would at least be bones."

He thought back to the battle and stood where he had before. Dead darklings surrounded that spot, but off to the side, two others had fallen. He had not killed those. The corpses were beginning to decompose, but he could deduce that those two had been slain by multiple sword cuts. Many sword cuts. Stavark.

He went to that spot. "Stavark fought valiantly here."

"Could he be alive? Gods, Medophae. Could Orem?"

"I would dare to say yes," he murmured. "But I cannot think of how. They were outmatched, and there were more that night than there are lying here. How could they have..." He left off as his gaze fell upon the door of one of the nearby shops. An open door with writing scrawled on it.

He jogged across the street and leapt onto the landing. What he had thought was crude writing was actually a scattering of small, bloody handprints smeared across the wood. The blood was long since dried, seeming like red ink. Stavark's handprints.

"Stavark?" he called out as he entered the dark shop, hoping against hope. She followed behind him.

"This was an herb shop," he said, squinting at the dark shelves.

"I don't sense anyone," she said. "Nothing living in here."

"Stavark?" he called out again, uselessly.

"He was alive," she said. "He made it through the battle somehow. He came here looking for something."

"A healing herb, probably. The question is: Did it save him?"

She smiled, and she did a girlish little jump up and down. "He's alive. I know it. We have to find him!"

"We can't," he said. "We're being hunted, and we could be found at any second. If Stavark was here, and if he survived, he has gone elsewhere. He's a quicksilver. The woods are home to him. If we went searching for him, not only might we get caught, but we might bring more trouble down on him, too. If he's alive, he's probably safer without us."

"Or he could be dying right now."

His shoulders felt tight. "It's a bad idea."

"We have to try," she said.

It could take forever to find a quicksilver in the woods, especially if he didn't want to be found. "Come on. Let's get about it."

"Where should we start—" she asked.

He motioned for silence with a quick swipe of his hand. That peculiar noise, the clacking wind chimes, sounded in the distance, louder.

She heard it this time, too. "What was that?"

A chill ran down his back. He grabbed her arm and moved her towards the door. "We have to go. We'll come back to search for

Stavark later."

Cursing himself for letting her come into the city at all, he set off at a jog. She followed.

The clacking sounded again, much closer this time. Those weren't wind chimes. That was some creature. It sounded like an avalanche mixed with a horse's whinny. It was heading straight for them, coming from somewhere to the north.

Sprinting, they turned the corner and saw the edge of the forest, which had invaded the closest buildings of Denema's Valley. They were just about to plunge headlong into the trees when a loud voice pulled them up short.

"Golden King!" a deep voice called to them.

Medophae spun about. He kept his hand casually at his side, close to the long sword they had bought before leaving Gnedrin's Post.

The newcomer who had called out sauntered around the corner of the nearest building. A Sunrider, of all things!

He was tall, powerfully built, with a strong jaw line, dark eyes, a mane of dark hair, and the proud, hawk-like nose of a Sunrider chieftain. He walked forward with casual confidence, his hands loose at his sides.

He wore a pair of leather riding pants and black riding boots. His chest was bare, save for the leather strap that held a sheathed greatsword across his back.

"Mirolah," Medophae said. "Go to the portal—"

"I'm not leaving you. That man's not normal. In my threadweaver sight, he looks like..." There was fear in her voice. "He has...black fire surrounding him."

Medophae kept his gaze on the smiling man, who stopped a dozen paces away.

The clacking neigh rose on the air, louder this time.

"Please, Mirolah! I'll be right behind you."

"The Spirit wants a word with you, Golden King."

The Spirit. Zilok Morth. This man was with Zilok. They were caught.

With quiet authority, Medophae spoke once more to Mirolah. "Trust me, please. If it's working, use the sequence we talked about."

She paused, then made the right decision. "I'll be back for you."

"Not if I catch you first," he murmured. She turned and sprinted into the woods.

The Sunrider raised his eyebrows and watched her run away, as if she didn't matter at all.

"So you are the one my people hail as a god?" the dark-maned Sunrider said. "The Spirit said your real name is Medophae. That much is true, yes?"

Medophae said nothing.

The Sunrider leaned against the wall of the house. "Not going to talk?"

"I am no god," Medophae said.

"Oh, I know. The Spirit explained how it works. You are a foreigner who was given more power than you deserved. But my people think you are a god. They believe your spirit lives within us all. Our warriors offer prayers to you when they ride into battle. I used to offer those prayers." He paused. "Perhaps now they will offer prayers to me?" He flexed his hand and a crackle of black fire flickered across his knuckles.

Medophae went cold. It was suddenly hard to breathe. Zilok hadn't just cut him off from Oedandus. Had he somehow...given Oedandus to *this* man?

"It's like fire in my veins. Did you know I can uproot a tree as tall as ten horses?" He chuckled. "Well, of course you do."

Medophae fought for composure. He made his lips move, forced his voice to work. "Who are you?"

"I am Vaerdaro, second son to Raedir-ba. According to the legends, I am your great-grandchild. The matron of my line was one of the original Three Mothers. It seems that some of our legends are true, after all."

"The Three Mothers..."

"Tell me that you remember, oh Golden King. The three daughters of the One Sun, the Uniter of the Tribes, Raegilan the Mighty. You bedded each of them to cement the treaty between Calsinac and our people. We share blood, great-grandfather."

Blood. Medophae's blood. Oedandus's blood. "That is why you

can—"

"Why I am the new Golden King?" Vaerdaro grinned. "So the Spirit tells me."

Medophae's mind whirled, but he had to take control of this situation. He couldn't sit here and wait for Zilok to show up.

"You have made a dramath's bargain, Sunrider," he said. "Zilok Morth helps only one person, himself. Whatever deal you made will cost you more than you imagine."

"Desperate words from a desperate man," Vaerdaro said. He gave Medophae a disappointed frown. "To be truthful, I had hoped for more." He sighed. "The way my people talk of you..."

Medophae took a step backward into the woods, and Vaerdaro pushed away from the wall. "The unholy woman may go where she wishes," Vaerdaro said. "The Spirit doesn't care about her and neither do I. But you must stay."

Medophae felt like a rabbit readying to fight a skin dog. What chance did he have? Was this the same feeling others had felt when they faced him across a battlefield? He took another step backward, gauging the distance between them.

The clacking neigh split the air. Whatever that creature was, it was almost here.

Vaerdaro spared a brief glance toward the direction of the noise, then looked back at Medophae. "The Spirit said he is bringing something called a spine horse to track you. That must be it."

Medophae turned and sprinted into the woods. Vaerdaro launched himself into a mighty, distance-spanning leap, and he pulled that greatsword from its sheath. But the moment the Sunrider left the ground, Medophae turned and drew his own blade.

Vaerdaro was caught in mid-air, and Medophae lurched to the side as Vaerdaro swung.

The greatsword clipped a lock of Medophae's golden hair and whisked past his shoulder. Medophae spun, throwing his momentum into his strike, and landed his blade precisely where he wanted it.

It sheared through both of Vaerdaro's wrists. The Sunrider's hands spun away from his arms, trailing spurts of blood. Vaerdaro crashed into the ground, sucked in a breath, and screamed.

Medophae kept moving, swiveling again and bringing his blade down on one of Vaerdaro's ankles. Bone cracked and the foot came away. Vaerdaro's second scream cut off as he lost consciousness.

Medophae did not hesitate. He turned and sprinted into the forest. Vaerdaro had Oedandus's power. He wouldn't die of those wounds. And if he reattached the hands, they would heal. Zilok had obviously told Vaerdaro of his invulnerability, but what Vaerdaro could not know was that while Oedandus healed the body, he did not spare the pain. Vaerdaro would be unconscious for a while.

A clacking neigh from right behind him stopped Medophae's self-congratulations.

The sun had finally set, and through the darkness, a glowing spine horse stood next to the unconscious lump of the Sunrider, glaring up the slope at Medophae with its lava eyes. It turned its head skyward and let loose that monstrous clacking sound, like flat stones falling from the sky onto a boulder. Its diamond jaws parted and glowing saliva slid from its lips.

It lunged up the trail after him.

67

MIROLAH

THE PORTAL WAS ALIVE when Mirolah reached it. Before, it had been a dark archway of flat stone. Now it shimmered like the surface of a lake. Her curiosity flared; she wanted to explore this. She wanted to know how it worked and how it had been made. If Medophae wasn't facing a twisted version of himself, she would have spent the time required to explore every single twist of fiber that comprised this. At a glance, the handiwork was beautiful.

With her threadweaver's sight, she gave it a quick look. It was ready to accomplish its purpose, to transfer a human body from one location to another, but it had a trigger, something specifically designed to work it. The sequence Medophae had mentioned. The seven large symbols on the archway glowed, and there were threads tying those symbols to the shimmering, watery portal.

A bloodcurdling scream ripped through the forest.

"Medophae!" She gasped, spinning around. She should never have left him! She abandoned the portal and started back down the slope.

Another of those clacking, wheezing sounds filled the air.

She skidded down the slope, but she hadn't taken a dozen steps when she saw Medophae scrambling up the slope, churning dirt with his feet, ducking branches and dodging brush.

Following him was a creature from nightmare.

It was twice as tall as the largest horse she had ever seen, and half again as wide. Its entire body was made of coarse plates of dark lava stone. Spikes of rock formed a row on its back. Between the plates, bright red lava glowed. Leaves withered and burst into flame and tree trunks cracked as it shouldered its way past. Its eyes were hollow recesses to its glowing core, and its gaze had locked on Medophae. It neighed again, stealing the breath from her chest.

"Gods..." she said.

No. Be surprised later. Right now, help him.

Mirolah divided herself into three nodes of attention, slipping into the threads of the air, the ground, and the trees.

"Mirolah!" Medophae huffed. "The portal! Did you tap the sequence?" He drew abreast of her and pulled her toward the gate, breaking her concentration.

The monstrous creature leapt up the slope, breaking branches. The brush it stepped on burst into flames, and heat preceded it in a wash.

"What is that?" she asked as Medophae lunged past her and touched the seven large symbols in sequence. The monster reared up before her, lighting the canopy of leaves on fire. She reached into its threads and yanked them apart...

...but they slipped through her fingers.

The huge head dipped and batted her aside. It was like being hit with a burning club. She screamed and flew sideways, tumbling to a stop next to tree.

Sparkly dots welled up in her vision, but she fought to stay conscious. Her shirt smoldered. Struggling to draw breath, she pushed herself to her hands and knees in time to see Medophae draw his sword. It seemed laughable, that tiny piece of sharp metal against that monster. Mirolah pushed down her pain and grabbed the threads around the beast, hardening the air and pushing it away.

The monster stepped through the spell like it was made of sand. It snapped at Medophae, but he managed to spin to the side.

"I can't fight it," she cried. "I can't hold it!" She forced herself to her feet.

"Mirolah," he said in a steady voice. With his sword in front of him, he beckoned her with his other hand. He kept his eyes on the creature and his back to the portal. It snapped at Medophae, but did not attack. It appeared to want to herd him away from the portal.

"Remember the battle in Denema's Valley?" he asked, keeping his gaze fixed on the creature. "What you did with Orem and Stavark?"

"Yes," she said.

"I will give you the opportunity. Take it. To our destination."

The creature cocked its head, as though it was listening to Medophae's words, trying to understand.

What she had done at the battle with the darklings...

"Yes," she called, scrambling back up the slope toward him.

Medophae stepped away from the portal, and the monster closed in behind him, herding him down the hill the way they had come. As they passed Mirolah, the monster suddenly lunged at her. It would have bitten her in half, but Medophae was there. His sword flashed forward, plunging into one of the creature's molten eyes. It gave a keening noise, jaws open a foot from Mirolah's face. Searing lava splattered the tree next to her, and she stumbled away from the wash of heat, tumbling to the ground.

It reared up with a great howl, bashing Medophae high into the air. She pushed up on one elbow, reached out and caught Medophae's threads. She yanked them and flung him at the glowing gate with the speed of a hawk in steep dive. He vanished through the shimmering water.

The wounded monster came out of its fury. Its punctured eye leaked lava, but it leapt uphill toward Mirolah, right behind her. Hot breath blasted her neck. Diamond teeth combed through her hair as its jaws snapped on air.

The portal shimmered as she plunged through.

Then, darkness...

68

MIROLAH

"MIROLAH?"

"Medophae..." She strained her eyes against the darkness. The stone underneath her was smooth, polished. She looked behind her. Through the archway, the dark forest rippled like a reflection on water. The nightmare horse snapped at them, trying to bite through the portal, but it couldn't. It shone scant light into the dark room she was currently in. They could see the thing, but they couldn't hear it anymore. The only sound was their own breathing.

Medophae jumped to his feet and touched the same sequence upon the glowing sigils on this side of the archway. The portal shimmered, and the silhouette of the nightmare horse vanished, leaving only the silvery water.

He stepped back, then he laughed. Her eyes were beginning to adjust, and she could make out some of his grinning face in the shimmering light.

"Why didn't it come through with us?"

"That was a spine horse," Medophae said. "They're immune to threadweaving. Can't use a portal that runs on GodSpill if you're immune to threadweaving."

"That's why I couldn't do anything to it."

"Zilok was counting on that, I'm sure. But he didn't count on the portal. Or on how resourceful you could be." Again, he laughed as though he couldn't believe they had made it.

It was infectious, and she began laughing, but stopped at a sharp pain in her side. The creature had broken her ribs. By the gods, how many times was she going to do that? She was getting tired of bigger creatures throwing her around. She should come up with some permanent spell to stop that from happening. Or an artifact that made her physically slippery like the spine horse was slippery to her threadweaver fingers.

"We shouldn't waste any time before—"

"Wait," she murmured, drawing GodSpill from the threads of the stone and the air. "Just...give me a minute." She put her attention into the threads of her own body and repaired the damage to her ribs. She also had some contusions on her arm and head from when the spine horse had batted her into the air, and torn muscles in her shoulder from when she landed. She spent a few minutes healing herself. As soon as could take an easy breath, she said, "Okay."

"Are you all right?" he asked.

"I'm good now."

"Well, I hate to press you, but we should just destroy this portal. Zilok often looks through the eyes of his creatures. He may have been watching from the eyes of the spine horse. I don't think he was, because he would have joined that fight. But if I'm wrong, he might have seen me tap out that sequence. He'll follow us."

"Yes," she said. She reached out and disconnected the threads that bound the glowing sigils to the water. The stones of the archway melted smooth, erasing the carvings. The shimmering moonlit water became flat stone.

She turned, finally inspecting this dark room they'd tumbled into. It was circular, with a dozen other portals shimmering, glowing softly.

"One moment and I shall have light for us," he said. His shape was shadowy, but she saw him wrench a torch from the wall, then kneel. Flint struck steel, and in a moment, a warm glow filled the room. Medophae held the torch high above his head. He had taken it from a sconce on the wall. A long, steel spear leaned against the wall next to it, like someone had put it there lifetimes ago, and it had been the sole sentinel in this room. Medophae picked it up in his other hand, felt the weight, then kept it.

"All of these gates go somewhere?" she murmured, walking up to one. "How long did it take you to build all of these?"

"Many years," he murmured, tapping the butt of the spear on the ground. "But we had many years then. When Bands and I began this room, some of the cities had not even been settled. Now, I cannot think of one that isn't a ruin."

"Some of the gates are just stone," she said, slapping a hand against the stone of the archway next to the one from which they'd emerged.

"I'm guessing those were found on the other side, and someone defaced the runes."

"So if you scratch away one rune, the gate goes dark?" she asked.

"Well, yes, but it wasn't that simple in the Age of Ascendance. The archways at each destination were protected by spells. Nothing short of dragon fire could destroy them. But during the years we went without the GodSpill, they were just normal stone." He turned. "Come, you're tired and so am I. Let's find rest and in the morning, we can see what time has wrought with my once-beautiful Calsinac." He headed toward one of the darkened archways. It looked like all the rest, but as he drew closer with the torch, she realized it was just a normal hallway.

He guided her down the dark passageway, the torchlight pushing back shadows, revealing paintings on the walls. On her left they passed a sculpture of a woman with a spear.

In the stories she'd read, Calsinac was a mythical city, but the dark tour, uncovering forgotten pieces of artwork one at a time under the flickering orange light, made her feel more like she was in a tomb.

They ascended stairs that started with walls on either side. After a time, the walls went away, and it felt like she was climbing into the air. There was no rail, and the torchlight reached into absolute darkness. Warm air wafted up around them.

"Where are we?" she asked.

"The vents," he said. "Warm air flowed up through this tunnel and into other smaller tunnels. It kept most of the palace warm."

"Why are there no rails?"

"There was something about the danger that appealed to the architect. No one ever fell, so far as I know. One does get very aware when walking onto these wide steps. Maybe that was the point. This circular room we're in lights up when the sun rises; there are windows everywhere. It's quite spectacular, actually, and it only goes on for a little while."

She looked up, keeping herself from looking with her threadweaver sight. She wanted to see what a normal person would see, and she thought she could make out a starry night sky through small, circular windows high above.

Moments later, the walls closed in on them again, and the stairs ended onto a flat hallway. To her left, Medophae's torchlight swept over the sculpted face of a knight, carved in bas relief right into the wall. She wanted to see it all, but instead the torchlight only tantalized her with hints. What other statues stared at her from alcoves? What other paintings adorned the walls?

Her curiosity damped as two skeletons appeared at the edge of the circle of light. They sprawled across the floor with their frozen grins and sightless eyes. Medophae paused, then nudged them out of the way with his boot. Bones clacked and tumbled down the steep steps. Mirolah stepped aside, not wanting to touch them. Part of her was curious, but another part revolted. It seemed a part of her now to want to know about everything she encountered, but the idea of poking through the bones of a dead person did not appeal to her.

She reached out with her threadweaver sight, finding skeletons in almost every shadowy corner. This room had two big archways, one through which they had come, and one on the other side of the room. The other two walls had three arched fireplaces each, that began at about waist level. There were six tall, rectangular tables taking up most of the center of the room. A dozen skeletons lay scattered on the floor. There had been some kind of battle here, many years ago. Mirolah ran her ethereal fingers over the fallen corpses and found, in some cases, arrows lying among the bones. There was a broken sword near one of them, but if the dead had had any weapons, they had been looted after the attack.

"These were the kitchens," Medophae said softly.

"What happened here?"

He knelt and picked up the broken sword handle. His thumb rubbed the symbol of a sun on its hilt. "Sunriders," he said. "Long ago. They swept through Calsinac, killing everyone. Come on." He moved past the skeletons and into a huge dining room. There were skeletons in here as well. Had they been caught during a feast?

"This way," he said, seeing her discomfort. He led her out of the dining hall into a foyer, up a sweeping staircase to an open arcade of pillars and archways that looked out over the dark city. Smaller buildings crouched before the front of the palace, some still intact, some crumbling to ruin. They looked like giants cloaked and crouching in the darkness. She couldn't see the ocean from here, but she could smell it.

He led her away from the arcade into a hallway, choosing a small room with an arched window that looked out onto the city just as the arcade had done. There were no corpses here.

He fixed the torch in a sconce on the wall. "We're safe for now. We can sleep easy tonight. We are far enough away that Zilok won't find us for a few days at least, a few weeks at most."

He stripped the dusty, rat-chewed blankets from the bed and inspected the mattress. Rat holes riddled the cloth that had once kept the straw inside. What remained was rotten and moldy. The rats had apparently abandoned it long ago. He hefted it over his shoulder and walked to the window.

"Wait," she said. She reached out with her threadweaving fingers. She altered the old straw, recreating more out of the mold, the rat droppings, and the air, and revitalizing the existing straw. She re-knitted the cloth wrapped around it all, recreating the threads of actual threads, which amused her. In minutes, it looked as if it had just been fashioned by a mattress maker.

He tossed it back on the bed and bowed to her. "I'd forgotten the comforts of traveling with a threadweaver. Would you care to sleep, milady?"

"It has been a long day. Still, there's one thing I'd like to do first."

"Is there?" He gave a wry smile.

"Lie down. This may take a while."

He sat down on the bed. "I thought sleep would be more alluring than—"

"It's not what you think." She gave him a tired smile in return. "As pleasant as that sounds."

His brow wrinkled in confusion. "Then what?"

"A precaution. Zilok Morth is fond of traps. Let's prepare one for him." And she began threadweaving.

69

MIROLAH

MIROLAH HAD BEEN ASLEEP for less than an hour when her fears came true. She had wanted to believe Medophae when he said they were safe, but she didn't. So she took steps, weaving a spell around Medophae. After, she allowed herself to pretend they were safe, and she fell asleep in his arms, her head snuggled into his shoulder.

Mirolah had learned to divide her attention into multiple pieces in Ethiel's castle. And after, when her soul had become one with the Fountain and then miraculously escaped back to her body, she felt as if the air, the stone walls and floor, the mattress and the bed, even the sandy beach outside the window, that all of these things were a part of her now, that she was connected to them. Her awareness of them wasn't as acute as when she was consciously focusing on a task. Rather, it was as if she was a cat with a million tails, softly swishing, and she could tell when someone walked near one of her tails.

A new presence had entered Calsinac.

Without moving or even opening her eyes, she reached into the threads of the air, a light and buttery yellow color—almost white—

and created a barrier similar to the one she had constructed in Ethiel's prison cell, the one that kept her threadweaving from being discovered. She made it seem as though the area around the bed was empty to one with a threadweaver's sight.

She whispered, "He's here," and touched Medophae gently on the chest. The spell she had hung over him before they'd gone to sleep activated. She had been fascinated by the trigger spell at the portal, and had wanted to try one. Before Medophae could even nod, her trigger spell activated. He flew out the window, down, and out of sight.

As she had feared, the presence sensed her, and shot to the room with the speed of thought.

She sat up.

"Well..." the voice came, so familiar. Smooth, cultured. "A merry chase, Weaver of Rith. Well done."

She could see his hovering bright blue eyes with her threadweaver sight, but he formed the construct of himself in front of her regardless. Obviously, it gave him satisfaction to imagine himself in human form. That was curious.

The man coalesced in the room, visible with her normal vision. It was the man she had met in the Fountain, the man who had helped her defeat Ethiel.

"I know your name now," she said. "Zilok Morth."

He bowed low, holding one hand over his stomach and the other out to the side. He straightened and his hand moved up to stroke his short beard.

"Except you were wrong," she said. "You said the next time we met, I wouldn't want to be in that room, and I'm exactly where I want to be."

He gave her an amused smile. "You amaze me, Lady Rith."

"And this is the part where you kill me?"

"I did promise you," he said. "And as a rule, I dislike those who go back on their word. But I've had a change of heart. You are a diamond in the sand. So unexpected, and you glitter so brightly. I find I'm having a hard time casting you away. I have questions. When no one else could, you destroyed my grandson's fountain. That is an achievement. I should love to see your power at its

418

height."

"You will," she promised. She stayed loose, keeping her attention in every thread of this room, waiting for what he did, ready to counter it. In addition, she tried to probe his threads, ever so gently. There was a little cluster around those blue eyes, but not much else there. He hadn't seemed to notice what she was doing, which was encouraging, and she was afraid to probe deeper. It was more important to stall for time.

He laughed. "Threats? Please. Let us be civil. I am not the Wildmane. I don't leap to violence out of hand. You and I, we have helped each other in the past. We could help each other now. We could be allies. I would like that, I think."

"'Great weavers are never friends,'" she quoted.

"Oh, well done." He seemed to take genuine joy in his words being flung back at him. "But great weavers also change the rules. That's what we do. I have admitted that you've done something I cannot do. I would learn from you. Aren't you curious what you might learn from me? Think of all the knowledge I could give you, grander than a hundred libraries. I could fill your mind until that thirst for knowledge was, at last, sated."

She felt the itch at the base of her skull. Zilok would have knowledge unlike anything else she'd ever experienced. He was a threadweaver who had walked the path almost as long as threadweavers had existed. She could only guess at what he knew.

She clamped down on her desire as he gave her a knowing smile.

"How did you find us?" she asked.

"Ah yes. Question number one. Once they start, it's hard to make them stop. There are so many trapped behind your eyes, like horses in a corral, waiting to break out. How did I come here? The GodSpill, of course. The threads of Amarion. Join me, young Mirolah, and I will show you how. We will enrich each other."

"Okay," she said. "I will."

He seemed surprised, and then he smiled. "I hadn't expected you to see reason so quickly."

"I will join you. I'll tell you how I destroyed the Fountain. Just leave him alone."

His smile flattened to a sardonic curve of his lips. "From delightful to predictable, alas. That, I'm afraid to say, is impossible."

"You've taken away his power. Let him live. He'll die in another sixty or seventy years, and then you'll get what you want anyway. The world will know that the great Wildmane was killed by Zilok Morth. What else do you need? What can those sixty years matter?"

He sighed. "He has sunk his hooks into you. Young Mirolah, this is my first lesson to you. Listen and learn it well: Medophae is a liar. He will make you feel loved, but it is not love. It is an enchantment. It is the tainted blood of a god working on your mortal mind. And once you serve him like a dog serves his master, he will send you to your death. Or he will kill you outright." He shook his head. "I am rescuing you from your fate. Justice must be done upon him. You'll see, when he confesses his wrongs, that everything I say is true."

Mirolah suddenly realized something. "You're the same."

"Excuse me?"

"You and Medophae, you're the same. You linger in this state of bitter hatred because of him. He lingers in a state of self-loathing because of her. You can't let go. He can't let go. You spin and spin in the soup of your past. You drown in it." She wondered if it was a curse of immortality, that the moment you became immortal, you were stuck, forever, unable to change.

"I am nothing like him," Zilok Morth said in a low voice. "I do not lie to those closest to me. I do not betray those who love me best."

"You're still doing it," she said. "I don't think you can *stop* doing it."

"Child," he said. "This 'good man' was my best friend. He would be in the grips of eternal torment at the hands of Dervon the Dead if not for me. I protected him, bled for him. I saved his life, and when it was my turn to need his help, he stuck his burning sword through my stomach."

"How many times have you relived that moment?" she asked. "How many times has he relived the loss of Bands?"

He waved a hand dismissively, seemingly bored. "It is simple.

Learn with me by joining our knowledge. Or learn from me as my enemy."

"I think—"

White knives like icicles formed in the air and shot at her. They almost got her, a dozen coming close enough that they pierced her clothing and pricked her skin before her quick manipulation of their threads turned them to water.

By the gods, he was fast! If she hadn't been feeling every thread in the room, vigilant for his attack, she would be dead.

He would stop time next, she knew. If he couldn't kill her outright, he'd threadweave that spell he'd done in Ethiel's throne room. She had to look for that change, that ooze of gray-black that he created to stop time for everyone else but him.

She'd distracted Zilok for as long as she could. She only hoped he hadn't seen her send Medophae away. That he was here, in this room, talking with her, seemed proof of that. If Zilok knew where Medophae was, she assumed he'd just got here. She hoped that Medophae was ready with their plan. She had days of time to study Ethiel through her handiwork and even her physical presence as she talked in her throne room. She didn't know how to defeat Zilok. She hadn't had a chance to study him at all. Her one meeting with him had gone so quickly, amidst such towering stress, that she hadn't even thought to find his weaknesses. After all, until the last moment, she'd thought he was befriending her.

What she needed was more time to watch him, to find his weaknesses, and the only way to do that was to set him back on his heels. If she could hurt him, make him cautious, even make him run away, she might chase him, might discover more about him.

So, after Mirolah had put the trigger spell on Medophae, which would send him out of their little room to the great room downstairs, she wove a spell around the head of the spear he had found in the portal room, an attack that, once activated, would repeat over and over and over. It had taken most of an hour to get it right. When the spearhead struck the spirit of Zilok Morth, and the spell activated, it would grab the spirit's nearest thread and pull it away, a thousand times in one instant.

When Mirolah had fought Ethiel, the most effective attack she'd used, aside from tossing the Red Weaver into the maelstrom of GodSpill, was to pull her threads apart. Without a physical body, Ethiel's presence was based solely upon her will to remain intact. Once she had been disconnected from the Fountain's power, her threads came apart like bits of fluff. Mirolah was gambling that Zilok Morth shared that same weakness.

The first step of her plan was to get Medophae out of the room, into the greatroom below and—most importantly—away from Zilok Morth. Once Zilok got his "hands" on Medophae, the fight was over. The spirit would flee with his prize, leaving Mirolah behind if he could.

The second step was to delay, to play for time so Medophae could get in place with his spear, which they'd hidden in the second-story arcade of the greatroom.

The third step was to get out of this room to their chosen battlefield.

These thoughts went through Mirolah's head in a fraction of a second, before the icicles had even fully turned to water.

She tapped her own chest, activating the same spell for herself that she had used on Medophae, and flew out the window, down to the first floor, into the open double doors beneath her room and into the great room.

She landed in the center, spinning to face the doors, and she pulled GodSpill from the threads all around her. She fragmented her attention into three parts and floated above herself in a triangle. One fragment was to attack Zilok. One was to defend herself. The third was to look for opportunities.

The long walls were bordered with arched arcades, above which were galleries with smaller arches. Her gaze flicked briefly to where she and Medophae agreed he would hide with one of her camouflage spells wrapped around him. She couldn't see him with her threadweaver vision or her naked eyes. When Zilok entered and came close enough, Medophae would spear him.

The blue eyes descended through the high stone ceiling, and Zilok's illusion of a body formed shortly thereafter.

He stared at her, but she knew he was searching the room for Medophae. She prayed her spell held together under his scrutiny, and that Medophae waited until she had his full attention.

"This seems planned, young threadweaver," Zilok said. "Is this where you want your last stand?"

"This is where I give you your last warning," she said, and he drifted down, almost in position. "Leave Medophae. Go live your life, such as it is."

"No."

She attacked, sending herself into his threads, trying to pull them apart. As she expected, he was deft at turning her aside, and she couldn't do it.

He descended lower, coming closer.

Medophae popped up and threw the spear with deadly accuracy.

Black ooze spread out from Zilok. His time-stopping spell!

Mirolah focused on the threads being saturated with this gray-black color. She reached into them, turned them back, turned them.

No! He hadn't changed the color. It was something else! She put all of her focus into understanding it.

Zilok loomed over her, blue eyes burning bright.

What had he done? The texture? Did the threads have facets? Had he angled them differently? Had he—?

70

ZILOK MORTH

Z<small>ILOK LOOKED</small> at the frozen threadweaver, concentrating so hard. Her lips were tight together, her brow wrinkled in concentration, her tumbling brown hair framing her young face. He supposed she was trying to understand his time-stopping spell even as Zilok wove it. So brave. So ambitious. So foolhardy. It had taken him ten years of study to understand how to affect time, another two years to finally perfect it. And in the end, he could only do it for a very limited span.

He loved her a little bit, he suddenly realized, for believing she was a match for him. For being so ferocious. Perhaps that was what allowed her to accomplish the miracles she'd already achieved. To have done so much in such a short time, it invigorated him like few things ever had. This pup of a girl had slain the Red Weaver, destroyed Daylan's Fountain, and sparred with him competently. On top of it all, she'd fooled him. She had effectively hidden Medophae in this room for several long seconds. Zilok had scanned it, and he had overlooked where Medophae crouched behind the stone, invisible to his threadweaver sight.

He turned, looking at the head of the steel spear, hanging in mid-air mere feet from him. Alas, the moment the spear left Medophae's hand, it left the protection of her spell, and he felt it coming. Medophae had thrown it with unerring accuracy. Even as a mortal, Medophae was impressive at any contest of arms.

Zilok looked at the spearhead, but he didn't inspect it too closely, certainly didn't touch it with his ethereal fingers. He could see it was wrapped tightly with an intense threadweaving that was, no doubt, prepared to trigger when it hit him. He wasn't able to decipher the purpose of the weavings, not with the short amount of time he had, but he didn't need to know the particulars to know that he dared not touch it.

Instead, he reached out to Mirolah with his ethereal hands and moved her into the direct path of the spear.

We must be careful with the threadweavings we toss around, young Mirolah, he thought. One never knows when our creations may turn on us.

He smiled, then leaned over and kissed her on the forehead.

"So much potential," he said aloud. He floated back a good thirty feet, enough to be clear of the backlash, then waited to see exactly what kinds of spells she had put on the spearhead.

71

MIROLAH

ZILOK LOOMED OVER HER, blue eyes burning bright.

What had he done? The texture? Did the threads have facets? Had he angled them differently? Had he—?

Zilok vanished, and the room shifted.

The spear slammed into Mirolah's chest, knocking her off her feet. She hit the ground, impaled, as the spearhead cracked the flagstone behind her.

Medophae shouted in anguish.

Then the pain came, bursting like lava throughout her body.

She opened her mouth to scream, but nothing came but blood.

Zilok Morth watched her from a distance, watched her dying. The light of the room began to fade. She couldn't think straight.

I'm in shock. I have to heal myself. Yes. Heal...

It took a moment to find her threadweaver vision. The shock of the spear punching through her body had stripped away the bright bridge, her connections to the threads. But they were still there. She just had to reach out...

She touched the spearhead with her threadweaver fingers.

And her trigger spell activated.

It tore her apart, yanking away the threads that made her. It was like being unmade in Daylan's Glass, except, instead of a huge wave washing her away, a thousand clawed hands grabbed at her, ripping, tearing. She screamed, and the threads around her vibrated with her agony.

The same calm that had come over her in the Fountain came over her now. She fragmented her attention into a thousand different places, and let a few of them feel the agonizing pain while she set to making things right. She kept her arms and legs together, her organs and blood, her face and nose and hair together. She dove into every piece of herself, giving it strength, trying to undo the hideous spell she had created, replacing the pieces as they were torn away.

Finally, the spell reached its end, and Mirolah had somehow managed to keep up with it. She had healed faster than it could hurt. The clawed hands came less frequently, then stopped. She kept healing, healing, healing. She'd kept her body together. Now she could get ahead of it.

She curled her fingers around the haft of the spear and yanked it out of her chest. It clattered to the stones and she began repairing the wound, knitting flesh and bone back together. The pain began to recede and, as it did, a slick, insidious snake slipped inside her mind. She tried to stop it, but she was already overtaxed, and it was too fast, placed too perfectly. He had been waiting, and now she felt Zilok's "fingers" coil around her mind. She scrabbled to stop him, but he batted aside her feeble defense.

She let out a mute gasp. And then, lassitude.

Zilok Morth came closer. "How do you feel?"

"Oh," she murmured. "Wonderful." She could not remember a time she had felt so good.

"I would prefer it, Mirolah, if you would address me as your master."

"Yes, my master," she intoned.

"That's better." He paused. "Did you see him? He ran away. Your noble hero threw a spear into your heart, then he ran away."

"I told him to," she said, revealing the back-up part of their plan.

"Did you?"

"You can't see him with your threadweaver sight. He's going to ambush you."

"With that mundane sword at his hip, I assume?" he said.

"I enchanted it. It can hurt you, like the spearhead."

"So clever of you."

"Yes, my master."

Zilok turned, and Mirolah saw what he was looking at. Beyond the double doors that led farther into the palace, she could see the burning black fire that surrounded Vaerdaro. A second later, the double doors burst open and slammed against the walls. Vaerdaro strode through. A taller, but thinner, man walked next to him. The new man's head was shaved and his eyes had a dull cast. He wore a belt and black leather breeches, but was bare of chest except for an X harness bearing a large blue sapphire in the center.

"Excuse me one moment, Mirolah."

"Yes, my master."

"Spirit," The tall, powerfully built Sunrider exclaimed.

"Vaerdaro, I trust that Sef led you in the correct direction."

"I don't appreciate being left behind in a maze of dead hallways," he snarled. He glanced at Mirolah, narrowed his eyes. "I see you found the girl."

"Mirolah is now our ally," Zilok said.

"You've made her an idiot, as well?" He gave a contemptuous wave at Sef as he came forward.

Zilok shook his head. "Your rude behavior impresses no one, Sunrider."

"I am not your lackey, to be left in the bowels of this castle following a simpleton through the dark! I am the Golden King."

"Trust me, my muscular friend. Soon, you can rage to your violent heart's content."

"I want to kill him," Vaerdaro said abruptly. "I want to make him suffer for what he did."

"Oh, he will suffer," Zilok said.

"By my hand."

Zilok chuckled. "I will let you know if I need assistance."

Vaerdaro clenched his jaw. He glanced at Mirolah. "Then I want her. She was his woman. She can be mine now."

"Let us ask her, shall we? Young Mirolah, would you like to serve the Sunrider when my business here is complete?"

"No, my master," Mirolah said.

"You see then?" Zilok said.

"You mock me, Spirit. You push me too far."

Zilok walked forward. "Shut your mouth," he said. "You have already received your prize. You have the power of a god. All your petty dreams will soon come true. Appreciate what has been given you."

"This is my birthright. You think I should thank you?"

"You should fall on your knees and worship me."

Vaerdaro drew his greatsword. "You are an unholy spirit, hanging on by a thread. I am the Golden King—"

Suddenly, Vaerdaro yelled and fell to his knees. One hand went to his head, but the other remained clenched on his weapon.

"I could make you as tractable as Mirolah," Zilok said. "Is that what you wish?"

Vaerdaro growled, pounding his head with a fist.

"Did you think I would simply give you the power of Oedandus without a way to control you?" Zilok asked. "Your mind belongs to me, Sunrider. Be respectful, or I will make you."

Vaerdaro huddled into himself, fists clenching as he shuddered.

"Do you understand me?" Zilok said.

"I...understand...more than you think," Vaerdaro said through gritted teeth. Dark fire exploded around him. Zilok's image vanished and reappeared a dozen feet away. Vaerdaro rose. He pointed with his sword, which was as long as he was tall and as wide as his arm. "The power inside me lives, thinks. And it hates you, Spirit. It calls you unholy. It demands justice. It whispers your weaknesses in my mind, tells me to kill you."

The image of Zilok waited for Vaerdaro, unafraid, but the blue eyes that represented his true form stayed well out of range of that sword.

Vaerdaro raised his sword, as if to strike Zilok's image, but he spun and hacked into the tall, thin man instead.

"No," Zilok shouted. Blue lightning lanced around the man, a protective shield of some kind, but Vaerdaro's flaming sword shattered it like glass, cutting deep into the tall man's neck. He choked and stumbled backward, blood running down his chest. He crashed to the floor.

Zilok's human image shimmered and vanished. The blue eyes became smoke twirling upward toward the ceiling, toward something beyond the ceiling.

"You fool!" Zilok's voice was thin, like it came from a long distance away. Mirolah felt the surge of GodSpill that Zilok drew, and blue fire exploded all around the Sunrider.

Vaerdaro yelled, his black hair and skin burning, but he stepped forward and delivered the finishing cut to the tall man's neck, and his head rolled away from his body.

Zilok's ice-blue eyes flowed upward, a coil of gray smoke and blue lightning spun around in a swirl.

The fist around Mirolah's mind unclenched. She gasped and wobbled on her feet. The horror filled her then, that Zilok had made her a puppet, that she would have happily done anything he said. It was like Ethiel all over again. But this time, he had simply owned her, had turned her into a different person and he had made her love it—

Vaerdaro charged her, grabbed her around the throat, and lifted her off the ground.

She choked, feet flailing in the air as he slammed her against a column. The Sunrider's singed hair grew back, sprouting from his head as Oedandus healed the damage Zilok had done. "I am the Golden King," Vaerdaro snarled.

She grabbed at his threads, but the black flame flared and batted her efforts aside. She clawed at his hand, but could not stop him from choking her.

"You are an abomination," Vaerdaro sneered at her. "You should die for your unholy nature, but if you please me, I will let you live."

She kicked him between the legs.

He grunted, and his grip faltered. She tried to win free, but he threw her to the floor, almost snapping her neck. She hit hard, groaned, and rolled over onto her back. She scooted away, trying to reach out to the threads, but her wits were scrambled.

Two fuzzy Vaerdaros bore down on her. They both caught her foot.

"I will use you," he hissed. "And you will bleed before you beg for death. I am a god!"

"Vaerdaro!"

The Sunrider turned. Medophae stood in the shadow of the open doors. His mane of golden hair glowed like a coin caught in the sunlight. A long sword extended from his hand, touching the marble floor.

"Bare your steel and show me what manner of god you are."

72

MIROLAH

VAERDARO SMILED. "So, you show your face at last. You would have been wiser to run."

"Not from you, Sunrider."

"You tricked me the last time we met," Vaerdaro said.

"I wish I could say it was hard."

Vaerdaro growled. "The last one who mocked me was the dark spirit. And I have killed him."

Vaerdaro strode toward Medophae, who stepped between two columns and into the arcade bordering the big room. He brought his sword up.

Mirolah pushed herself to a sitting position. Her head rang, but her vision was clearing. She had seen Medophae slice through a dozen darklings with the power of Oedandus raging through him. How long would it take Vaerdaro to slice through one mortal man?

She could barely hold her head up, but she reached out and changed the colors of the threads all about Vaerdaro's body like Zilok had done. Fire erupted around him. He roared, backing away. His hair burned like a torch, but he swiped his hand across it, putting out the flames.

Medophae leapt from the shadows of the side aisle, using Mirolah's distraction. He cut at Vaerdaro's neck, but the Sunrider moved inhumanly fast and blocked. Steel clashed, and the shock threw Medophae back a step. Vaerdaro lunged. With a grunt, Medophae leapt to the side, but Vaerdaro was faster. The Sunrider's greatsword clipped Medophae's arm, and blood flecked the pillar.

Again, Vaerdaro's sword came around. Medophae ducked. The six-foot blade cut halfway through the pillar and stuck there. Vaerdaro abandoned his weapon and reached for Medophae with bare hands.

Mirolah pulled the threads of the floor upward, launching Vaerdaro backward onto a pillar of rock. Vaerdaro roared as he hit the ground and slid, but he quickly rolled to his feet.

The distraction gave Medophae a blessed second, and he leapt forward even as Vaerdaro stood up, and kicked out the Sunrider's knee. It bent sideways. With a yell, Vaerdaro dropped back to the floor. Medophae lunged, stabbing him in the chest.

Vaerdaro howled, backhanding Medophae, who flew away and hit the ground hard. He rolled, rising to his feet, but he was much slower to recover than Vaerdaro had been. Sweat shone on his face and shoulders, and his breath came quickly.

Vaerdaro pulled out Medophae's sword with a gasp and let it clang to the floor. Blood gushed from the wound, then slowed to a trickle, then stopped. He leaned over. Black fire raged around his leg, and a popping sound came from his knee as it moved back into place.

He chuckled—a dark, horrible sound.

"You taught me well," Vaerdaro said, standing upright again. "When you severed my hands, I thought I would die, but you knew I wouldn't. It was only a trick to keep me from following you. But I am wise to your tricks now." He grabbed the hilt of his greatsword, stuck in the stone pillar. With a mighty wrench, he pulled it the rest of the way, cutting the pillar in half at an angle. White rock exploded, and the pillar skidded sideways, then ground to a stop, misaligned. A section of the overhanging gallery sagged, rock grinding against rock, but it did not fall. Vaerdaro glanced upward as dust floated down around him, then he looked back at Medophae.

With a smile, he picked up Medophae's bloody blade and tossed it back to him. Medophae snatched it deftly out of the air by the hilt.

"Have your weapon," Vaerdaro said. "Use all the tricks you want."

With a cry, Mirolah changed the threads of the floor, melting it under Vaerdaro's feet. He sank, and she made it solid again, trapping his legs in stone.

She strained to keep her focus. She'd been stabbed and her body pulled apart. She could feel her insides still ragged, still raw. She'd barely healed enough to survive before Zilok stole her mind. She wanted to sleep, and it was a fight just to keep her eyes open. Every little thread in her body cried for her attention, cried out for her to make them whole and healthy, but she didn't have the time. The fight between Vaerdaro and Medophae would be over in seconds. She had to help him now.

With a powerful shrug, Vaerdaro ripped one leg free of the stone, then the other. Rock chunks flew up, and he clambered out of the hole.

Mirolah fell onto her stomach, breathing hard. *Get up. Medophae needs you.* Clenching her teeth, she pushed herself onto her elbows.

"You're next, abomination," the Sunrider said.

"Medophae," she yelled. "I can't stop him!"

"It's okay," Medophae said. "Stand up, Mirolah. Run and hide so he can't find you. Don't wait. Go now."

"No."

"Mirolah!"

She just shook her head. She didn't have the strength to talk anymore.

With a flick of her threadweaver fingers, she uprooted a flagstone and sent it at Vaerdaro's head. It smacked him down, and he howled again. But he jumped up, the wound healing. She had to come up with something better, but she couldn't think.

"Fine. I'll kill you first," Vaerdaro said, stalking toward her.

"No!" Medophae ran forward, putting himself between Vaerdaro and her.

The Sunrider grinned, like this was the plan all along, and lunged at Medophae. Medophae parried the strike and swung at Vaerdaro's head. He blocked it, cutting at Medophae's waist.

Somehow, Medophae's sword was there, but the parry was hasty. The Sunrider's greatsword struck the center of Medophae's blade and sheared through it.

Medophae yelled and tried to leap, but the flaming blade sliced him open from shoulder to hip.

Mirolah screamed.

Medophae's hands went wide. He stared down at his bloody torso with a surprised look, then staggered backward.

Vaerdaro laughed, swinging his sword casually back and forth as he followed, watching Medophae with cruel amusement.

Through tears of despair, Mirolah reached into the threads and tore away the top of the column that Vaerdaro had severed. The gallery sagged, and she hurled the chunk of stone and wall at Vaerdaro. It blindsided him and smashed him into the ground, burying him.

Medophae took a step forward, then a step backward. He looked drunk. Putting one hand to his chest, he brought it away soaked with red. His entire right pant leg was already slick with his own blood. Somehow, he managed to find his balance. He gritted his teeth and staggered toward Vaerdaro, gripping the broken sword.

Mirolah's vision darkened, and she fought for consciousness. She reached into the threads and wrenched the other half of the pillar from the floor, but her concentration slipped. The half pillar moved a little, then fell back into place.

"Medophae..." She reached into the threads again, but she couldn't hold them. She couldn't feel them.

Vaerdaro burst out of the debris, looked around, and spotted Medophae. He looked ready to pounce, then he saw Medophae's pitiful progress, staggering forward, stopping, catching his balance, then taking another step. Vaerdaro let the godsword fade and crossed his arms, content to watch Medophae struggle.

Medophae's progress was torturous, but he eventually closed the distance. He tried to say something, but he choked and blood came out of his mouth. He swung his half sword. Vaerdaro caught Medophae's hand and twisted it. Bones snapped. Medophae spat blood upon Vaerdaro's chest. The Sunrider laughed and lifted Medophae off the ground by his neck.

Medophae's hands fumbled against Vaerdaro's face, trying to grab his neck. Vaerdaro continued to laugh.

"Where is your mocking now?" Vaerdaro said, and slid the greatsword through Medophae's stomach. "I want to hear your taunts now." A shudder wracked Medophae's body, and he coughed. The black fire leapt about them both. Medophae twitched, then hung limp.

Mirolah gave a strangled cry.

Vaerdaro pulled his sword out, still holding Medophae up by the neck. The Sunrider turned him this way and that, like he was inspecting a shank of beef.

Vaerdaro flung the body across the room. It hit the weakened gallery, and the whole thing finally fell, burying Medophae under tons of stone and a cloud of dust.

Mirolah cried quietly, head on the floor. It didn't matter anymore. Nothing mattered anymore. They had lost. He was dead.

Vaerdaro's footfalls scuffed the stone as he approached and stopped in front of her.

"I was thinking..." Vaerdaro said. "If I am to be the god of the Neverending Plains and Amarion, I may need one of your kind, like the Spirit, who can twist the natural order." He lifted her shoulder with the toe of his boot, then kicked. She rolled onto her back. He stepped on her chest and drove the air from her lungs.

"What do you say, unholy woman? Swear fealty to me, and I will let you live."

"Let me live, and I'll find a way to kill you," she said through her teeth.

Vaerdaro pursed his lips. "Very well."

He brought his boot up over her face. It crackled with black fire.

But it did not descend.

Vaerdaro grunted. His foot seemed stuck in midair, ablaze with black fire. He strained to bring it down, but he couldn't.

With a cry of frustration, he stepped away from her, and he could control his foot again. The black fire faded. Mirolah wearily pushed herself up on her elbows.

"What?" Vaerdaro growled. He stared at his hands in disbelief.

In the silence of Vaerdaro's shock, Mirolah heard a very quiet sound, like a spoon scraping against rock.

She looked at the crumbled gallery. A small stone at the top tumbled down the pile to the bottom.

Vaerdaro followed her gaze.

A larger stone shifted, slid down the pile to the bottom.

"No..." Vaerdaro murmured.

A tall, flat slab rose up and fell longwise over itself. Through the settling dust, Mirolah saw an arm burst up. It burned with golden fire.

"Medophae," Mirolah cried. Relief washed through her like warm water.

Medophae shrugged, and stones skidded away from him. Golden fire crackled about him. He climbed out of the debris and set his feet solidly on the floor.

"No!" Vaerdaro shouted.

Medophae strode out of the dust. The cut across his chest was a huge scab. The hole in his stomach had closed.

"You and Zilok had him fooled," he said through clenched teeth. "He thought you were me, but he sensed the difference when you stabbed your sword through me, when you stabbed *him* through me. What else did you do, Vaerdaro? What last crime did you commit that made him turn from you?"

"There is no *he*! I am the Golden King!" He charged, swinging his greatsword in a huge arc.

Medophae waited for the attack. At the last second, he held up his fist, and the godsword exploded to life. Vaerdaro's greatsword shattered upon it. He staggered forward, off balance. Medophae grabbed him by the chin and yanked him up, bringing their faces level.

"He doesn't like you, Vaerdaro," Medophae whispered. He

shoved Vaerdaro backward. The Sunrider crashed to the ground near Mirolah.

Medophae watched the truth dawn on Vaerdaro. He crouched down onto his hands and feet like a cornered rat.

"Leave now, Vaerdaro," Medophae said. "Go back to the Neverending Plains."

"This is a trick," Vaerdaro said. "Another of your tricks!"

"No. It's Oedandus's will. He wants to kill you, Vaerdaro, for using him. I can barely hold him back. Go now."

"You've tricked me into giving up my power somehow, but you will give it back. You will give it back!" Vaerdaro sprang upon Medophae, but Medophae caught his wrists. The Sunrider's face turned red as he strained. Medophae slowly pushed Vaerdaro to his knees.

With a strangled cry of rage, the Sunrider leapt away. Spit gathered in the corner of his mouth. "You're unholy creatures," he hissed. He took two quick steps back and grabbed Mirolah by the hair, yanked her upright. He yanked the dagger from his belt, held it to her throat.

Mirolah took a swift breath as he bent her head back.

"Don't," Medophae said sadly. He didn't seem scared. "Go your way. We will let you leave."

Mirolah changed the threads of the knife and blunted the edge.

"You may kill me," he growled, "But she dies first." He pulled the useless knife across her throat.

He only got halfway. His arm froze, unmoving. A flicker of black fire flickered across his forearm. He screamed.

Vaerdaro backed up, looking about himself in horror. The black fire surged away from him in a streak, then returned like a striking snake. Vaerdaro screamed again and spun across the floor. He slammed into the stairs of the dais.

"No," Medophae yelled. "Oedandus!" He started forward, as if to shield Vaerdaro. "It was Zilok—"

Medophae stopped as if he had hit an invisible wall. His arms went wide, palms upward. He threw his head back and opened his mouth, but no sound came.

Snakes of golden fire leapt off Medophae, turning black in mid-air, then struck Vaerdaro again and again, passing entirely through his body. He screamed and shook with each strike. Soon, his body rippled like a pennant snapping in the breeze. The scream became inhuman, like it was rising from a deep well. He and Medophae floated in the air and the fire streaked between them, like lightning between two clouds. With every exchange, Medophae burned brighter and Vaerdaro became more insubstantial, rippling like a mirage.

Finally, the Sunrider exploded like a popping log. Medophae swirled within the maelstrom of Oedandus's fury, the black fire returned to him and changed to gold once more. Mirolah could hear Medophae shouting, but as with Vaerdaro, it seemed to come from far away.

She struggled to get to her feet, reaching out to him with her ethereal fingers, trying to help. Would Oedandus attack Medophae? What was happening?

But before she could even try to do something, the unnatural wind ceased, and Medophae fell to the ground.

73

OREM

OREM'S LEGS BURNED as he continued moving them back and
forth, pushing hard against the rock. His ankles were bound with
thick rope, and his movement was hampered by the length
connecting those ankles to his bound wrists.

"Come on," he whispered, sawing as quickly as he could
manage. The sharp chunk of rock he was using had blown off the
scrying pool Zilok Morth had been gazing into before he bathed
the Sunrider in flame. Orem had seen where it landed and waited.
He hadn't dared to hope he'd have a moment alone, but it had
finally come. They were all gone: the Sunrider brute, Zilok, even
the creepy, bald, tall man who kept saying, "Yes, my master," to,
apparently, no one.

Orem hadn't wasted a single moment of his luck. With
torturous struggles, he had moved his bound body as close to the
rock as he could. He was connected to a ring set in the wall, but if
he stretched, he could reach the chunk of rock. He had kicked it
until it was braced against the wall so that he could put pressure on
this sharp edge.

He felt the rope begin to fray, so he ignored the burn in his thighs and went faster. The rope gave, freeing his ankles, and loosening the entire binding. He gasped. Now he just needed to lock his legs around that stone and pull it close enough for him to get his hands on it—

A wisp of a breeze seemed to flutter over his mind. Orem twitched, looking toward the door. Nothing.

"Come on, come on," he said, wrapping his ankles and feet around the stone. It looked a hundred pounds at least. He pulled, the rock tilting toward him, but he slipped. The rock thumped back.

"Dammit!"

Good… the word whispered in his mind.

Orem went still. The hairs on his neck stood up. Zilok Morth. The spirit was back. He looked at his ankles, wondering if he could hide them, hide the progress he had made. He pulled his knees up, tried to scoot his ankles behind himself.

It is good… the voice whispered in his mind again. A heavy hand seemed to grasp Orem's brain. Blue lightning flashed inside his mind.

He thrashed.

"It is good I kept you," Zilok's voice said, no longer a whisper. It was as strong as if the spirit was hovering right next to Orem. "Even I didn't know how I would need you, but now it all comes clear."

"No!" The blue lightning became black ooze, and it felt like it was coating him, trickling down from the crown of his head to his temples and forehead, down behind his ears. "No…" Orem whispered.

"You have such fervor. Such desire. Be calm, Portnoy Orem," Zilok said. "I am about to grant your dearest wish. You have always longed to be a threadweaver. I am going to make that possible."

Orem bowed his head. "Yes, my master."

"There, isn't that better?"

"Yes, my master."

"Good. Well, this was an unmitigated disaster. But what is

failure if not an opportunity to learn?"

"As you say, my master."

"Yes, Orem. As I say..."

74

MEDOPHAE

MEDOPHAE STOOD on the red beach alone, tears running down his face. Blue-green waves stretched back farther than the imagination, continuing to the end of the horizon. The wind whipped through his hair, and clouds bunched on the flat, blue horizon. A storm was coming.

His waves of grief came, one after the other, and he let them. He remembered standing on the balcony of Tyndiria's castle just like this, thinking these same thoughts. A lifetime ago.

He remembered the cage he saw around himself then. Orem had tried to free him with dreams. Tyndiria had tried to free him with kisses. But only when Zilok stripped Medophae of Oedandus, only when Mirolah had reminded Medophae of what he had wanted to be as a young man, did the cage door finally open.

He remembered what it was to be a man again, rather than an immortal. A man suffered. A man made mistakes. A man was broken. But the sun rose on a new day, and a man could make new choices. A man could change.

Because of Oedandus, Medophae had remained stuck in the

same horrible mistake he had made, unable to change the past, and unable to move on. Orem had berated him for it. Tyndiria had begged him to let her help. But Mirolah rekindled the memory of what it was to need that change, the thrill of leaping into the unexpected. She had brought hope back into his life.

Now that hope filled him when he looked at her. There was a future, and she was his.

And so...

Medophae opened the pouch and let the ruby fall into his hand. Mirolah had found the gem on the dead body of Zilok's servant, the tall one with no name who wore the X harness. As ever, the ruby was warm.

Does that mean you are alive, my love? I do not know. I cannot know.

A sob wracked him.

"I cannot help you, Bands," he whispered. "Gods, I hope you understand. I had become nothing. I fell into darkness so deep I forgot what light was. But I can see it now, and if I don't follow it now, I never will. I'll return to nothing again." He paused. "I wish you could hear me. I wish I could see your face. Of all the betrayals I have ever made, this is the worst."

He stood.

"I will love you always. When forever takes the lands, I will stand at the edge of time and cry out that I loved you..." He choked on the words.

He shouted as if he were leading an army into battle and cocked back his arm. Golden fire danced about his trembling muscles. Moments dragged by as he struggled with himself.

He snapped forward, hurling the stone to the horizon. It flew straight and far, through the light of the setting sun, flipping over and over, flashing red until he lost sight of it.

With an anguished cry, he fell to his knees and sobbed.

The sun set, and a storm came, vicious and wild. Lightning danced on the ocean. The dark clouds roiled low, pelting the earth with sheets of rain.

Eventually the storm spent its fury and moved on. Clouds parted, the stars came out shone down upon him, shuddering with wave upon wave of grief.

He was still hunched over, weeping like a wounded child, when Mirolah came for him in the night. She brought a blanket, and she wrapped him in it.

She sat next to him as the sun rose over the mountains behind the white castle of Calsinac. She said nothing. Sometime around midday, he reached out for her hand, and she took it.

They rose together, and she led him up the beach.

EPILOGUE
SARAPHAZIA

THE WHALE ROSE SILENTLY, head above the waves, and looked toward the distant shore. It was so far away that mortal eyes could not see it. They would only see her mighty waters, but Saraphazia could see whatever she wanted to see. Medophae had cast away his gemstone, letting it go at last. He was in love again. With a human. He had solved the Red Weaver's riddle and broken the fearsome enchantment.

Saraphazia dove deep. She descended through the fathoms quickly. It was as black as a starless sky when she reached the bottom of the True Ocean. Even her greatest whales could not dive this deep. They would be crushed by the weight of the water, but this was her ocean, and she could do whatever she wanted to do.

She hovered above the ruby that had come to rest in those dark, soft sands.

Red light flashed, and suddenly a thousand bubbles burst outward. She manipulated the threads, holding the dread weight at bay.

A light-green dragon with dark emerald bands circling her neck emerged in a flurry of bubbles, as did Saraphazia's curly-haired, curly-bearded brother. Saraphazia shifted the threads to protect Randorus Ak-nin Akli Forkandor—or as the humans called her, Bands—from the water. For any other dragon, contact with the True Ocean was death, but for this dragon, Saraphazia made an exception.

Tarithalius looked around himself, saw her, then grinned. It disgusted her how much he loved that weak human form, flashing those white teeth all the time as if he was proud of them. Unlike Bands, Tarithalius didn't need her protection. He cheerfully inhaled a lungful of water and started to speak, but she left him on the bottom and swam quickly through the water with Bands in tow.

Bands burst through the surface of the water and drew a long breath. She spread her wings and flapped urgently away from the True Ocean as if it was poison. Her long, sinuous neck curved around as she tried to get her bearings.

"You are safe," Saraphazia assured her. At her command, a portion of the ocean stopped moving, becoming as solid as rock. "You have my permission to alight."

Bands hesitated, then landed gently onto the indicated spot. She neatly folded her wings.

Tarithalius arrived a moment later. He broke the surface and flew into the air, his golden armor gleaming, standing as if someone was going to paint his portrait. He landed on the plot of still ocean.

"Well, that was an experience," he exclaimed.

"Quiet, Thalius," Saraphazia said.

Bands stared at the horizon. She had not moved since she had landed.

"Would you like to see them?" Saraphazia asked.

"Yes, if I may," she said politely.

She gave the dragon her vision, enabling her to see miles away as though it was ten feet. The lovers sat on the beach together. Medophae pressed his palms to his head, crying. Mirolah sat next to him, patient, silent, her head bowed.

"He loves her," Bands said. Saraphazia wasn't certain what emotion floated on the dragon's voice. Non-whales were so difficult to read.

"Of course. The enchantment could not be broken unless the riddle was fulfilled," Saraphazia said.

"I forget, what was the riddle again?" Thalius asked.

Saraphazia snorted. A geyser of mist shot into the air. "My idiot brother... Perhaps you should go back into the gem for another four centuries."

"I only remember things that pertain to me." Thalius grinned, showing his teeth again.

"It does, if you had the wit to see it. Do you think you were thrown into that ruby by chance?"

"Who would want to imprison me?"

"Who *could*?" Saraphazia turned her tail to him.

"Not Avakketh?" Thalius said incredulously.

She didn't answer him. Thalius was such a dullard sometimes.

He pursed his lips thoughtfully. "Well, I suppose I shall have to pay him back for that."

"Unless you forget."

"Oh yes, which brings us back to the confounded riddle. It certainly took our boy a long time to figure it out."

"He couldn't figure it out. If he had figured it out, he couldn't have solved it. A human cannot force himself to fall in love," she said. "Idiot."

"Ah! The answer was *love*, was it?" Thalius scratched his beard.

Saraphazia closed her eyes and wished him away. He didn't go anywhere.

Bands's clear voice recited the riddle that had kept them imprisoned for four hundred years. "*You must give to someone that which you have already given away. And you must cast away what now sustains you,*" she said quietly.

"That's *love*?" the bearded man asked.

"We spoke of this before," Bands said quietly. "We talked of it many times."

"Oh. I forgot."

The corner of the dragon's long, scaly mouth curved upward in a smile. "He needed to fall in love with someone else. Ethiel was cunning. She thought it was the one thing he could not do." She paused. "But he did it." Saraphazia detected admiration in her voice this time.

"And so," Saraphazia said, "her master spell is broken. Go to him."

The dragon watched as Mirolah took Medophae's hand and they walked up the beach. She let out a long breath. "No."

Saraphazia was disappointed. "Your restoration is his prize. He has longed for you for four hundred years. He has lain in torment for you. Will you not give him what he craves?"

"He has found what he craves."

"The girl? She is a human. You are the one he wants."

Bands slowly shook her head. "Not true, Saraphazia. She is the one he wants. She is the one he needs, otherwise Ethiel's trigger spell could not have been tripped."

"Then the Red Weaver wins," Saraphazia said, disgusted.

Bands stretched her wings, flapped them three times. "No. The poor woman, she never won anything she really wanted."

"Then you will forsake the man you love for some foolish sense of fair play?"

"What you said was right, Saraphazia. Mirolah is human. I am a dragon. What is a human life span to me? Seven decades is a short time to wait."

Saraphazia shook her head. "You make no more sense than the humans do."

Thalius laughed.

"Begone from my ocean." Saraphazia waved impatiently. "I tire of you."

Bands leapt into the air, flapping her wings and hovering. "I thank you beyond words for your assistance, goddess."

Saraphazia said nothing. She turned her tail up and dove into her ocean.

TARITHALIUS'S flippant mien faded once his sister was gone. He looked at Bands solemnly. "And so you feel no pain in having to wait for your lover's words in your ear, for his touch on your skin?"

"Oh, Tarithalius. Don't mock me or I shall break. I must be strong for him. For her. For me. It would be a shabby victory to claim him by casting her out. She sacrificed everything to come to this shore. I have waited four hundred years; I can wait seventy more for the sake of the woman who saved us."

"Can you?" Tarithalius asked, his voice low.

"Stop it, Thalius. Please stop."

He nodded. "Very well then."

Mailing List/Facebook Group

MAILING LIST
Don't miss out on the latest news and information about all of my books. Join my Readers Group:

https://www.subscribepage.com/u0x4q3

FACEBOOK
https://www.facebook.com/todd.fahnestock

AMAZON AUTHOR PAGE
https://www.amazon.com/Todd-Fahnestock/e/B004N1MILG

AUTHOR LETTER

Wildmane is the most personal project I've ever worked on. He's been in my life for as long as I can remember. The character was born in 1986. I was a junior in high school then, and on the weekends I would play Middle Earth Role Playing (MERP—anyone remember MERP?) with my friend and roommate Marvin. Initially, I wrote half a novel of how Wildmane came to be a demigod, of how he and his band of friends set out on the legendary quest to destroy the god Dervon the Diseased. The story was a summer project, brainstormed with Marvin during those lazy teenage days when it seemed all we had was time.

But when summer ended, so did the book. I moved out of Marvin's house, began the series of misadventures that would comprise my youth, and I left the unfinished story to gather dust. Six years later, in college, I wrote a new story with Wildmane, set 1,400 years after he gained his immortality. During those college years, I lived in several big houses with my friends, and I would read chapters to them. Wildmane became a part of our daily vocabulary. When we would meet a rude person or get into a scary situation, we would say, "This story needs a Wildmane!", meaning that Wildmane could overcome any obstacle, and was particularly good at putting rude people in their places. As my skills as a writer improved, I continued coming back to the story, rewriting it again and again. Some of those versions made my friends gnash their teeth as I took the characters places they didn't like. But that first attempt in college, that first version, though it has been rewritten dozens of times, is the essence of the book in your hands right now. I'm happy to say that most of those college friends are still a regular part of my life. That they get to see this book in its final form makes me smile.

So, welcome to the land of Amarion and to the story of the unstoppable Mirolah and the immortal Wildmane. Thank you for coming. I hope you enjoy your stay.

-Todd

ALSO BY TODD FAHNESTOCK

Tower of the Four Series
Episode 1 – The Quad
Episode 2 – The Tower
Episode 3 – The Test
Episode 4 – The Nightmare
Episode 5 – The Resurrection (Forthcoming)
The Champions Academy (Episodes 1-3 omnibus)

Threadweavers Series
Wildmane
The GodSpill
Threads of Amarion
God of Dragons

The Whisper Prince Series
Fairmist
The Undying Man
The Slate Wizards (Forthcoming)

Standalone Novels
Charlie Fiction
Summer of the Fetch

Short Stories
Urchin: A Tower of the Four Short Story
Royal: A Tower of the Four Short Story
Princess: A Tower of the Four Short Story
Parallel Worlds Anthology: *Threshold*
Fantastic Realms Anthology: *Ten for Every One*
Dragonlance: The Cataclysm – *Seekers*
Dragonlance: Heroes & Fools – *Songsayer*
Dragonlance: The History of Krynn – *The Letters of Trayn Minaas*

ABOUT THE AUTHOR

TODD FAHNESTOCK is a writer of fantasy for all ages and winner of the New York Public Library's Books for the Teen Age Award. *Threadweavers* and *The Whisper Prince Trilogy* are two of his bestselling epic fantasy series. He is a finalist in the Colorado Authors League Writing Awards for the past two years, for *Charlie Fiction* and *The Undying Man*. His passions are fantasy and his quirky, fun-loving family. When he's not writing, he teaches Taekwondo, swaps middle grade humor with his son, plays Ticket to Ride with his wife, scribes modern slang from his daughter and goes on morning runs with Galahad the Weimaraner. Visit Todd at www.toddfahnestock.com.